Solaris Saga book 2

Janet McNulty

Solaris Seeks
Copyright © 2015 Janet McNulty

ISBN-10: 1-941488-01-3 (MMP Publishing)
ISBN-13: 978-1-941488-01-0

Library of Congress Control Number: 2015937492

Printed in the United States of America

First Edition

I am an avid reader and love science fiction, especially adventure stories. I hope you enjoyed Solaris Seethes and that you find yourself getting lost in the journey as it continues.

Contents

Solaris Seeks

Chapter 1
SOMBER MOOD

The emptiness aboard Solaris permeated every aspect of the ship, soaking through the metallic walls and attacking everyone's mood. Brie's absence left a gaping hole. Each member of the crew hid in their own nook of the ship, not wanting to associate with the others, never noticing that several weeks had passed. Even Solaris retreated within herself, preferring her own cyber systems over the company that the flesh and blood beings on board had to offer.

Rynah took Brie's death the hardest and locked herself in her room, refusing to leave. Her anger, her impatience, drove Brie to prove herself. *I killed her;* Rynah berated herself, repeating the message over and over again until she almost believed it. She knew it wasn't entirely true, but felt she deserved the brunt of the responsibility.

Wondering what had become of Rynah, both Tom and Solon stopped by her door, but she refused to answer, remaining motionless in her room until they gave up and left.

Clinging to her glumness one day, she rose from her bunk and sauntered over to the window, looking out at the darkest and furthest reaches of space. There was no color; only distant specks that resembled stars. Her breaths fogged the window. Rynah reached up with her index finger and drew her initials in them, her signature. Memories of her grandfather doing the same when she was a small child flooded her mind and she touched the bracelet he had given her long ago as she thought about him, rubbing the tips of her fingers over the tiny engraving on its edge. Taking in a sharp breath, she breathed on the glass, covering it with the vapors from her mouth. More determined, Rynah drew her signature again.

She wandered over to her desk and automatically clicked on the console; a holographic screen popped up, awaiting a command as files lined across it. Rynah scrolled through them, but her eyes focused past the holoscreen, not wanting to focus on the mess of files that beckoned to be opened. She didn't know why she bothered with her console. Perhaps her mind wished to focus on something other than the loss of Brie, or maybe, her fingers needed something to do in their effort to deal with her brooding mood.

One file caught her eye. Rynah tapped the screen and opened it. Her grandfather's voice filled the speakers in her room as his holographic image materialized—another of his bits of wisdom that he had left for her.

"Hello, my dear." His well-remembered hoarse voice sent shivers down her spine. "I know that the task I left you is difficult and there will be times when you will face loss. The loss of a friend or loved one is never easy to bear, but you must prevail."

Rynah stopped the recording. *What did he know?* She stared at the image of Marlow, every line, every wrinkle on his aged face, and the gray eyes that once twinkled, but now held only sorrow. He pleaded with her to continue; his piercing eyes bored into the depths of her soul. Infuriated at him for leaving her with such a mess, Rynah clicked off the screen and jerked to her feet, pacing the small room, hands clasped behind her back, mumbling and grumbling to herself.

"I know that is easy for me to say."

Rynah whirled around. The holographic screen had turned back on, replaying the recording. Once again, she stared into the ancient eyes of her grandfather, his calm demeanor filling her with equanimity and courage.

"But I have lost loved ones as well. Your mother being one. Your grandmother being another. But this thing is bigger than all of us and more important than our own wants and desires. I know that it is easy for me to say. I am an old man, and by now, I am probably dead.

"But, you must continue, Rynah. I wish more than anything that I did not have to leave this task to you. I am sorry. Do not let the sacrifice of those we love be in vain. Loss is a part of life. You know that better than most. If your roles were reversed—if you were the one who had died and your friend survived—what do you think he, or she, would do? Would they mope and wallow in their self-pity? Or would they continue with their search for the crystals?

"I know you think this is easy for me, but making these recordings is the hardest thing I have had to do. It means that I have failed and must leave you to undo the damage I have wrought."

"You," she whispered. Rynah didn't believe what she had heard. Her grandfather was responsible for all of this?

"When I was still at the academy, I discovered something in the ancient texts, something that only I would have recognized. That is when my search into the crystals and their power began. My zeal to find them increased when I met a man who claimed to have seen one. Oh, they are not magical by any means. It is pure technology, but one that is even beyond our capabilities.

"You may be wondering what this has to do with everything. My research, my quest for knowledge, brought to light the power of the six crystals and the weapon they are said to create. I was so focused on discovering their capabilities, and where they were, that I never stopped to ask if I should—if maybe there was a reason they were lost in the first place. I remained unaware of the eyes that watched me, nor was I aware of the consequences of discovering such knowledge.

"My experiments led to the deaths of innocent people. I tried to create my own crystal to match the one in the geo-lab, but it had disastrous consequences. The crystal imploded, causing an explosion that wreaked havoc on the Brestef region. But, then, I did the most shameful thing imaginable: I covered it up. I destroyed all of the evidence linking me to it. I destroyed people's lives, but could not face the magnitude of what I had done. I was a coward.

"That was when I realized the true nature of these crystals and, that if they were ever united, it would mean devastation for our race. I realized that the crystals had to be protected. If I could become lost in their majestic properties, someone else might as well.

"When I was tried for attempting to steal the crystal from the lab, some at the trial had already guessed that I had something to do with the explosion at Desmyr. They only lacked conclusive evidence. But there were those present at the trial who had suffered losses at Desmyr.

"I tell you all of this, Rynah, so that you do not make the same mistake I did. When you find the crystals, do not be tempted by their power, by the technology they hold; it will only destroy you. I tell you this so that you know why I believe so strongly in you.

"During my search, I stumbled upon something: a small symbol, which most scholars had passed off as nothing more but a watermark. Something benign and easily ignored because of its unimportance. But one day, your mother put you in my care, while she went out shopping and that mark became clear. Oh, how the fates must be laughing at the trick they pulled. You will know soon enough what I mean and you must discover it on your own. When you do, you will know why I have complete faith in you. You, Rynah, bear a strength that I never possessed.

"Do not let grief con you into carrying the weight of the dead. It will serve you little in the end."

The recording ended and Marlow's holographic face faded. Rynah stared at the blank holoscreen, trying to comprehend what he had just told her.

Desmyr. She remembered watching the news reports that covered the devastation and its unknown cause. Desmyr was the most populous city—though small by her planet's standards—in the Brestef region where a terrible explosion destroyed the entire city and thousands of people had died. Families had been torn apart. The authorities never found the one responsible and, in the end, they admitted that they had no information to go on and filed it away as a freak accident. The nuclear power plant had exploded; that was the story released to the press. People believed it because no one could imagine one person causing such desolation.

My grandfather killed those people!

Rynah couldn't believe it. She refused to believe it. How could he have done such a thing? Though if it were true, that would explain his withdrawal from the world.

Rynah remembered, when she was still a child, how Marlow always pored over dusty volumes of books—images of him hunched over a hefty volume in the dim lamplight filled her mind—written in a language she could not read. When she had asked him about the books, he told her to learn the language first. So she did, though he still refused to talk to her about it, insisting that his discoveries would change the world. She left it at that, concluding that his books were just the hobby of an old man.

Rynah stared at the holoscreen as one of those memories rushed back to her, propelling her into the past, as only memories can.

She had just been commissioned as a Lieutenant in the Lanyran fleet and accepted a post on General Delmar's vessel: the Protector. That was when it had happened, when his withdrawal had begun.

"Rynah, have you heard?" asked Gresef, a fellow Lieutenant, recently commissioned like her.

She shook her head.

Gresef seized her arm and dragged her over to a holoscreen that portrayed the most recent news reports. "It's unbelievable," he said.

Rynah dropped her duffle bag as she watched scenes of explosions, charred bodies, and tremendous plumes of smoke that filled the air as rescue crews attempted to douse the fires.

"Reports of the wounded and dead from this devastation continue to come in," said a news reporter; the camera panned across the valley, now a desolate place full of ash and smoke. "We do not have the number of those who have died…"

The reporter ceased speaking as an earsplitting explosion drowned her voice, forcing her to hunker low and cover her head with her arms.

"It appears that… gas… gone." The camera cut out and the holoscreen went black.

"I can't believe it," whispered Gresef. "All of Desmyr is gone and Brestef will be uninhabitable for years."

Rynah's private communicator buzzed. Seeking a secluded corner, she answered it; her mother's face, now with bits of white hair framing it instead of the sage color she used to have, appeared in a small holographic form.

"Rynah, you need to come home immediately."

"Mother, I can't," said Rynah. "I have just arrived at my post, and now with what's happened in Brestef, they won't let me leave."

"Rynah, your grandfather has gone insane!"

"What do you mean?"

"He just came home and went straight to his workshop. He's in there now, mumbling nonsense and throwing his notes and sketches into the fire! I don't know what to do."

"Three and four do not work!"

Rynah heard her grandfather's erratic statement over the communicator. "What is he talking about?"

"I don't know! He just keeps repeating the same sentence over and over again. Rynah, please."

"I'll see if I can get an assignment there."

"Hurry."

Rynah clicked off the communicator and hefted her duffle bag on her shoulders, heading straight for the first officer's office.

The memory ended.

Infuriated, Rynah clicked off the screen. She hated secrets, and the secrets he had kept from her were no small matter. *He killed those people.* She still couldn't believe that her grandfather was responsible for such a tragedy, though it explained his reclusive manner. She marched to the window again, trying to process this information with the ever-present sadness of Brie's loss.

"I didn't know either," Solaris said over the speaker, her voice soft.

"What? Know what?" demanded Rynah.

"About Desmyr."

"But you recorded these."

"Your grandfather recorded these videos and downloaded them into my systems with the express wish that I only watch them if necessary."

"And how was this one necessary?"

"Because you needed to know the truth, and because you needed motivation to find the other crystals."

Rynah fumed. She hated people always deciding when she needed to do something.

"I have been hiding as well," said Solaris. "You are not the only one to suffer from Brie's death, but you cannot hide in here. That was the point Marlow tried to make on that recording. He tried to hide from the world when Desmyr happened, but the world continues and will find a way to pull you back in."

"So you say," snapped Rynah.

"So life says," retorted Solaris. "You can stay here and wallow in your grief, but Klanor still searches for the crystals and he will find them if no one stops him. Can you forgive yourself if that happens?"

Rynah slumped on her bunk. She hated pep talks. She hated being wrong, but what she didn't know was that Marlow had made a similar video for Solaris, programmed to play if she ever ceased in her role as Rynah's guide.

"You're right," relented Rynah. "Nothing will bring Brie back and I cannot let Klanor win, but where is the next crystal?"

Rynah's console screen flicked on again as Solaris projected digital scans of the ancient text. "You will have to search."

"Solaris, the watermark my grandfather talked about, do you know what it was?"

"No."

Rynah noticed a tone that implied she did not wish to talk about it. "Can you bring it up?"

"Unfortunately, no. The scans do not show things like smudges or watermarks."

"Are you sure?" asked Rynah, with the distinct feeling that Solaris held something from her.

"Certainty is an impossibility," said Solaris, repeating one of Solon's phrases. "To find the watermark, you will need the actual text."

Figures, thought Rynah. "Do the books still exist?"

"Most likely they were destroyed when Lanyr was. Marlow had one, which he gave to you. He had claimed that it was the original book written, which he had restored."

"I no longer..." Rynah gasped as she thought of something. "Klanor has it!"

"How do you know?"

"He has to. It's the only explanation."

Rynah thought about it and Solaris' statement made sense. "Thank you, Solaris."

"For what, dear?"

"For the pep talk."

Chapter 2
HARD LESSON

Klanor watched in triumph, Stein by his side, gloating as the sleek, black tube was brought aboard his ship. He waited as the technicians unhooked the cables before approaching it. One of his men waved at him. With purposeful steps, he neared the missile tube, a smug grin pasted to his face. The top of the tube slid open. Inside laid Brie's body, though it lacked the usual signs of decay.

A woman approached with a medical scanner. It beeped as she ran it over Brie's body before bringing it up to read the results. "I do not understand, sir, but she is not dead."

"Not dead? Then why did they leave her?" Klanor demanded.

"There seem to be nanobots in her blood system, sir, but these are odd... unlike any I have ever seen."

Klanor stared at the medical technician before him with a quizzical look. They all had nanobots in their bloodstream; such a thing was standard practice to make it easier for individuals to live in space for prolonged periods of time.

"Explain," he said.

"These are not your standard nanobots; they are more advanced—more specialized. Though her lungs are full of poisonous gas, these nanobots seemed to have slowed her system to the point where all of her vital functions have stopped, except the neurocenters of her brain remain intact, preserving her higher brain functions. In essence, they have put her in a sort of stasis. Such a state resembles death."

"And why would they have not detected this?"

"Their medical equipment must not be as advanced. Their ship is old after all."

Klanor thought about it. Rynah's ship was outdated and outmoded, lacking many of the advancements that his vessel possessed, but how did she get possession of these more advanced nanobots?

Only one answer came to mind: Marlow. The old geezer must have created them and then left them on the ship, and Rynah had no idea what they were. He knew that administering nanobots to combat space-sickness was common practice. Marlow must have switched them out with his experimental ones, but Rynah had no idea.

Klanor's smile widened.

"Get her to the medical bay. I want her cleaned up and made well." He touched the pendant in Brie's stiff hands, his victorious demeanor faltering as it reminded him of the ring he had given to Rynah, and kept when it had fallen from her finger, before ripping it away and shoving it in his pocket.

"You want me to treat her?" asked the medical technician.

"How can I question her if she is in a coma?" Klanor's harsh tone frightened the woman into obedience.

"Yes, sir. Right away."

The woman motioned for three others to help her. Together, they placed Brie on a gurney—though this one hovered instead of using wheels—and moved her down a long, well-lit corridor and to the medical bay. Klanor watched with a mixture of exuberance and sorrow; now he would learn about these new arrivals from some distant planet, and learn of Rynah's movements as well, but his mind remained focused on the pendant in his hand. Someone had placed it in Brie's slender fingers with care, an act of affection that gnawed at his heart.

"Stein, I want you to keep an eye on her."

"Yes, sir," replied Stein, choking back tears, and memories.

Klanor gave him a questioning look, but refused to address the somber note he heard in Stein's voice, as his fingers reached into his pocket and fiddled with the ring that he kept there. "I have matters to attend. Inform me when she is ready for questioning."

"Yes, sir."

Stein waited for Klanor to fade from sight before stalking away from the cargo hold of the ship and down two hallways, until he found a secluded corner, concealed in shadow, where his caged emotions escaped. Unable to hold them in, they burst from him, reducing him to a bout of weeping, which made him appear pitiful, instead of the strong man he prided himself being. Brie's serene, and seemingly lifeless, form reminded him of his tortured past, and the horrendous events that he longed to forget.

With shaking hands, he reached into his pocket and pulled out a crumpled photograph; its edges still black from where the flames had singed it in his failed attempt to purge the woman and child smiling back at him from his memories. How he longed to forget.

Stein stared at the image of his wife, holding their child; a mixture of emotions (hatred, envy, anger, and sorrow) etched his face, creasing his forehead. He remembered the day that photo was taken, the day they went to the lake. It had been a beautiful day with a bright sun, with a warm and gentle breeze, as most days on Lanyr were. The leaves brushed against one another, singing to them as they shared a picnic lunch on the sand.

Stein remembered that his son had taken his first steps there, the joy he felt as he watched the small child try to walk, his unsteady steps leaving tiny footprints in the magenta sand. It had been a perfect day; that day, he was a loving husband and father.

His hands shook as he recalled the day of the explosion. Many dead, killed before they even knew what had happened. That day was forever seared into his memory. His wife, his beloved Ofylia, had gone to the daycare center to pick up their son, and it happened. An explosion, the likes of which no one had ever seen before, rocked the entire city of Desmyr, in the Brestef region. Buildings toppled, crushing any in their path.

The impact had knocked him back several yards, and his side still ached from where his ribs had cracked. Stein screamed Ofy-lia's name. He rushed to the daycare center as smoldering chunks of concrete and steel rods blocked his path, ignoring the pain in his body and the blood that dripped from a wound on his left temple; the scar was still there. He charged through the smoke that reached for any in its path, past people who wandered in a catatonic state, unable to comprehend what had occurred.

Then he saw it—a sight that never left him, but burned a hole through his heart. A lifeless Ofylia lay on the floor, surrounded by charred debris and floating embers, clutching their son.

The next few months remained a blur, the only constant being that his wife's brother harassed him for living while she had died. Rage filled him as Stein remembered his brother-in-law's words about how he should have been the one killed. He took it to heart. Those arguments drove him to the lake that day—the same lake his son had taken his first steps—to end his life, and where he met Klanor and received his new purpose in life.

Stein kissed the photo before tucking it back into his pocket. "We will all be together again. I promise," he whispered.

Dragging feet reached Stein's ears. Straightening his shirt and pants, he rose to his feet, a hardened expression, for which he had become well known for, clouding his face. He whirled around and saw Gaden, the man who had stayed behind on Lanyr in case Rynah returned, rounding a corner. Gaden stopped, star-tled by Stein's presence.

"What do you want?" demanded Stein.

"No—no—nothing, sir." Gaden fled from Stein's ominous presence.

Stein glowered at the spot where Gaden had been. He did not know why Klanor had brought the man aboard the ship. He would have left him to rot with what was left of that miserable planet, but then, Klanor did have a soft spot for troubled individuals, always thinking he could give them purpose.

Stein touched the side of his pocket where he kept the photo of his wife. He had a purpose. He would find a way to restore what had been taken from him. If he failed, Great Ancients, help those who would suffer his wrath.

Tom rummaged around in the storage area of the ship, looking for a way to occupy his mind. He hated the solemnness that seemed to surround everyone, though he himself felt glum. He liked Brie. Of all the people brought here, she did not deserve death, but where one died, perhaps he could give another life, so to speak.

Remembering that Solaris had mentioned wanting a physical body, Tom thought he would try to give her one—the old parts on the ship seemed like a good place to start. Discarded tubing, plastic sheeting, wires, a piece of moldy cheese (Tom used scraps of paper to move it to the waste chute, while holding his nose), scraps of synthetic material used for clothing, and useless computer components buried him to his waist in the disordered room.

He loved putting things together. Whenever he felt sadness or anger, Tom retreated to his workshop and dreamed up another invention. Now, he would do the same, except this time a specific individual would benefit.

He chuckled as he thought about Solaris as an individual. Who would have thought that an artificial intelligence, a computer, could be so human? Even in his time, computers had not reached such heights, though Solaris had reminded him more than once that she was unique, the only artificial intelligence on her planet. Marlow had created her and kept her a secret. Tom pondered why he would do such a thing.

"Ah, perfect," he said as he found something that he could use for an arm. After more rummaging, he found bolts, nuts, and even discarded memory chips. Tom piled everything into his arms and headed for the door. He paused. He needed a lab to work in if he were to complete this task. He turned in a circled, while clinging to his "junk".

"You may set up shop here," said Solaris.

Tom frowned. "Is there ever a time when you don't spy on people?" he asked her.

"No."

"I'll remember that the next time I shower," mumbled Tom.

"As though anyone wants to see you naked."

Tom studied the huge space that had been turned into a storage area. It would provide the necessary room. "I'll take it."

"Good. And I can show you how to grow skin and hair for my body."

"How did you…"

"All of the components in your arms indicate that you are planning to create a synthetic body. Since I am the only non-living member on this ship, I must assume it is for me."

Tom hated it when his secrets were discovered. "You know this was supposed to be a surprise."

"I will squeal with delight when you are finished, if that will make you feel better."

Tom chuckled. *So, Solaris had learned sarcasm.*

"There is a workbench to your left and a tool box to your right."

"Thanks," said Tom, putting his items down, "you are most helpful."

"You're most welcome."

Tom's face fell as he remembered the time he had joked to Brie about what it would be like if Solaris had arms and legs. Instead of laughing, Brie had thought it a good idea and encouraged him to consider the matter.

"Have I done something to offend you?" asked Solaris, concerned.

"No, I..." said Tom, "was just thinking about Brie. This ship is empty without her." Tom realized how his words must have seemed to Solaris and added, "I didn't mean..."

"You're right," said Solaris. "It is empty without her presence. I had become so used to her that I never thought about..."

"Tom," Solon entered the storage area. "Tom, Rynah has called a meeting."

"Now?"

"She was insistent." Solon glanced around the room and Tom's somber demeanor. "Am I interrupting something?"

"We were talking about Brie," said Tom.

Solon's small frown displayed understanding. He missed her as well.

"I should have done more," said Solaris, more to herself than the others.

"You could not have made her decision for her," said Solon. "Brie's choice was hers to make, and she chose our lives over her own. Come, we mustn't keep Rynah waiting...and someone must still summon Alfric."

"Yeah...uh...you can do that," replied Tom. "He's been a bit moody lately. More than usual."

"I will inform him of Rynah's summons," said Solaris. "He will be there when you two arrive."

Tom dropped everything and followed Solon up the steps and to the gathering area, which was where they also held their meetings. Alfric, who was there before them, as Solaris had promised, and Rynah waited for them as Tom and Solon took seats near the Viking.

"I thought we should meet," said Rynah. "I know things have been difficult without Brie, but I have realized that it is time to end this grief of ours and decide what to do next."

Rynah scanned the faces staring at her. "I have decided to continue my search for the crystals and to stop Klanor. However, I realize that I do not have the right to ask you all same. I never had the right to pull you all here in the first place, so I am offering you a choice: you can return home, or remain. I will not think any less of you for leaving. This is my fight, not yours."

Silence filled the chamber as she stopped speaking. Rynah hadn't expected them to answer right away, but she thought they might say something.

"To return home without avenging Brie's death would be dishonorable," said Alfric, breaking the silence with his deep voice.

"Revenge is a very cold dish," said Solon.

"Cold or not," said Tom, "we can't just leave you here to clean up this mess. I'm staying, for Brie."

"I am sure your noble dish would have a more desirable taste," mused Solon. "I can do no less than the others. I will remain."

Rynah stared at all of them. She hadn't expected them to stay. After all, she had kidnapped them from their planet, from their time, and plunged them into her problems. "Are you certain?"

"Yes," Tom, Alfric, and Solon said in unison.

"I thank you for not asking my opinion, but I think I will remain just the same," said Solaris.

"My apologies," said Rynah. "Solaris, would you like to continue on this foolish quest for the crystals?"

"Yes."

"Do you know where the next one is?" asked Solon.

"No," said Rynah. "I am still studying the text."

"Then I will help you," Alfric offered.

"But..."

"Your ancient text is a story. Such tales are full of symbols that most miss. I can be of assistance."

Rynah never took the Viking as being someone who was interested in stories, but there was much about his world she didn't know.

"I accept. For now, we must make the necessary repairs. When I learn the location of the next crystal, I will inform you all."

The meeting adjourned and everyone pushed back their seats to go about their business, with Tom racing back to the storage area to work on his new "project".

Chapter 3
PRISONER

Bright lights filled Brie's eyes as she opened them. Still groggy, she looked around, trying to focus. As her vision cleared, she noticed people, who looked a lot like Rynah, wearing white coats, oblivious to her movements. *I'm not dead?* Confused, Brie tried to sit up, but restraints prevented her from doing so. She looked down. Leather straps lay across her chest and hips, as well as her wrists, pinning her to the medical bed.

She glanced at the people standing around. Still unaware that she had awakened, Brie squirmed under the straps, noticing that she had some freedom of movement. Whomever had secured the restraints did not make them very tight. She wriggled her slender wrist as she slipped it free of the strap's grasp; her skin burned from the effort, but she didn't care.

Once free, Brie reached over and undid the other strap. Voices grew louder. She turned in their direction. Though the people within the room had not noticed her, they did approach the bed. Desperate, Brie freed her other hand and began working on the strap around her chest. The buckle popped.

"She's awake!"

Cursing that she had been discovered, Brie sat up and undid the final strap. She jumped off the medical bed, her unsteady feet refusing to support her weight, staggering until she found her sense of balance again. Men ran for her. Brie shoved the floating table at them, forcing them to stop and dive out of the way of the gurney.

Brie raced for the exit. The doors slid open and she burst into a busy hallway with people moving about their business. Most wore uniforms, while others wore white and blue labs coats; all of them remained incognizant to Brie's sudden presence. The bustle of the hallway disoriented her as her brain still remained foggy from having just become conscious again, but voices behind her alerted her to her current predicament.

Brie bolted. She shoved people out of her way as she ran, not caring where she went, so long as she could escape. Guards pursued her. Not slowing her pace, Brie raced down the hallway past confused onlookers, who had never seen someone with such white skin before, a stark contrast to their purple pigmentation. A set of doors loomed before her.

Glancing behind, she noticed that the guards neared. Brie grabbed the person closest to her and threw him at her pursuers as she ran through the doors. She stopped. Above her was a dome ceiling that also served as a window. Stars filled it. A transparent balcony rail was in front of her, overlooking the main floor and reminding her of the mall, which she only visited on days the weather was poor while waiting for her sister to get out of school. People walked by her, and below her; she leaned over the railing, studying their movements, trying to find an exit. As she studied the scene surrounding her, Brie realized that she was on a ship, but one that resembled a space station more than a small craft.

The doors popped open behind her. Brie dashed down the walkway and through the crowd. She found a set of stairs leading to a lower level. Taking them two at a time, she raced down them, almost knocking someone over.

"Stop her!" shouted one of the guards.

Alarms sounded overhead, alerting everyone aboard about her escape.

Brie ignored them. Heart pounding, she ran faster, looking for a way to flee her new prison. Nothing. Guards appeared before her with weapons raised. Skidding to a halt, Brie turned and veered to her left, dashing through another set of doors and into a long hallway. Her bare feet pounded the linoleum floor as she ran. Glancing all about, she spotted a promising sign.

A man appeared in front of her from around a corner. Brie ducked low, dodging his attempt to capture her. He lunged for her again, but his clumsy movements made him stumble. She spotted what looked like a fire extinguisher and snatched it. Swinging with all her might, Brie smashed the man in the chest with it. Without thinking, she pulled the pin and sprayed foamy, white liquid in his face, forcing him to stagger back and bring his hands up in an effort to block her assault.

She dropped the fire extinguisher and ran. More shouts and angry voices raged behind her as the alarm continued its onslaught of ear piercing noise. She turned another corner and passed a sign: *Level 12*. Brie refused to stop.

Another set of doors greeted her. She pushed the button to open them. With a hiss, they slid open, allowing her to pass. Brie hurried into the room, only to be stopped by a man dressed in black. His soulless eyes forced her to freeze. Frightened, she turned and went back through the door, but the way had been blocked, as the guards had caught up with her.

She froze. Turning in circles, the realization that she was trapped filled her. Brie made one last effort to get away, but hands seized her and forced her to stop.

"I must say," said a snide voice, "that was a daring escape attempt. Though I wonder, where you were planning to go once you got off the ship?"

A man with the same complexion as Rynah stepped in front of her. Klanor. She recognized the voice and the face from the images Rynah had showed her and the others.

"Let me go," said Brie.

"And where would you go?" replied Klanor. "Back to Rynah and the others? They abandoned you in space and left you here to my mercy."

"You're lying."

"I'm afraid not. That is how I found you. You have me to thank for bringing you back from the dead."

Brie glared at him. Rynah and the others never would have abandoned her. She tried to remember the last day she had seen them, forcing her mind to focus: Klanor had attacked them; she had decided to stop the engines from imploding while surrounded by clouds of poisonous gas. Rynah's sorrowful face as she watched, helpless, through the window filled her mind.

"They thought I had died," she whispered.

"And you certainly would have if I had not found you," said Klanor with a smug expression, but his voice betrayed him with a note of regret.

"What do you want with me?" demanded Brie, not knowing where this newfound rebellious attitude came from.

"Information," said Klanor, hardening his voice. "I have no desire to keep you here any longer than is necessary. However, I do require information."

"What sort of information?"

"I wish to know what Rynah knows. I wish to know about you and the others she brought aboard."

"And why would I tell you?" hissed Brie.

"I have no desire to be enemies," answered Klanor. "We can be friends. Just tell me what I want to know. Then, I will take you anywhere you wish to go. Of course, you are welcome to stay aboard. I'm sure we could find a use for you here."

"And if I refuse?"

"A foolish course of action." Klanor closed the gap between them, taking her chin into the palm of his well-muscled hand. "I have ways of making you talk, and I advise you not to force me to use them. Others have lost their minds because of it."

Brie jerked her head away. "Never."

"Suit yourself. Stein, see to it that our guest is given the best accommodations in our detention center."

The man in black, whose cold and soulless eyes filled Brie with fear, stepped forward. "Yes, sir." He flicked his hand at the guards holding her arms, and together, they hauled Brie away.

Chapter 4
Another Mission

Locked away in her quarters, Rynah studied the text of the ancient myths of her people. She hated the constant use of euphemisms or imagery that were more symbolic than literal. "Why couldn't they just say where the crystals were? Or not mention them at all?" she asked herself in the darkness.

"Because then it would be too easy," replied Solaris.

Rynah groaned. Even when she thought she was alone, Solaris always showed up. "I thought you were preoccupied."

"I was," said Solaris, "but now I'm not. How is it coming?"

"Slowly." Rynah read more lines of text.

> On the planet of eternal light
> lies an object black as night.
> A gift it is from the gods
> of stark material bold and odd.

Rynah reread the passage. *Could it be the location of the next crystal?* She read it a third time before moving to the next.

Light cannot thrive without the darkness.
Night cannot thrive without the sun's rays.
A gift this is, with a price. So beware.
What seems far away is actually near.

Keep the gods' gift close to thee
for its blackness is the key
to your salvation
and all of its revelations.

Rynah pursed her lips. *What does all this mean?* How could some crystal be her salvation, much less reveal anything to her? She hated riddles.

The door slid open with a hiss and in walked Alfric, back from his rounds. "Any progress?"

"Not really," said Rynah. She read the lines of text to him.

The Viking's eyes unfocused as he concentrated on the words. "Eternal light. It may just mean a place where there is no night, or where the sun seems to never set. In my homeland, we have a period where the sun does not rise for 30 days. Maybe the crystal is buried in a place where the sun does not sink below the horizon."

"That's a possibility," said Rynah. "Solaris, are there any planets around here that seem to always be covered in daylight?"

"Let me check." Several minutes passed as Solaris searched her immense database. "There is a trinary system in the Pryser Sector—a three-star solar system." Solaris brought up a holo-image and showed them the system she referred to. "It has a planet that is positioned in the center of the circles created by the three suns. Because of its distance, it does not overheat, but stays at an even 80 degrees Fahrenheit. There are no seasons and no nights."

"So, this planet has perpetual sunlight."

"Yes," replied Solaris. "The planet is called Cien and has a 36-hour day, and because of the position of the three suns, it never experiences darkness."

"The place of eternal daylight," muttered Rynah. "What about this other part?"

Alfric listened as she read the rest of the passage. "The crystal could be a literal key," he said. "We won't know until we have acquired it. As for the rest, it could mean anything and was probably put in there by the poet to fill the verse."

Rynah doubted that, but she knew that poets often added verses to their literary works to fill space, or add confusion. The study of literature was never her strong suit, as she always preferred direct approaches to problems and found poetry to be too metaphorical.

"At least we know where to begin the next search, though we still have the problem of getting back the crystals that Klanor stole," she said.

"An issue we shall overcome once we have found this crystal," Alfric said.

Rynah agreed.

"Uh, there might be a slight problem," said Solaris.

"What sort of problem?" asked Rynah.

"The planet is controlled by a Fredyr Monsooth."

Rynah cursed. She had heard the name, most everyone had, though she had no idea he lived on that planet.

Fredyr Monsooth was what some would call a mob leader, but not in the sense we know of. He literally controlled the planet of Cien and all its economic activities. No one landed there without his permission. No one left without it either. The man started out selling precious gems to anyone with a deep pocketbook. Once his wealth grew, Monsooth bought up every legitimate business there was on Cien until he owned everything.

His empire stretched beyond Cien, being found in other sectors, but Cien remained its heart. Pirates traded with him, though even they were careful not to intrude on his territory, or renege on a deal. Though a man with fair business sense, he detested any who crossed him. Stories were told of a man who stole one pound of flour from Monsooth's flour mill. The next day, they found his body parts floating in the Cygor River. The entire populace knew what had happened and who was responsible, but none dared do anything. The authorities always gave Fredyr Monsooth a wide berth and ignored his transgressions. He owned the planet of Cien, hence, why Rynah was dubious about going there.

"Who is this Fredyr Monsooth?" asked Alfric.

"A man you best wish you never meet," replied Rynah. "How are we supposed to search for this crystal on Cien?"

"You won't have to," said Solaris. She pulled up news articles and images of a black crystal. "Mr. Monsooth is having a celebration to honor the find of a rare artifact, the crystal we are looking for. It was found three weeks ago by some archeologists that he allowed on his planet. Of course, anything they found became his property."

"Why is he celebrating the find of some innocuous crystal?" asked Rynah.

"Because it is worth a lot of money. According to these reports, many have already begun bidding on it, and I have a feeling that Klanor will be there as well."

"Was he invited?"

"There are over a thousand guests on the list, and any who can provide a substantial amount of money will be allowed in."

Rynah thought a moment. She had no idea how to break into a security system such as the one that Fredyr Monsooth had in his home, nor did she have the funds to buy her way inside. "Solaris, I think it is time for you to hack his systems."

"Understood."

"I have some interesting news for you, sir," Stein strolled into the interrogation room where Brie sat strapped to the chair with needles in her arm.

At first glance, one would think that he had walked into a medical bay, with the long table (just to the left of the chamber's exact middle) full of syringes, vials of liquid (which Brie had no desire to learn what they were), and monitoring equipment. The sterile, colorless walls, the chair which Brie had been strapped to, resting to the right of the table, and the harsh, uninviting lights gave no doubt of being in an interrogation room; and unbeknownst to all, except Klanor and Stein, a small panel in the far right corner of the room was a two-way mirror, but well-disguised as part of the wall.

"What news?" demanded Klanor; his grumpy tone at being interrupted evident.

"The next crystal has been found." Stein handed over the holopad with the latest news posted on it. "The fool actually announced his finding and the fact that he plans to auction it off."

"Maybe not so foolish," mused Klanor. "He knows the value of his treasure. Fredyr Monsooth."

"Should I prepare a team to go in and steal it?"

"No," said Klanor, "Mr. Monsooth is not a man to be crossed. He has his own private army, and we would do well to do this his way. See to it that I am on the guest list."

"Yes, sir," said Stein. He took the holopad from Klanor and stalked out of the room, disappointed that Klanor had dismissed his suggestion.

"Now, my dear," said Klanor to Brie, "let us begin."

Chapter 5
DARING PLANS

Rynah stood at the head of the table in the briefing room, which often served as the social area as well. She eyed the others in the room, formulating her words as they waited for her to speak, but decided there was only one way to tell them.

"Alfric and I discovered where the next crystal is."

"Really?" Tom's enthusiasm filled his voice.

Rynah moved over to the holoscreen on the wall and turned it on, bringing up images of Cien and Fredyr Monsooth; his burnt orange hair, and purple skin, though a much darker complexion, provided a glaring contrast to Rynah's heliotrope skin tone. Beady eyes, the sort that picked up the minutest of details, stared back at them, giving Solon the unnerving feeling that Monsooth's image actually glowered at him. Alfric noted the fine, leather material of Fredyr's suit coat: gold beads lined the edges of the collar, accentuating the tan, silk shirt he wore underneath, marking him as a man of great wealth and power who enjoyed flaunting his riches.

"This is Fredyr Monsooth, owner of the planet Cien. Yes, I said owner. He owns every trade and transport business, every ounce of the economy on that planet."

"Why would people put up with that?" asked Tom.

"Because he provides stability," answered Rynah. "So long as you do not steal from him, you can have a fairly decent living, luxurious by some standards. Monsooth provides stability and protection. No one—not even pirates—dare attack the planet of Cien because of the retaliation he would bring. Study his face and memorize it.

"Monsooth is hosting the social event of the century. He holds titleship to the crystal, meaning that legally he owns it."

Another image popped up on the screen, showing the black crystal encased in a gilded cage.

"Diggers found it a few weeks ago, and it now resides in Fredyr's floating mansion."

Another image of his home appeared. It looked like an apartment complex that hovered in the sky. Rockets formed the base, firing thrusters every so often, but a series of powerful magnets also provided a polarity which created a repelling force from the planet's natural gravitational pull, thus allowing it to hover. It stood high up in the clouds, allowing Fredyr Monsooth to look down upon his empire.

Balconies and porches surrounded the marbled building with plants and topiaries for decoration. Even a green yard filled the center, providing some semblance of nature's natural beauty. Domed ceilings lined the top of the mansion, looking more like gems as they sparkled in the sunlight.

"This is where the celebration will take place," continued Rynah, "in his home."

"It's like a floating city," breathed Tom.

"Almost," said Rynah. "It has every security measure you can think of, and since the crystal is to be auctioned off, there will be even tighter security. This is where it gets tricky. We are not on the guest list, but Solaris has found an area that is hardly patrolled where we can slip in."

"And that would be…" began Tom.

"The garbage chute," Rynah replied. She pressed the screen and a diagram appeared, illustrating her point.

"The chute's opening is at the bottom of the base. We will go in through here, climb up into the main building, and mingle with the crowd."

"And how will we do this without smelling like refuse?" asked Solon. "We will need to blend in."

"Precisely," answered Rynah. "We will wear coveralls over our party outfits. They are made of a material that repels everything. Once inside, you three will keep Fredyr Monsooth distracted, while I locate the crystal and steal it. Solaris has already pinpointed the most likely area, and with her help, I shall be able to crack the combination to the safe."

"You alone?" asked Tom.

"One person can move around more easily than three. Now, Alfric will pretend to be a king from a distant land."

"There is no deception necessary," said Alfric. "I am a king in my land and it is far from here."

"Yes, my apologies," said Rynah. "Tom and Solon, you two will pretend to be his bodyguards."

Solon's face fell a bit. He had never been a soldier, always a scholar. "I'm not sure I would be believable."

"Nonsense!" Alfric clapped him on the back. "Because of my training, you have built muscle! You will soon be a warrior worthy of my kingdom! Consider this a test to prove your strength and your honor."

Solon grimaced. He had never done anything to prove his honor, and just hoped he could complete this mission.

"Now," continued Rynah, "Alfric, you will need to befriend Mr. Monsooth. Keep him distracted and see to it that he does not auction off the crystal before I have a chance to acquire it."

"It shall be done," said Alfric.

"Good. When I have the crystal, I will send you a sign. We will all go down to the shuttle bay; it houses many of Monsooth's most prized shuttlecraft. The guards there will be minimal, as most will be focused on the guests upstairs and on the entrance. We can steal one of Monsooth's shuttles and meet up with Solaris who will be standing by."

"Sounds simple enough," said Tom.

"The simplest plans have a way of going awry," added Solon.

"That is why if anything goes wrong, or even seems the slightest bit off, I want you three to get out of there," said Rynah. "Do what you have to do to escape and do not worry about me."

"We'll not leave you behind," said Alfric.

"I mean it," insisted Rynah. "I can take care of myself."

The others reluctantly agreed, though their grumblings told her that they did not like the idea of leaving her behind.

"And if Klanor is there?" asked Solon.

"That we will have to deal with, if it happens. He would be foolish to try anything."

"And we're not?" scoffed Tom.

Rynah gave him a piercing glare. "If we know about this auction, chances are Klanor does too. We will have to hope that we do not run into him."

"When is this party?" asked Tom.

"In two days."

"Then I guess we better get started."

The rest of the day was spent with them poring over the plans of Monsooth's home and finalizing the details of their heist.

Chapter 6
QUESTIONED SANITY

The blaring alarm clock assaulted Brie's ears as it released its fury, reminding her to wake up or face being late. Groggy, and still wishing she could sleep, she threw off the covers of her bed and looked at the clock. Seven fifteen. Blinking, Brie looked out her window and at the small unit next to theirs. A flood of memories rushed her brain; she bolted to a sitting position. *Was it all a dream?*

Brie looked around her room. Her sister slept in the bed on the other side, oblivious to her worries. A pile of dirty laundry rested in a corner. *Forgot to wash those.* Her desk was under the window as it had been since the day her mother moved them there. Everything seemed normal.

Thinking that she must have had the most vivid dream of all time, Brie crawled out of bed. "Hey, sleepyhead," she whispered to her sister, "time to get up."

Six-year-old Sara stirred, clutching her *Dora the Explorer* sheets even tighter.

"I mean it, or we'll be late."

"No."

"Come on you little, munchkin," Brie urged as she tickled her sister. "If you don't get out of that bed, I'll have to tickle you to death."

Her sister laughed with glee as she squirmed to escape Brie's onslaught of unrelenting tickling. "I'm up!"

"Good," said Brie. She looked into her sister's deep brown eyes, having inherited their father's. "Up and at 'em. I want you dressed and teeth brushed in the next 10 minutes."

Her sister jumped out of bed and ran to the bathroom, while Brie dressed in the only clean clothes she could find in her dresser: a pair of jeans with a hole in the knee, sneakers, and a washed-out tee. She checked her book bag, making certain that all her books and homework were in there. A few pages of completed math work filled her hand. She didn't even remember doing it, much less picking it up. The nagging feeling that something wasn't right gnawed at her.

"Brie!" her mother's voice echoed from the kitchen.

Brie hitched up her bag and ran into the kitchen.

"Oh, good, you're up," said her mother as she placed some toasted pastries on a dish. "I'm sorry I don't have time to make a real breakfast for you. Mr. Carrow wants me in early today." She placed her nametag on her blouse. "I'll probably be home late again. I need you to take your sister to school and pick her up today."

"No problem," Brie mumbled with her mouth full.

"I'm sorry I have to do this to you," her mother caressed her hair. "It shouldn't be like this. If only…"

"It's okay, mom," Brie interrupted, not wanting her mother to start crying again. "I don't mind taking Sara to school. You go on to work now. I'll finish up here."

"You're such a dear," her mother said. "I'll try not to be too late tonight."

Brie watched as her mother left for work, racing to the bus stop. A small bit of jealousy brushed her as she thought about how some of the kids at school who had parents that did everything for them. Shaking it off, she turned her head as Sara walked into the room. "Ready?" Brie asked as she handed her a pastry.

"Yeah."

"Let's go."

Brie shuffled her sister out the door and locked up. They raced to the bus stop as she pulled the passes from her pocket, just as the bus with its roaring engine belching black smog arrived. For a brief moment, Brie wondered how taking a bus was good for the environment as she choked on the smoke that the wind always blew into her face. Once aboard, she steered her sister to an empty seat in the back.

The trip took only 10 minutes. Most of it was spent being jostled about by the bus's worn-out shocks and the potholes that littered the paved road. Brie hugged her sister good-bye as they pulled up to the stop, one block from the elementary school. "I'll be here at three."

Sara hopped off the bus, waved, and walked to her school with her group of friends.

Sighing, Brie nestled into her seat. The vacant eyes of the man in front of her grabbed her attention. He stared right at her, and through her, at the same time. "Hey, you're creeping me out," she said.

The white haired man continued to stare at her with those vacant eyes, so Brie faced the window in an effort to ignore him.

The bus shifted gears and the engine spat as the driver pulled into the stop near the high school. Desperate to get away from the man looking at her, Brie hurried off the bus and ran to the school building. She glanced back as the bus drove past; the same man still gave her his vacant stare.

"Hey."

Brie jumped. Heather, her only friend at school, had walked up to her. Brie settled her nerves.

"What's wrong? You look freaked."

"Nothing," said Brie. She shifted her bag on her right shoulder and headed to the glass doors of her school. High school, her most dreaded prison. Brie couldn't wait for graduation, but two years was a long way away. She spotted Jenny. Brie darted behind some trash cans, pulling Heather with her.

"You know, some day you really need to stand up to her," Heather whispered as they watched Jenny and her friends walk by.

"I know, but I just don't know how."

Brie jumped. On one of the lockers in front of her was the face of a man with a beard, icy blue eyes (that bore a gentleness she didn't expect), and a stern expression that read her innermost thoughts: Alfric's face.

"Make me stop," he said.

"Hey," Heather pulled her from her mind, "where'd you go?"

"What?" Brie looked around, but the Viking's face had disappeared.

"Are you alright? You look like you've seen a ghost."

"I'm fine. Come on, I don't want to be late for homeroom."

Brie headed for her first period class, which was next to the water fountains. As she and Heather strolled past, she noticed that the fountains were different. The metal gleamed and reflected the sun, except Brie never remembered them being so clean. A group of boys raced by them, laughing and high-fiving one another.

"Since when has Jonathon been friends with Billy?" asked Brie.

"Forever," replied Heather.

Wary, Brie eyed them. The football star never hung out with the captain of the debate team. They were mortal enemies who hated one another, yet now they acted like the best of friends. The more Brie thought about it, Jenny gave up too easily. Most days, Brie and Heather hid for at least 10 minutes in the bathroom, waiting for Jenny to forget her reign of terror.

"What is with you?" demanded Heather.

"Nothing," said Brie.

"You're not acting like yourself."

"I just feel weird today," replied Brie.

The bell rang and everyone darted about as they hurried to their classes. Heather snatched Brie's arm and pulled her along as they entered their English classroom and sat in their seats, waiting for the others to settle down.

"Just try to forget all of that," said Heather.

Brie didn't answer. She watched her classmates participate in their usual behavior as they waited for the teacher. Mrs. Ophala arrived in her normal brisk manner and sharp outfit, the door slamming shut behind her. "Good morning, class."

The students settled down.

"I hope you all enjoyed your weekend."

Wasn't yesterday Wednesday? Brie thought to herself. She was certain that today was not Monday.

"Today, we will be starting a new chapter in our book," continued Mrs. Ophala. "Today, we will be learning about ancient myths and objects that were believed to possess magical power."

"Yeah, right," said a boy in the class. "I'd love to have something that would turn this desk into gold, if you know what I mean." He and his friend high-fived one another as they laughed.

"I can assure you, Mr. Dankins, that that will never happen," said Mrs. Ophala. "Today, we will read about the Grimsalga, the divine crystals who possess such power that they could destroy entire worlds, or heal them."

Brie's ears perked up. Crystals? She had dreamed about magic crystals and…

Brie jerked her head to the left and stared out the window. What had been a small grassy area, leading to the street, had now become a jumble of stars and ships darting about in chaotic zigzags. Each ship dove for her, shooting lasers. Brie watched, horrified, as one with a skull on it headed straight for her. It fired.

"Pirates!" Brie ducked under her desk, covering her head as an explosion rocked the classroom and the pirate ship veered away. She jumped back to her feet and ran to the window, watching as the pirates zoomed about in a mass of fire and exploding rockets. Heavy boots on metal forced her to turn around. Rynah's face filled hers.

"To the weapons array! Now!" Rynah ran off, sliding down more steps and disappearing around a corner.

Solon stood next to Brie. They locked eyes for a moment before he vanished.

The sounds of gunfire and grenades stopped as the scene outside the window returned to the grass and the street. Brie glanced around the room. Twenty pairs of eyes stared back at her; each thought she had lost her mind.

"Brie, honey, is everything all right?" asked her teacher.

Brie continued to study the scene before her. "This isn't real."

"What do you mean?" asked Mrs. Ophala.

"None of this is real," repeated Brie. "None of you are."

"Of course, we're real."

"No! You're not real!" Brie's screams echoed off the walls as the scene before her disappeared and she found herself strapped to a frigid, leather chair with a needle in her arm. A metallic band hugged her forehead, generating electrical pulses to her brain.

"Remarkable," said one technician. "She has a very strong will."

"I don't care about her will," said another voice, cold and callous, like the room she was in. "I want to know what she knows."

Brie screamed and struggled against the leather straps that held her into the hard-surfaced chair as her violent movements rocked it from side to side. "Let me go!"

"Increase the dosage," said the technician in charge.

Gloved hands seized Brie's wrist. She tried to pull away, but the straps and the hands held firm. Sharp pain struck her as a needle pierced her skin, injecting its poison into her veins. Growing drowsy, the people and the room faded until blackness took her.

Chapter 7
A Heist

Three suns illuminated Cien, outlining its edges in an orange glow, as Solaris arrived within range of the planet. A wide variety of ships darted about, zipping past them as they entered and exited the planet's atmosphere. No shadows could be seen on the surface of the planet as it basked in eternal daylight from its three suns.

"We have arrived," said Solaris.

"How much time until the social event of the year?" asked Rynah.

"Two hours. I will set us just out of range of their radar systems."

"Very well. Okay, fellas, it's time for us to get dressed."

Alfric entered his room, its sparse decorations mimicking his personality, as he was one who never bothered with trifles or luxuries. He grimaced. He detested the outfit that Rynah had picked for him to wear and had placed on his bunk. Satin shirts were not his idea of clothing.

"You must wear it," she had told him when she first showed it to him. "A king in this sector wears satin. You must look and play the part."

Picking up the shiny material in his meaty and calloused hands, he studied the flimsy fabric. Resigning himself to the fact that he had to wear it, Alfric tore off his fur vestments and slipped on the shirt. He picked up the pants that Rynah had included. *Too feminine*, he thought. Groaning, he put them on as well. The snug fabric hugged his muscular legs so tight that Alfric pulled uncomfortably at the material.

"Men do not know how to be men in this sector," he said to himself.

Alfric looked in the single mirror in the room. What he saw almost made him rip the clothes off, but the mission at hand stopped him. He snatched the comb off the side of the sink and smoothed out his hair and beard. Once done, Alfric left his quarters and joined the others.

"Look at you," teased Tom. "You clean up nice." He and Solon wore black suits, typical of security personnel.

Alfric glowered at him.

"Alright," said Rynah as she walked in, carrying four coveralls and wearing a purple dress that hugged all her curves and revealed the tops of her breasts. The darker shade of the gown accentuated her paler skin tones. She had even painted her lips a burgundy red and added blush and eye shadow to complete her look.

The others gawked at her as her dark emerald hair, which she had tied in a loose bun with a few curled strands hanging loose, swayed in tune to her movements.

"What?" asked Rynah.

"You look gorgeous," said Tom.

Rynah eyed him, a doubtful expression covered her face.

"You look like a queen," said Solon.

Rynah looked at herself in the metal siding. She hadn't expected their reactions to be one of shock and surprise. "I feel ridiculous in this getup."

Alfric understood how she felt, but kept that to himself. "My lady, tonight, you look like a goddess, as fair and beautiful as Freya herself."

"Thanks," said Rynah. "Okay, enough compliments. Let's get to business. Solaris?"

"We will arrive at Fredyr Monsooth's home within 10 minutes," said Solaris.

"Good," said Rynah. She tossed a set of coveralls to each of them. "Put these on."

The others obeyed, slipping the slim and form-fitting outfits over the ones they wore for the party; the smooth material hugged their bodies.

"And you'll need these. They are earpieces, which will allow us to communicate with one another at the party."

Tom put in his earpiece. Alfric and Solon studied theirs for a moment, having never seen one, much less heard of the concept. Trusting Rynah, they stuck them in their ears.

"Follow me," said Rynah as she zipped her coveralls closed.

She led them down to the cargo hold of the ship. Once there, Rynah grabbed four masks from a storage compartment and security lines. "Strap on these lines and put on the masks. You're going to want them for crawling around in the garbage."

The others took the masks and rope, securing themselves.

"Solaris, are you ready?" asked Rynah.

"Yes," replied Solaris.

"You know what to do while you wait for our signal?"

"Yes. I have found a place to hide undetected."

"Good. Wish us luck."

Rynah opened the hatch. Air roared around them, whipping their clothes with such violence that it almost knocked them over. She snapped her line in place. "Follow me," she said as she reached out and grasped one of the rungs that climbed up the side of the ship.

Solon went next. He reached out and wrapped his fingers around a metal bar. With a great leap, he jumped out, placing his feet on another set of rungs.

Tom followed, with Alfric taking up the rear.

Howling winds raged around them as they climbed up the side of Solaris, making their way to the top. Rynah glanced behind. The others still followed. She looked up at the garbage chute to the floating mansion. It loomed above her as Solaris maintained her position. Rynah grabbed another rung and pulled herself up. As she reached the top of the ship, she turned back to the others.

Solon's hand slipped. Before he could slide off, Rynah dove for him, snatching his arm and pulling him to safety.

Tom came next, positioning himself beside Solon.

Alfric's bulky form appeared over the ridge of the ship, and he held his position as he waited for Rynah to issue the next set of orders.

Satisfied that they had all made it, so far, Rynah reached up for the opening in the garbage chute. "Hold steady, Solaris."

"What do you think I've been doing this entire time?"

Rynah twisted the wheel on the hatch. It wouldn't budge. Cursing her luck, she twisted again, putting all her strength into it. It held firm. Frustrated, she slumped back and noticed that black gunk had crusted over the hinges and the gears. Using her hand, she picked at it until she had peeled most of it away.

Rynah tried the wheel again. It moved an inch. Relieved, she twisted as hard as she could until the wheel turned with ease. The hatch popped open. She unhooked herself from her safety line, pulled herself inside the garbage chute, pressing both her hands and feet against the sides of the metal chute, and inched her way upward.

Solon entered the chute next, followed by Tom and Alfric, who closed the hatch.

"All right, Solaris," said Rynah in her earpiece, "we're in."

"Acknowledged," said Solaris.

They heard her engines as she flew away to the agreed hiding place.

Grunting, they climbed upwards, inching their way through the garbage chute amidst decayed debris and piles of black mold. The slow going seemed to take hours, but in actuality, it only took them 20 minutes to make their way to the top.

"What if someone decides to throw some garbage in here?" asked Tom.

"You best hope that they don't," replied Rynah as sweat dribbled down her neck and back.

The four of them in such tight quarters increased the temperature of the chute, causing their breaths to fog the visors on their masks, adding to the heat. Solon's arms tired. He slipped again, but managed to catch himself before he knocked Tom and Alfric down.

"We don't have very far to go," said Rynah, as her arms and legs begged her to rest.

She crept upwards. Light spilled in from just above her head. Rynah climbed another foot. She pushed against the place where the light came in. The flap opened. Realizing that they had reached the top of the garbage chute, Rynah grasped the opening and hauled her way through it. She scanned the hallway she had found herself in. They were alone.

"Solaris, did you get the cameras?" whispered Rynah in her earpiece.

"Yes," replied Solaris. "All they see is an empty hallway, but you need to hurry because two guards are rapidly approaching your position."

Rynah reached back into the chute and heaved Solon out. She did the same for Tom, but Alfric refused her assistance as he crawled out of the dark hole and into the light of the hallway with its embroidered carpet.

They stripped off their coveralls and shoved them back into the garbage chute. Footsteps sounded from around a corner. Rynah motioned for all of them to follow her. They ran to the end of the hall, stopping at a door. Locked. Using one of her hairpins, Rynah picked the lock and ushered them inside, shutting the door just as the two guards rounded the corner.

"I'm telling you I heard something," said one.

"You're imagining things," said the other.

"No, I heard something."

The second guard spoke into his radio. "Central, have you noticed anything unusual in this area within the last hour?"

"No," came a crackled reply. "Just you two."

"Understood," said the second guard. He turned to his buddy. "Come on."

Rynah watched through the slit in the door as the two security guards disappeared again. "Solaris, is it clear?"

"Yes," replied Solaris. "I have switched the cameras back, so now no one will see you."

"Quickly," said Rynah as she left the room.

The five companions raced down the carpeted hallway to where the guards had disappeared. Rynah peeked around the corner. Clear. She and the others hurried down the corridor. Faint music touched their ears. Knowing they were close to where the party was, Rynah quickened her pace; their footsteps made little sound on the carpeted floor.

The music grew louder. Rynah stopped as they reached another corner. She peered around it. They had reached the celebration area. Sunlight spilled through the domed ceiling, its tinted glass turning the white rays to a rose color, illuminating the balcony of the second floor and the ballroom below. Guests, who were unaware of their presence, strolled up and down the stairs.

Rynah noticed a group passing near their hiding place. "Blend in with the crowd," she whispered to the others, indicating the group of guests walking by. As one, they darted out from behind the corner, mixing in with the crowd. Making certain no one spotted their movements, Rynah and the others meandered down the flight of steps to the room below with the group of guests that giggled and chatted among themselves. Once at the bottom, they peeled away from the group.

Solon and Alfric looked around at the floating fountain (Truly, it had to be made of gold!) and its 12 spouts that streamed frothy, amber colored wine. A chandelier, just as elegant and magnificent as the fountain, hovered four inches from the arched ceiling above it (which had ivory braiding lining its seams), providing a warm and inviting yellow light on the celebration below—much like candlelight, yet brighter. People ambled past, but they looked nothing like the people back home, or even like Rynah. A pair of women, with ears that resembled those of a dog and even possessing pug noses, giggled as they meandered by, their eyes roving over Alfric and his satin attire.

"You seem to be attracting some admirers," mused Rynah.

Alfric frowned. He'd rather be admired for his skill in battle, not his strange—and much too womanly, in his opinion—attire.

"Just go with it," urged Rynah. "Here, kings dress as such and"—she snatched a pair of gloves from the pocket of another passing guest—"they do not have such hardened hands. Put these on."

Alfric obeyed.

"Now we just need to find Mr. Monsooth," said Rynah, as she surveyed the crowd. She needn't have worried about finding the host of the party, because at that moment, Fredyr Monsooth strolled by. Rynah's stunning gown caught his eye as she was the only one who wore purple, aside from him.

"Pardon me," said Fredyr Monsooth, "but I do not believe we have met."

Rynah couldn't believe her luck. "We haven't," she said, holding out her hand. "My name is Rynah, Mr...." She allowed her voice to trail off.

"Monsooth. But you may call me Fredyr." Fredyr kissed her hand, the gentleness of it marveled her. "I must say that your dress is striking. And bold."

"Bold?"

"No one else here is wearing such a color, as it is fit only for royalty."

"Should I change?" Rynah asked, feigning apology.

"Not at all," said Fredyr, "as that outfit suits you."

"I am pleased you like it. Oh, allow me to introduce Alfric, King of the Viking Clan, and his two bodyguards. He never goes anywhere without them."

"A wise policy," said Fredyr. "Will you and your friend join us?"

"It would be our honor," said Rynah. She allowed Fredyr to lead her by the hand to the far side of the ballroom, where an enormous table sat piled with food and drink.

Alfric walked with them, while Solon and Tom trailed behind with stern faces, doing their best to play the part of hardnosed bodyguards.

Once they reached the table, Fredyr held out a chair for Rynah and motioned for a servant to do the same for Alfric, while Solon and Tom took their place near his chair with stoic expressions. Their eyes roamed every inch of the party, keeping aware of the exits and the movements of the attendees.

"So tell me, Alfric, King of the Vikings, what is your homeland like and where is it?" asked Fredyr as a waiter poured wine into his gold plated (with diamonds lining the bottom edges) glass.

"My kingdom is far from here, Mr. Monsooth. It is cold and dark, but fit for a man to prove his honor," answered Alfric.

"Indeed," said Fredyr. "I would like to see such a place."

"Perhaps one day you shall."

"I noticed you carry a dagger with you."

Alfric frowned; he had thought he had concealed it. "A man in my position must always be prepared in case a traitor shows himself."

"I see that you and I think a lot alike," said Fredyr. "I too carry a means of self-defense." He pulled open his jacket, revealing a knife, the likes of which Alfric had never seen. Its light blade, made it easy to carry, but its sharp edges, made it lethal. "This little beauty has a companion known as the *Kresnyr* sword. Are you familiar with it?"

"No."

"To fight using the *Kresnyr* sword is an art form. The blade has three points, and made from a metal that is indestructible. Any who can use it is a worthy opponent."

"As would any who can defeat such a blade would be," said Alfric, intrigued by this weapon that Fredyr had described.

"Do you know that art of swordsmanship?" asked Fredyr.

"Indeed I do," replied Alfric. "In my homeland, one is expected to know the sword regardless of their station. My father gave me my first blade when I had reached my fourth winter."

"Perhaps we should match our skills," said Fredyr. "It is difficult finding a worthy opponent."

"Indeed."

"And you, my dear," Fredyr said as he stroked Rynah's arm, "what do you do?"

"I am a wanderer," replied Rynah.

"You never stay in one place?"

"Only if I have a reason to," Rynah teased.

"Perhaps, I can give you one," said Fredyr, with a hungry look in his eyes.

Rynah smiled as she sipped her drink, its charm concealing her desire to shove his face into the glass table. She watched the party guests frolic and talk amongst themselves as though they hadn't a care in the world. Many seemed glad to relieve Fredyr of his drink and lavish food.

"You seem distracted," Fredyr said.

"Only by your magnanimous presence," said Rynah.

"You have rich accommodations," said Alfric, "far greater than I thought possible."

"Does that surprise you?" asked Fredyr.

"Yes," replied Alfric, "but it proves that you are a far greater man than some have led me to believe."

"And what people are they?"

"Outlanders mostly. The envious type."

"The universe is full of those. I trust the food is to your liking."

"Very much." Alfric raised his glass and took a sip.

A group walked up with one man they all recognized in the center, Klanor. Tom almost choked when he saw him, but regained his composure. Rynah lowered her glass. She had hoped to avoid running into him, but at the moment, luck was not on her side. Hers and Klanor's eyes locked.

"Mr. Monsooth," said Klanor, with gratitude flowing from his lips, "I cannot thank you enough for granting me an invitation to your party."

"I must say, Klanor, that your message intrigued me. So you really think that someone will try to steal my crystal on this night?"

"I do," answered Klanor, glancing in Rynah's direction.

"And do you know who these thieves are?" asked Fredyr.

"I have my suspicions, but they are only that."

Rynah watched the proceedings, prepared to flee with the others if Klanor gave her away.

"Only suspicions?" continued Fredyr.

"At this point," said Klanor.

"They will never get past my security," said Fredyr.

"I believe they are closer than you think," replied Klanor, "but I fear that I am interrupting your guests."

"Not at all. Please, sit down."

Klanor took the seat that Fredyr had indicated, graciously accepting a plate of exotic food and a glass of sparkling liquid.

"It is fortuitous that you have come here tonight," said Fredyr. "I'd like you to meet Alfric, King of the Viking Clan. He has traveled far just to gaze upon my crystal."

"Indeed," said Klanor, raising his glass in Alfric's honor.

The Viking returned the favor, playing his part in the charade.

"And this lovely creature is Rynah," Fredyr said, infatuated with her.

"Rynah," said Klanor, "your beauty stands alone in this room and none can match it."

"That is quite a compliment," said Rynah. "I thank you." Her voice portrayed honey, while her eyes betrayed her, showing hatred. Reminding herself why she was there, Rynah smiled, softening her eyes, and pretended to enjoy herself.

"I beg your indulgence, Mr. Monsooth, but might I ask the lady for a dance?" said Klanor.

"By all means," said Fredyr, "but do not keep her long. I have plans of getting to know her more intimately."

Knowing she had to play along, Rynah grinned and accepted Klanor's hand as he led her to the dance floor. Music flowed over them, playing an energetic tune for the dancers. Klanor wrapped one arm around Rynah's slender waist, while his other hand took her left. He whirled her, though taking great pains to be gentle, before bringing her back into his arms.

"I must say that I am impressed that you have managed to get this far," he said. "How is it you plan to steal the crystal?"

"I could ask the same of you," spat Rynah.

"Such spite. Careful, Rynah, Fredyr Monsooth might see it."

"Only if you tell him."

Klanor dipped Rynah, bringing his lips to her ear. "You do smell lovely." He pulled her back up and they drifted across the ballroom floor with a grace many had never seen.

"Why didn't you tell him?" asked Rynah. "Why didn't you tell him who I was?"

Klanor's face twitched, but he quickly regained his composure. "No need. If you do manage to steal the crystal, you will have garnered a dangerous enemy. Besides, I am most curious to see if you can pull it off."

"I bet you are."

"I never meant to hurt you, Rynah."

Rynah's eyes widened. "Never? What did you think would happen when you stormed into the geo-lab and stole the crystal? You destroyed our planet for your gain and used me to do so."

"But you could have joined me," said Klanor. "I even asked you to."

"When you asked me to start a new life with you, I assumed you meant marriage, not this."

"My fault entirely," said Klanor. "You could still join me, Rynah."

"Never."

"Give up this foolish quest of yours. You cannot win."

They continued dancing to the music, ignoring the others that whirled around them, lost as they were in their argument.

"Foolish it may be," said Rynah, "but I will never assist you in your venture to build a weapon of indescribable power."

"But do you know what kind of power that is?"

Rynah said nothing.

"What do you think the crystals are?" asked Klanor.

"A weapon."

"A weapon, yes, but they are much more. Marlow understood them better than anyone. Together, the crystals can do more than create a weapon. Once together, they can be used to create a new world. Think about it. With them, we can bring back Lanyr and all who were lost.

"They can even turn back time and literally create something from nothing. Think of all you could do with that sort of power. You could use them to stop the destruction of Lanyr. You could even use them to erase Marlow's shame."

"You're insane."

"I'm serious, Rynah. With the crystals, we can create a new universe, one we want."

"No one should have that kind of power."

"At one point, someone did."

"And what do you intend to use them for?"

Klanor's lack of response told her what she already knew.

"I thought so. You have chosen your path, and I have chosen mine."

"Then I wish you well," said Klanor.

Rynah studied his eyes and saw sincerity there. Confused, she broke from his embrace and stalked away from the dance floor to the stairs. "Alfric, it's time," she whispered into her earpiece.

Alfric heard Rynah's command in his earpiece and nodded at Tom and Solon. The two of them moved further away to get a better view of the ballroom, but not too far from Alfric, where they might attract attention.

Klanor sat back down at the table.

"Where is Rynah?" asked Fredyr.

"She apologizes, but she felt a bit dizzy and has gone to the lounge to freshen up and regain her composure."

Alfric raised an eyebrow, curious as to why Klanor had lied.

"I do hope she feels better soon," said Fredyr, anticipating a chance to be alone with her.

"Mr. Monsooth, if I might ask," said Alfric, "but how is it you came by such a wonder as this crystal? I have never seen anything of its kind."

"That is a most intriguing tale," replied Fredyr.

"I wish very much to hear it," prodded Alfric.

"Then I shall tell it, if you tell me more about your homeland."

"We have a bargain," said Alfric. He glanced over as Klanor

motioned to Stein to leave. Unable to do anything, he hoped that Rynah had planned for all variables, while keeping a watchful eye on Klanor.

Rynah hurried up the steps, doing her best to act casual. The last thing she needed was for Fredyr's security detail to notice her movements.

"Solaris, do you have it?"

"I have the map pulled up," replied Solaris. "You will need to take the first hallway on your right."

Rynah reached the top of the stairs and moved down the second floor balcony to the hallway Solaris had indicated. Two security guards blocked her way. Thinking quickly, Rynah feigned losing her balance as she neared them, forcing one to catch her.

"I'm sorry," she said, "but I feel a bit faint. Is there a place where I might rest? Too much wine, you know."

The two guards looked at each other, unsure if they should let her pass.

"Please," pleaded Rynah, doing her best to appear ill, "even a restroom would do."

"Down that way and to your left. First door on the right," said one of the guards, taking pity on her.

"Thank you very much," said Rynah. She staggered down the hall, maintaining her charade as she rounded the corner on her left.

She stopped and peered back down the corridor. The two guards had gone back to their usual pose, paying no attention to her. Rynah darted across the hall and to the corridor that Solaris had told her to go down. She was alone.

"I have control of all the cameras," said Solaris, "but you don't have much time until they realize that I have looped the video feed."

"Understood."

Rynah ran down the hall, her heels making soft plops on the plush carpet. Tables and plants of every variety from the Twelve Sectors lined the way, but she ignored the paintings and sculptures, concentrating only on the task at hand.

"Solaris, I need some direction."

"Take the next left."

Rynah did. Still, she remained alone in the vast labyrinth of corridors that lined Fredyr Monsooth's home.

"There should be a door at the end."

"There is."

"You'll need to go through it."

Rynah reached the door and tested the gold knob. Locked. She took her shoe off and pulled the heel out. On the revealed tip was a slender disk, which she inserted into the slot between the doorframe and the door. A holoscreen turned on as a series of numbers raced across it.

"Hurry up," hissed Rynah, growing impatient.

"I can only go so fast," said Solaris. "This is a very complicated key code."

Noise, like rattling disks, sounded from the other end of the corridor. Rynah crept closer, peeking around a corner. She watched as three waiters carried trays down the hallway and disappeared through a door. Rynah went back to the locked door. The light turned green and the lock popped. Relieved, she took the disk out of the slot and put her shoe back together before entering the room.

She shut the door behind her and pulled out a tiny flashlight. Shining the powerful beam around the dark room, Rynah looked for anything that resembled a safe, checking the giant portraits of Fredyr that hung on the wooden walls. *Conceited*, she thought to herself. She pulled it away to peek behind. No safe. Rynah checked another portrait of Fredyr in the room. Nothing. Growing frustrated, she rifled through a pile of loose papers on his desk, each slip making swishing sounds.

As she rummaged through his office, her foot stepped on a small mound underneath a purple rug filled with gold-embroidered, geometric shapes. A panel on the top of the desk opened and a holoscreen appeared, flickering before her eyes, asking for a command.

"Solaris, I think I found his console, but it wants a password."

"I am running the decryption program now. One minute."

Heavy footfalls echoed outside as a guard strolled past. Rynah froze. She watched the shadows caress the light that spilled under the door, only releasing the breath that she had been holding, once the shadows disappeared.

"Got it," said Solaris.

The holoscreen flashed images across it as it logged onto Fredyr Monsooth's network. Rynah studied the files that appeared, looking for anything that referred to the crystal. She found three. She touched the screen, opening the first one. Images and documents about the dig that had excavated the crystal appeared. As she scanned them, Rynah realized that they had nothing to do with the crystal's current location.

She opened the second file. All it revealed were inventory registers and bankrolls, but nothing about the crystal.

"Third time's the charm," she said to herself as she opened the third, and final, file.

A high resolution image of the black crystal filled the entire screen. "Got ya!"

Rynah scanned through the documents, hoping to glean information about its whereabouts. Something caught her eye. In the center of the image was a red dot. *Odd,* she thought. It didn't seem to fit. She pressed the dot on the screen. Suddenly, the desk rose five inches above the floor as a poof of pressurized air escaped. Its slow rotation forced Rynah to step back. As the desk moved away, a staircase leading downward to another level revealed itself, with bluish-white lights lighting the stairs, beckoning her to enter.

"Rynah, is everything all right?" asked Solaris with concern.

"I think I found where he hid the crystal," said Rynah as she placed her heeled foot on the first step. Making certain that no alarms went off, Rynah hurried down the stairs, holding her dress up so she wouldn't trip over it. A cold, concrete room greeted her when she reached the final step.

An empty case stood in the center of the room. Rynah ran to it, but her hopes at succeeding in her venture were dashed. She stared at the vacant case with fury. The crystal had been there; the papers and holopads revealed as much, but it wasn't there now.

"Rynah, do you have it?"

"No," said Rynah. "It was here, but not anymore."

Disappointed, Rynah searched the room, hoping to find a clue to its current location. Nothing. In anger, she smashed her fist on the counter, causing a holopad to land on the hard floor with a clank. Curious, Rynah picked it up. A map appeared on its screen accompanied by the name of a room.

"Solaris," said Rynah, "I am sending you the contents of this holopad. See if you can gather any information from it about the crystal."

"Affirmative."

Rynah's impatience showed as she waited for Solaris to finish her decryptions and analysis of the pad's data core; the seconds ticked by at an agonizing pace.

"Got it," said Solaris as she came back on the radio. "It appears that the crystal has been moved to another part of the complex. It is in the Ante Room, where it is to be auctioned off and is heavily guarded."

"I need you to take me to it," said Rynah, running up the stairwell and back into the dark office. The floorboard over the secret room replaced itself and the desk moved back into its original position just as she exited.

"Rynah," said Tom over the earpiece, "Fredyr is starting to wonder about your absence."

Rynah cursed. This was taking longer than she had planned. "You'll have to make something up. The crystal isn't in his office. It's in another part of the complex. I'm on my way to it now."

She opened the door a crack, peeking out. The hall was empty. Seizing her chance, Rynah slipped out of the office and shut the door before hurrying down the hall.

"Solaris, now would be a good time for directions."

"Go straight," said Solaris. "Take the first left and the second right."

Rynah rounded the corner, following Solaris' instructions and took the second right. *Why does this place have to be a maze?* "Now where?"

"There should be a door straight ahead, with one off to the right. Take the one on the right. It will take you back to the party. Walk straight through, until you come to the double doors and go through them."

Rynah quickened her pace. She dashed through the door that Solaris had instructed her to go through. Music and the chattering of party guests filled her ears. A waiter with a tray passed in front of her; Rynah swerved so as to avoid him—and making a mess in the process—and hurried straight ahead to the glass double doors, her heels clicking on the ballroom floor.

Glancing around, Rynah kept her head low, while she looked for anyone who might recognize her. She spotted Alfric at the table with Fredyr and Klanor, engrossed in conversation, while Tom and Solon maintained their positions as bodyguards. Alfric looked up and noticed her. Rynah motioned for him to keep talking as she dashed through the crowded room.

"I'm on my way to the crystal," she said in her earpiece. "Keep them busy a little longer."

Solon nodded his head, acknowledging her orders.

Rynah reached the doors. They stood twice as high as her, with planters hanging from the arched ceiling. A guard stood there. Rynah strolled up to him. "Excuse me, but I think that man over there is trying to steal some of the silverware." She pointed at a random guest who had needles for a beard.

The guard summoned two others and went to the man after thanking Rynah. Pleased that her ruse worked, she bolted through the glass doors, unaware that Stein had seen her from his corner of the room.

"Now what?"

"Take a left," said Solaris, "and a right. Go straight, and then another left. That will take you past the pool and straight to the Ante Room."

Rynah ran as fast as her fancy shoes would allow. She didn't dare take them off, fearing that she might drop them if she tried to carry them. She found the turn and took it. Thanking her luck that no one patrolled the corridors, being too preoccupied with the social event of the year, Rynah quickened her pace.

She almost stopped when she entered the pool area. It was large enough to fill an entire football field with waterslides and sectioned-off areas for more intimate occasions. Rynah couldn't believe it. Fredyr Monsooth knew how to live as a wealthy tycoon who believed he owned the world. Of course, in this case, he did own the planet of Cien.

Rynah glanced up at the bright sky and the wisps of clouds as she caught her breath. Hiking up her dress, she dashed across the area by the pool, hoping that no one from the party had decided to take a quick dip. Her breathing quickened as the altitude began to wear on her from all her exertion.

Her shoes clicked on the marbled area by the pool as she rushed past lounge chairs and a bar, which was closed at the moment. Chill winds tickled her cheeks, but she welcomed them as they comforted her warm, and reddened, face.

"I'm in the pool area," Rynah said as she ran.

"The doors straight ahead will take you to the Ante Room. According to the security footage, the crystal is there, but there are security guards."

"I need you to get them out of there."

"How?"

"Pull the fire alarm if you have to, but figure out a way," insisted Rynah.

"I am hacking into their communications," said Solaris. "Attention! Attention! Disturbance in the kitchens. All security detail report. Repeat, all security report to the kitchens."

Rynah reached the doors to the Ante Room out of breath. She stopped short and watched through the window as the guards in the room listened to Solaris' message that played over their earpieces and left.

"Good work, Solaris," praised Rynah.

"I have my moments, but you don't have much time. They'll soon learn that it was a hoax."

Rynah slipped through the door and into the empty room with its rows and rows of chairs. In the front of it stood a pedestal with a gavel and a giant, velvet curtain draped behind as a backdrop. Knowing that behind the curtain was where the crystal lay, Rynah raced to the front of the room and up the steps to the podium. She darted behind the curtain. The black crystal loomed before her, emanating a soft glow of its own, a testament to its power.

She approached it.

"Wait!" Solaris stopped her. "According to my readings, there is a protective forcefield around it."

Rynah slapped herself. How could she be so stupid? Of course Fredyr Monsooth would have taken extra precautions. She took out her palm-sized flashlight and shone it on the crystal. A mesh of green lines appeared. "How am I to get through this?"

"One moment," Solaris said as she ran schematics of the crystal's casing through her database. "Just below the glass, there should be a panel."

Rynah approached the case with caution. She walked around it, looking for the panel that Solaris had said was there. Growing more agitated as the seconds ticked by, Rynah began to think that maybe Solaris was wrong when something snatched her attention: a small square on the pedestal of the crystal's case. Rynah hiked up her dress, revealing the small pouch of tools she had tied around her thigh, and yanked it free, pulling out a screwdriver and used it to pry the panel off.

"Now what?"

"There should be two wires, one green and one yellow. Cut the green one."

Wiping the sweat from her hands, Rynah removed the small scissors from the pouch and placed them on the green wire. Bracing herself for the alarm, she cut it. Nothing happened. Relieved, Rynah relaxed her tense muscles. "Done."

"Okay, now you will need to strip the casing off the yellow wire, but do not cut it."

Rynah did as instructed. Once the wire had been exposed, she told Solaris.

"Now tie the green wire to the yellow wire. Once you do that, you will need to slip a metal object in the righthand corner of the box. There should be a slot of some kind."

Rynah focused the beam of her light on it. There was a tiny slot, but what could she use to slip in there? She searched and searched, but found nothing. But an idea struck her. She took apart the back of her flashlight, revealing the small power cell and the thin metal plate that held it in place and completed the electrical connection. Wishing she didn't have to sacrifice her light, Rynah pulled the metal plate free.

"Hurry," urged Solaris.

"Rynah, we have a lot of activity here," said Tom.

"I'm almost there," said Rynah.

Flexing her fingers, Rynah calmed her nerves as she tied the green wire to the exposed yellow one. Being extra careful, she positioned the metal piece from her light in the slot and let go; it clicked into place and the green laser lights switched off.

Glad that something had gone right for a change, Rynah tore the glass case off the crystal. She hiked up her skirt again, revealing the small bag she had tied to her other thigh. Yanking it free, she blew it open. With nimble hands, Rynah reached for the crystal, and as her fingers wrapped around its cool exterior, a slight tingle danced up her arm, surprising her, since the previous crystals hadn't done it. Ignoring it, Rynah grabbed the crystal and stuffed it in her bag, securing it.

"I got it," said Rynah as she ran off the stage and back the way she had come. "Alfric, Tom, Solon, get out of there now. Meet me at the hangar bay."

She burst through the doors to the pool area. Rynah paused, trying to remember where the hangar bay was, having gotten all turned around in her efforts to locate the crystal.

"Solaris, help."

"There should be a door behind you. Take that and go out the other side. Then hang a left, and it should lead straight to the hangar bay."

"Thanks."

Alfric glanced at Tom and Solon after Rynah had informed them that she had acquired the crystal. Now he had to think of a way to get out without making a scene. "I must say, Mr. Monsooth, that this food is quite enticing."

"Yes, it's a delicacy here," answered Fredyr.

Stein hurried to the table. He leaned over and whispered into Klanor's ear.

"Indeed," whispered Klanor with a grin.

"News?" asked Fredyr.

"Well, yes," replied Klanor. "It appears my associate here has seen your mysterious minx go through those doors a moment ago and she hardly looked ill."

Fredyr's face darkened a bit. "She came with you, didn't she?"

"Yes," answered Alfric, "perhaps she just needed a bit of fresh air. Crowds can be stifling."

"Perhaps." Fredyr's voice betrayed that he did not believe Alfric's suggestion; his sense that not all was right had engaged.

"I'm sure it's nothing," said Klanor, "but maybe you can take us to the crystal, and along the way, we may pick up your intriguing guest."

"That is an excellent idea," Fredyr stood up. "This way, gentlemen."

"As enticing as that sounds, I must rest a little myself," said Alfric, hoping they bought his excuse.

"It isn't far," said Fredyr.

"Yes, but perhaps a moment of..."

"I insist," Fredyr's voice had grown hard.

"Very well." Alfric followed, with Tom and Solon close behind.

"Without your bodyguards," said Fredyr.

"I never go anywhere without them."

"Mine will be sufficient."

Knowing he would not win this with words, Alfric nodded at Tom and Solon, who stepped back.

"Now what?" whispered Solon.

Tom didn't answer. He looked around the ballroom for anything that would allow Alfric to break free. Something red—and very familiar looking—snatched his attention. "Unbelievable," he whispered as he hurried over to it.

A small sign read, "In case of fire." Tom grabbed the small crowbar and smashed the glass, exposing the alarm. He pressed the red button; the moment he did, squealing bells raged around them, as blinking, red lights popped out of the floor, forcing everyone into a panic.

"Come on," Tom said to Solon as he ran for Alfric.

The moment the alarm sounded, Alfric seized his chance. He picked up Stein with ease and threw him into Fredyr, Klanor, and the guards that accompanied him, before running in the opposite direction. He found Tom and Solon. Together, they raced out of the ballroom and into a hallway packed with panicking guests.

"Follow me," said Tom, taking the lead. He had memorized the schematics for the complex and knew exactly where the hangar bay was.

Rynah burst through the steel door and into a locker room— its opulence stunned her—full of plush, red couches, ivory towels with Fredyr's insignia embroidered in gold and silver in their center, and gold showerheads. Gold lined lockers, with ruby-colored nameplates, protected people's belongings behind a glass panel which a code opened. Rynah ignored it all. She hurried past the showers and toilets as she beelined for the door on the other side of the room.

Voices spilled from beyond it. Scrunched against the door, Rynah listened as two security guards jogged through the hallway— their feet pounded the floor with hard thumps—speaking into their radios. Time ran short. Once they had gone, Rynah yanked the door opened and darted out. She turned in the direction Solaris had told her to, running as fast as she could.

Shouts behind her forced her to turn her head. The theft had been noticed. Rynah whirled around just in time to see two people kissing in the hallway. She couldn't stop, crashing into both of them, knocking them to the floor as she sprawled across the carpet; a loud rip alerted her to a tear in her dress. Without a word, Rynah jumped to her feet and took off.

"Hey!" shouted one of the two she had knocked to the ground.

His insults fell on deaf ears as Rynah hurried to the hangar bay. "Alfric, where are you?"

"We are not far," came his reply.

A guard appeared before her. Without slowing her pace, Rynah swung the bag with the crystal, striking the man in the face. He fell to the floor, unmoving. She ran even faster, her feet pummeling the floor the way a stampede shakes the earth.

"*Belgryr!*" she cursed as she missed her turn.

Her feet skidded on the floor as she came to a halt and turned, darting around the corner just as more guards showed up. Tom and the others appeared further down the hall. Rynah ran as fast as she could. She zipped through the hall, shoving people out of her way, not caring if she injured them in the process.

"You're late," teased Tom as she reached them.

"Yeah, well, I got distracted by all the beautiful things in this place," Rynah replied. "Come on!"

Together, the four of them ran through the corridors crammed full of fleeing guests, pushing and ramming their way through the mass of bodies. Shouts and whistles sounded behind them as the guards spotted their presence. The hangar bay lay just ahead.

Shlomp!

Glass, security doors slammed shut, cutting off exits and escape routes. Rynah stopped.

"What are you doing?" demanded Tom.

"Take this," she said, handing Alfric the crystal. "Steal a ship from the hangar bay and get out of here. Solaris will meet you at the rendezvous point."

"What about you?" Alfric grabbed her arm as she turned to flee. "I'll distract them," said Rynah. "Now go!" She ran away.

"But…" Tom protested, but Alfric seized him and shoved him onward.

Rynah paused further down the hall and watched as they entered the hangar bay with guards hurrying after them. She pressed another alarm bell, causing a glass security panel to seal the doorway to the hangar bay and cut off the guards' pursuit. Pleased that the others had made it, Rynah turned and ran.

Alfric and the others bolted into the shuttle bay among a crowd of others pressing against them to get to their ships, and away from what they knew was certain danger. They stopped. Together, each glanced around at all of the spacecraft, wondering which one to take.

"Perhaps we should convince someone to give us passage from this place," suggested Solon.

Tom noticed a man in a bright blue outfit, with squiggly hair and an elongated face, fiddle with his pocket. He pulled out a control pad and pressed a button, opening the hatch to a nearby ship. "There!"

Alfric ran over to him, grabbing the man's hand, and pried the control pad from him.

"Hey!"

Alfric's murderous glare stopped any protests.

"Take it," said the frightened guest as he ran away.

Alfric handed Tom the control pad. "Can you operate this vessel?"

Tom studied the item in his hand. "I'll have to," he said as guards entered the hangar bay and headed straight for them.

The three men scrambled aboard the tiny ship, squeezing into the cockpit, which was quite a feat, considering Alfric's bulky size took up most of the space. Tom pressed the ignition button. The engines roared to life as fire spilled from the booster rockets.

"Fasten your seatbelts," said Tom as he pulled back on the controls and shot forward. They raced down the hangar bay, past the other ships that awaited their owners, and out the open doors. Once freed from the confines of the hangar, Tom took them high into the sky and veered to the left.

"What are you doing?" demanded Alfric as he hugged the crystal close.

"Going for Rynah," answered Tom.

Alfric placed his hand on Tom's shoulder. "She ordered us go to the rendezvous point."

"But we can't just leave her," said Tom.

"Trust her," Alfric said. "She will find a way."

A disbelieving look crossed Tom's face.

"I believe he is right," said Solon. "We cannot risk losing the crystal. Rynah would not want that."

"Fine." With reluctance, Tom steered away from the floating mansion and headed straight upward until they had broken free of Cien's atmosphere. He punched the rendezvous coordinates into the computer's navigation system. "I hope you're right."

Alfric prayed that he was also correct.

"There!" shouted a guard.

Rynah ran faster. A man blocked her path. Pulling her fist back, she punched him in the jaw as she rushed by. His staggering body slowed the guards down, but not by much. More joined the pursuit.

Rynah spotted a laundry chute. She dived into it headfirst, sliding down several floors until she popped out the other end and crashed into a full laundry cart. Catching her breath, she saw faces appear above her. Rynah scrambled to her feet and dashed through the steam-filled laundry room, ignoring the odd glances she received from the employees.

"Solaris," said Rynah into her earpiece, "change of plans."

"What?"

"Alfric and the others will meet you at the rendezvous point. I'll find another way out."

"Rynah, this wasn't part of..."

"No time! Just go! I'll meet up with you somehow."

"What are you planning?"

"I'll think of… something."

Rynah stopped. She watched as some of the workers strapped on parachutes and jumped through an escape hatch. *Of course,* she thought, *even they would need a way out if there ever was an emergency.* She spotted one in particular who struggled to fasten his chute's harness. Rynah dashed past the enormous washing machines and tackled the man. They rolled across the floor. The man stood up, dazed. Rynah pounced on him. She swept his feet out from under him before jumping on his back and securing her arms around his neck in a chokehold. The man struggled, trying to strike her, but Rynah remained just out of reach. He fell to the floor, unconscious, allowing Rynah to strip the parachute off him.

"She's over there!" Security guards had appeared in the laundry area.

Glancing over her shoulder, Rynah snatched the chute and ran. She jumped over carts and darted past hanging sheets as she searched for the exit. Laser fire zipped by her. Dodging their attack, Rynah swerved around a full laundry cart, turned, and shoved it into a guard that had neared her. He hunched over as the cart struck him in the stomach.

Rynah took off. She found a door. Her heart pounding in her ears as she ran, she burst through the solid, steel door. Once it shut, she locked it so no one could get through; banging and angry shouts raged on the other side.

A whistle touched her ears. Another guard had appeared in the same hallway she had entered. Growing tired of running into security, Rynah turned and ran in the other direction. Her eyes searched for anything that resembled an exit. More laser fire whizzed past her head as the security guards pursued her. She quickened her pace.

Rynah racked her brain as she tried to remember the maps she had studied of Fredyr's complex. She spotted a sign. "Level One," it read. Now knowing where she was, Rynah veered to the right and then to the left, going down a narrow, and shadowy, hallway. Once on the other side, she turned another corner until she spotted what she searched for. A giant door four times as wide as her, and three times her height, loomed before her.

Rynah slammed her hand against the red button that controlled the door. More alarms and lights sprang to life as the door rose, revealing the outside world, its harsh light hurting her eyes. Furious winds howled around her, whipping her hair and dress. Rynah fastened the parachute to her body as the guards neared her location.

"Stop!" yelled one.

Rynah glared at him.

Fredyr Monsooth shoved his way past his guards and to the front. His furious gaze bore into Rynah's. "You thought you could just steal my property and get away with it?"

Rynah didn't answer. She glanced outside, gauging the distance to the engines so that she would not hit them when she jumped.

"Just give me the crystal," said Fredyr, "and I'll go easy on you."

"I don't have it," said Rynah.

"You know the sort of enemy I can be," said Fredyr.

Rynah placed her hands on the sides of the doorway. "You know the sort of woman I am."

She jumped. Wind whistled past Rynah as gravity pulled her down to the surface of the planet. She spread her arms and legs to slow her descent. Once she had cleared the hovering complex, Rynah pulled her chute. It shot out, opening above her and jerking her body as it slowed her fall. Rynah's adroit skill showed as she used the handles on each side to control where the parachute carried her.

A glint of metal flashed just below her. "Solaris?"

"I am directly below you. The main hatch is open."

Solaris ascended, matching Rynah's position as she circled around. Rynah spotted the opening and steered her way towards it. Her hair smacked her face as the wind beating her attacked with all its might. Solaris hovered in the sky. Knowing she'd only get one chance, Rynah veered toward the open hatch and headed straight for it.

Her feet crumpled beneath her as she landed on the lowered ramp. Before she had time to relax, the wind caught her chute and pulled her away. Desperate, Rynah held onto the rivets of the ramp as she pulled out her knife and cut her chute lose. It whipped away. Freed, Rynah pulled herself up, until she lay on the ramp.

"I'm here," she said, breathless.

In response, the ramp raised until it closed out the outside world.

Rynah took a moment to catch her breath before speaking. "Get us out of here."

"I'm already on it. A course has been set. We shall meet up with Tom, Solon, and Alfric within a few hours."

"I thought I told you to leave."

"I couldn't leave a friend behind," replied Solaris.

Rynah's face fell a bit. She had never thought of Solaris as a friend, even though she was the closest thing she had to a friend, or family. Humbled by Solaris' statement, Rynah whispered, "Thank you."

On one of the many balconies of Fredyr Monsooth's floating complex, Klanor watched as Rynah's ship disappeared into the sky. "Well played," he whispered, touching the ring he kept hidden in his pocket; a forlorn look etched his face.

"I can have Mr. Monsooth send his own men after her," said Stein from behind.

"No need," replied Klanor, regaining his stoic features, while yanking his hand out of his pocket and away from Rynah's ring.

"But, she is getting away with the crystal."

"True," Klanor faced Stein, "but we have someone she wants, even if she doesn't know it yet."

Chapter 8
INTERROGATION

Brie struggled as two men, dressed in body armor, hauled her through the interrogation room and to the icy, leather chair.

"Let me go!"

She twisted, desperate to wrench herself free, but her efforts only resulted in the guards tightening their grip. They flung her into the cold seat, tightening the callous straps around her thin wrists and ankles until they cut into her delicate, white flesh. Brie screamed and kicked.

"Now, my dear," said Klanor, "there is nothing to fear."

Fury erupted from her eyes as she glared at the people around her.

"I simply have a few questions for you," Klanor said in a calm voice.

"I'll not tell you anything," spat Brie.

"You really are being obstinate." Klanor sat in a metal chair beside her. "After all, it was I who saved you."

Brie said nothing.

"Your friends left you for dead," continued Klanor. "They had put you in a missile casing, ejected you into space, and abandoned you. If it wasn't for me, you would still be there as a corpse."

"Why did you bring me aboard your ship?" asked Brie.

"To help you," said Klanor.

Brie's doubtful look did not go unnoticed.

"We do not need to be enemies," said Klanor, his tone sincere. "We could be friends. Just tell me what you know."

"I don't know anything."

A grim line crossed Klanor's lips. "I think otherwise. You have spent many weeks on Rynah's ship. I am certain that you picked up a few tidbits of information that would prove most useful. And I am very interested in your home."

Brie remained silent.

"Come now, you can't tell me that you feel any loyalty towards Rynah."

"I have more reason to trust her than I have to trust you."

"Really? Did she tell you that I only care for power?"

Brie's expression answered his question.

"She probably even told you that I plan to rule the universe and she—the noble heroine—has vowed to stop me. But, did she inform you that she is the reason I was able to acquire the crystal in the first place?"

"You knew about it because of her grandfather's trial."

"I learned of the crystal's existence then, but not how to attain it."

"Does it matter?" asked Brie.

"Perhaps not," answered Klanor, "but I'm sure it does matter that she is also tempted by the power of the crystals and has her own plans for them. In any case, returning the one to our people would restore the honor that her family lost due to Marlow's rash actions."

"I don't believe you."

"Believe what you will, but I still require information from you, and one way or another, I will get it."

Brie clamped her mouth shut.

Klanor waved a medical technician over. The man walked up with a needle and injected its contents into Brie's veins. Another placed a metal band around her head and flipped a switch, turning it on.

"If you will not tell me willingly," said Klanor as he placed a similar band on his head, "then I will get it from you this way."

"No!" screamed Brie.

"I will see you in your dreams."

Brie's mind left the lab and the chair, being transported to her internal memories of home. Soon, she found herself walking along the street on her way home from school; the lab and the chair she was imprisoned on became a vague thought as a cloud of black smog fluttered over her when a city bus bounced down the road past her. Coughing, Brie hurried away. She stopped. Confused, she looked all around her as construction workers repaired a sidewalk and people darted by on their way to an important engagement. *How did I get here?* Mystified, Brie stared at the activity surrounding her, not remembering leaving school and taking this path home.

It's okay, said a voice in her head. *You've come this way before.*

Brie shrugged it off. The beating noise of a jackhammer followed her as she trotted down the walk to the complex her family lived in. A sign stopped her. On it was the picture of a strange crystal and the words, "Where is it now?"

Brie studied it. She didn't remember the giant sign, or the store, being there.

"Care to come in?" said a man, holding pamphlets.

"Excuse me?" Brie stepped back, wary of him.

"Here, take one." The man handed her a brochure.

Brie took it and flipped through the colorful pamphlet as it referred to some crystal from space. "What is all this?"

"To learn that, you should come inside." Noticing Brie's hesitation, he added, "I promise it's perfectly safe." He pointed at an old woman seated at the clerk's counter. "She's my mother."

Relenting, Brie agreed; stepping through the doorway, she felt that she had traveled to another dimension. Whirling lights hummed as they hung from the ceiling. Giant pictures of ships, planets, and star systems lined the wall as shelves of strange gadgets filled the small shopping space.

"What is all this?" asked Brie. "I don't remember this place being here."

"I just opened," said the man, his sparkling purple suit wrinkling with every flamboyant movement he made.

"What do you sell?"

"Well, you can buy any of these strange gizmos, or you can come in here to learn."

"Learn?"

"Why, I have a library here." The strange man spun around and whisked his way to the back of the shop, where a heavy, velvet curtain hung. Brie stared at it for several moments. She didn't remember it being there a moment ago, and it seemed to have magically appeared. The strange man yanked it back. Brie's eyes opened wide in amazement. Awed, she stepped into the back room overflowing with books—not standard paperbacks, but leather-bound editions with frayed edges. She pulled one from the shelf almost crumpling under its weight. Brie opened it, remarking at the artwork and calligraphy on the yellowed pages.

"How old are these books?"

"Very," said the man, "but I offer knowledge, and anyone can come here to learn."

"Learn what?"

"Anything. Everything. Whatever it is they don't teach you in school."

Brie continued to flip through the pages intrigued by its contents. "And you let anyone come in here?"

"Only those who care about the truth."

Brie's excitement waned. She put the book away. "Truth?"

"About the crystals," the man pointed at the brochure in her hands. "These crystals have existed on our planet for a long time, but the government is conspiring against us to keep it a secret."

"Right," Brie replied in a drawn doubtful tone.

"No, really." The man grabbed her arm and turned her back to him. "Haven't you ever seen this before?"

Humoring him, Brie studied the picture in the brochure. It did look familiar, but she couldn't remember where she had seen it before. "Maybe."

"I knew it." The man jumped and hopped with excitement.

"What does it matter?"

"Do you remember reading a story in the news a while back?"

Brie thought for a moment. "Well, there was this short report about some quartz object being discovered at an archeological dig in Guatemala, but I didn't pay much attention."

"Where is this Guatemala?"

Brie's eyes narrowed. "What do you mean? Everyone knows where Guatemala is."

"Yes, yes, I know that. What I meant was, where in Guatemala?"

"Don't know. Why don't you look it up yourself? I'm sure you could do a web search."

The man eyes' seemed confused when she mentioned the vernacular phrase for researching something on the internet. She ignored it.

"I just wanted to see what you knew first," said the man, "because you must assess your own knowledge before you can add to it."

"Okay. Look, I need to go."

"No, no, wait!" The man jumped in front of her. "There is so much I could teach you. Here. Why don't you take a book with you? Any one you want."

Brie thought about it and decided that his offer seemed genuine. She noticed a book on a lone table, sitting wide open. Curious, she walked over to it. Unlike some of the other books, this was in excellent condition. She touched one of the delicate pages and turned it. It was a poem.

"Rynah mentioned a poem," said Brie as she closed the book and looked at the cover and the emblem on it. "This seems a lot like what she talked about."

"Not that book!" The man snatched the volume from her.

"You said…"

"Sorry, but this one is an old family heirloom."

"Sorry."

"Rynah?" said the man. "Who's Rynah?"

"Wha… no one," answered Brie, wondering why she had said the name. "Just a story I must have read somewhere."

"Tell me about it."

"It's nothing really," said Brie. "It's just a name of a character in some story about an adventure and some crystals."

"How interesting," the man leaned closer, wanting to know more.

"Yeah, there was this one chapter where this Rynah and some people go underwater and battle a shark…"

Memories of being underwater and chased by a man and sea creatures flooded Brie's brain. Vivid images of the crystal being ripped from her hands plagued her, forcing her to stop her story. Confused, she turned in a circle, seeing the small shop and its hidden library in a new light.

"How long did you say this place has been here?" she asked.

"A few days," answered the man. "Now tell me more about this Rynah."

"I… I need to go," Brie grabbed her school bag and ran out.

"No! Wait!" the man called after her.

Brie ignored him. She raced for the exit, but the looming figure of the old woman blocked her path. Brie halted.

"Going so soon?" said the woman.

Turning, Brie noticed the strange man coming straight for her. She smacked the old woman with her backpack and shoved her out of the way. Shouts filled the space she had vacated as the man pursued her. Fear filling her, Brie's only thoughts were to get away.

She ran out into the street, pushing a passerby out of her way. The man's angry shouts drew her attention back. Brie turned around and watched as the shop owner exited the store before the blare of a horn forced her to look to the right. A bus headed straight for her. Before Brie had time to react, her world went black.

Back in the interrogation room, Brie woke with a start, her mind still blurred from the drugs.

"She's fighting the serum," said a voice.

"Then give her a stronger one," roared Klanor.

"We can't," said the technician. "If we do, we could kill her. She seems to know when she is in a dream state."

Klanor studied Brie, whose clouded mind tried in vain to grasp what happened around her. "Then we will have to try another approach. If she won't talk with a stranger, then perhaps she will talk with someone she trusts. Get her ready for another session."

"She needs time to rest, sir. If we push her too hard, we will kill her."

"Very well," growled Klanor. "Take her back to her cell."

Two guards released the straps that restrained Brie and heaved her out of the chair. Her head flopped to the side, her mind still engulfed in a haze. Klanor watched as the guards hauled Brie away, looking forward to the next session, but disturbed by how the book, which he had stolen from Rynah and kept locked in his room, had appeared. He knew that Brie had no knowledge of it.

He pulled out the ring that had fallen from Rynah's finger that day he betrayed her, twirling it as his eyes focused on the shiny band. Memories of their time together, and her smile, filled his mind as he looked past the ring and into himself. Though he was never one to brood over his choices in life, guilt panged him as he held Rynah's engagement ring.

Harsh footsteps jerked him from his thoughts and he shoved the ring into his pocket, hoping no one had seen him with it. He had a job to do.

Chapter 9
CODED VERSE

Alfric stood poised as he balanced on one leg, his sword held straight out. He twisted and stepped lightly as he whirled around and struck the empty air around him. Thoughts of Brie floated through his mind with each move as he hacked the air before him, until he leapt and plunged his blade into the metallic floor of the ship.

An image of Brie laying cold and pallid in her coffin consumed him. He had given her his pendant—his most prized possession, as it had been blessed by the wise man of his village.

"It can turn back death," the man had told him.

"Then why did it not save her?" Alfric mumbled to himself.

Feeling he had grown weak, he jumped to his feet and charged through the cargo room that he practiced in. His breaths filled the empty space around him as he ran until he reached the end. He turned and raced to the other side, his sword held before him. Again, images of Brie overwhelmed him: her smile, her laugh, her very demeanor reminding him of one he loved and lost. A horrific roar escaped his lips as he charged, raising his blade high above his head.

Sparks flew as the steel blade struck the interior wall of the ship. Alfric collapsed to the floor, breathless. All the guilt, the pain which he had kept hidden deep within, spilled forth, desperate to break free.

"You know, I would appreciate it if you wouldn't scratch up my walls like that," said Solaris.

"My apologies," said Alfric. "I should not have let my anger drive me so."

He rose to his feet and sheathed his sword. As his breathing slowed and he regained his composure, the Viking seized his fur cloak and wrapped it around his shoulders.

"You are forgiven."

Alfric groaned at being forgiven by a voice he could not see.

"What troubles you so?" asked Solaris.

"Brie," said Alfric. "Why is it I was unable to save her? I gave her my talisman, and even it could not protect her."

"Necklaces have no power. They are merely objects. Brie is dead. It is time for you to move on."

Anger flared within Alfric. "How can you be so callous?"

Silence followed. Alfric regretted yelling at Solaris. She was a machine, that much he understood, and therefore incapable of emotion. Being a king in his homeland, circumstances forced him to keep his emotions buried deep within and act as aloof as Solaris was, even though he wished to scream in frustration.

"Do you know what Brie said to me once before she died?"

Alfric shook his head. "No."

"She told me that I was the closest thing to a friend she ever had." Sorrow filled Solaris' voice; something that Alfric never thought possible. "You are not the only one to feel guilt, nor does the blame solely rest with you. She made her choice to save all of us. It was hers to make in the end."

"Perhaps, but it should not have ended that way," whispered Alfric. "I have dreams of her. I dream that she is locked in a room with white walls. I dream that each day she undergoes the horrors of the underworld when she should have been welcomed in Valhalla and the halls of Odin."

"They are only dreams."

"Then why do they feel so real?" Alfric walked to the exit. "I must go."

"Go where?"

"There is something amiss," answered Alfric. "I must find it."

"Did you ever wear the helmet?" asked Solaris, referring to the device that linked an individual's mind telepathically to her.

Alfric paused, surprised by her sudden question. "Why do you ask?"

"Just answer it."

"Yes," replied Alfric, "for a moment. I was alone and allowed my curiosity to get the better of me, but I wore it for only a few seconds. Why?"

Solaris didn't answer. She had overheard Tom and Solon whispering about dreams of Brie or hearing faint echoes of her voice that were so shortlived that they passed it off as their mind playing tricks on them in their time of grief. The only person to not have mentioned experiencing something similar was Rynah, but questions had arisen in Solaris and she intended to find answers.

Once again, Rynah pored over the words on the holoscreen. She read and reread the lines of the verse over and over again, but could not make out what it meant. She had hoped to learn the location of the next crystal, but feared that Klanor would get to it first. A console beeped. Annoyed, she pushed the flashing button and up popped another holoscreen with a wanted poster and her picture. *Great*, she thought. Fredyr Monsooth had placed a bounty on her head of 1,000 scillions, a value of $500,000 on Earth.

She flicked off the screen. Just what she needed. Every mercenary in the Twelve Sectors would hunt her now, something Klanor would take full advantage of. She turned back to the ancient text.

Most tricky will be the sixth
as it lies deep in fiery mist.

Gods of fire, you will face their wrath
and delve deep within the mountain's cast.

But more than courage you will need.
Friends' devotion and the girl who heeds
the call of sacrifice and pendant's glare.
Only she will escape the enemy's snare.

Frustrated, Rynah rubbed her hands over her face. "Why must it always be in riddles?" she said aloud.

Deep down, she knew the answer. That was how they told stories in the ancient world. She just wished the poet could have pointed her to a map and said, "Go there."

Rynah continued on.

Read well and remember this,
Numbers that most will miss.
thirty-five, sixty-eight, nine;
fifty-two, one and twenty's bind.

Mark and trace as you go.
A circle each forms with arcs that flow;
and crossroads that one seeks
the way one climbs the highest peak.

Rynah paused as she pondered the numbers. They seemed familiar in the way they had been written. She twirled the necklace around her neck, her fingers caressing every curve of her grandfather's amber ring. *Of course!* Rynah jumped from her seat and went to the pile of maps that she always kept, a habit that she had learned from Marlow, who always preferred real maps, as he called them, over digitized ones.

She searched through them, flinging the old paper maps everywhere until she came upon the one she sought. She remembered her grandfather poring over the same maps, losing himself to them, never understanding why, until now. Could he have discovered the location of the sixth crystal?

Rynah cleared a space on the table and placed the crinkled map upon it. She snatched a pencil. Using a ruler, she marked the numbers on the map, which were coordinates, and circled the points. She snatched a compass and drew circles around each mark, noting where the circles intersected.

"Crossroads," she whispered. But which point should she go to?

Reading the verse again, Rynah realized that the word "peak" didn't seem to fit. There are no peaks in space unless...

She rushed over to her books and snatched a heavy volume. Her grandfather's scrawl filled the margins as she flipped through it until she landed on the page she searched for. On it was the picture of a green mountain capped in snow. It's location was on the planet of Sunlil, which also corresponded with one of the intersecting points on the circles she had drawn.

Rynah tapped the holoscreen, bringing up the planet. Her face fell as she looked at the images that filled it. Sunlil had suffered a series of catastrophes and was no more than a barren wasteland. "This has to be it," whispered Rynah to herself. She stared at the image of the highest peak on the planet.

Rynah bolted from her room, running straight into Alfric.

"Sorry," she said. "Where are you off to?"

"My quarters," said Alfric in a low tone.

"No time. Grab the others. We have work to do."

"You have discovered something?"

"I know where the final crystal is," said Rynah. She noticed Alfric's downcast face and placed a gentle hand on his shoulder. "I know you still feel upset about Brie, but think of what she would want."

"I will summon the others."

"Thank you." Rynah sped off.

Chapter 10
Obiah's Search

Obiah steered the small vessel through a maze of ships in space dock, searching for a place to park his shuttle as he pulled into the space station, now turned into a saloon. An open area caught his attention. Obiah pulled into it before someone else could. Metal upon metal scraped together as the chute attached to the hatch of his ship.

Obiah unbuckled himself and opened the hatch. Hundreds of voices and music filled his ears as he stepped out of his ship and into the space port. No one looked in his direction, no doubt thinking he was just another traveler seeking rest and entertainment. Obiah closed the hatch.

Rumors had spoken of a Lanyran survivor who frequented this place. Obiah planned to see if it was true. Since he had left Rynah, he had actively sought survivors of Lanyr. So far he had found none. Obiah hoped these rumors would prove useful.

He moseyed through the space station to the saloon. Loud music escaped from the swinging doors as he walked through. People of every race and planet lined the bar or occupied every table in the room. Not liking this place, Obiah walked inside. He had a mission. He approached the bar.

"What'll you have?" asked the bartender in a raspy voice.

"Malted mead," said Obiah.

The bartender groaned, disappointed that Obiah hadn't ordered a more expensive drink. He snatched a glass from the counter and wiped it out with a gray, and odor-ridden, dish towel before filling it with foamy liquid. A distinct slunk sounded as he plopped it on the sticky counter in front of Obiah. "Three bromas."

Obiah dug into his pocket and pulled out three bronze coins and tossed them on the counter, allowing them to clink and jingle. The man moved to scoop them up. Obiah snatched the bartender's freckled arm and yanked him close as he leaned in so he could whisper in the man's ear.

"I hear there is a man here from Lanyr."

"Lanyr is gone," hissed the bartender.

"That may be," continued Obiah in a low voice, "but that doesn't mean there aren't survivors."

"No one could have survived that chaos." The bartender desperately tried to pull away, but Obiah's grip held firm.

"Don't toy with me," Obiah warned. "I have reliable information that there is a man here from Lanyr, seeking any who survived the planet's demise. Now I want to know where he is."

Obiah never noticed a hooded figure moving away from the bar and approaching him.

"I don't know of anyone," said the bartender. "People come here for a drink and I don't ask questions."

Obiah knew the man held back information. He squeezed harder, leaning closer. "That may be, but the fact remains that someone is spreading the rumor about a man from Lanyr. Now I know that you would not allow anything to happen in this place without you first getting your cut. Tell me where he is."

"Let him go," said a deep voice behind him.

Obiah turned his head. The hooded figure stood a few paces away. "Who are you?"

"I could ask the same of you," said the stranger.

People backed away from them, sensing trouble and not wishing to be part of it.

"There is no need to antagonize the man," said the stranger. "I am the one whom you seek." The stranger removed his hood, revealing the purple face of all Lanyrans and his burnt orange hair.

Obiah released his grip. The bartender backed away, hurrying to the far side of the bar to help another customer.

"Why don't we sit over here," said the stranger.

Raising his drink, Obiah followed the newcomer to a secluded table in a dark corner of the room. As they sat down, the stranger glanced around, making certain that no one listened to them.

"Who are you?"

"Obiah."

"And you survived the devastation on Lanyr?"

"Yes, in a manner of speaking," answered Obiah. "I was not on Lanyr when it was destroyed, but I heard of it. I also heard that there were other survivors."

"You seem to hear a lot."

"I didn't catch your name."

The stranger smiled at Obiah's way of asking indirectly.

"You can call me Merrick."

"Well, Merrick," said Obiah, "have you heard of Klanor?"

"I have."

"He is the one responsible for Lanyr's destruction. He is also looking for six crystals that are said to give one ultimate power."

"I'm not one to believe in children's stories."

"Well, he does, and that should concern you."

"Why's that?"

"Because Klanor's belief in the crystals is what possessed him to destroy our planet," said Obiah. "It will also lead him to destroy countless other worlds and lives."

"And why does it concern me?"

"Because he may come after any who survived our planet's destruction."

"Why would he do that?"

"Why does any man do anything?" Obiah took a sip of his malted mead. "Look, someone I know believes in what Klanor is trying to do. At least she believes in it enough to try and stop him."

"Who is this person?"

"Her name is Rynah."

"Rynah?" said Merrick. "Wasn't her grandfather brought up on charges for trying to steal the crystal from the geo-lab some years back?"

"Yes."

Merrick mused over that bit of information. "Figures she would believe in these crystals."

"You are aware of the one in the lab," said Obiah.

"Yes, but that was one. I doubt that there are six."

"Rynah has found four of them."

Merrick's eyes lit up. "Four? Are you serious?"

"I have seen them. Merrick, Klanor means to get all six and use them for whatever they were meant for. If he succeeds in obtaining this powerful weapon, he will be unstoppable and destroy entire solar systems. The man is power mad. Do you really think that he will leave your band of survivors alone?"

"It is not for me to decide," said Merrick. "I am here to guide any who wish it to a camp where there are other survivors, but the council will have to decide."

"The council?"

"Some members of it survived and have established a working government, for now. But you must understand, Obiah, that even if we wanted to help you, there are few of us left. We haven't the manpower that Klanor has amassed."

"Rynah cannot do this on her own," said Obiah. "She will need help. If we are to bring justice for what was done to us, we need to help her. Let me come with you to speak to the council."

Merrick pondered over what Obiah had suggested. "They will not be happy to hear about these crystals."

"I'm aware of that."

"However, since you are a Lanyran, you have the right to be with your people. I will take you to them. Meet me at Dock B in one hour."

"Thank you."

"I warn you, they won't be as open-minded as I am."

"I will deal with it."

Together, the two men finished their drinks as Obiah thought about what he would tell the council. He hoped he could win their support for Rynah's sake.

Chapter 11
DEAD IN SPACE

"**W**e shall reach the planet's outer atmosphere in about four hours," said Solaris.

"Good," replied Rynah. She couldn't wait to get this search for the final crystal over with.

"Any news?" asked Alfric as he entered the pilot's area.

"We're almost there."

The Viking nodded his head before leaving.

"You can stay," said Rynah. "You do not have to always be so distant."

"Much plagues my mind."

"You miss your home," said Rynah. She had seen that look in Alfric's eyes numerous times before, though it had mostly been in Brie's."

"Yes."

Rynah remained silent, hoping that it would encourage him to continue.

"I wonder how my people are faring without me. Did my kingdom survive the attack by King Sveth? How are my children? These questions torment me each day I remain here."

"You have children?"

"Yes," said Alfric. "A son, who shall grow up strong like his father, and a daughter, whose beauty surpasses her mother's."

"I did not know," Rynah looked down at the console. The realization of the enormity of what Solaris had done when she pulled the four earthlings from their home struck her. "You will return to them."

"But there is no guarantee," said Alfric as he thought about Brie.

"I will do what I can to ensure your safe return to your family and your people," Rynah reassured him.

Alfric smiled at her offer. "I shall hold you to it."

"This is all very heartwarming," Solaris interrupted them, "but have any of you seen that menace of an inventor around?"

They shook their heads. "I haven't seen him all day," said Rynah.

"I will search for him and see to it that he sets nothing afire." Alfric left the command center, his heavy boots stomping down the steps.

"That boy is going to get us all killed someday," quipped Solaris, with a minute amount of affection.

"You can quit bellyaching," said Rynah, "I know you like him."

Solaris grunted.

"I meant as a friend," said Rynah.

"I know what you meant."

Rynah laughed as she turned back to flying the ship.

Alfric found Tom in an abandoned cargo hold surround by piles of metallic debris and trash, working on a piece of equipment with wires slung around his shoulders and wrapped around his waist, with such punctiliousness that, for a moment, Alfric admired the young man. A screwdriver was stuck behind his ear; his tongue poked between his lips as he concentrated on the task at hand.

"What is all this?" asked Alfric.

"Huh?" Tom looked up. "Oh, nothing."

Alfric put his hands on his hips in disbelief.

"Okay, okay, I'm trying to build a body for Solaris, but it's supposed to be a surprise."

"A body?"

"A cybernetic life form," said Tom. Upon noticing the confused look on Alfric's weathered face, he continued, "Right now, she lives inside the ship, but cannot interact with us the way we can with each other. So, I am attempting to give her something she doesn't have, a body. In short, I am trying to make her human."

Alfric picked up what looked like an arm. The synthetic skin, which looked and felt like real skin, had been tinted a pale purple to match Rynah's skin tone, and that of her people. Tom had also added another unique feature to the skin: nanotechnology.

"So you are attempting to make her flesh and blood."

"Yes," beamed Tom. "Right now, I am working on her face." He lifted up a head. It had two eyes and a nose, but the mouth had not been finalized yet. "The thing is, I don't want her to look like a robot. I want Solaris to pass for a human so people don't stare. I hope she likes it."

Alfric put the arm down. "I am certain that the spirit of Solaris will greatly appreciate your gift."

"I found it!" Solon entered the room, waving what looked like a circuit board.

"Excellent!" Tom jumped up and grabbed the object, mumbling technobabble to himself as he stripped pieces away and popped out a tiny disk. He placed the quartz disk into the robotic head and powered it on. The others watched, mesmerized, as the eyes blinked and the robotic face made a series of expressions ranging from happy to sad.

"You know, if I keep this up, she will have a body in a few weeks."

"Anything else you need me to find?" asked Solon.

"No." mumbled Tom as he concentrated on his work.

"Very well," Solon walked off. "I am going to study Rynah's ancient texts some more."

"I will leave you to your work." Alfric left the room.

Tom never noticed their departure; his mind was too focused on his project.

Rynah stared out at the vast reaches of space that stretched before her. The trip to the planet had been uneventful, and she felt confident that no trouble would arise. In the back of her mind, she wondered why she had not heard from Klanor in a while. If she had discovered the location of the final crystal, he should have as well. She shrugged it off, thinking that maybe she had gotten lucky.

"Rynah," said Solaris, "I am picking up strange readings on my sensors."

"What readings?"

"An unusual amount of electromagnetic activity. I suggest that we divert our course and wait until it passes."

"We haven't time," said Rynah.

"Rynah, you must trust my judgment."

"If we divert now, Klanor will…"

The ship lurched as the engines shut off.

"Rynah," Solaris' voice faded, "we are caught in a gravitational ion storm. We need to…"

Solaris's voice disappeared.

"Solaris!" Rynah jerked upright in her seat. She grabbed the controls and yanked them back, forcing the ship to go upward just as a series of neon green rocks pummeled them. Desperate, Rynah steered to avoid the barrage of space rock.

Bang! Bang! Bang!

The constant noise pounded her ears as giant bits of rock slammed into the hull, rocking it back and forth and threatening to cause a breach. Rynah maneuvered the ship to the left, avoiding a deadly blow, before veering to the right to avoid another. Before she knew it, they had entered a hailstorm of space rock and electromagnetic pulses. The power fluctuated.

"Hold together," whispered Rynah.

The pugnacious force of the storm roiled the craft as she gripped the controls to maintain her course. Rynah looked up. Her mouth dropped open at what she saw: a giant cloud of luminescent gas and fierce winds heading straight for her. She had flown right into a storm without realizing it. Knowing she would never be able to outrun it or escape its path, Rynah turned on the intercom. "Brace for impact!"

She strapped herself in her chair and wrapped her fingers around the controls. Hoping that they would survive this, Rynah turned into the wave and braced for hell's fury.

The storm crashed into the small vessel, tossing it as though it were nothing more than a slight annoyance. Rynah held on as they were jostled and shaken from the ion storm's tumultuous wrath; thunderous roars raged outside the ship's hull, warning her of the danger they were in.

A screw popped free of its hold and a hissing noise filled the area as air leaked out. Rynah watched, helpless, knowing she could do nothing until the storm had passed. "Come on, hold together," she pleaded.

Her stomach lurched as the storm flipped the ship like a pancake, tossing it back and forth. They rolled and reeled, unable to stop the onslaught. Squeezing her eyes shut, Rynah clung to her chair as screeches escaped her mouth, while she waited for the inevitable that never came.

Down in the cargo hold, Tom had little time to react after Rynah's announcement. He had just seized hold of a rail as the ship jerked to the side, tossing him about like a ragdoll. "Alfric!"

Alfric clung to the edges of the doorway. His sweaty fingers slipped. Another jerk of the ship racked his body.

Wasting no time, Tom let go of the rail and allowed himself to fall towards Alfric, crashing into the wall with a grunt. Ignoring the bruises and the pain, Tom scooted along the wall as the force of the ship's movements squeezed him against it.

Alfric's hands slipped some more. "Do not worry about me," he said to Tom. "Help the others."

"No!" Tom scooted closer. Just as Alfric let go, he reached over and grasped the Viking's hand, holding as tight as he could.

A loud thud echoed around them, causing Tom to tumble over

and both he and Alfric fell through the long hallway. They stopped. Weightlessness overtook them as their bodies floated in midair.

"Quickly," shouted Tom, "grab hold of something. The gravity centers of the ship have been damaged, but in moments, we'll be propelled downward again."

Not arguing, Alfric clung to the handle on the side of the wall as Tom found another rail. The ship lurched before turning end over end, flinging their bodies around.

It stopped. Deafening silence loomed over all of them as the ion storm passed and the ship stilled. His head aching, Tom pulled himself to his feet as artificial gravity restored itself on the ship. "Solaris?" he called.

Nothing. The ventilation had stilled. The engines had silenced. A sinking feeling filled Tom's stomach.

"Are you all right?" Tom asked Alfric.

"Fine."

"The ship is silent," said Tom. "We should find the others."

Alfric agreed.

They found Solon in his room, laying on the floor underneath layers of debris. Despite a slight headache, he was fine. "What happened?" he groaned as they helped him to his feet.

"Not sure," answered Tom. "We should find Rynah."

Rynah rubbed her temples as she opened her eyes and they slowly focused. Blackness filled the window before her. No stars twinkled to provide any comfort. It was as close to a black night as one could get in space.

"Rynah!" Solon's voice echoed up the stairwell to her.

She moved her arm, only to cry out as a sharp pain shot up it. A long, jagged cut stretched down her right arm, with blood oozing from it.

"Rynah!"

"Over here!" she called.

The others crashed through the doorway to the pilot's center in response to her call.

"Are you all right?" asked Tom.

"I'll be fine," she said.

They helped her to her feet as Solon wrapped a piece of cloth from his shirt around her arm to stem the bleeding. "We should get you to the medical bay."

"No," said Rynah, "we need to get the ship running." She had noticed that no sound came from the engines. "Solaris?"

No response.

Rynah clicked on a few buttons and frowned. "We're dead in space," she said.

Worried looks crossed all of their faces as the news sunk in.

"What does that mean?" asked Solon.

"It means," answered Rynah, "that if we do not get Solaris' systems running soon, we will be dead within a few hours. We have no life support, so no air to breathe. It's going to start getting very cold in here."

"We need to get the air working again," said Tom.

"My thoughts exactly," said Rynah. "Once we get the life support systems back online, then we can work on repairing the engines."

"Where is the main system?" asked Tom.

"In the belly of the ship," said Rynah. "A place Solaris never allows anyone to go."

"Do you think she will make an exception this time?" asked Tom.

"She'll have to," replied Rynah.

Chapter 12
A Test

Klanor stared out at the mass of pirate ships below as he stroked the crystals in his hands. The pirate base had been built into the canyon walls of the seemingly lifeless planet, though clusters of sagebrush dotted the landscape; giant arches indicated hangers with showers of sparks sputtering from them, and on C-shaped platforms rested the parked vessels in groups of three. Klanor placed the ancient crystals in the mechanism that he had created, using the ancient texts, which would utilize them and turn them into a weapon. Though he missed two, he hoped that the machine would still work, even if not at full power, and what better place to test it than on a pirate outpost?

"We are ready," said one of his men.

Klanor did not answer. Something held him back, warning him that what he was about to do was unforgivable. He shoved it aside.

"Sir?"

"Do it," ordered Klanor.

The man at the weapons' console punched a button. The device whirred to life as it turned toward its intended target. Another button was pushed. Lights flickered as zaps sounded in rapid succession of one another; a bright glow surrounded the device as it aimed at its target and fired an intense beam. Fire and explosions erupted on the surface of the planet below and frantic people scurried about to escape this newfound terror.

Klanor noticed a few ships leave their station. "Destroy those," he said.

Those under his command shifted the weapon's targeting parameters to attack the departing pirate vessels. Another beam of light spilled from the weapon, vaporizing everything in its path.

"The targeting scanners seem to be off. We need the other crystals to use this device to its full power."

"Understood," said Klanor. He smiled as he realized just how deadly a weapon the crystals formed. If only he had the other two; then he would be unstoppable, and all those who had laughed at his quest to find the crystals and their ultimate source of power would regret their taunts. He, Klanor, would dictate life and death in the universe; he would be the law.

Another set of thoughts (regret, guilt, and innocence lost) entered his mind and his smile faded. He touched the outside of his pocket and felt the slight bulge of the ring. Ever since he had danced with Rynah at Fredyr's Monsooth's celebration, Klanor had not been able to get her out of his mind. He had offered to let her join him, yet she had refused his sincere invitation. The hatred in her eyes when she had looked at him gnawed at his heart. He dismissed his musing, knowing that he had to keep his emotions in check, but Rynah's eyes and the loathing within them plagued him.

He turned around to find Stein standing a few feet behind him, watching the devastation with interest. The man's unreadable eyes betrayed nothing, but Klanor paid little heed to it.

"How does it feel?" he asked, trying to make his voice sound light and excited.

"Invigorating," answered Stein in a low, flat tone.

Klanor turned back to the window, wishing he could read Stein's mind.

As Stein watched, his mind only thought about his family. *How could a weapon of such power bring them back?* he wondered. The more he thought about it, the more he realized that Klanor could not help him and nothing would return what was lost. Stein's eyes observed every detail of the fires below him and what had once been a pirate port. Such power could prove useful, even if it couldn't restore what had been taken from him. He kept this thought to himself.

Chapter 13
DOLPHINS IN SPACE

"**G**ive it a try," said Tom as he called up from amongst the inner workings of Solaris.

Rynah pulled a lever. A series of—SSSSSS—filled the air as the gears ground together, bringing the fans to life. Fresh, invigorating air poured through the vents, bringing relief to all of them. "We have air," she called back.

"Good!" Tom crawled out of the tube he was in. Alfric reached down and helped him up.

"Though having air to breathe is nice," said Solon, "if we do not find a way to get the engines working, we will be stranded here and eventually die." He had gleaned that much information after listening to Tom and Rynah for the last two hours.

"Always so cheerful," said Tom.

"But he is right," said Rynah. "How bad did the damage look?"

Tom didn't answer right away. "Bad," he finally said. "Many of the components have been burnt through or melted. If we had new parts, we could replace them in a matter of hours."

Rynah's face fell. She stood up, wiping her hands over her face, pondering their dismal prospects of survival. "We can't even get the computer working so that we can talk to Solaris."

"Do you have a new acryllian chip?" asked Tom.

"No," said Rynah. "Solaris is lost."

"No she's not. Once we repair the ship, she will come back."

"But I have no new parts, or spare parts," Rynah said.

Solon and Alfric watched the exchange between Tom and Rynah, unsure of what they meant, having very limited knowledge of spaceships or computer systems.

"You have nothing that can be of use?" asked Tom.

"This ship is old," said Rynah in frustration. "It was decommissioned as a military vessel decades ago. It was considered new in my grandfather's day, but no one owns a B-class ship anymore. They're obsolete. Solaris is probably the last. If we were in port, I could probably fashion new parts, but out here, I cannot."

Tom's face fell. He had thought he had been onto something, but now that hope had been ripped away. "It appears all I did was buy us time."

"Time can be useful," said Solon. "With it, perhaps we can think of a solution."

"Dolphins," said Alfric.

Everyone turned towards him. "What?"

"When I was still a boy, my father took me with him on an oversea voyage. We ran into a terrible storm, which destroyed our mast and rendered our ship useless. We had no knowledge of our location and feared getting lost at sea. Then, dolphins appeared, frolicking about, curious as to why we were there. A sign of good luck. We used oars and followed the creatures as they guided us back home."

"I doubt that we will find any dolphins in space," said Tom, "but it was a good idea."

Rynah released an exasperated sigh and stalked away. She stared out a small port window at the few twinkling stars as darkness loomed over them. *Dolphins,* she thought. It was a nice story. A memory of one of her grandfather's stories jolted her brain. Years ago, before she had left home, Marlow had told her about creatures in space whom many spacefarers regarded as lucky. What was it that attracted them?

"Some believe that the electrical components of the ships brought them to you," her grandfather had told her once.

Rynah spun on her heels, "I need some wire. Lots of it."

"For what?" asked Solon.

"We're going to get ourselves a dolphin, except here they are called 'ackmyra.'"

"And how exactly are you going to lasso one of those things?" asked Tom.

Rynah grabbed the helmet of a nearby spacesuit. "Suit up."

Tom grimaced as he took the helmet; he should have known.

"Come on, we haven't much time. I need those wires. The generators are producing enough electricity to run the ventilation system. Touch one end of the exposed wires to it, while I touch the other end to the wall of the ship. It should electrify the outer hull."

"How does that help us?" asked Tom.

"They are attracted to electricity. Now hurry up! We haven't much time."

"How will we be protected from electrifying ourselves?" asked Tom.

Rynah snatched some rubber gloves from a storage locker and tossed a pair to each of them. "These, and the soles of our shoes, ought to protect us. Not that it matters much. If this doesn't work, we're dead anyway."

Alfric and Solon jumped into the small tube that Tom had been in earlier. Together, they yanked whatever wires they could, making certain not to touch the ones that Rynah had said supported the ventilation system. She leaned over the opening, snatching the wires as they handed them to her.

Knowing he had little choice, Tom went into the cargo bay,

sealing the doors behind him, put on the spacesuit, and crawled through the hatch of the ship. "You know, some would call this a bad idea," he said into his radio as he climbed the side of Solaris and positioned himself on the top.

"Quit complaining," said Rynah. "You have the harness?"

"Ready and raring to go," said Tom. "By the way, you owe me big time for this."

Rynah's laughter spilled over the radio. She turned back to Alfric and Solon. "Ready?"

Alfric nodded.

Rynah touched the charged wires together, emitting sparks. Satisfied that power flowed through them, she scrupulously placed them on the exposed side of the ship. Shocks of electricity shot through the metallic plating, sending an electrical charge throughout as sparks erupted from exploding lights, with one spark igniting next to her face. Rynah pulled back.

"Are you all right?" asked Alfric.

Rynah ignored the question, and the newly formed burn mark that singed her cheek. She touched the wires to the side of the ship again. Again, jolts of electricity surged through it.

Tom stood on the bow of the ship as yellow and orange sparks flew all around him. Jagged lines of lights spread across the hull beneath his feet in patterns and to a rhythm that only they understood. He watched, awed by the show, realizing for the first time how beautiful electricity could be.

Movement caught his eye. Tom spun around. Far in the distance rested a single speck of light. Entranced, Tom watched as that small speck grew larger with each passing second, splitting into many colorful and twinkling dots. Soft pressure prickled his skin as something brushed against him, forcing him to turn his head.

Right in front of him floated a luminescent creature with the body of a fish and fins that bobbed up and down in synchronized movement. Spikes spotted its back—each glowed a different color—

as the somewhat transparent scales transformed into a rainbow: red, blue, yellow, and green. Awestruck, Tom watched as the fishlike creature—he had no other way of describing it—floated past him, waving its massive tail in gentle strokes as it joined its companions.

"Rynah, I think it worked."

Back in the ship, Rynah pushed her face against the port window, straining to see the strange creatures. She gasped as a glowing green and yellow creature moved past. "Look!"

Solon and Alfric ran to another window. Their faces lit up as the luminescent "dolphins" floated past, their numbers growing with each passing second.

"You were right, grandfather," Rynah whispered. "They're beautiful."

Song filled the intercom system as the radio sparked alive and transmitted the creatures' vocal sounds.

"Tom," said Rynah, "you only have one chance at this."

"I hear ya," said Tom.

He held up the harness in his hands. Another of the creatures floated by. Stretching out as far as he could, Tom placed the loop around the being's neck, making sure to keep it loose enough so as not to choke it. The creature swayed a bit, but continued onward, ignoring the ship and Tom.

The vessel shifted. As the space dolphin moved forward, it pulled the ship with him. Tom held on to maintain his balance. Amazed their plan had actually worked, he watched in astonishment as they moved onward. Another approached him on his left. Tom reached out to touch it, pleased when the animal pushed into his hand, enjoying the attention as he rubbed its snout.

"You're kind of friendly," he whispered.

"Tom, you best get back in here," said Rynah. "Hate to lose you."

"Sorry, fella. I've got to run, but you take care now," said Tom. He navigated his way back down the rungs on the side of the ship and back to the open hatch. Once inside, he closed the outer hatch and waited for the room to repressurize before taking off his helmet.

Once the air had flowed back in, Rynah and the others ran into the room and clapped him on the back amidst praise and cheers.

"You did it!" she said.

"Did you think I wouldn't?" asked Tom.

A broad grin stretched across Rynah's face as she hugged him.

"Congratulations," said Alfric. "From now on, I shall call you dolphin singer."

"Thanks," said Tom, not sure how he liked being given a new name, but accepted it as high praise coming from the Viking.

"Where will they take us?" asked Solon.

"Hard to say," replied Rynah. "Hopefully, they will take us near a settlement, but for now, we might as well enjoy the ride."

They each went back to the command center of the ship where they could watch the strange creatures, glad for the tow.

Chapter 14
AN OFFER

The door to Brie's cell slid open as two well-armed guards stood there with their arms crossed. She sat up on her lumpy bunk, blinking in the bright light that spilled in.

"Up," said one of the guards in a gruff voice; his swarthy face betrayed no emotion.

Still groggy with sleep, Brie forced herself to stand, wondering what they had planned for her now. She placed herself between the two men as they walked out of her cell and into the sterile hallway. Moving only her eyes, Brie read the signs that they passed and counted the number of steps. "Twenty-two," she said to herself in a low whisper.

The elevator doors slid open, revealing the cramped space inside. The guards pushed her in. Still wondering what would become of her, she watched the counter above the door as numbers flashed. Floor two. Knowing that that was not the floor where the interrogation room was, Brie realized that something else would be done to her. Once the doors slid open, the two guards shoved her through them and marched behind her, steering her down another sterile corridor. Doing her best to observe every inch of her new surround-ings, Brie peeked every so often to make certain her efforts did not attract the attention of her guards.

More signs greeted them. Brie committed their words to mem-ory. They turned right at a sign reading, "202-209." As Brie thought about it, she realized that they were room numbers. She glanced at the doors. As though to prove her theory correct, each door pos-sessed a number and counted up.

The guards stopped before another door with the number 209 on it. One seized her shoulder, yanking her to a stop. The door slid open with a soft hiss and the guards shoved her inside a darkened room. Masks and plants lined the wall, though Brie recognized none of them. Lamps were nestled in each corner of the room, providing some light and bringing life to the rust-colored rug in the middle of the metal-plated floor. The only other light in the room was the lamp on a desk as it illuminated a book with worn and crinkled pages and a small mound of black cloth.

"Leave us," said a voice.

Brie turned her head. Klanor stood in the shadows with a glass of red liquid in his hand.

"But, sir," protested one of the guards.

"She is hardly a threat here," said Klanor. "Wait outside."

The guards saluted and marched out of the room, taking their positions on each side of the doorway, hands behind their backs.

Brie turned back to Klanor. "What do you want with me?"

Klanor ambled over to the desk and flipped the archaic volume closed. In a brief second, Brie noticed the writing on it. It matched the writing in the ancient poems that Rynah had read to her and the others ever since she had been yanked from her home, but some-thing else seemed familiar about it; it was the same book that she had seen during one of Klanor's interrogation sessions.

"It seems to me that we got off on the wrong foot," said Klanor. "You are unusually resistant to the questioning."

"You mean the mind games."

"If you wish to call them that."

Klanor sipped his drink before walking over to another table with a carafe and glasses on it. "Drink?"

Brie remained still.

"I assure you, it isn't poisoned."

"How can I trust you? You hold me prisoner."

"A wise question." To ease her fears, Klanor picked up the carafe and poured its contents into an empty glass, lifting it up to her in a toast, and drank from it. After several seconds, he held it out to Brie. "Seems perfectly fine to me."

Gauging her options, and Klanor's true motives, Brie took the offered glass. She sniffed it. It had a fruity smell and she guessed that it was some sort of wine. She pretended to drink it.

"Ah, see, we can be friends," said Klanor in an unusually cheerful voice.

"You have a strange way of making friends," Brie replied.

"I'll admit that keeping you locked up in a cell was not the best thing for me to do. However, we could start anew. I know what Rynah has told you about me and the crystals."

"You mean how you used her and then stole the very thing that kept your planet alive."

"Such disdain," scoffed Klanor. "Good. I like that. For a while, I thought the only emotion you could express was fear, but there is something else about you. A sort of kindness masked in loathing."

Brie stared at Klanor, unsure of what he meant.

"I know about the girl you saved from being sacrificed to her gods on that planet," said Klanor. "Do you know what they call you now?"

Brie shook her head. In everything that had happened since, she had forgotten about the girl.

"*Megula*. It means honored mother," replied Klanor. "Curious, isn't it?"

"How is she?" asked Brie, curious about the child's wellbeing.

"Quite well," said Klanor. "When I realized that you all had gotten the crystal first, I left the planet exactly as I found it. No one was harmed."

Thankful for that, though somewhat doubting Klanor's word, Brie pretended to take another sip.

"You can finish your drink."

"I've never had much tolerance for alcohol," said Brie.

"Pity."

"Why have you called me here?"

"That is what I like about your race," said Klanor, "you're to the point. Very well." He waved Brie to him, and curiosity getting the better of her, she walked over to the desk the old volume and bit of cloth rested on. "This is the ancient text of my people. I am sure you are familiar with it as Rynah has, no doubt, told you about it, and read some passages to you."

"I know of it."

"Good. Then believe me when I say that she has not told you everything."

"What do you mean?"

"You know that the crystals can be turned into a sort of weapon if placed properly in a certain device, as described here"—Klanor held up another book, its leather binding tattered, which discussed the construction of the weapon he spoke of—"I happen to have built that device. Using the specifications from other ancient texts and scholars, I built it. The original has never been found and probably no longer exists."

"And what does all this have to do with me?"

"Did you also know that one of the crystals has the ability to turn back time?"

Brie's widened eyes told Klanor that she didn't. "Are you serious?"

"Outlandish to think about, I know, but time travel has long been sought after, no matter what planet you are from. Many wish to undo the past."

"But how do you know all this?"

"From here."

"Rynah never spoke of a crystal that could control the streams of time," said Brie, still doubting what Klanor had just told her.

"There are two possible reasons," said Klanor. "One, she doesn't have a complete copy of the text. Or two, she doesn't wish you to know."

Brie remained silent as she thought about all of this new information. *Turn back time? Is it possible?* she asked herself. "It seems too good to believe."

"Another piece of wisdom from one so young. You are correct, of course. It does seem too good to be true, but what if it is possible? You could have your father back."

Brie dropped her full glass of wine. It shattered on the floor, sending shards of glass everywhere as the red liquid seeped through the fibers of the rug. "How do you…"

"I know a lot about you, my dear. Courtesy of the mind games, as you call them. Once your mind is linked with another, it isn't difficult to glean information from them without their knowledge, so long as you keep them distracted."

Now Brie began to understand the illusions she had often found herself in whenever they strapped her to that chair. "I know you didn't call me here for a social call, so what is it you really want?"

"You could tell me how to find Rynah."

"I'm not sure how."

"Of course you are. You know how she thinks. You know about the crystals. Where would she most likely bunk down for the night?"

In reality, Brie had no idea where Rynah would go. They had never been close, and Rynah despised her most of the time. "I'm not certain."

"Come now. If you help me, Brie, you will find the rewards worth it."

"Rewards?"

"Yes. You could have your own room, much like this one, with the luxuries and comforts that far surpass your home. I could bring your father back by going back in time and stopping the very incident that robbed him of his life, and your family of his presence. You never would have had to move into that dreadful government housing, as you call it, and go to that school with that… Jenny. Yes, I know all about it. You could be a family again."

Tears welled in Brie's eyes as she thought about the possibilities. To have her father back and still be living in the house that she had loved so much. She never would have had to grow up so fast, nor would she have been forced to change schools and leave many of her friends behind. She could just be a normal teenager. The endless possibilities surrounded her thoughts as she dreamed of having back what had been taken from her.

"Think about it," whispered Klanor. "What has Rynah ever done for you?"

Klanor pulled back the black cloth, revealing five crystals, one of which looked familiar. She reached out to them before yanking her hand back in fear.

"Go ahead," encouraged Klanor. "I'm sure you recognize them."

Brie knew them. She stretched out her hand and touched the one that she had lost while on Aquara, the same one that Rynah had entrusted her with, and the same one that Stein had stolen. Her fingers wrapped around the once luminescent crystal, which had greyed and turned dull. The moment she took hold of it, it brightened, turning a pale blue with specks of white light that sparkled, something that Klanor took notice of.

Without warning, her mind filled with thoughts of Rynah, but they weren't just thoughts, it was as though she could feel Rynah's presence. "Rynah?" she whispered.

Mental images of Rynah walking through a strange town with a man that looked as alien as her consumed Brie. Soon, they vanished and her heart filled with dread as she sensed the cold presence of Stein and the growing darkness that consumed his heart. As fear filled her, the crystal in her hand warmed, calming her, reminding her of who she was, and who she had become.

Thoughts of Tom, Alfric, and Solon filled her mind. If not for Rynah, she never would have met them. She would not have learned to be strong, due to Alfric's teachings. She would not have learned to laugh, as Tom had taught her how, nor would she have learned the bits of wisdom that Solon possessed and shared with her. Most importantly, she never would have entered a different world and seen the endless possibilities of the universe… and what of the girl whom she had rescued? Brie shuddered at the thought of the child's fate if she had not been there.

Klanor took the crystal from her, and the moment he did, an image flashed in Brie's mind: a simple ring in the palm of a hand accompanied by intense emotional pain. She did not understand the message, but knew what her answer was.

"Your offer is tempting," said Brie.

Klanor smiled at her statement as he placed the crystal back on the desk.

"But at what cost?"

His grin evaporated.

"You are correct to assume that I would desire to have my father back, and perhaps you could give me that gift. But such a gift should come without a price tag, and you place a hefty one upon yours."

"You may wish to reconsider," Klanor's voice deepened in tone.

"No, I do not." Brie placed her arms by her side, doing her best to look resolute, even though deep inside she shook with the fear of what he would do to her.

"I will not make this offer again."

"Good, because I would hate to refuse you twice."

Klanor closed the distance between them. He cupped her chin in his strong, purple hand and forced her to look into his eyes. A crooked grin crossed his lips. "Yes, now I see it. There is something there, something within your eyes that was not there before. Be certain that you have made the right choice."

Klanor released Brie and marched to the doors. They hissed when they opened and the guards faced him in attention. "Take her back to her cell."

In obedience, the guards each seized one of Brie's arms and dragged her out of the room. Brie managed to glance back and noticed a series of buttons being pushed on a holographic keypad to Klanor's room, and as they hauled her away to her fate, she committed the sequence to memory.

Seething, Jifdar wandered through the smoldering remains of one of his pirate bases as he eyed the damage that had been dealt. Mangled bodies hung from wires and railings, as bits and pieces of ships lay strewn across the smoke filled area. He puffed out his scaly cheeks as he surveyed the smoke-ridden place.

"This is the third one of our bases to be destroyed. Who would do such a thing?" he demanded of his first mate, Heller. Though a pirate—and one who had committed similar atrocities—to be forced to see his own people suffer infuriated him.

"I have my suspicions," answered Heller.

"Then voice them."

"Klanor."

"Why do you say so?" Jifdar kicked a piece of scrap metal and sent it skittering across the debris-ridden ground.

"He has a most powerful weapon."

"Built on foolish, ancient tales."

"Maybe they are not so foolish."

Jifdar glared at his first mate. "What are you trying to say?"

"Remember when we captured that archaic ship with the strange crew?" asked Heller.

Jifdar remembered. He would never forget the Viking that managed to kill one of his best men, the girl with the pale skin, the boy with the scrawny build, or the man with the skin as black as night. No, he would never forget them. "Why do you ask?"

"Remember that their captain said something about a crystal and a weapon they hoped to stop the development of. What if they told the truth? She mentioned Klanor's name."

"She did," mused Jifdar. "Are you saying…"

"There has been a lot of talk lately about the planet Lanyr and how it was destroyed by none other than someone named Klanor. I think he has built this weapon and is testing it."

"But why on us?"

"Does he need a reason? We are pirates."

Jifdar mulled over Heller's words. His first mate had a point. Pirates were considered the scum of the universe, and what a better place to test a newly developed weapon. "If this continues, there will be none of us left."

"We need to form an alliance with the other pirates," said Heller.

"If they have not already been destroyed," said Jifdar.

"Or perhaps we should form an alliance with the crew we abandoned on Ikor since they did manage to escape from there and steal their ship back."

"That they did," muttered Jifdar. Though angered at losing to them, he admired them for what they had done.

A soft cough coming from under a teetering pile of rubble caught his attention. Jifdar raced to it, heaving a piece of metal off one of his men.

"Captain," said the pirate as he coughed some more, "they came unexpectedly… from nowhere. We were… unable to…" A fit of coughing stopped him midsentence.

"Easy, man," said Jifdar. "You fought bravely. You're a good pirate and shall be well rewarded."

"I fear I'll not be able to spend that reward."

"Just take it easy." Jifdar turned to Heller. "We need a doctor over here!"

The dying pirate coughed some more before going still. Enraged, Jifdar laid him on the ground with a gentleness most would think a pirate incapable of expressing before facing his first mate. "I want that man to pay. I want that ship found."

Chapter 15
REPAIRS

The ship bobbed up and down, mimicking vessels that sailed the waves of the ocean as the dolphins in space towed them closer to a small, yet out of the way, settlement. The four companions stood in the command center glued to the window and the luminescent beings that helped them. As the small space station neared, Rynah realized the time had come to release their strange saviors.

"Detach the cable," she said.

Solon pressed the button that Rynah had told him to push upon her orders. A loud pop sounded as the cable snapped loose and left the ship; each of them watched as the "dolphins" left.

"I never would have believed it if I hadn't seen it," said Tom, still marveling at the whole affair.

"Not every creature needs oxygen and a pressurized atmosphere to survive," said Rynah.

"If only Brie were here to see this," muttered Solon.

A pang of guilt struck Rynah's heart as she remembered the

way she had allowed Brie to die. She found herself desiring the girl's presence more than the others. "Me too," she whispered.

"Unidentified ship," came a voice over the radio, though scarcely audible, "what is your purpose here?"

Rynah jumped over the pilot's chair and pressed the talk button on her radio. "Our engines are dead and we barely have enough power for life support and communications. Request assistance to land on the planet below and conduct repairs."

"Where are you from?"

"Survivors, from Lanyr," said Rynah. She figured a half truth was better than nothing. Besides, she had no desire to tell anyone about her friends from Earth.

"Lanyr?" came the static reply.

"Yes," said Rynah. "Please, I don't know how much longer I can keep this transmission going."

"Prepare to enter orbit."

"Thank you."

Within seconds, two ships appeared alongside them, each emitting a tractor beam to guide them into orbit. The ship jolted and bounced. "Hang onto something," said Rynah.

They each grabbed hold of the sturdiest thing they could find.

Outside the window, the brown planet grew larger. Flames swept across the outer hull as they entered orbit, only to disappear once the gold clouds greeted them. Rock encrusted hills increased in size, changing from pinpricks to mammoth-sized mountains with each passing second.

"This last part may get a bit bumpy," said a voice over the radio.

With one final drop, the ship landed on the ground with a force that almost knocked Rynah out of her chair. "A bit," she grumbled.

"Please open your rear hatch," said the same voice over the radio.

Rynah jumped from her seat. "I guess it's time to meet our hosts. Do not, under any circumstance, tell them where you are from. We are merely passing through."

"Understood," said Alfric.

"We are going to stand out, you know," Tom said.

Rynah stared at him a moment, knowing he was right, but aware that there was little she could do about it. "Just, leave the talking to me."

They all trooped down to the main hatch and allowed those waiting outside to enter. Three stepped inside the ship. Their leader took off his helmet, revealing a man with skin that possessed a yellow undertone and brown hair.

"My name is Usef," he greeted them. "You all look like you have had a time of it."

"That barely begins to describe it," said Rynah. "We need a new engine to get this baby running again."

"Can she refer to Solaris as 'baby'?" Tom whispered in Solon's ear with the feeling that Solaris would not appreciate being called "baby".

Solon shrugged in response.

"I'm afraid we can't help you there," said Usef. "This is a remote settlement. Mostly farmers and miners—people looking to get away from everything and live where not many questions are asked. Our supplies are limited, but you are welcome to stay as long as you need to. You may have to assist in a few chores to earn your keep."

"Fair enough," said Rynah. "What supplies can you give me to conduct repairs?"

"Tools, mostly, but I'm not sure how that will replace your engine."

Tom had an idea. He ran up to Rynah and tapped her on the shoulder, not stopping until she turned to him and hissed, "What!"

"I know! When you brought me here, I had an engine in my hands. It was experimental and didn't work half the time; of course, I didn't have access to some of the technology you have, but I might be able to fit it for Solaris. With a few modifications, I could get her up and running again."

"Solaris?" asked Usef.

"It's what we named the ship," explained Rynah, not wanting to tell him that Solaris was an artificial intelligence with a mind of her own, and a stubborn streak that would put any donkey to shame.

"Ha-ha! Yeah, I named my ship Belfi. She's temperamental, but she'll treat you well."

Rynah smiled. "You go work on your engine," she said to Tom.

Beaming, Tom ran off. "Solon, come on!"

"Keep an eye on them," Rynah said to Alfric.

Groaning, Alfric hitched up his sword and followed after the over eager "children" as he referred to them.

"You all are not from Lanyr," said Usef.

"No, I am. I met them as I searched for a place of safety. They, too, have suffered losses and just wish to start over. We've formed an unlikely friendship."

The explanation seemed to have satisfied Usef as he nodded his head. "I'll show you around."

Rynah walked beside Usef as he led the way around the small settlement. Once they left the landing area, buildings surrounded them as they trekked down a gravel path. Smoke spilled from the chimneys of some, while others had wide, open doors to allow the arid air to flow through in a cross breeze. The banging and clanging of hammers filled the air as two men attempted to fix the axel of a wagon.

"Do you not believe in technology?" asked Rynah as she watched others hack at the ground with hoes and mix in manure from the farm animals that roamed freely.

"We do, but out here, luxuries are difficult to come by," said Usef, "so we make do with more 'primitive' ways."

"Who are all these people?" asked Rynah.

She watched as different races from the various sectors worked together to eke out a living on what many believed to be a lump of rock. They managed it, to some degree, as patches of emerald grass poked out of the ground, and one woman in her 70s, with a scarf containing her frizzy red hair, watered a patch of wildflowers.

"Many of them are exiles, or people looking for a new life," said Usef.

"Exiles?" Rynah was unaware that some systems still practiced such punishments.

"Yes," said Usef. "Jon, here, fell in love with the daughter of a wealthy benefactor on the planet of Flynyr. Unfortunately, her father disapproved of the union and put a price on his head. So, he ran away with her, and they came here."

"And no bounty hunters have shown up?"

"Most people ignore this place. It is an arid planet, and we work hard to scratch out a living, but as you can see, our efforts have paid off. Besides, we leave breadcrumbs to keep the bounty hunters, and other undesirables, away."

They continued, their boots crunching on the gravel path that curved as it wound its way through the compound; tufts of fluffy moss edged the walk. Rynah looked around at the pumps that drew water from deep under the planet's surface; their rusted sides shone in the sunlight from droplets of condensation. Farmers hacked the ground with garden hoes and shovels, planting young plants which had been grown in the greenhouse—a building that resembled an antiquated barn with plastic for walls, instead of wooden planks.

Rynah observed the settlers as they strolled by with baskets on their shoulders or bundles in their arms—their clothing simple and adapted for the arid environment, blocking out the sand that drifted across the path or filled the air. The walkway forked as they neared a water fountain: simplistic, made of copper, with two spouts from which clear, refreshing water poured forth.

"This is the center of town, if you will," said Usef.

"It's amazing how you have turned this place into a home," said Rynah, noticing an oval flower garden filled with petunias, morning glories, and zinnias, bringing color to the brown planet.

"We do what we can. This is the town's fountain. Most come here for water, and though some have their own wells, we have found that a communal well provides much needed socializing. And look…"

Usef pointed at small streams of water that moseyed toward the gardens.

"An irrigation system," said Rynah.

"Precisely."

"And your gardens, are they communal as well?"

"Yes, and no. We have found that it is best to have them all here, where we can put these panels"—Usef held up a metal sheet—"around them to protect them from the sandstorms, but each individual, or family, owns their own plot, which they can till as they like. We are all landowners and are responsible for our own well-being. Slovenly behavior is not tolerated."

A commotion arose nearby and Usef ran towards it with Rynah right behind him. When they reached the circled area where angry shouts echoed around them, Rynah's face contorted in a mixture of frustration and laughter. Surrounded by a crowd of irate settlers were mounds of grain, and in the center was Tom, humiliated, standing with a livid Viking.

"That was this year's grain!" yelled one angry man.

"I didn't mean…" began Tom as grain dust fell from the top of his head and shoulders with each movement he made, making him cough.

"Enough!" shouted Usef.

The crowd settled down, but some within it still shot menacing glares in Tom's direction.

"I had told him that some things are best left alone," said Solon, walking up to Rynah, "and Alfric tried to stop him."

Rynah didn't bother asking; she had already guessed what had happened.

Needing water and some tools that he could not find in the hangar, Tom and Solon went to the little town in search of them, when he noticed a four-poster building, having no exterior walls, but possessing holoscreens and flashing lights, with a high, pointed ceiling. Curious, and thinking that such an innovative and highly technological building didn't belong in the middle of a place full of farmers, he decided to investigate. Once underneath the vaulted ceiling, Tom found a lone button. He did what most inquisitive people do when they find such a button, he pushed it, releasing a lever that dumped the grain which had been stored in the attic above him.

Rynah shook her head, unable to fathom why Tom loved to fiddle with things that most people left alone.

"What do you have to say for yourself?" demanded Usef after listening to Tom's explanation.

"Oops," said Tom.

"Oops?" Usef raised an eyebrow. "This is our only grain supply and you dumped it all over the place!"

"I'm sorry," Tom said.

Before Usef could admonish the young inventor any further, Rynah grabbed his arm. "I do apologize for my friend, here. He is a bit… curious and tends to let that get the better of him. I'm certain that he will clean this up."

"Happy to," squeaked Tom, hoping to not be hung for his mistake. Within moments, shovels were thrust into his empty hands.

"I want this cleaned up by morning, "said Usef.

Rynah stifled a yawn, but Alfric had seen it.

"My apologies," Usef said to her, regaining his amicable composure. "I don't normally lose my temper."

Rynah said nothing as she reached for a shovel to help Tom clean up the piles of grain before the wind had a chance to carry them away. A firm hand seized the shovel before she had a chance to scoop some up.

"The soothsayer and I will assist our undisciplined friend," said Alfric. "You need some rest."

"I'm fine," protested Rynah.

"You are exhausted." Alfric turned to Usef, and saying in that commanding stature of his, "You will take her to her quarters where she may rest."

Knowing it was best not to argue, Usef led Rynah away. "I will show you to your rooms where you and your friends may spend your time here."

Usef led Rynah back to the hangar where a single floor building stood next to it. "This is our guest's quarters, if you will. I figured you would wish to be close to your ship. Normally, this is where the pilots who bring us supplies sleep, but…"

"It will do just fine," said Rynah.

The building had three rooms, each with a single cot and a table with a washbasin and pitcher on it. She had already decided that she and Alfric would have their own rooms, while Tom and Solon would bunk together, as they seemed to get along so well, and perhaps Solon could curb Tom's impulsive behavior.

"I do apologize…"

"Don't worry about it," interrupted Usef. "It's not the first time such a thing happened. Another inquisitive youth did the same."

"Who?"

"Me. I'll give you your privacy now."

Usef left Rynah to rest and she stretched out on the springy cot—its comfort surprised her—falling fast asleep.

Chapter 16
A Request and a Feast

"**L**and right there," said Merrick as he pointed to three protruding boulders form the rocky ground.

"That doesn't look like a landing strip," commented Obiah.

"Just do it," said Merrick.

Obiah adjusted his controls and slowed down as he lined up for a landing. A red light flickered at him, warning him that he had forgotten the landing gear. Irritated, he pulled the lever that controlled it. A screeching hum reverberated on the interior walls as the gear lowered and prepared for landing. Obiah held his ship steady as he lowered in altitude and approached the designated landing area.

Suddenly, lights spilled from the pointed tips of the rocks, focusing their beams on his vessel. "What's this?" he demanded.

"They're just scanning the ship," answered Merrick.

Annoyed at not being warned about such things, Obiah held his tongue as he kept his ship level, while he neared the ground with plumes of dust and sand swirling around them. The engines howled

as Obiah guided his ship. With a loud plink and a jolt, he touched
the ground and turned off the engines.

"Time to go," said Merrick.

Obiah followed Merrick to the hatch of his ship, allowing himself to be led, even though he started to wonder if he had made the
right choice in trusting this stranger he had met in a space outpost.
Too late now, he thought to himself. While Merrick busied himself
with opening the hatch, Obiah snatched a laser gun he kept hidden
in a secret panel. He had just finished putting it in his belt when
Merrick turned back around.

"Ready?" he asked.

"Yeah," said Obiah. "Let's get this over with."

Merrick took the lead and plopped his heavy boots on the first
step as he walked outside. Obiah followed. A single door lay in front
of them that led to an underground bunker.

"Halt!" yelled a stern voice. Men, with the same skin pigmentation and hair as Obiah and Merrick, raced out from behind the
rocks, releasing a series of clicks as they armed their weapons, taking
aim at Obiah. "Hands up!"

Obiah thrust his hands above his head, while shooting a glare at
Merrick, whose arms remained by his side.

"I'm sorry," Merrick apologized, "but I had to warn them. We
have to make sure we can trust you."

"Apparently, I cannot trust you," growled Obiah.

The barrel of a laser gun poked the tip of his nose as a
Lanyran soldier pushed it in his face. Another lifted up his shirt
and jerked his weapon free of its hold. "I knew he was armed,"
said the commander.

"Of course I'm armed," said Obiah.

"Silence!" yelled the commander. "Name?"

"*Grergisda*," answered Obiah, which, roughly translated, means "F you".

The commander raised his fist.

"Stop!" shouted Merrick.

The commander hesitated as he lowered his hand, while glaring at Obiah, the dislike in the man's eyes prominent. "Take him to holding."

Hands seized Obiah's arms and shoved him through the only door and into the darkened interior. Damp stairs descending downward led them the rest of the way as they marched deep underground, with nimble trails of work lights that lit their path, illuminating a dismal atmosphere of darkness and hopelessness. Obiah moved his eyes all around, taking in every detail of his surroundings. Forlorn faces, aged before their time, lined the hallways; each possessed hollowed eyes that watched him. As Obiah took note of the ragged people around him, he understood his less than cordial reception.

His guards jerked him to the right. Again, they walked down a winding corridor (jagged edges of roughhewn rock marked the walls and were as welcoming as Obiah's captors), pushing him along until they came upon a rusted and brown metal door, which had been built recently and bore a pinprick of a window for one to look through, and shoved him into the dingy cell behind it. The distinct click of the lock warned Obiah that he would be going nowhere.

He meandered over to the far side of his prison. Only solid rock supported his feet. No windows. No light. Obiah brushed away the fine dust that littered the ground and sat cross-legged, knowing that eventually someone would come for him. Someone always did.

Sparks flew from the flamethrower as Tom cut away a chunk of metal from Solaris' hull. They danced before the dark glass of his welding helmet as he attempted to carve away the damaged pieces of the ship. They had been there for over a week, and still, Solaris was not back online. A part of him missed her sarcastic voice and teasing, though another part of him was glad that she had been silenced for a while.

A jolt of electricity shot through the exterior of the vessel, creating a shower of sparks around him.

"Hey!" shouted Tom as he shut off the flamethrower and lifted his visor. "What are you doing?"

"Sorry," apologized Solon. Tangled wires trapped him in a tight fitting suit. "I tried to put these the way you said I should, but this electricity, as you call it, is still quite new to me."

Tom put down the flamethrower and jumped off his perch on the ship.

"Here," he said as he untangled Solon from his wiry mess, "let me help you with this before you get us both killed."

"It has the power to do that?" asked Solon. "Amazing."

"Yeah, real amazing, except when you're dead."

"How exactly are you going to bring Solaris back?" asked Solon as he tried to wipe a black smudge from his olive-colored skin, but instead, managed to smear it across his cheek.

"These magnets"—Tom pointed at his engine—"are going to do that. I am going to use them to create a reverse polarity, which will, in turn, generate a small gravitational force that will be the power-house of the engine."

"Uh-huh." Solon's confused look relayed that he understood none of what Tom had said.

"It will work," said Tom.

"If you say so."

"Get back to those wires." Tom picked up his flamethrower and climbed back to his perch. "I need them fixed before I can install the new engine."

Solon gave Tom a disbelieving look, but continued with his task. He hoped his friend was able to accomplish the job he had set before himself, otherwise, they would all be stuck there.

In another part of the hangar, Rynah scoured through scraps, looking for anything that could be used to fix the flight controls of the ship. Usef had said that she might not find anything, but she searched anyway. Many of the wires in the ship had shorted out. Her hand grasped an odd looking pipe. She studied it a bit before tossing it aside, allowing it to clank on the cement floor.

"No luck?" said Usef as he approached with a jug.

"Unfortunately," muttered Rynah.

"Here"—he handed her a glass and popped the cork on the jug—"this should help."

Rynah took a sip. Her eyes watered as her throat burned from the liquid that trickled down it. "What is this stuff?"

"Moonshine," said Usef. "Homemade malt liquor. We don't get many supply ships here, so we have to do what we can with what we have."

"I think I'll pass." Rynah handed him back her glass. "It's a little too strong for my taste."

"That's all right." Usef emptied her glass. "I'll drink for the both of us."

Rynah chuckled. "You really need to work on your pick up lines."

"Oh, that wasn't one." Usef put the glass and jug down. "This is a pick up line: 'We're having a celebration tonight, and I would look great on your arm.'"

Rynah burst out laughing until her sides ached. "It still needs work."

"You're probably right," conceded Usef, "but will you come to the celebration? A couple are getting married and it's a great time to feast and relax. My sister has some clothes you can borrow, and I'm sure I can work something out for your friends."

"Speaking of my friends," said Rynah, "have you seen Alfric?"

"He's helping someone repair a wheel on his cart. They don't have a lot of technological conveniences where he's from, do they?"

"What makes you ask that?"

"Well, the man knows about more axels and rudimentary tools than our best engineer, and he is able to lift amounts that make most men crumble. When asked to fix and engine's computerized parts, he has no idea what we were talking about. Instead, he had a strange response."

"Such as?"

"Get a horse."

Rynah chuckled.

"So? You coming to the celebration?"

"We'd love to. And I'd be honored to have you adorn my arm."

Usef beamed. "I'll see you around seven then."

"See you." Rynah watched Usef leave, still giggling to herself at the way he asked her to the wedding. She turned back to the scrap heap and continued her search for anything that could be used to fix Solaris. As a bout of melancholy struck her, Rynah turned toward her grandfather's ship. She brushed the hair from her face as she thought about how attached she had become to it. "Come back to us, Solaris," she whispered. "Please."

The metal lock clicked as someone opened the door, allowing the unoiled hinges to squeak. Obiah shot to his feet, regaining his composure. In marched two guards, and Merrick.

"Are you my escort?" asked Obiah with a note of distaste.

"I do apologize for this," said Merrick. His expression indicated that he was sorry for the way Obiah had been treated. "I had to radio ahead and let them know we were coming, but I never thought they would lock you up in here. You see, we've had others come to us, claiming to be survivors, but they were actually working for Klanor. We have to be careful."

"I have never lied to you."

"But how can I be certain of that?"

Obiah closed the distance between him and Merrick, stopping when the guards pointed their weapons at him. "I spoke the truth when I talked to you in that bar. I must see the council."

"That is where I am to take you." Merrick waved his hand and the two guards each took a position by Obiah's side. Again, they stepped out into the feeble light of the corridor and trekked its winding path until they came to a set of stairs.

The steps had been carved out of the rocky wall, their unevenness making the climb challenging. The guards' steps fell in time with Obiah's as he ascended the stairwell until he entered the beam of light that lay above him. His jaw almost dropped as he walked into the council chambers. Giant, glassless windows lined the wall, allowing the sun's rays to fill the room, a stark contrast to the catacombs he had just vacated. Particles of dust danced in the light, oblivious to the tension in the air. Grim faces lined the long table before him; each bore hardened eyes that studied Obiah's every move. He ignored their scrutiny and strolled to the center of the room, his hubristic manner disquieting them. Silence loomed.

Obiah glanced around at the gathered crowd. People had filled every open crevice within the chamber, eager to hear what he had to say. A warm breeze flowed through the open windows, brushing his cheeks with its embrace. Obiah turned back to the council members. "You summoned me."

His voice echoed through the room; the challenging tone did not go unnoticed.

"I believe it was you who asked to see us," said one member, sitting in the center of the table. His gray-streaked, auburn hair swayed in the wind.

"And is this how you greet your citizens?" challenged Obiah. "With shackles?"

"We have reason not to trust people these days," said the same council member, whose name was Hylne. Obiah recognized him.

"Have I given you reason not to trust me? I came here peacefully with news and a request."

"Klanor was once one we trusted, yet he stole the crystal, thus damning our planet to a horrendous fate," Hylne's voice boomed through the chamber.

"I am not he," said Obiah. "Now remove these shackles, unless I am to remain your prisoner." He held out his hands.

Hylne nodded at one of the security guards. A tiny holopad appeared, allowing the man to type in a code, unlocking the handcuffs. Thankful, Obiah rubbed his wrists.

"Members of the council," Obiah addressed the others with more respect, "I have come to ask you…"

"Yes, about that," interrupted Hylne. "Merrick told us why you have come. You believe some silly story about a bunch of crystals and wish us to go chasing after them."

"Silly stories? Is that what you believe destroyed our planet? Klanor doesn't, and he is pursuing them as we speak. Besides, you will not have to chase after them. Rynah has already located them. She, and she alone, has pursued Klanor in an effort to stop him before he rains more devastation upon us and other innocents."

"Considering who her grandfather is," said Hylne, "I am not surprised that she chose to believe this nonsense."

"Marlow warned all of you, all of us, about the dangers of keeping that crystal. We should have moved to a different home long ago, but instead, past members of the council chose to utilize a piece of technology for which they had no understanding of. Now we have reaped the rewards of such stupidity."

"How dare you!" roared Hylne.

"How dare you, President of the Council!" Obiah shot back. "I came to you in peace to ask for your help, and yet you rebuked me."

Obiah turned away from the council and faced the gathered crowd. He noticed the pain in their faces, mixed with interest in his words. His heart bled for them.

"There is still a chance for all of us to stop Klanor," said Obiah, "before he has a chance to harm others. We will find a new home, but we cannot do that until we remove the threat that Klanor poses. He believes in the crystals and the power they are supposed to hold. Rynah, Marlow's granddaughter, has studied the legends and believes that they form a weapon, the technology of which we have yet to understand. But she knows this. If Klanor gets hold of it, he will turn against us and others.

"Will we stand idly by while he delivers the same punishment to other civilizations that he has dealt to us? If we do nothing, are we not just as guilty? I pose this choice to all of you. We have survived the destruction of Lanyr, and I know that you are all afraid, but don't let that fear drive you because, if you do, it is only a matter of time before Klanor finds us and finishes what he started."

"Nice speech," said Hylne. "How do we know that you did not lead him here?"

"Because if I did, we'd all be dead," replied Obiah. "Is this what we have come to? Are we so frightened that we accuse any newcomers amongst us of disloyalty and then imprison them? Are we so frightened that we allow evil to flourish?"

"You have said your piece," said Hylne, "now the council will vote on it."

"One moment," said a low voice as a single man rose from his chair dressed in the uniform of the Lanyran fleet with medals pinned to his chest. Obiah almost gasped when he looked at the man that had been his commanding officer during his first few years of active service in the Lanyran fleet. He had not seen him earlier and scolded himself for being so unobservant.

Hylne backed down.

"My name is Delmar," said the man, "general of the Lanyran fleet. I have commanded our ships for over 30 years and been in the fleet for 70, and never once saw the devastation that I witnessed back on Lanyr. Councilman Hylne, you are wise to practice caution, but unwise to ignore Obiah here. We ignored Marlow to our misfortune. Now Obiah seeks our help to hunt down Klanor and bring him to justice. Members of the council, I propose that we help him. I implore you all to consider his request carefully. Do not make the same mistake again."

General Delmar took his seat. No one spoke, as his presence commanded obedience. After several seconds passed, Hylne continued, but with more reserve. "By a raise of hands, who wishes to grant Obiah's request?"

Two hands, General Delmar's and a woman's, rose into the air among the council. Within the gathered crowd, whose votes were not counted, more rose, outnumbering those who refused to help.

"Motion denied," said Hylne as he smacked the gavel on the table. "You are dismissed." He stood up, sweeping his robes around his feet and marched out of the room.

Obiah had expected this decision. Disappointment filled him, as for a fleeting moment, he thought he might have gotten through to them.

"I am sorry," said General Delmar, approaching from behind. "I tried to help."

"It's not your fault."

"You have come a long way from that cocky upstart I trained all those years ago."

"Years?"

"It's been nearly 52."

"That long?" scoffed Obiah. "I hardly noticed."

"Your hair says otherwise."

"So does yours," laughed Obiah. "So they made you a general? I got out of the service before they could pin that torture on me."

General Delmar chuckled. "Perhaps you got out too soon."

Obiah didn't answer.

"What will you do now?"

"Meet up with Rynah. It shocked me to hear that she had left the fleet to become a security officer in the geo-lab."

"Not surprising if you think about it. A lot of things changed after Marlow's trial," said the general. "You know, we could use a good pilot, especially since we have been almost entirely obliterated."

Obiah clapped a hand on the general's shoulder. "I appreciate the offer, old friend, but I can't. I abandoned Rynah once. I'll not do it again."

"How will you find her?"

"Not sure, but give me my ship back, and some supplies, and I will."

"There's the Obiah I know. You will have your supplies and your ship."

"Thank you." Obiah turned to leave, but General Delmar stopped him again.

"Obiah, I'm sorry about Marlow. I should have stood by him." General Delmar's face fell as he remembered the trial and his refusal to defend a man he had once called a friend. Just as he had once been Obiah's commanding officer, he had also been Marlow's, but he always found Marlow's love and knowledge of Lanyran lore fascinating, and when Marlow left the fleet, they became friends. There was always something about Marlow, something General Delmar respected. He remembered when Marlow had come over to his home, excited that he had a granddaughter. Then, the time between their get-togethers lengthened as Marlow delved deeper into his books and his workshop. When Marlow tried to steal the crystal from the geo-lab, General Delmar didn't want to believe it, but when Marlow confessed to the crime, like Obiah, he turned his back on his friend and never spoke to him again, a guilt that plagued him since.

"We all should have. Perhaps this is our opportunity to atone for that."

They shook hands and Obiah left. Though exhausted, he did not wish to waste another moment getting to Rynah. He pushed his way through the crowd and raced down the steps back into the corridor. As he turned a corner, he bumped into Merrick. "You!"

"Hear me out." said Merrick, holding up his hands. "Please."

Against his better judgment, Obiah allowed Merrick to speak.

"I honestly had no idea they were going to lock you up and treat you like a criminal," said Merrick. "The rules are that whenever I find survivors, I am to let the people here know before I bring them. Normally, people are welcomed and given food and shelter. I don't know why they treated you differently."

"Because of Marlow," said Obiah.

"I am sorry," said Merrick. "We are struggling to survive here. There is barely enough running water for the amount of people

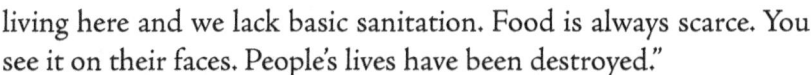

living here and we lack basic sanitation. Food is always scarce. You see it on their faces. People's lives have been destroyed."

"What do you want?" demanded Obiah.

"Let me come with you," said Merrick.

Obiah crossed his arms as a doubtful look filled his face.

"I know these parts," said Merrick. "I know this section of space, and I am on friendly terms with some of the pirates that roam here. You need me."

"Why do you wish to come?"

Merrick's face fell. "I had a sister who was killed because of that crystal. I wish to see some justice for her death."

Obiah softened his face. "I intend to bring him back to stand trial. We still have laws."

"I understand," said Merrick.

"If you cross me..." began Obiah.

"Understood," Merrick interrupted.

The two ran down the hallway to where the landing strip was. When they reached Obiah's ship, they found that General Delmar had kept his word and had fitted it with supplies.

Alfric growled as he looked into the distorted mirror and the ensemble that Usef had brought him to wear to the wedding. He hated frilly outfits, always preferring the simple attire of a Viking. Solon and Tom wore similar clothes, which made him feel better, considering they were as uncomfortable as him.

"Ready?" asked Rynah as she stepped inside the small room.

"Yes," answered Alfric. He followed her outside into the setting sun where Usef waited. The man held his arm out for Rynah, who took it.

"Here," said Usef, handing them each a basket of white flowers. "Once the couple has made their vows, we will throw these in the air. It's tradition."

They each took their flowers and followed Usef to the cere-
monial area where they joined the others and watched as the bride
moved forward to the front in her wedding dress: a simple, white,
yet elegant A-line gown made with a cotton over-lining that resembled lace, purple flowers embroidered along the hem line, and a pale
green ribbon tied around her waist. The veil drifted in the twilight
breeze, her smile visible through the transparent material. The
groom waited at the front in his black, dress slacks and black jacket,
though no tie. Rynah smirked as she watched him shift from one
foot to the other. When the bride reached him, they clasped hands.

"Merya and Stolson," said the white-haired man at the front,
"you two have agreed to be joined together in this union."

"Yes," said both bride and groom.

"Do you both vow to be honest with one another and to forsake
all others?"

"Yes," they said in unison.

"Then, as leader of this community, I declare you husband and
wife, bound together for the rest of your days. May they be blessed."

Once the pronouncement had been made, Stolson kissed his
bride without waiting to be told to do so. Laughter emanated
from the crowd.

"Now," whispered Usef.

Rynah, Alfric, Tom, and Solon joined the others in tossing their
flowers into the air. The calm breeze carried them to the newly married couple, allowing them to float to the ground. Joy etched on their
faces, the couple laughed with the rest of the crowd.

"That was very short," said Rynah.

"Most things are out here," said Usef. "We keep the niceties to
separate us from the savages, but life is too short to waste on pomp
and circumstance. Come. The feast awaits."

Usef led them to the banquet area. A single table lined with roast-
ed meat, squash, and bread awaited them. A roaring fire, reminding
Alfric of his home, filled the center as more meat was cooked. Alfric

headed to the beverage area, filling a large glass with their moonshine, and drank it in one gulp.

Tom sipped some, gagging from the alcohol as it burned its way down his throat.

Roaring with laughter, Alfric patted him on the back. "'Tis good for you. It will put hair on your chest."

"I don't see any on your... uh... yeah, thanks," said Tom as he rethought his response. He glanced at Solon, who had not touched his drink, and they both dumped their beverages. "I don't think I'll ever develop a liking for this stuff."

"Wine is a better drink," said Solon. "My father makes the most delicious wine and stores barrels of it." A sad note entered his voice. "Sorry."

"Don't be. You'll see them again."

"Do you not miss your home?"

"I do, but most of the people I care about are gone. Besides, I think they were glad to be rid of me. The Academy couldn't wait to find a reason to expel me. Something about my inventions always not working out. Come on. Let's find some ladies and hit the dance floor."

"Hit the dance floor?" asked Solon, confused.

"I'll show you what I mean," Tom replied.

Rynah and Usef watched from a table as the newly married couple danced to the effervescent music, staring into one another's joy-filled eyes.

"Where will you go from here?" asked Usef.

Rynah didn't answer.

"Sorry. It's a secret. I know."

"It isn't really. It's just, Klanor has a lot of spies and..."

"You don't fully trust me."

"It's not that," said Rynah.

"I'm not offended," said Usef. "I wouldn't trust me either. How about we just enjoy this moment?"

"Agreed."

Usef stood up and held out his hand. "Join me?"

Smiling, and not wanting to be rude, Rynah placed her palm in his and allowed herself to be drawn to the twirling people, while Usef placed a hand around her waist and guided her. As they danced to the jubilant music, images of Klanor filled her mind as Rynah remembered the times they had danced together: their first dance at a local club, their dance at a friend's birthday celebration when she had been overflowing with joy, before thoughts of them dancing together at Fredyr Monsooth's banquet entered her head. Klanor had asked her to join him. At the time, she had thought that he was just trying to distract her, but the more she pondered it, the more she realized that an underlying need and sincerity had filled his voice. Could he…

Usef leaned in to kiss her. Startled, and still reeling with mixed emotions about Klanor, Rynah broke away, running away from the crowd to find solitude, leaving Usef alone in the frivolity around him.

The strap of one of her shoes broke as she dashed down the walk and away from the wedding celebration. Angered at its failure to remain intact, she ripped off both her shoes and tossed them away, where they thumped in the soft silt that glided over the ground in the breeze. Rynah ran again, heading back to the hangar where Solaris remained lost to her. She reached it in the pale glow of twilight as she leaned, panting, against the edge of the hangar door.

She looked at her ring finger, as though seeing it for the first time. She had never even noticed that she had lost her engagement ring, the ring that Klanor had given her with promises of eternal love and happiness. Fury welled up within her as she thought back to that moment, the last moment where she had been filled with joy and contentment. The moment that he had ripped away from her with his betrayal.

The sunlight glinted off Solaris' hull, attracting Rynah's attention. "You left me," she spat at the ship, knowing, deep down, that that was not entirely true.

Rynah spotted a broom. She snatched it and slammed it against the Solaris' metal side with repeated force, releasing all of her anger that she had kept locked within herself and allowing it to cloud her mind, thus directing her actions. Sandaled feet stopped her. Looking up, Rynah dropped the broom and stared into Solon's concerned eyes.

"Am I interrupting something?" he asked with sincerity, knowing full well that he was.

"No, I… I was just…" stammered Rynah. "It's nothing."

"Such displays of emotion are never nothing."

"What are you doing here?"

"Tom tried to get Alfric to… disco," replied Solon, saying that last word with confusion. "It did not end well."

Despite herself, Rynah cracked a slight smile as she pictured Tom's fruitless effort to get Alfric to have fun, and the Viking's reaction.

"Might I inquire as to your presence here?" asked Solon as he observed the dented and scuffed markings that Rynah had left from her emotional outburst.

"Just leave me alone, please," said Rynah.

Solon started to abide by her request, but stopped, having an inkling of what troubled her. "He is attracted to you."

"What?"

"Usef," answered Solon. "I see the look in his eyes when he looks at you, the same that was in my brother's when he met his future wife."

"Future wife?"

"Yes, their wedding is set to take place upon the spring equinox." A note of sadness filled Solon's voice as he thought about his home and the people he had been forced to leave behind.

"I'm sorry," said Rynah. She glanced at her ring finger and the missing ring, wondering if it remained on Lanyr, consumed by the very fires that destroyed her hope for the future.

"Hearts do mend, if you allow it," Solon said.

Rynah looked up at him, trying to hide the tears that filled the corner of her eyes, but one escaped and left its trail down her flushed cheek.

"I'll leave you to your thoughts." Solon left the hangar, strolling into the last vestiges of the sun's light, no doubt thinking of his family and how her rash actions had ripped his future away from him.

Rynah looked at the damage she had inflicted upon Solaris' outer hull—no doubt Solaris would have words with her about it when she came back online—before watching Solon's fading form and then staring out at the settlement's center where the wedding feast still lingered. She thought of Usef's kindness in letting them land and make repairs. She thought of how understanding he had been about her attachment to Solaris, even though, to him, Solaris was just a ship, not an intelligent being. Could Solon be right? Could her heart truly mend?

Chapter 17
INTERROGATING ILLUSIONS

Brie stared at the dangling rope before her as it swayed in the breeze created by the air conditioning vent. She hated gym class and detested the thought of climbing the rope.

"Hurry up!" yelled the gym coach as he blew on his whistle. "Start climbing, Reynolds!"

Brie eyed the rope again. Didn't they do this yesterday? Rope climbing was always done on a Tuesday and she knew this wasn't Tuesday. Or was it?

The coach blew his harsh whistle again.

Brie took the rope in her hands and jumped up, wrapping both her feet around the roughhewn cord. She pushed herself with her legs, while holding on with her hands as she climbed.

"Look, she's actually doing it," said one of the other students.

"Faster!" shouted the gym coach, blowing his whistle again.

Brie wished she could shove that whistle down his throat. Deep down, she thought that he loved tormenting students with daunting physical exercises. Sweat dripped down her neck as she climbed higher towards the bell at the top. Suddenly, an ear splitting noise surrounded her, swirling around her, forcing her to look all around as her confused mind tried to comprehend what was happening. As Brie jerked her head around, trying to see what had caused the terrible commotion, she almost lost her grip. The rope lurched as she fought to maintain her hold on it, while the others at the bottom stared at her, oblivious to what had startled her.

"Did anyone hear that?" she asked.

"Hear what?" the coach called back. "Keep climbing!"

Brie couldn't believe that no one had heard the explosion. She looked around, but the gymnasium seemed normal. Pushing her worries aside, she climbed higher. She was only inches from the bell when the rope pitched with such ferocity that it forced her to let go. Weightlessness gripped her for a moment until she plunged to the ground, striking the mats below.

"You almost had it that time," scoffed the gym coach. "Almost. F for the day."

Rubbing her sore rear, Brie scowled at her teacher. Green hair snapped her attention. Brie whirled around just in time to see Rynah running through the gymnasium, shooting her laser pistol at something that chased her from behind. Brie watched as Rynah paused before the only plant in the gym—one that had been put there as a memorial to a student who had died—and stood ready to defend herself. To Brie's astonishment, the plant sprang to life; huge jaws appeared with razor teeth as it dived for Rynah. Horrified, Brie watched as it attacked, but Rynah leapt away, firing her laser pistol at it, stunning it.

"To the cave!" she yelled. "Brie, come on!"

Brie couldn't believe it. This person knew her? The plant lunged for Rynah again. Without thinking, Brie sprinted for Rynah, snatching a pole from the floor, used by the pole vaulting class, and rammed it into the carnivorous plant, striking it in the head just as it dove for Rynah a third time. Infuriated, the plant turned its attention to Brie. She jabbed it again with the pole and railed into the plant, hacking away at it as leaves flew in every direction. Brie continued her incessant strikes until...

"Brie?" Heather stood by her side; concern filled her face. "What are you doing?"

Brie glanced around the gymnasium. All eyes were upon her. Terror filled some, concern others. Brie turned back to the plant. It looked like it should: no teeth, no eyes, and no leaves missing, as though she hadn't touched it.

"Reynolds," said the coach as he walked up to her, "what is the meaning of all this?"

Brie dropped the pole. She would have sworn that her teacher had been wearing a green shirt just a minute ago, not yellow.

"Back to the rope!"

Brie didn't budge. Something was not right.

"Reynolds, I said back to the rope," said her coach, his hawk-like eyes boring into hers.

Brie looked about her. Her eyes locked with Jenny's. Where did she come from? Concern filled Jenny's eyes, and Brie knew something was amiss. "None of this is real."

"Not that again," said another of her classmates.

"Brie," Heather now appeared by her side, "I know you had a mental breakdown last week and perhaps you shouldn't have climbed that rope, but we are real. We're your friends."

Brie backed away. "We're?"

Heather never included others when she reminded Brie that she was her friend; she always used the word "I". Shaking her head, Brie struggled to discover what was happening around her. "No! I'm not at school—I'm on a ship!"

"Brie," Heather reached out for her.

Brie slapped her hand away. "Get away from me!"

"Reynolds, you need to calm down," said the coach.

"No!" screamed Brie, pushing her way past everyone and racing for the exit. As she burst through the doors, strong arms caught her. Brie's vehement struggles proved useless, since with each movement the grips of those arms tightened. "Let me go!"

The walls of the school melted away, leaving only a forbidding room with a chair and medical equipment. Brie's eyes shot toward the exit. She looked through the small window into a corridor with people ambling by. Before she could get a better look, the men that had captured her dragged her away.

"No!"

Brie managed to free her left arm and rammed the heel of her hand into the nose of one of her captors. Stunned, the man staggered back, and Brie punched another. More hands seized her, pinning her arms behind her back and forcing her back into the leather chair.

"Let me go!"

Brie kicked at anyone who strayed too near. Despite her efforts, she felt her body being lifted into the air and dumped on the chair. Cold leather wrapped around her wrists and ankles.

"How did she get free?" demanded Klanor as he threw a helmet off his head.

"I don't know, sir," replied a technician. "Somehow, she realized that it was an illusion, but I have no idea how she managed to get free of her restraints."

"Help me! Somebody help me!" screamed Brie.

"Well, figure it out," growled Klanor. "And shut her up!"

A man with a needle approached Brie. He checked the syringe making certain all air bubbles were gone.

"No!" Brie's vicious movements rocked the chair. Two pairs of hands reached out and held her down as the man with the needle pricked her arm and injected the serum.

"RYNAH!" Brie screamed before going limp.

Another man in a white lab coat checked her vitals. "She is unconscious."

"I want her ready for another interrogation before the end of the day."

"Yes, sir."

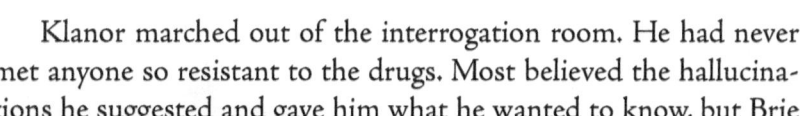

Klanor marched out of the interrogation room. He had never met anyone so resistant to the drugs. Most believed the hallucinations he suggested and gave him what he wanted to know, but Brie proved to be a challenge.

He slumped against a lone wall, concealed by dark shadows, fumbling with the ring he kept in his pocket: Rynah's ring. Sweat dripped down the sides of his face as he thought about Brie's resistance, something he would have relished, but now, it pained him, and with each interrogation, he felt guilt. Then, she had said it, Rynah's name, and all of his veiled emotions broke free. The more time he spent inside her head, the more compassion he felt for her, something that had never happened before.

Footsteps turned the corner. Klanor straightened himself, wiping the sweat from his face and putting on his nonchalant mask.

In another part of space, asleep in her bunk, Rynah awoke suddenly and sat up. As the wave of dizziness from her sudden movements subsided, she whispered, "Brie! You're alive!"

Chapter 18
LINES CROSSED

Stein bent over the holopad in his hands with the text of the ancient poem filling its screen. Following Klanor's suggestion, he had spent every hour he could spare studying the myth of the crystals, hoping to find some insight into how to get his family back, but no matter how much he stared at the words and memorized them, he found only one passage that might help, though it remained unclear.

A gift from the crystals' hand,
a guide in a foreign land.

On the surface, it appeared that the author was saying that the crystals could give gifts, but how? Could Klanor have been right all along? Would he be able to use the crystals and have his family returned to him? Could the crystals somehow turn back time? He would only need a few minutes, just long enough to convince his wife to never go into that building.

But they did not have all the crystals. Stein slammed the holopad down on a table, infuriated at being kept from what he wanted most. Once again, he pulled out the crumpled photograph of his wife, holding their only child. It was her birthday. In the past, they had always gone to the lake to celebrate, and he would be there now, holding her in his arms as they nestled by the fire, telling one another stories if it hadn't been for that explosion. He stared at the picture, remembering how her long hair once swayed in the breeze, cupping her jovial face. How he missed running his fingers through her silky tresses; how he longed hearing his son's laugh. Stolen from him they were because he could not save them.

Regret boiled within him, filling his mind and his heart, bringing with it anger, sorrow, guilt, and a desire for revenge. How Stein loathed seeing smiles on the faces of others. What right did they have to be happy, while he remained miserable? The only joy he ever felt was when he intimidated those around him, removing the smiles from their faces.

Seething from his guilt-fueled rage, Stein stormed out of his room, almost running into a young man, bearing a message.

"What do want?" demanded Stein, his harsh voice causing the messenger to jump.

"Sorry to disturb you, sir, but Klanor has requested that you conduct today's test of the weapon, as he is busy interrogating our prisoner."

"Requests?" said Stein, his mind still focused on his wife and child.

"Yes, sir," said the frightened young man as Stein enjoyed the way he cowered before him.

"Very well," Stein said.

He left the messenger and hurried to the elevator, taking it up to the command center. Once there, a hushed silence overtook him as he entered the room—people huddled over their holographic consoles in an effort to become invisible—his heavy boots clomping on the hard floor, each step sending an ominous echo. His sharp eyes scanned the room as he felt some form of elation over the fear of the people that surrounded him.

"Scan for suitable sites," he ordered.

Room-sized holoscreens appeared with images of the surface of various planets filling them (deserts, ice worlds, gas giants, barren rocks with no atmospheres) in rapid secession, until one caught his notice.

"Stop," he said. "Focus on that one."

Several images filled the holoscreens, each with people in them, laughing, joking, relaxing, and enjoying themselves. The envy Stein felt for such people, mixed with his own misery, reeled within him as he looked at the jovial faces before him. How dare they be so happy, while he had lost everything he held dear? He wished they could feel his pain and know what tortured him every minute of every day.

A thought struck him. Perhaps they could, and what better place to test the new weapon than on a populated area? A small part of him warned him against such actions, but Stein shoved it aside as his dark thoughts possessed him.

"Prepare to test the weapon," he said.

"But, sir," said one crewmember, "that is Neblar, a civilian population."

"Set the parameters," Stein ordered.

"But, sir…"

"You have your orders!"

"I won't do it," said the same crewmember as he stood up and walked out of the room.

Stein glowered at the faces staring back at him. Another left his post and placed himself in the vacated seat.

"Target set," he said, his voice cold and void of emotion.

Taking one last glance at the naïve faces in the holoscreens, Stein issued his final command. "Fire."

Within seconds, a stream of light burst from the ship, soaring through space as it raced for its target. Stein turned back to the holoscreens. He watched as the jovial faces before him reacted in terror and screamed as they tried to outrun the devastation that overtook them. Fires filled the screens as people burned alive; their haunting screams pierced the ears of those in the room, but Stein watched, unaffected by the horror before him. He knew he should have felt something, some measure of remorse, but he didn't. Once he had seen enough, he turned to the man that had obeyed his orders. "Come with me."

Stein led the man into the corridor, where they could converse in private. "Why did you obey my orders, when the others would not?"

"Because my only function is to obey your orders," replied the man.

"And you were not bothered by them?"

"No, sir."

Stein studied the man's face and the eyes that displayed no guilt, matching his own, and found validation in them. "I want you to do something for me. Go to Neblar and wait."

"What am I waiting for?"

"A single, archaic ship, piloted by a woman from Lanyr, accompanied by three others, the likes of which you have never seen before."

"What should I do when they arrive?" asked the man.

"Watch them and then contact me," replied Stein.

The man saluted and sped off, taking the elevator to the flight deck.

Stein stole one last glace towards the sealed door of the command center. A part of him told him that he should not have harmed an innocent population, but a larger part didn't care, believing that there was no such thing as innocence. The only innocents in the universe were his wife and son, but they were dead.

Stein stormed away, hurrying back to his quarters, unaffected by guilt.

Chapter 19
A Friend Returned

Solon handed Tom a wrench as he watched his friend work in the engine compartment of Solaris with assiduousness. Tom grabbed the tool and tightened a bolt, while cursing the fact that his engine refused to turn on.

"You might want to calm down," suggested Solon.

"The darn thing won't work!" exploded Tom, who had spent the entire night trying to figure out why his engine suddenly decided not to turn on. They were running out of options and he knew it. "I can't understand it."

"Anger never solves anything."

"But it's so… frustrating!"

Solon understood that part. He was aggravated as well and wished he could help his friend, but his knowledge of ships and engines remained rudimentary at best. "Maybe you should take a break."

"I can't!" yelled Tom. "We've been here long enough. If I can't get this thing working, we'll never get Solaris back and we'll never be able to leave this place."

Solon took the wrench from Tom. He fingered the indented metal as he thought about what he had seen some of the people around the small settlement do. "Maybe you should just hit it with this." He held the wrench out to Tom.

"I thought you said anger never solved anything."

"It doesn't, but hitting things seems to be a technique used in abundance around here. At this point, what do you have to lose?"

Tom took the wrench. He raised it high above his head and struck his magnetic engine with as much force as he could muster. Nothing happened.

"Feel better?" asked Solon in a calm voice.

"A bit. Yeah."

A small hum filled the air. Both Tom and Solon looked down at the engine as a series of lights sparked to life and the magnets turned. The hum grew louder until it sounded more like a roar.

"I did it!" exclaimed Tom. "I actually did it! Your idea worked!" Tom sprang to his feet and embraced Solon in a giant bear hug before releasing him. "Sorry. Got caught up in the moment."

"What are you two doing?" demanded Alfric as he marched up to them, thinking they had been playing games.

"I got it to work," said Tom.

Alfric stared at the ship as the lights flickered on. A smile crept across his stern face. He had grown tired of remaining still and looked forward to continuing their journey.

"Hello?" said a familiar voice. It sounded faraway, but soon strengthened. "Is anybody there? Rynah?"

"Solaris?" Rynah walked up with Usef, who had been showing her some star-charts, charts with coordinates that most conventional charts did not possess, having heard the commotion. "Solaris, is that you?"

"Yes. Did we escape the ion storm?"

"Yes, barely. It's so good to hear your voice again." Rynah's voice choked a bit as she swallowed back a few tears. "I missed you."

"As did I."

"Come on," said Tom to Solon. "I need to check the internal power relays and make sure everything is functioning properly." He hurried off with Solon in tow.

Rynah remained rooted to the ground. Though pleased to have Solaris back, a part of her felt sorrow, an emotion that did not go unnoticed.

"What's wrong?" asked Usef. "I thought you'd be thrilled."

"I am," said Rynah, "It's just…"

"You're short a crewmember."

"Something like that."

"I understand," said Usef, who had lost friends of his own, and knew the pain of such loss well.

"I thought I heard her voice the other night."

Alfric turned his head in her direction upon hearing Rynah's statement.

"Come on," said Usef. "Let's get some grub." He led Rynah away while Alfric stood alone, pondering Rynah's utterance.

Stein stalked through the pristine corridor on his way to Klanor's quarters, knowing why he had been summoned. He reached the metal door just as a holopad sprang up. Stein pressed a button, which rung the bell. The doors opened. Stein stepped inside, stiff and regal, his eyes taking a quick sweep of the room; the lights were brighter and the book that Klanor always hunched over, engrossed in its words, was missing.

"You wished to see me," Stein said.

Klanor stood in the center of the room, an irate expression on his face. "Did you think I wouldn't find out?" he asked.

"Find out what, sir?" Stein said that last word with a touch of sarcasm.

"The test on Neblar."

"You had asked me to perform a test of the weapon that day, to further measure its abilities. I chose a target with a suitable population, much like you have done."

"Pirate hubs are one thing, but civilian populations are another."

"Both have generous populations to demonstrate your power."

"Everyone on Neblar is dead!"

"The test proved most successful."

"Innocent people are dead!"

"There are no innocents," said Stein, his callous voice chilling Klanor to the core.

"Were your wife and son just as guilty that they deserved the same fate?" said Klanor, wishing he could take it back the moment the words left his lips.

Anger flashed in Stein's eyes. He knew what Klanor was trying to do, to connect what he had done with what another had done to his family. A distant memory of Brestef surfaced and how the bodies that littered the ground before his feet that day with their vacant eyes watching him had horrified him, but as he thought about it, an emptiness took hold of him, shoving any previous reservations about such atrocities aside. He did not know the people on Neblar. They meant nothing to him. Rage roiled within him as he thought about their joyful faces as they laughed with one another as though sorrow and despair never existed there.

Then, the geo-lab and Klanor's theft of the crystal there filled his mind. What of the people of Lanyr? They were just as dead. How dare Klanor question his morals when Lanyr was his doing? "Did you feel the same abhorrence when you condemned Lanyr?" challenged Stein.

"That is not the issue," growled Klanor.

"It is no different."

"It is!"

"Billions died so that you could have the crystal!"

"Not all…"

"Innocents! Just like the ones you claim were on Neblar."

"I did what was necessary!"

"As did I. Now everyone will know the power that we possess."

"Do you not understand what you have done? Do you…" Klanor

stopped speaking, desperate to keep his remorse from exposing itself. Long nights he had spent telling himself that the destruction of Lanyr was necessary, that it was for the greater good, but in the end, despite his efforts, guilt plagued him.

"I cannot undo what has been done," Stein said, his voice hollow.

Klanor glanced at Stein, looking into his dark eyes. Gone was the man that was tortured by regret and hopelessness. "You knew the preferred targets, yet you chose to ignore them."

"A grave mistake."

"A mistake can be remedied, but this…"

"I seemed to have upset a delicate balance between us," said Stein, reading the meaning behind Klanor's words. "Let me prove myself to you."

A second chance. Klanor debated with himself over whether he should give Stein a chance to redeem himself. Thoughts of Brie entered his mind. She believed in Rynah, defended her, despite the treatment she had received from her. Perhaps, there was some merit in awarding someone a second chance; besides, he needed Stein. And the man had a point. No one would question his might after the incident on Neblar.

"Very well," Klanor said, "Rynah will not give up her search for the final crystal. I want you to leave her breadcrumbs and lead her into a trap, where she, and her crew, can be captured."

"Consider it done."

"There are a group of mercenaries, not far from here, who will be more than willing to do the job, for the right price."

"Yes, sir."

"And, Stein, I want her brought back here, understand?"

"Perfectly." Stein left the room unabashed by his actions towards Neblar, while Klanor wrestled with the nagging guilt about Lanyr and his betrayal of Rynah.

Rynah walked to her quarters, feeling invigorated since she had eaten, though a nagging sense that she should be doing something plagued her. Alfric's bulky arm appeared before her, blocking her path. "Alfric?"

"You heard her voice?"

"What?"

"Brie's. You said you heard her the other night."

"Yes," replied Rynah, "but I was dreaming."

Alfric's gruff features portrayed disbelief. "You were not dreaming. I believe Brie might be caught in a world between worlds."

"What? This is madness!"

"Is it?" Alfric lowered his arm. "You are not the only one to hear her sometimes."

"Alfric, are you saying…"

"You injected us with something when you first brought us aboard your ship," continued Alfric. ""What was it?"

Rynah thought for a moment. "Nanobots. It's standard procedure."

Soon after the words had left her, a thought struck Rynah. She ran from Alfric and through Solaris' open hatch, heading for the medical bay. Alfric pursued her. Rynah went to the cabinet and tore it open, rifling through the vials that still remained there. She stopped. A multitude of vials (reds, yellows, and greens) stared back at her, but she could not find a particular one, one she hadn't thought about until now, the purple vial.

"Solaris?"

"Yes," replied Solaris.

"Where is the purple vial?"

"You must have used it."

"What was in it?" asked Rynah.

"It contained a series of experimental nanobots that your grandfather invented. Supposedly, when injected into someone who was mortally injured, they would put the person into a comatose like state, but keep him alive until a medical facility could be reached. But they had never been tested."

"How many of these vials were there?" asked Rynah.

"Only the one. Why?"

"When did you last see the vial full?" asked Rynah.

"The day you brought the others aboard," answered Solaris.

"Solaris, this is important," said Rynah. "Did I inject the contents of that vial into one of them?"

Solaris scrolled through a bunch of video footage in her memory databanks before stopping the recording. "Brie. But how can this be? I checked her… checked all her vitals and nothing!"

"Solaris?" said Rynah, growing concerned about Solaris' unusual outburst of emotion.

"There was no heartbeat, no pulse! She was clinically dead. She…"

"SOLARIS!" screamed Rynah, stopping Solaris' rambling. "What are you saying?"

"Before you ejected Brie into space, I ran scans of her body, searching for any indication that she still lived, but each scan came up negative."

"Solaris," said Rynah, "your medical scanners are at least 50 years old and, at the time, you had suffered a lot of damage to those same systems. Isn't there a chance that they could have been wrong?"

"Yes," said Solaris in a whisper.

"Do you have any ideas as to why Alfric and I have been hearing Brie's voice in our sleep?" asked Rynah.

Solaris composed herself, and spoke in a more steady voice, "You all have worn the helmets that telepathically link you to me, and each other. There is a possibility that a residual link has remained, even when you're not wearing the helmets. If Brie were to suffer some kind of emotional distress, you may be picking that up while you are asleep because that is when your conscious mind is inert, while the subconscious is active. It's pure conjecture, but…"

"It'll do," said Rynah, her heart sinking. "There is no way of knowing…"

"If there is the slightest chance," interrupted Alfric, "we owe it to her to save her from her plight."

"I think I know who has her," said Rynah.

Chapter 20
UNEXPECTED INSIGHT

The drone of the television filled Brie's ears, though she paid little attention to it. Her mother should have been home an hour ago, but once again, was late. Brie wished her mother could get a better job. She pushed such thoughts aside. At least they had income. Some people didn't have even that, though she could do without the government housing. Brie turned back to the TV as the man on it talked about a quartz crystal that had been discovered in the Yucatan Peninsula.

"Scientists are still unsure of the significance of this crystal to the Maya, but scholars believe that it might have been part of their ritual sacrifices."

"Oh, whatever," mumbled Brie. "It doesn't even look sharp."

She watched as the screen paned over the quartz crystal, remarking at how its shape was reminiscent of the SD card in her camera. Her mother had bought the camera for her for Christmas as a special gift, and though it was the only present she received, she appreciated it.

The lock in the door clicked. *Finally!* Brie turned off the TV and ran to the door, yanking it open before her mother had a chance to get the key out of the lock.

"Oh, there you are, honey," greeted her mother. "I know I'm a bit late, but we just got busy and they asked me to stay." She unfastened her name tag and kicked off her shoes. "Oh, I'm exhausted."

"I saved some supper for you." Brie pulled a covered plate from the refrigerator and popped it in the microwave.

"Thanks. Your sister?"

"In bed and homework done."

"You're too good to me," said her mother. "Anything interesting happen at school today?"

"Define interesting."

"Brie."

"No, nothing. Just the usual stuff." Brie filled the coffee maker with water and turned it on. A small bit of peeling wallpaper attracted her eye. *Didn't I already fix that?* Shrugging it off, she poured her mother a cup of coffee and set it on the counter with the plate of food.

"Thank you, dear. You're too good to me," said her mother as she shoved a forkful of food into her mouth. "It's good."

"New recipe." Brie sat next to her mother. "How was work?"

"The usual. Mr. Carrow stayed in his office, Sal was cranky, as always, and Jose managed to drop three bottles of Tequila today."

"Jose? I thought you said he quit and moved to California." The gnawing feeling that something wasn't right rose in Brie's stomach.

"Did I say Jose?" her mother replied, "I meant Tim. New guy, you know."

"But didn't you say that your boss wasn't going to hire any more people for a while and that was why you've had to work late?"

"Well, he must have changed his mind."

Brie frowned. Her mother seemed a bit dismissive and different. She hadn't even given Brie a hug or checked on Sara, something she did every night the moment she returned home.

"Tell me about your television program," said her mother.

Figuring that her mother was just tired, Brie pushed her worries aside. "They were talking about some crystal."

"Well, where is this crystal that they found? Do they know what it does?"

"I'm not sure where they put it," replied Brie. "Some museum I guess."

"Weren't you paying attention?"

"Not really." Brie shifted in her seat. Why the sudden interest in what she watched on TV?

"Well, you should," said her mother. "How are you to learn anything if you don't pay attention?"

"It was only TV, mom," said Brie. "Aren't you going to check on Sara?"

"In a moment, dear." Her mother took another bite of her supper. "So they have no idea what this mysterious crystal is?"

"Well, no," Brie said, "that was what the documentary was about, all of the possibilities. Some of them are pretty out there, but interesting. They found another one in India a few years ago, dating back a thousand years, but I don't know where it is either, and they concluded that it had been formed using the rudimentary tools of the time."

"Too bad," mumbled her mother. "If they were at the local museum, we could all go down and look at them."

"I suppose they'll show up at the Smithsonian at some point."

"Smithsonian?"

Brie eyed her mother. Everyone knew what the Smithsonian Museum was and where it was located. Her mother especially, since she had grown up in the Washington D.C. area and worked as an intern there during her college days. "You don't know about the Smithsonian?"

"Well, I suppose I might have heard of it."

"You grew up there." Caution filled Brie's voice, something her mother noticed.

"Oh, that, yes. I just wanted to make sure you knew about it."

Brie watched as her mother took two more bites. Something was wrong. She glanced at the peeling wallpaper again and she knew she had fixed it. "Aren't you sure you shouldn't check on Sara?"

"When I'm finished, sweetheart," replied her mother. "I wanted to talk with you a bit first. I don't see much of you. So, tell me more about the quartz disks."

Brie's head shot up. She never said anything about a disk. She hadn't even mentioned that the things were made of quartz. "But Sara had another nightmare," lied Brie.

"Nightmare?"

"Yeah, you know, about the bad men that keep coming for her. She woke up screaming and I had to comfort her, but you know she always feels better after you tuck her in."

Her mother put her fork down. She scrutinized Brie's face, trying to discern if she spoke the truth. "I guess I ought to check on her then."

She stood up and walked towards her own bedroom. Brie jumped to her feet and snatched a knife from the sink, pointing it at her mother. The woman turned around. A smile crept across her lips as she laughed with a male voice.

"You really are smarter than I had first thought," said the woman who looked like Brie's mother. "Lying to me to see if I am who I seem." Brie's mother slowly morphed into Klanor.

Brie backed away.

"Unlike some of my other subjects whom I have subjected to this, you are most resistant, but you will tell me what I want to know."

"Get out of my head!" yelled Brie.

The apartment melted away and she found herself in a room she did not recognize. Drapery and silver vases lined the far window as purple-tinted sunlight spilled through. Voices emanated from the adjoining room. Brie crept over to it. She gasped at what she saw: Klanor and Rynah lay on a bed together, looking at pictures and laughing.

"Come on," said Rynah, "you'll love it."

"I'm not big on the country," Klanor said.

"Do it for me?" Rynah gave him a puppy dog look.

Chuckling, Klanor tossed a feather pillow at her. "Fine. For you, I'll do anything, even a weeklong vacation in the middle of nowhere."

"Good. Now you make the reservations and I'll make sure that I get off work for the week." Rynah glanced at her watch. She jumped off the bed and put on her uniform jacket. "I'm going to be late!"

"Story of your life."

Rynah threw another pillow at Klanor.

"Hey," Klanor grabbed Rynah's slender, but toned, arm and pulled her close, giving her a long, deep kiss. "I love you."

"And I love you." Rynah grabbed her key card. "Now, don't forget."

"I won't."

The room faded, and before Brie knew it, she found herself in a darkened room full of smoke, while dancing shadows covered the floor and walls. Eerie silence filled the room, broken only by the hushed voices of two men.

"Everything is arranged and on schedule," said one.

Brie crept closer. She stopped. Stein stood in the room with Klanor; she would never forget the man that had attacked her on Aquara.

Klanor said nothing.

"Some members of the Lunyra Movement have agreed to help us break into the Geothermic Lab. They think that they are merely going to upload a virus into the computer systems and destroy a few pieces of equipment."

Klanor remained unresponsive, his eyes focused straight ahead.

"Klanor," said Stein.

"Yes, thank you."

Sensing that Klanor's mind remained preoccupied by Rynah, Stein stepped closer. "We are ready to proceed with our plans. Everything is set."

"I heard you the first time," Klanor replied in irritation.

"You cannot falter now," continued Stein. "You knew this day would come."

"I know," said Klanor. "I just hope we haven't forgotten anything."

"All has been accounted for. The only thing we need now are the security codes for the lab."

"Already acquired, and I know for a fact that the lab will be undergoing a systems check next week, meaning that security will be too preoccupied to pay attention to a simple glitch in their system."

"Next week, then."

"Make sure all of our men wear the armbands," said Klanor, "and, Stein, you do realize that once we have done this, there will be no going back."

"There was never any going back for me. You will be able to bring them back?" Stein's voice had taken on a darker tone.

"Once we have acquired all of the crystals," answered Klanor.

Stein moved away from Klanor before being stopped.

"Do you ever wonder if perhaps there is another way?" asked Klanor.

Perplexed by the man's change in attitude, Stein faced him, hands clasped behind his back. "There is no other way. You taught me that. Only the crystals matter."

"Yes," breathed Klanor, as though reminding himself of his original mission, "only the crystals matter."

The scenery changed again, as Brie found herself standing outside, the sun shining so bright, its warmth tickled her skin, even though she was in another's memory. Giant buildings made of stone and glass surrounded her as she stood on a walkway that looked as though it had been carved out of marble. Purple-tinted grass, bearing none of the ash and soot she had seen upon her one visit to Lanyr, stretched before her, a carpet meant for royalty.

"Don't go to work today," came Klanor's voice.

Brie spun on her heels. Before her stood Klanor and Rynah, holding hands as he whispered to her, but not with the sweet sentimentality of love, but with worry and pleading.

"Klanor, you know I have to."

"I mean it," he said.

"You already begged me not to go in once today. What's wrong?"

Klanor took her hand, and touched the ring on her finger, his eyes bearing mixed emotions, as though he wished to tell her something, but couldn't. "I just think that you should take today off."

"You know I can't. We're doing a systems check today and I have to be there. I'll be fine." Rynah kissed him. "See you for dinner."

Rynah hurried away, her jovial mood radiating from her as she skipped to the building where the Geothermic Lab was kept underground.

Turning back, Brie looked at Klanor and the mixed emotions on his face as he struggled with what he had spent years bringing to fruition.

Once again everything vanished, plunging Brie into darkness until she found herself thrust into the Geothermic Lab, lights crashed on the split concrete floor as orange flames and molten rock spewed forth. Men scurried about, desperate to escape the planet's revenge, but that wasn't what captured Brie's attention. Klanor's demeanor grasped hold of her, forcing her to ignore the laser fire, explosions, screams, and instinctual actions of those around her.

She watched as Klanor picked up a ring, holding it before his face, his eyes focused on something in the distance. Brie turned. She caught a quick glimpse of Rynah dodging a steel support that had almost toppled on her. Rynah glanced back at Klanor and her fallen comrades before diving through a hole just as it sealed itself. Brie looked back at Klanor. He stood, lost in the moment as though time had stilled around him, holding the ring and staring at where Rynah had just been; a mixture of regret, sorrow, guilt, anger, and loathing filled his face, and in that instant Brie understood: Klanor loved Rynah and hated himself.

Klanor pocketed the ring, abandoning the woman he loved for the promise of ultimate power. Unable to move, Brie remained among the sparks that showered over her as electrical wires snapped. She never noticed the spray of water that erupted from broken water pipes, her mind consumed by what she had witnessed. In that moment, Brie understood Klanor. Their minds connected. She felt the pain he struggled with each day; she recoiled from the remorse that filled the core of his being each time he tested his weapon, thus destroying innocent lives, but telling himself that such sacrifices were necessary. Though the more he committed them, the less he believed it.

"Enough!" The real Klanor appeared beside her, having broken her unintentional—and mysterious—hold on his memories.

The underground laboratory disappeared and Brie found herself in the interrogation room strapped to the same leather chair she had been in for the past several weeks.

"How did you do that?" demanded Klanor.

Confused as to how she had managed it, Brie didn't answer.

"How?" demanded Klanor. He threw the helmet off his head and stepped toward her until his face hung inches from hers.

"I don't know," wailed Brie.

"How!"

"I don't know!"

"I want to know about those disks."

"Then keep looking because I can't tell you what I don't know," said Brie.

Klanor slapped her so hard that her head jerked to the side; a burning, red handprint marked her cheek.

"You used her," said Brie. "That's why Rynah hates you so much. You pretended to love her and then betrayed her for your own gain."

"You know nothing," hissed Klanor.

Brie remembered the pained look on Klanor's face as he watched Rynah escape the underground bunker. "You do love her," she whispered to him. "Despite your best efforts, you fell in love."

Klanor placed his lips near her ear. "You know nothing," he hissed.

"That is why you couldn't kill her, despite all of the opportunities you've had."

"Silence!"

"You are tormented each day by what you did to her, but you continue to do it. It is eating away at you and will continue to do so until you make amends."

"Enough!"

"Now I understand," continued Brie, ignoring Klanor's harsh commands. "You do care. You feel everything."

"SILENCE!"

Klanor's eyes roamed the room, glaring at all the people whose vacant expressions stared back at them. "What are you looking at? Get back to work! And take her back to her cell."

Guards seized Brie's arms and heaved her out of the chair, dragging her back to her cell, but they could not undo what had been done. She knew Klanor's heart.

Klanor swiped his hands across the nearest table, knocking its contents onto the floor, allowing their rancor to echo around him. He slumped in a chair. Ignoring all who watched him, Klanor propped his elbows on the bare, yet scratched surface of the table and placed his face within his cupped hands.

Stein watched Brie and Klanor from the window of an adjoining room; no one knew he was there, much less that he had the key to get inside. Klanor thought that only he possessed the key to the small chamber that allowed one to spy upon the proceedings in the interrogation room. Grinning with satisfaction, Stein realized that Klanor had a weak spot, thus realizing why he struggled with doing what was necessary to acquire the crystals. Klanor's weakness would rob him of his family once again. Stein watched as guards dragged Brie from the room and back to her cell.

Knowing that within moments Klanor would ask to see him, Stein slipped out of the cramped room and locked the door behind him, tucking the key in a secret pocket on the inside of his leather coat.

"Let me go!" Brie screamed as her guards hauled her away.

She rammed her bare heel into the shin of one. As he buckled under the pain, Brie slipped from the other's grasp and punched him in the face before darting away. Fortunately for Stein, she ran right towards him. Brie didn't realize her mistake until it was too late. She tried to dodge Stein's grasp, but his lightning fast movements seized her and brought her to a halt. Brie's desperate struggles proved useless as Stein's grip held firm.

"Continue moving and I'll break your collarbone," he hissed into her ear, relishing the power he had over her.

Brie ceased, going limp.

"Good girl," said Stein, failing to notice that Brie's eyes focused on the sign to his right with the words "Level 10" on it. "Guards!"

The two men hurried over.

"Make certain she doesn't get away from you again. Or are you both incapable of watching a girl?"

The guards saluted and wrapped their gloved fingers around Brie's arms as they yanked her away from Stein and towards her cell.

Stein's cold eyes watched as Brie disappeared; a plan formulated in his calculating mind. Realizing her strength, he knew that he had a use for her.

Klanor stepped out of the interrogation room. They locked eyes a moment before he turned and walked away. Confident that Klanor did not know his plan, Stein hurried down the corridor and to his quarters. He entered the elevator at the far end of the hall. "Level 6," he said.

The hum of the elevator filled his ears as it whisked him to his floor. The doors slid open.

"Level 6," said the robotic voice.

Stein marched out of the elevator and turned the corner. Technicians and low ranking crewmembers hurried by him, too afraid to be caught alone with his foul mood. Stein smiled. He loved the amount of fear he exuded. He stopped. Where did that fear come from?

Stein thought back on his past. There was once a time when he would have been amicable with the other members aboard the ship, but all of that changed the day his family died, the day of the explosion. Shaking off his reminiscence, Stein strode through the winding corridors to the doors of his quarters. They slid open. Going inside, he glanced around. No signs of anyone having been there.

Not a trusting person, Stein always rigged a few booby-traps to inform him if his place had been searched. So far, no one had dared to go in there uninvited, not that he would ever welcome company. Sighing, he sat down at his desk and pulled open the top middle drawer. Inside rested a photo, the only object within the shadowed confines of the drawer.

With a gentle touch that none would have ever thought possible, Stein picked it up. A woman with pale purple skin and gold hair stared back at him, holding a child. A single teardrop plopped on the photograph. Stein wiped it away before it could stain the image. *My dear Ofylia.* He looked up, allowing his eyes to roam the corners of his darkened room until they rested on the window that looked out at the stars. His face changed into a hardened expression as the rage over losing his wife and child filled him. The universe took his family from him and only the crystals could bring them back.

A thought occurred to Stein. He tucked the picture in his pocket and closed the drawer. Sweeping out of his room, Stein rushed down the corridor back to the elevator. The doors slid open, allowing him to enter before shutting behind him.

"Level 12," he said.

The elevator hummed as it took him to his desired destination. When it stopped, he raced to the medical bay. Empty. Stein hurried to a cabinet where most of the medications were kept. He rifled through them as he searched for one in particular: a truth serum. Once he found it, he snatched a needle from a nearby drawer and filled it with the serum. Footsteps sounded outside the room. Before he could be discovered, Stein placed the needle in one of his many pockets and the vial of serum back in the cabinet.

He crept to the door. Peeking around the corner, he spotted no one. With long, hurried strides, Stein made it to the elevator once again.

"Level 14."

Again the elevator hummed as it took Stein to his destination. Once there, he hurried towards the detention area. A guard stood erect in front of the door.

"Authorization?"

"I don't need any authorization," spat Stein. "Don't you know who I am?"

The guard gave him a bored glance. "I need your authorization to be in here, sir."

Fuming, Stein brought his face closer so that the guard could get a good look. "I am Stein and subject only to Klanor's command. So let me pass, or I assure you, that by tomorrow morning, you will be working in the tubes."

The guard's face flinched and Stein knew he had struck a nerve. The tubes were the most disgusting, and dangerous, area of the ship where only troublemakers and criminals worked, and no one wanted to be sent there because of their tendency to shorten one's lifespan. The guard stepped aside, allowing Stein to pass.

With a quick scan of the registry, he found the cell where Brie was kept; his brisk movements carried him down the narrow corridor lined by steel doors. He found her cell. Punching the button, the door slid open, revealing Brie as she sat on the cot, hugging her knees. She unfolded them, straightening her back at the sight of him.

Stein shut the door.

"What do you want?" demanded Brie.

Stein pulled the needle from his pocket. Brie's eyes widened as she realized his intentions. She sprang from her bed and hugged the wall. Stein stepped closer. In a desperate attempt to get away, Brie tried to go around the man. He shot out an arm and seized her wrist. With a flurry of movements and expertise, Stein whirled Brie around until he had pinned her against the wall, but not before she had raked her nails against the side of his neck, drawing blood and leaving deep gashes. Breathing hard, Brie tried to push him away. No effect. A clack sounded as Stein popped the cap off the needle, allowing it to drop to the floor. Still struggling, Brie bit her tongue as the needle pierced her skin and the solution entered her veins with a burning sensation.

Stein released her. Brie faced him and started to charge when she stopped. Staggering, her mind refused to focus, and she crumpled to the icy floor.

"Now," said Stein with satisfaction, "tell me about your home."

Chapter 21
SEARCH FOR BRIE

R ynah shoved a loaf of stale bread into her pack. She snatched a few apples from a bowl on the counter and packed them as well. After examining her weapons and charts, Rynah heaved her bag on her shoulders and headed for the exit.

"Are you sure you should be doing this?" asked Solaris.

"I have to find her," replied Rynah. "It's my fault that Brie has been taken prisoner."

"Yes, but you shouldn't go alone."

"You cannot abandon the search for the last crystal," said Rynah. "I want you, and the others, to find it and keep it from Klanor. I will find Brie. You have the coordinates of where we should meet."

"And if you do not arrive?"

"Then continue without me." Rynah stuck a second laser pistol in her belt. She reached for another when Alfric's hand held it out to her. "Alfric? What are..."

"I can't let you go alone," he said.

"None of us can," said Solon as he and Tom entered the room.

"Who told you?" demanded Rynah.

"I might have accidentally let it slip," replied Solaris.

Rynah pursed her lips. Solaris never did anything by accident. "You're not going to stop me."

"Wouldn't dream of it," said Tom.

"I have to search for Brie," Rynah continued.

"We're coming with you," said Alfric.

"Five minds are better than one," added Solon.

"No," said Rynah, shaking her head. "I can't allow that. You all need to search for the crystal. We cannot allow…"

"And for what?" demanded Alfric. "At what cost? The cost of our friend? I made that mistake once and have regretted it since. I'll not make it again."

"Regret has a way of turning a person's heart towards darkness," Solon added.

"But I can't…" began Rynah.

"It is not your decision," said Alfric, "but ours."

Rynah stared at all of them, knowing she was about to lose this argument. "What about the search for the crystal?"

"It can wait," said Alfric. "The life of our friend is more important. You, apparently, believe the same, as you are preparing to sneak away in the dead of night."

Usef stepped into the lamplight from around a corner where he had been hiding, listening to their conversation. He had been on his way to see Rynah with a flower in his hand, but the voices of the others had stopped him. Once, he had been the captain of a ship and was responsible for a crew of 50 men. They had been attacked, their ship had suffered irreparable damage, and against insurmountable odds, he survived, but he never forgot the ones under his command that he had lost. Their faces plagued him each night, and as he listened to Rynah and the others, moved by their commitment to one another, he remembered each of those faces and decided to make his presence known.

"If it is a rescue you are planning, you will need more provisions than have currently been supplied."

"Usef?" said Rynah, astonished that he was there. "What are you doing here?"

"I was on my to see you, but it seems that you have more important matters."

"And where will we garner these provisions?" Alfric asked.

Usef eyed the Viking, appreciating the man's habit of getting to the point. "I will give them to you from my own personal stores, and I offer my services as well."

"You've already…"

"You misunderstand me," said Usef, "I am coming with you."

Rynah's eyebrows arched in surprise. "She is not your crewmate."

"No, but she's yours," said Usef, remembering the crewmates he had lost in the past and understanding the nightmares that Rynah had each night. "You can use the help."

"Face it," said Tom, "we're coming with you."

Rynah relented. She lost and she knew it. "Fine. Alfric, will you help Usef bring the extra supplies to the ship?"

Alfric nodded and left with Usef, grabbing both Tom and Solon by the shoulders and forcing them along."

"All you had to do was ask," commented Tom as they walked off.

"You planned this whole thing," Rynah said to Solaris, once they were alone.

"My lips are sealed," said Solaris.

"You don't have any lips," chided Rynah.

"Destination?" asked Solaris.

Rynah thought for a moment. "Tre," she said. "He monitors all of the communications in the Twelve Sectors. He might be able to tell us where Klanor is."

Solaris entered the course into her databanks and started her engines. "Destination set."

A pale peach-colored spot caught Rynah's attention. She strode over to it and picked it up, holding it in the light; her eyes narrowed. It was a petal. Rynah found the orchid it had belonged to, lying in the shadow near the wall that Usef had hidden behind and scooped it up, cradling it in her palm. Her head shot up as she looked in the direction Usef and the others had gone as she realized for whom the orchid was meant for, torn between her hatred for Klanor and the possibility of accepting Usef's affection for her.

Stein swept through the corridors of the ship, his mind muddled with thoughts; thoughts about Brie and what she told him about her home planet, and what uses he would have for such information; thoughts about his family and his failure to save them; but what weighed most on his mind was Klanor. Since the theft of the crystal from the Geothermic Lab, Klanor had not been the same. At first, it had been little things, a reminiscent pose, or a blank stare. But now he fiddled several times a day with the engagement ring he had once given Rynah, something he thought no one noticed, but Stein had, and remained increasingly reluctant to put Rynah in her grave. Rynah had been a thorn in Stein's side the moment she escaped Lanyr on that wretched ship. What did Brie call it? Solaris.

The more Stein watched Klanor, the more he felt himself losing faith in the man. Klanor was weak, his attachment to Rynah made him so, but Stein had nothing to keep him grounded in the confining morals of those around him. All that he cared about had been ripped away from him. The more Stein pondered Klanor's willingness to do what was necessary to acquire all six crystals, the more he concluded that Klanor was not worthy of such a task. Someone whose will was iron was required to complete the job.

Movement stopped him in his tracks. Stein's eyes focused on the shadowed figure that slipped behind a corner with care, making certain that no one noticed. With stealth, Stein crept to the corner and peeked around it. Gaden. Stein had seen him before, a weasel of a man, whom he had no patience for, sneaking around the ship. This time, he followed him.

Gaden went to a service elevator used by maintenance crews, avoiding the main one. Curious about Gaden's secretive movements, Stein watched as Gaden entered the elevator and stared at the screen above it as it counted down until it stopped. Once he had the deck number, Stein rushed into a nearby stairwell and hurried down the metallic steps until he reached the desired level of the ship. He ripped the door open and stepped out, being careful not to make any noise, finding himself thankful that, for once, the hinges on the door had been oiled. A scratching noise told him he was close. Stein darted into a darkened corner, and when he felt safe, he craned his neck to see who had made the sound. Gaden hunched before the door to one of the storage rooms, with the holopad pulled out with the wires cut and reconnected, thus undoing the lock. Once opened, Gaden snuck inside.

Anger boiled within Stein as he watched Gaden leave the room, redo the wiring so that the lock worked, and hurry away with his arms full of rations. *Scum,* thought Stein when Gaden had disappeared. He loathed those who filled their stomachs, putting their greed and comfort above the others aboard the ship. Food in space was limited, and thievery could not be tolerated. He hurried to tell security of it and stopped once he reached the stairwell. Stein knew that his time as the executer of Klanor's will was drawing to a close, since Klanor hadn't the will to do what was necessary to take the crystals and learn their secrets, and to kill Rynah.

Stein knew that whenever he chose to take matters into his own hands, he would need someone to dirty their hands so that he wouldn't have to. *Even garbage has its uses,* Stein mused as he stared down the hall that Gaden had disappeared in. Gaden would pay for his theft, but Stein wished to make certain that such payment would benefit him and no other. For now, he would watch, and wait.

Tom sat in the pilot's seat, navigating the ship to where Rynah had directed him. They flew past bits of rubble as they neared what appeared to be an abandoned space station. The windshield of a ship floated by, bumping into them, before scraping against another chunk of derelict metal. Tom watched as a few sparks flickered from the contact.

"Go there," said Rynah, watching over his shoulder. "Move slowly. If you approach too fast, he might think we're here for less friendly purposes."

"A bit paranoid, isn't he?" asked Tom as he steered the ship.

"That is putting it mildly," said Solaris.

Another piece of space junk floated past them. Alfric and Solon sat in the command center as well, each strapped to a chair as they waited for them to reach their destination.

"Tre doesn't like strangers. Actually, he tends to prefer to live alone," said Rynah.

As Tom looked around at all of the debris that surrounded them, he felt that the man had achieved that goal.

"Is he a hermit?" asked Solon. "A thinker of sorts who prefers his mind over the company of others?"

"That is one way to put it," said Rynah. "Tre once lived on Lanyr, like me, but he has always been a bit odd and paranoid. He got the idea in his head that one day the world would end and he didn't want to be around when it did."

As Rynah finished her sentence, she couldn't help but feel that Tre had been onto something when he had left home. "Some years back, he left Lanyr and came out here. He lives a solitary life in this junkyard to disguise his whereabouts. Must work, though, because very few people seem to know he is here. Even pirates go right past this place."

"So where am I taking the ship?" asked Tom as he moved the controls to miss another piece of floating debris.

"Just keep heading for the center," said Rynah. "Pretty soon, we should hear from him. He doesn't like it when people get too close."

"Hear from him how?" asked Solon.

As though in answer to his question, a laser cannon fired at them from a seemingly innocent looking bit of rubble. It detonated just off the bow of the ship, scorching the exterior, but not causing any sustainable damage.

Tom's muscles tightened as he struggled to keep Solaris steady.

"I am going to have words with that maniac," quipped Solaris.

"Fly straight," Rynah instructed.

Tom did as ordered, though he thought she was crazy.

Another cannon blast jostled their ship, knocking Rynah off balance. She soon regained her feet as she gripped Tom's chair.

"That was close," said Solaris. "If you are going to do something, do it now."

"Just wait," said Rynah.

The others looked at one another, wondering what her plan was and what she waited for.

"Rynah…" began Alfric.

"Patience," Rynah cut him off.

Another cannon blast ricocheted off the ship, rocking it side to side. Rynah remained stoic.

"Are you sure we shouldn't do something?" asked Tom.

"Just stay on course," said Rynah. "The cannons are not positioned to hit us, so long as you maintain this position."

"How do you know all this?" asked Solon.

"I just do," said Rynah.

A fourth blast detonated just off the stern of the ship, sending vibrations through the hull. Rynah remained undisturbed. Alfric and Solon clung to their seats, wishing that she would do something, but her impassive face indicated that she wasn't worried.

Tom's sweaty hands slipped from the controls. He wiped them on his pants so that he could grip them better. Beads of sweat dripped from his face as he grew more and more nervous, while he glanced at Rynah who maintained her stance, not bothering to look at him.

"Any minute now," whispered Rynah.

The radio cackled to life as a gruff voice filled it. "Who are you? What do you want?"

"We wish to speak with you, Tre," said Rynah.

Silence ensued for a moment until…

"Who is this?"

"Rynah."

"No! Go back, or I'll fire on you!"

"Like he hasn't been already?" mumbled Tom.

Rynah glared at him before speaking into the radio again. "Tre, you and I both know that your cannons are rigged so that ships charting the same course as us will not be harmed. They are merely there to keep people away."

"Well, they're not working at the moment!" yelled Tre over the radio.

"Because I know you too well," said Rynah. "Let us dock."

"Never! Now go away!"

"Tre," Rynah's voice took a dangerous edge, "I will disable all of your weapons and your entire space station if you do not let us dock."

More silence loomed as Tre thought about her proposal. "You wouldn't."

"Would you rather risk it?" asked Rynah.

"Leave me be!" Tre yelled over the radio.

"I am ready when you are, Rynah," said Solaris, playing a role in Rynah's bluff. "Target selected."

"No tricks," said Rynah. "We just want to talk."

A snort sounded over the radio, indicating that Tre did not believe her.

"Tre…"

"Fine! Continue your current course. You may dock, but I want no tricks."

"Continue your present course," said Rynah, "There should be a docking station straight ahead."

"How do you know all this?" asked Tom.

"Tre and I have a history together," said Rynah. "Not like that," she added when she noticed the looks on the others' faces. "We went to the university together. That is where I met him."

"What happened?" asked Solon, while Tom mimed floating hearts with his hands.

"He built an underground bunker in preparation for an alien invasion and I joined the Lanyran fleet."

They glanced from one to the other before Solon said, "And?"

"And we had a falling out," said Rynah, in a tone that conveyed she wished to end the discussion.

All three men leaned forward in anticipation of her continuing the story.

"Oh, for crying out loud," said Rynah in frustration. "When Tre built his bunker, he started stockpiling everything. After a while, someone was sent to make sure he wasn't building a weapon of mass destruction."

"Let me guess," said Solon, "that someone was you."

"Unfortunately," said Rynah. "When I saw his place, I grew concerned. Tre could never intentionally harm another soul. However, he had bags upon bags of fertilizer, which he used for his underground garden. Fertilizer can be flammable, and he had it sitting near the gas line. I accidentally knocked a lamp over. It landed and broke near the fertilizer, sending a couple of sparks. One was all that was needed. The entire place went up in a pile of smoke. We were unharmed, but the damage had been done."

"What do you mean?" asked Tom.

"The accidental explosion was seen as proof by the government that Tre was plotting some bit of terrorism. Despite my report, they refused to believe otherwise, thus forcing him to leave. He blamed me, of course, and perhaps he's right, but it was a complete accident. Anyway, last I heard, Tre came out here and built this space station, and my little bit of clumsiness made him a bit more paranoid."

"No wonder he doesn't want to see you," said Alfric. "You have soiled his name and reputation."

Rynah's face contorted upon Alfric's statement. Though the Viking was correct, she did not like his choice of words.

"Here we are," said Tom as he neared a grungy looking space station with the docking arm waiting for them. He maneuvered the vessel to the arm, lining up the opening with the hatch. With a few quick jerks, the docking arm and the ship connected, releasing a loud hiss that echoed around them as the arm pressurized itself so that they could open the hatch.

"I caution all of you to watch your step," said Rynah.

"I thought you two knew each other well," said Tom.

"Which is why you should exercise caution," replied Rynah. She threw on her jacket and zipped it up, making certain that her laser pistol remained secure in its holster. Another quick check told her that the knife in her boot was also there. "Let's go."

They opened the hatch and exited the ship, entering a room with sparse bulbs lining the ceiling. They walked with caution as they moved further into the station; their eyes roamed every dark corner.

"That's far enough!" said a voice.

"Tre?" Rynah questioned.

"Don't move! I mean it!" A man stepped out of the shadows and into the dim light. His tattered clothes hung loosely from his bony frame, forming bags; a few rips and tears lined the bottom of his yellowed, grease stained shirt.

Rynah slowly put her hands up. The others followed suit. "Tre, I just want to talk."

"Oh, yeah? You sure you're not going to blow up my place again and have government agents throw me in prison?"

"It was an accident!"

"One you caused! I can never go back home!"

"There is no home to go back to," said Rynah. "How did you get out of the detention facility anyway?"

"That is my secret," said Tre. "Wait. What do you mean there is no home to go to?"

"You don't know?" Tom blurted out.

Alfric gave him a scolding look.

"Sorry," mumbled Tom.

"Don't know what?" Tre demanded, his voice growing higher in pitch.

"Lanyr no longer exists," said Rynah.

"You're lying!"

"That is partly why we're here," Rynah continued. "I know that you monitor all of the communications in this sector. Tap into the footage of our satellites. You'll see that I'm telling the truth. Either way, you can put down that bolt gun."

"Why would I do that?" asked Tre as he aimed the bolt gun, threatening to fire.

"Because it's not even loaded," Rynah answered.

Tre glanced at his weapon and at her. He tossed the bolt gun aside as though it was mere trash, and it banged on the metallic floor, sending a deafening echo throughout the room. "Who are they?" he asked, pointing at Tom, Alfric, and Solon.

Usef stepped forward to stop him, but Rynah held up her hand. "Friends," she said.

Tre aimed a light at their faces. Upon seeing the different pigmentation of their skin, he knew they were not from any of the Twelve Sectors. "Aliens!" he cried. "They're here! The invasion has begun!"

Tre darted to another part of the room, his frantic hands rummaging ally through a teetering pile of garbage before he ran back to them, wearing a tin foil hat and aiming a crossbow in their direction, with a potato gun stuck in his belt.

"What are you doing?" demanded Rynah, flabbergasted.

"I'd say he's gone a little crazy," said Tom.

Rynah shushed him. "Tre, they are friends."

"But they're not from around here. What sector are you from?" he demanded of Tom, Solon, and Alfric.

"Tre, enough!" roared Rynah. "I brought them here."

"Actually," interrupted Solaris as she tapped into the space station's intercoms, "I brought them here. They are from the Terra Sector. I assure you that there is no invasion. Now put that damnable thing down before you hurt yourself!"

"Who said that?" Tre whirled around, searching for the source of the voice.

"That would be Solaris," Rynah replied. "She is a ship."

"A ship?" said Tre.

"Marlow created me," said Solaris.

"Marlow created you?" Tre lowered his crossbow. "He was a good man. If he created you, then I guess you're okay."

"You knew my grandfather?" asked Rynah, with curiosity. She had never introduced them and wanted to know how they could have met.

"No, not exactly," said Tre, "but I read all about his trial and how he tried to steal the crystal. You see, he knew that the aliens would want it. So he tried to protect it by stealing it. Anyone who is crazy enough to do such a thing is okay by me."

"Figures," mumbled Tom. "This guy is completely bonkers."

Rynah glared at him. "Tre, we need your help."

"Sure, why not," said Tre. "I was getting bored anyway."

"Are you sure you want help from this whack job?" whispered Tom to Rynah. "He's insane!"

"A little insanity is what we could use right about now," Rynah replied.

Tre led them through his home, displaying his stockpile of food and his hydroponics garden. "This garden will last forever. It's perfect for out here in the farthest reaches of space. You don't need a lot of soil or sunlight, though you do need these UV lights. I built them myself!"

"So you are an alchemist?" asked Solon.

"What?"

"An..."

"Inventor," said Usef.

"Yes," said Tre with enthusiasm, "I do build a lot of my equipment and add my own flair."

"Tre," said Rynah, "we don't have a lot of time."

"Yes, yes, here we are." Tre opened the door to another compartment of the station. Inside it lay computer consoles and holoscreens that filled the entire area, while wires draped from the ceiling as they connected to pieces of electronic equipment piled against the walls.

"Whoa," said Tom, mesmerized by the scene; his hand reached out to touch one of the screens, but Alfric's strong grip seized it, forcing him to stop.

Alfric and Solon both looked at the room with amazement. They thought they had seen all there was of Rynah's mysterious universe, only to find that there was more they had yet to witness. Alfric bumped into a humming tower, almost knocking it over—to which Tom chuckled—but caught it and set it back upright.

"Now," said Tre as he sat in his swivel chair, "you wanted me to tap into the cameras of Lanyr's satellites?"

"Yes," said Rynah.

"But weren't they destroyed as well?" asked Tom.

"They were," said Rynah, "but they would have transmitted their data to a Lanyran base."

"Just give me a moment and I will find it." A holographic keyboard popped up. Tre typed away at it, his hands punching the keys as he brought up screen after screen of data. "There!"

He pressed a button; a planet, surrounded by stars encompassed them, filling the entire room. They all watched, awed, as giant explosions filled it; except for Rynah, whose face grew somber as she watched her planet give way to death and destruction. Lava erupted from the planet's crust, sending its inferno rage into the upper atmosphere of Lanyr and spreading across space. With each passing second, the planet gave way to the forces that ripped it apart until nothing remained but bits of black, smoldering rock.

"I am sorry," said Alfric, placing a comforting hand on Rynah's shoulder.

"You have nothing to apologize for," said Rynah.

Tre's face also filled with sorrow as he watched his planet disintegrate. "I never knew."

"How could you?" said Rynah. "You have isolated yourself for so long that you had no cause to worry about home."

"But I should have known. How did this happen?"

"Klanor," said Rynah.

"What?"

"You know that crystal that my grandfather tried to steal?"

Tre nodded his head.

"Well, Klanor took it. It wasn't long afterward that our planet was gone."

"But why?"

"Are you familiar with the ancient myths?"

"Those things," scoffed Tre. "They can't possibly be true."

"This guy believes in alien invasions, but not some tale about magical crystals?" muttered Tom.

"But that's preposterous," said Tre.

"Not as ridiculous as you might think," said Rynah. "My grandfather believed in them and so does Klanor. Thus far, we have recovered five of them with one still remaining."

"Really?" Tre's eyes perked up. "They do exist?"

"Yes."

"And you need my help locating the last one," said Tre.

"That is where things get a little more interesting," said Rynah. "We know where the last crystal is, but we are searching for something else."

"Someone," interrupted Alfric.

"Yes," said Rynah. "Klanor took our friend hostage. We need to find her. I need to know where she is."

"I wouldn't know where to begin searching," said Tre.

"You must have some idea," said Rynah. "Klanor may be smart, but even he cannot encrypt all of his communications. Isn't there some way you can locate him by finding one of his older radio transmissions?"

Tre thought about it a moment as he brushed back strands of

his wild, gold hair. "I might be able to do a logarithmic search. I cannot guarantee success, nor can I say how long it will take."

"As soon as you can would be good," said Rynah. "She has been in his custody for almost two months. I can only imagine what he is doing to her."

"Her?" asked Tre.

"She is a girl of 16," said Alfric. "We want her back."

Tre studied the Viking a moment, noting his voice and overbearing stature. "Indeed. Let me work my magic. In the meantime, why don't you all eat something and get some rest. This could take a few hours."

"Thank you," whispered Rynah.

"Don't thank me yet," said Tre.

Chapter 22
LAST KNOWN LOCATION

Rynah paced the floor, her methodical movements wore a path in the metal grating, as she waited for Tre to finish his work. She hated waiting. Patience was never one of her virtues. With each passing second, she imagined what Klanor did to Brie, each scenario worse than the last. She wished Tre would hurry up.

"Calm down," she told herself, "he is doing the best he can."

"Here," said Usef, handing her a steaming cup of tea.

"Thanks," said Rynah, her voice hollow. Her worried face betrayed her thoughts.

"We will find your friend."

Usef's presence filled Rynah with both hope and rage, each battling with the other for control of her heart. "I cannot thank you enough for helping us."

"You don't need to thank me," said Usef. "Helping you find your friend is the right thing to do."

"The right thing," whispered Rynah.

"Yes," replied Usef, thinking of the losses he had suffered in life, but always kept as a well-guarded secret, "some people do that."

Rynah looked into Usef's calm eyes. They were brown, like Klanor's, but softer, gentler, and with a hint of pain. As she stared into his eyes, and the depth within them, she found herself attracted to him, pulled towards him with a mixture of desire and loathing, a desire for hope and a comforting embrace, loathing for allowing her heart to be deceived by Klanor's promises. Drawn to one another, they leaned closer, their lips almost touching, but just like at the colony, Rynah pushed Usef away, unwilling to allow her tattered heart a chance to heal.

A loud snore disturbed them. They turned and found Tom and Solon sprawled on Tre's patched and threadbare couch, asleep. Each snored in turn, mimicking the other. Chuckling, Rynah remained amazed at how the two had become fast friends. Each separated by time—by millennia—yet they acted as though they had known each other their entire lives. She suspected that Solon had some mischievous tendencies when he wasn't buried in his books, tendencies that Tom brought out.

Usef bowed his head and walked away, muttering something about needing to check on Solaris, disappointed that his kind gestures had been rebuffed. Rynah turned away from him and strolled over to the kitchen area. Tre had an assortment of exotic foods that he had grown himself, though she wondered about some of the stuff he had in jars. She rifled through a bowl of fruit and picked one up that look like an orange. At least she hoped it was an orange.

Something weighed her hand. Glancing down, Rynah realized that she still held the cup of tea that Usef had given her. She hadn't even bothered to sip it and taste its bitter, yet soothing flavor. Disappointed over her own lack of courtesy, Rynah glanced down the narrow corridor and the shadows that Usef had melted into. She thought of how he had volunteered to join her and the others in their search for Brie with no thought of compensation. The cynical part of her wondered about what he hoped to gain from it, but her mind forced such thoughts away.

Sometimes, people are kind, her grandfather's words, from when she had been a child and doubted another's sincerity, echoed in her head.

"Do you think he will find her?" asked Alfric as he approached from behind, ripping her from her fragmented thoughts and emotions.

Rynah whirled around, startled. She thought she had been the only one up, other than Usef. "I thought you were asleep."

"I do not sleep well in strange surroundings," said Alfric.

Rynah peeled her orange and took a bite. "I suppose not. Yes, I believe he will find her. Well, give a starting point in any case."

"And we will track her from there?"

"Yes. Look, I know this is hard, but we will find her. Even Klanor cannot remain hidden forever."

"I will snap his neck when we find him."

"Get in line," said Rynah.

"You have history," said Alfric, reading her body language.

"We do." Rynah turned away, not wanting to talk about it, while painful memories of Klanor crept into her mind, causing her shattered heart to ache all the more.

Alfric refused to be brushed aside. "Perhaps you should seek counsel. Anger and hatred buried deep within have a way of destroying us."

"You'd make a fair philosopher," said Rynah. "I thought I was in love."

"He courted you?"

"You could say that."

"And you accepted his gifts?"

"Yes," said Rynah.

"It was not arranged by your parents?"

"No. On my world, children choose their own mates, but, yes, he courted me and I accepted his summons. Then he betrayed me. He betrayed the people of Lanyr, and his act has caused the death of billions. I will never forgive him."

"A broken heart rarely does."

"He should burn in the fires that consumed Lanyr."

Alfric studied Rynah's face. "Your words scorn him, but your eyes do otherwise."

"I don't know what you mean."

"The only way for you to hate Klanor so is if you loved him in the first place, and still do."

"I do not..."

"Like hatred," said Alfric, cutting off Rynah's words and the growing wrath behind them, "love is not so easily dismissed."

Another bit of snoring interrupted them. Both Rynah and Alfric glanced over and watched as Tom and Solon shifted positions.

"Heavy sleepers, aren't they?" asked Rynah.

"Those two could sleep through an invasion."

Rynah laughed.

Alfric's face turned serious. "Someone told me once that in order to reclaim control over your life, you must calm the rage within you. It is sound wisdom."

"Who told you that?"

Alfric nodded in Solon's direction. "He did. For one so young, he possesses the wisdom of a man with many years."

"I hope his wisdom rubs off on Tom," joked Rynah.

Alfric smiled before turning away.

"And did you calm your rage?" Rynah asked, stopping him.

"It is easier to give bits of wisdom than to follow them. I have much work to do," replied Alfric, remembering his sister and the horrors she suffered because of his cowardice.

"As do we all," Rynah whispered to herself.

"I found them!" Tre ran into the room all excited.

Rynah and Alfric whipped around, facing Tre as he waved his arms.

"Where?" demanded Rynah.

Tre motioned for her to come to his computer console. He punched a few keys on the holographic keyboard, bringing up a cluster of stars that Rynah didn't recognize. "Here is where the signal originates," said

Tre. "I've tracked it and checked and double checked. There was a communication sent from here and it has Klanor's signature."

"You are certain?" asked Rynah.

"Positive."

Alfric leaned closer, observing the holograms surrounding them with the pinpricks of dots and nebulae clouds upon it. "The Eyes of Thjazi," he mumbled.

"The what?" asked Rynah and Tre together.

"The Eyes of Thjazi," repeated Alfric, as though they should have known the tale. "Thjazi was a giant who took the goddess Iðunn captive with the help of Loki. Thjazi kept her prisoner until Loki freed her, having been threatened with execution had he not. Thjazi perished in the attempt. The eyes are all that are left of him. I suggest we practice caution."

"We may not have the luxury of caution," said Rynah.

"Nevertheless, giants are ill-tempered and dangerous beasts. Untrustworthy and best avoided," said Alfric. "If Klanor is there, then we should be wary. I sense a trap."

Rynah mulled over Alfric's words, having grown to trust the Viking's judgment. "You're probably right, but we can't take the chance of missing this opportunity. Tre, chart a course. Wake the others."

Alfric nodded his head in compliance as he strolled away from the computer room and marched up to the still-sleeping Tom and Solon. With a nudge of his knee, he woke them both from their slumber.

"Shor… What?" Tom said as he sat up, rubbing the sleep from his eyes.

"It is time to wake," said Alfric.

"But it's still dark," blurted out Tom, his mind still fogged by sleep.

"It is always dark here," said Alfric. "Up, the pair of you."

"Yeah, sure." Tom flopped back down on the couch, as Solon rose to his feet, still groggy.

Frustrated, Alfric moved to the back of the sofa. He took one quick glance at Solon before gripping the sofa and turning it over, sending Tom flying.

"I'm up! I'm up!" yelled Tom. "You don't have to get violent about it."

Alfric grunted before clutching the hilt of his sheathed sword and stalking off, while Solon chortled at Tom's misfortune.

"Shut up," grumbled Tom.

Usef ran into the room upon hearing the commotion. "What's happening?"

"It is nothing," Alfric answered, strolling away, while Tom rubbed a newly formed bruise.

Rynah stormed into the room, zipping up her jacket. "Listen up! We have a possible location on Klanor. Where he is, Brie is most likely to be. Pack what supplies you can. We leave within the hour. Solaris?"

"Yes," came Solaris' reply over the intercom speakers.

"Do you have the coordinates?"

"Yes. I have entered them into my computer."

"Good. Prepare for departure."

The five companions bustled about, grabbing what provisions Tre would part with and storing them on Solaris. As the frenzy of activity continued, Tre skipped about in nervousness as he watched his supplies dwindle.

"Are you sure you don't want the kitchen sink?" he asked Rynah when they had finished.

"I've no use for it," she quipped. "Tre, I want you to keep in constant contact with us. Monitor the airwaves. If you have any news of Klanor, let me know."

"Will do, so long as you promise not to return here."

"Tired of me already?" joked Rynah. "I will repay you for the supplies."

"You just get your friend back," said Tre.

"Thanks."

Rynah hurried aboard Solaris as the engines hummed to life and went to the command center where Tom already sat in the pilot's seat, preparing to leave. "All set?"

"Yes."

"Let's go."

Tom clicked a few buttons and grasped the controls as he

disembarked from the space station. Within minutes, they were in space, far away from Tre's residence and the few comforts he provided.

Pink and orange vaporous clouds, much like a misty morning, but more colorful, drifted past the windows as they entered the Twelyr Sector. It lay on the furthest reaches of the Twelve Sectors. A solitary, burnt orange star stood before them as planets moseyed around it in elliptical patterns.

"That planet there," said Rynah as she double checked the coordinates Tre had given her.

Acknowledging her directions, Tom veered to the left, guiding Solaris to the fourth planet from the sun, which was larger than the one that gave life to Earth.

"Solaris, scans," said Rynah.

A few seconds passed before she answered. "There is nothing there."

"What?" Rynah couldn't believe it. The planet Neblar was always populated, a huge tourist attraction that bustled with life and activity. "I meant Klanor specifically."

"There are no signs of life," repeated Solaris, "including no signs of Klanor."

"That doesn't make any sense," breathed Rynah. "How can this be?"

"I have run my scans three times and each time it is the same, no signs of life."

The solar wing panel of a satellite dish swept past them as they neared the planet. Rynah stared at it with a blank expression as it shrunk into the distance. *An entire population gone?* She couldn't believe it.

"We still need to land," said Rynah. "Have you found a suitable location?"

"Yes," answered Solaris.

"Set us there."

Solaris flashed the coordinates on the screen for Tom and guided him to the specific landing strip.

"An entire civilization does not just disappear," said Solon.

'Precaution should be taken." He walked over to a storage locker where a couple of laser pistols were kept and tossed one to Rynah and the other to Usef.

"You indeed have developed a warrior's intuition," beamed Alfric at his student.

Solon smiled, somewhat embarrassed by the praise.

They zipped over the surface of the planet as they headed for a landing strip. Alfric and Solon peered through the window, studying the devastation that marked the ground.

"What happened?" asked Solon.

"War," answered Alfric.

Solon stared out the window as they passed smoldering fires and embers that had once been magnificent buildings. Rynah did as well. Tears burned behind her eyes as she remembered fleeing her planet and watching, helplessly, as it burst into millions of pieces.

A gentle thump rocked the ship as Tom placed Solaris on the cracked surface of the planet. He jumped out of the pilot's seat and strapped a laser pistol around his leg. "I think we better take a look."

"We should be careful," Usef said.

Rynah nodded her head. "Solaris, if we're not back in an hour, leave without us."

"Understood," said Solaris.

They each walked down the gangplank of the rear hatch as they stepped onto the surface of Neblar; tendrils of smoke swirled around them, creating waves of floating embers that danced in the breeze. Solon's foot crunched shards of glass. He removed it, kneeling down to study the jagged pieces. The tinted bits of glass reflected the sun's rays, crafting tiny rainbows, the only bit of beauty in the now desolate place that had once thrived with laughter and happiness. The broken pieces had once formed a stained glass window. With deft movements, Solon put them together like a puzzle, remarking at the image they formed.

"What happened here?" he asked for the second time.

"Klanor," spat Rynah. "He attacked this place."

"How can you be so certain?" asked Usef.

"I just know," replied Rynah.

"Certainty based on emotion is rarely correct," Solon reminded her.

"You want logic?" Rynah rounded on him. "Try this. We have a signal tracing his last location to this place. We know that he possesses most of the crystals and has been experimenting with them and the weapon they are to create. We also know that he has destroyed my planet already."

"I see your point," Solon conceded.

"We should head for high ground," said Alfric. "This area is too exposed."

Rynah glanced at the tall buildings around them. She agreed. If anyone had remained, where they now stood made them easy targets. "This way."

She took the lead, heading for a set of marbled stairs that led to a stone courtyard with topiaries lining the exterior amidst gardens, which had been reduced to ash. Burnt, scorch marks dotted the building they strolled past, blackening the white paint and darkening their mood. They did their best to ignore what emotions such devastation rendered.

The shrill scrape of metal radiated in the air, filling their ears. Each stopped in their tracks. The metallic sound grew louder as it intensified around them. Without warning, Usef grabbed Rynah around the waist and pulled her out of harm's way just as a flagpole crashed into the ground, sending pellets of dirt in every direction. They waited with baited breath as the noise echoed off the buildings and dissipated.

"Thanks," said Rynah. "I guess I owe you one."

"You owe me nothing," Usef whispered to her, before realizing that he still had his hands around her waist, and released her.

Rynah watched Usef as she regained her feet, as though seeing him for the first time, and that attraction (not physical, but more intuitive) towards him took temporary hold of her.

A scuffling sound echoed around them. They dashed across the courtyard and up a flight of stairs to a lone balcony. Nothing. Each took a separate corner to search, but no one was to be found.

"What was this place?" asked Alfric as he scanned the surrounding area.

"Many things," said Rynah. "Neblar was known for its sandy beaches, museums, fine dining, resorts, and centers of knowledge. It was a place people came to relax."

"So it possessed halls of pleasure," said Alfric.

"That's one way of putting it," said Rynah.

Solon wandered away from the group. A giant archway attracted his attention as it bore a resemblance to the library that the scribes spent their days in back home. He admired the columns before the entrance to the grand building, their structure reminding him of the temples near his home. He walked through them. A domed, glass ceiling loomed above him, allowing the sun's rays to spill through and fill the area with light as dust particles glittered in its softness.

"Good evening, sir," said a computerized voice as a hologram appeared. "Welcome to the Neblar Library, the biggest collection of books in the Twelve Sectors. May I help you locate a particular title?"

Solon stopped. "N—n—n—no," he stammered.

The hologram disappeared. Solon turned toward the center of the library and gasped. Before him, stood shelves upon shelves of books. He recognized the binding of the volumes as they were similar to the few that Rynah possessed.

Mesmerized, Solon allowed himself to wander among the shelves of books. He touched the leather bindings of the volumes as he strolled by, his eyes growing wide with each passing second. *How many are there?* he wondered. He had no way of knowing, but wished he had more time to spend in the library. Scrolls of knowledge always fascinated him as Solon believed that was the way one learned about the past, and the future. He heard the others' voices outside. Knowing that he should return to them before they started to worry about his absence, Solon headed back to the archway.

Something caught his attention. A lone book, sticking out from the even line that the others on the shelf formed, begged for his notice. He picked it up, staring at the embossed image on its plain cover, trying to remember where he had seen it before, and flipped it open. The pages crinkled as he rifled through them. One page in particular snapped his interest. It bore the same picture that was on the cover and—it hit him. He had seen that symbol before, on Rynah's wristband that she always wore. The marking on her band was small and had been surrounded by other symbols, but he had noticed it one day, passing it off as something important to her culture. Feeling that it was more than mere coincidence that he stumbled upon the book, and wanting to know more about the image on its cover, Solon tucked it under his arm.

"Hey, everyone," came Tom's voice from outside. "Over here!"

Solon ran out of the library and joined the others as they circled around Tom. Horror took their breaths away. Before them, stretched an entire expanse of corpses; flies buzzed around them, ignoring the stench and the newcomers. Solon placed his hand over his mouth in an effort to not vomit. Noticing his pale shade, Usef guided Solon away from the others so he could regain his composure with dignity. Only Alfric and Rynah seemed unaffected by the gruesomeness of the scene.

"What happened?" breathed Tom in disbelief.

"Annihilation," said Rynah; anger tainted her voice as her cheeks puffed out in her effort to contain it.

"Odin spare us," said Alfric, having difficulty grasping the scope of the death that loomed before him.

"Your gods have no power here," said Rynah. It came out ruder than she had intended.

Alfric glared at her, but kept his mouth shut.

"We should bury them," said Tom.

"There are too many," said Rynah.

"But they must be delivered to the underworld," said Solon when he returned with Usef.

"We cannot leave them," Alfric agreed. "The dead deserve peace."

Rynah remained unmoved, seething over what had been done and wishing the one responsible dead for it.

"Rynah," Usef said, placing a gentle hand on her wrist, "you know it's the right thing to do."

Rynah glanced at the half burnt bodies of what had once been men, women, and children; rage boiled deep within her as she thought about how she had once loved the man responsible for the horrific scene before her. She wanted to do as they asked, but at the same time, she wished to find Klanor. "We haven't time."

"Actually, you have plenty of it," said Solaris over the radio.

Rynah groaned. *Was there ever a time when Solaris didn't eavesdrop?* "But…"

"There is a fueling vehicle not far from you. You could bring it there, empty it, and burn the bodies," said Solaris.

"Fire is the proper farewell for the dead," said Alfric, "Preferable to their current state of shame."

Knowing she would lose the argument, Rynah relented. "Very well. Usef, you're with me."

Rynah and Usef found the fuel truck within minutes. They pried the doors open and jumped into the cab. Rynah started the engine, amazed that it still worked. Soon they hovered just above the ground.

Rynah unhooked the parking brake; the hover vehicle lurched as she put it in gear and steered it to where Tom, Solon, and Alfric waited. She maneuvered it so that when she dumped the fuel, it would cover the bodies and not them.

Once she turned off the engine, she jumped out. "Stand back," she said as she walked to the back where the release valve was.

The others did as ordered.

Glancing around one last time, Rynah opened the release valve, letting loose a stream of liquid fuel that gushed forth, smothering the dead bodies. Rynah hurried away from it, motioning for the others to do the same. Once they had reached a safe distance, she pulled out her laser pistol, aimed, and pulled the trigger. A single spurt of light burst from it, striking the flammable liquid. Flames erupted to life, engulfing the entire area, and the inferno spread with rapid speed. Mumbling caught Rynah's attention. She turned to find both Alfric and Solon muttering a prayer in their own language.

Something moved behind them. They each whirled around. A flicker of movement caught Rynah's eye. She looked at Alfric and he nodded, knowing what to do.

Rynah walked straight towards the commotion. "Hey," she called. "Who's there?"

Silence.

She glanced in Alfric's direction and noticed him jump over the low wall. "We mean you no harm."

Still no answer.

Usef and the others started to follow her, but Rynah waved them back. "You might as well come out. We know you are there."

She moved closer… her hand on her weapon.

"Hey! Ge—let go!" screamed the stranger as Alfric seized him from behind and dragged him out into the open.

"Who are you?" demanded the Viking.

"No one!" wailed the stranger.

"What are you doing here?" Rynah asked.

"I saw your ship land and I wanted to know more about you."

"We came looking for someone," said Tom.

Rynah glared at him, silencing him.

"Whom?" asked the stranger with a little too much interest.

"None of your concern," said Rynah. "How did you escape the devastation here?"

"I hid in an underground shelter."

"Are there others?"

"No."

"He's lying," spat Usef.

Something didn't seem right. "Who caused all of this?" asked Rynah.

The man refused to answer.

Alfric's grip tightened.

"Klanor! It was Klanor," he screamed.

"How do you know?" asked Usef. "Did you see him?"

"I didn't need to," said the man. "The armada, it was unmistakably his. He's got a weapon I've never seen before. So destructive. Killed everyone."

"Except you," growled Alfric, suspicion filled his voice.

"How long ago was this?" asked Rynah.

"About 10 days," said the stranger.

"Ten days?" said Rynah. She glanced down at the man's feet. His shiny, black boots reflected the light well, mimicking a mirror. "Your boots seem a bit clean for someone who has been here for so long."

Knowing his cover had been blown, the man jabbed Alfric in the face with his elbow, before lunging at Usef. Stunned, the Viking loosened his grip, allowing the stranger to escape. The man ran, fleeing across the courtyard and away from them.

"After him!" ordered Rynah.

"No!" Solaris yelled over the radio.

"Why?" demanded Rynah.

"If he is here, then Klanor and his armada cannot be far away. We best leave before we are outnumbered."

Though she wished to pursue the man, Rynah agreed. "Back to the ship. Now!"

The man ran until his legs carried him no further. He found his small spacecraft hidden among the rubble where he had landed after noticing Rynah's ship on his navigation screen. Stein had ordered him to remain in case she showed up. He ripped off a grimy, odorous cloak that he had pulled from a corpse and wrapped it around himself. Once in the pilot's seat, the man started his engines and took off.

Chapter 23
MUSINGS

Alone at last, Solon took advantage of the lull in the activities aboard Solaris to look at the book that he had procured from their visit to Neblar. He placed it on the one table in his room, careful not to disturb the pages or damage the frayed tips of the book's corners, though he could not help but rub the engraving on the cover, treating the volume with the gentleness that he treated the scrolls he copied for the library near his home.

Solon opened it to the first page. The words made no sense to him, not that he was surprised because he knew they would be different from his native language. A wave of disappointment hit him. He wished he could read the words and learn the secrets held within the pages of the book. Solon snapped out of his thoughts as he remembered that he was on a vessel like no other, one that had the ability of speech, and a personality to match.

"Solaris?" he called out.

"Something I can do for you, soothsayer?" came her reply.

"Soothsayer?"

"That is what Alfric calls you."

"I am no soothsayer," said Solon, "merely a student of knowledge."

"According to my research, that is what a soothsayer is, one who learns, is a guardian of knowledge, and in some cases, capable of performing magic. But I digress. You wanted something."

"Can you translate the words in this book?" asked Solon.

"Place it in the scanner, please."

A panel in the wall opened up and Solon put the open book in there, hoping that Solaris would be able to assist him. A beam of white light ran over the pages.

"How did you come by this?" Solaris asked him, her curiosity obvious.

"I found it," Solon replied, "on Neblar, in the library there."

"Why did you take this book?"

"Because of the symbol on its front."

"And you just happened upon this?"

"I'm not sure what you are implying."

"I'm implying nothing," said Solaris. "I am just curious as to, of all the books within the library, you found this particular one."

"Do you know what it is?"

"A most interesting book. A translation from a much older text and published in this format for others to read, much like the civilizations that come after yours will do with all of the stories told, and eventually written down, in your era. But it is not in my databanks."

Solaris' voice went silent for a few moments, prompting Solon to bring her back to the purpose of his calling her to his room. "Can you translate it?"

"Yes," said Solaris, abandoning her ponderings about why the book was not in her memory banks. She shook the thoughts away at Solon's impatient tapping of his foot. "Yes, I can translate this. Give me a moment."

The small hole in the wall that contained the book brightened as the lights within it flared up and the pages of the book itself flipped themselves until the very last had one had settled. Once done, the lights flickered in a random pattern before shutting off.

"In the drawer near your bed should be a holopad."

Solon walked to where Solaris had directed him. He pulled open the metal drawer, finding a paper-thin, transparent, rectangular shape.

"Remove the book and put the holopad in its place."

Solon obeyed. Once he had placed the holopad in the small opening, the lights flared up again and the holopad itself lighted up, until darkness consumed the area again.

"Finished," said Solaris.

Hesitant, Solon reached for the holopad, unsure of what he should do next. "I do not know how to use one of these."

"Just touch the top right corner."

Solon did so, and in an instant, a three-dimensional, and very realistic, image of the book appeared, surprising him and causing him to let go. The holopad clattered on the floor, but the image remained.

"You're not supposed to drop it," huffed Solaris. "Goodness me."

"Sorry," Solon apologized and picked up the holopad again, marveling at how the picture looked just like the actual book. He opened it. To his amazement, the pages looked like the original and even crinkled. "How did you…"

"One of my many talents. You should find that the words are in a language you do understand."

"Yes, they are."

"Do you require anything else?"

"No, thank you."

Solon placed the holopad on the table and turned to the first page, thinking that he was alone, but though Solaris had gone silent, she had remained, wanting to know why that book, which bore a marking she recognized, was not in her memory banks. Solon read the first few lines.

Many will read this text
And find themselves most vexed.

Though all can read what follows in this leaflet,
Only a child of Herclai will realize its secrets.

If you are one, read further and study well
For in the labyrinth this will be most helpful.

Solon paused. He did not know what a child of Herclai was, unless the lines of verse referred to what some in his world called demi-gods. Solon shoved his musings aside. The only way to fully understand a riddle was to listen to it over and over again until the meaning became clear. He continued reading and spent the next several hours poring through the book, unaware that Solaris watched over his shoulders.

Chapter 24
BRIE'S PLAN

The constricting straps dug into Brie's wrists as she awoke in the interrogation room, once again, after having fallen unconscious hours before. Voices permeated the fog in her brain. Keeping her eyes closed, Brie focused on them.

"Why does he keep her around?" asked one lab technician. Her purple-toned skin shone through the sheer lab coat.

"It is not for us to question," answered another technician.

"Why not?"

"Shhh! Remember what happened to Wren?"

That silenced the first technician for a while. "Do you think she is still unconscious?"

"Look at her? She's out cold."

The first technician leaned closer. "Why do you think he is so interested in these crystals? We have some energy crystals in the engineering section of the ship. Why does he need these? What makes them so special?"

"Keep your voice down," hissed the other one.

"But why?"

"I don't know. The crystals in engineering power the ship. Supposedly, these are different, the likes of which have never been seen."

"So these crystals are energy generators on a massive scale?"

Energy generators? Brie committed that bit of information to memory. "Something like that."

The doors slid open and the two technicians fell silent as Stein marched in, his very presence chilling the room. The two technicians hunkered over their tasks, hoping he would ignore them.

"Well?" demanded Stein.

"Sir?" asked one, shaking.

"Is she awake yet?"

The poor technician glanced over at Brie, who pretended to be asleep. "She doesn't appear to be."

Stein walked over to Brie, staring down at her sleeping form. Not fooled, he grabbed a metal lance and smacked it across the top of the chair, missing her head by an inch. Brie's eyes shot open in fear as she inhaled sharply before calming herself.

"She is awake now," said Stein, tossing the rod on a nearby table. "Take her back to her cell."

"Yes, sir."

Again, Brie found herself yanked from the interrogation chair and dragged back to her prison cell. Thoughts about the energy crystals bounced around in her head. If they needed them to power the ship, then perhaps she could steal one. *No*, Brie thought to herself, *it won't do any good if I cannot get off this ship.* Suddenly, Brie realized that Rynah had no idea where she was. She needed to send a signal. But how?

A sign caught her attention. Judging by the image accompanying the words on it, Brie realized that it led to the communications array, but going there would be too obvious. Unless…

"Where does that go?" she asked.

One of the guards laughed. "The flight deck? You think you're going to escape from here on a ship?"

Brie smiled. *So that is where they kept them.* "You never know."

"Shut up," scolded the other guard. He looked at Brie. "Why do you care where things are on this ship?"

"I wouldn't want to get lost," Brie said, with sarcasm.

The guard grumbled.

She didn't care if he believed her or not. A thought struck her. All she needed was to broadcast a message to let Rynah and the others know where she was. She knew that there was no guarantee Solaris would pick it up, but she had to hope they would. What did she have to lose? "I need the restroom."

The guards laughed. "You have a toilet in your cell."

Brie stopped. "Look, all of those meds they have given me have really made me have to pee, or do you want me to make a mess out here?"

The guards thought about it a moment. The last thing they wanted was for her to urinate on the carpeted floor.

"Look, guys, where am I going to go?" said Brie, waving her arms. "We're in the middle of space."

"Fine," said one guard as he looked around, "but make it quick."

They hauled her to a door with the unmistakable sign of being a restroom on it. Brie walked inside while they took up their positions outside. She sprang into action, searching the empty restroom for a place to hide. She had thought about the stalls. *Too obvious.*

"One minute," yelled a guard through the door.

Frantic, Brie searched for a place to conceal herself. She needed them to think she had escaped. She checked the ventilation. No use. Something glittery caught her attention. It was a doorknob. Brie pulled on it. Locked. Desperate, she glanced around for something she could use to pick it. She dashed into a stall and pulled the paper off the roll. Pulling the rod apart, Brie exposed a small spring. *Perfect,* she thought.

"Hurry up!"

Knowing she had little time, she straightened the spring into a slim, metal sliver and stuck it in the lock on the door to the janitor's closet. She twisted it until—click! She yanked open the door and shut herself inside just as the two guards stepped into the bathroom.

"Where'd she go?" demanded one.

The second one spotted the door to the closet and hurried over to it, pulling on it, but Brie had locked it just in time. "It's locked."

"Then she couldn't be in there."

They looked up and noticed the cover to the ventilation hanging ajar. "The ventilation!" said both of them, running out of the room.

After they stormed outside, Brie opened the closet door. No one. She dashed out and hurried to the bathroom exit and peeked through it. The guards were nowhere to be found. Seizing her chance, Brie ran from the bathroom and towards the communications array, hurrying up a flight of steps, her bare feet making little noise.

An alarm blared through the ship, warning everyone of her escape. Knowing she had little time, Brie quickened her pace.

Two crewmembers rounded a corner. She darted behind a bulkhead, squishing against the wall to make herself invisible. They strolled past her, unaware of her presence. Releasing a sigh of relief, Brie watched them continue on, ignoring the alarm. She ran. Her feet pounded the floor as she raced to the radio room.

Marching boots alerted her to danger. Brie dashed toward a set of doors that slid open and went inside. The darkened room was empty. She leaned against the wall, listening as the soldiers ran past. A map on the wall caught her eye.

Momentarily forgetting her mission, Brie walked over to the lighted map. After a few seconds, she learned the key and studied every inch of it until she discovered where she was on the map and how much farther she had to go to the communication center. It was only one more deck up. She studied the map a few minutes more. *There!* The engineering section was five decks below her current position. Half a plan formed in Brie's mind, but she forced it out. *One thing at a time*, she reminded herself.

Having wasted enough time, Brie ran out of the room and bolted down the corridor, hoping that she didn't meet any unexpected surprises. She glanced behind her every few seconds as she hurried to her destination. She needed to take the elevator up. Brie rounded a corner, heading straight for it. Stein, along with a group of armed guards, stood there. Frightened, she dodged behind another corner.

"Where is she?" stormed Stein.

"We do not know," said one guard. "We thought she was heading for the shuttles, but she's not there."

"You thought?"

"What does it matter?" asked a new voice.

Brie recognized that voice. She peered around the corner and saw Gaden standing before Stein. She couldn't believe it. *How did he escape Lanyr?*

"What does it matter?" Stein asked with a dangerous edge to his voice. "That girl is a valuable commodity."

"She can't go anywhere," said Gaden.

"No?" said Stein. "Check the cameras. I want her found! And get this filth out of my sight."

Armed soldiers ran off in obedience of Stein's orders. He shoved Gaden out of his way as he stalked off. Brie watched as Gaden remained, alone, by the elevators. She crept up behind him and tapped him on the shoulder. Gaden turned around. With as much force as she could muster, she punched him in the face, sending him flying backward. Brie pushed the button to open the elevator doors.

"Over here!" yelled Gaden.

Brie kicked him in the stomach, shutting him up. A magnetic passkey caught her attention. Reaching down, she jerked it free of Gaden's belt, slipping inside the elevator as the doors opened, and closed them just as four guards arrived. Brie breathed a momentary sigh of relief. She rethought her plan. Escape wasn't her present goal, but she needed them to think it was. She stopped the elevator. *If I go to the communications array, they'll know I was sending a message.* A new idea formed in her mind. She needed them to believe that she wanted to leave.

Brie punched the button for the flight deck. The elevator hummed as it descended. The doors slid open as it stopped. Brie rushed out into the empty hall. Remembering the map she had found earlier, she darted to her right and ran down the cold hallway to where the ships were. She ran underneath a camera, on purpose, and looked at it; whoever monitored them would see her. She knew it wouldn't take long for them to send guards.

Doors opened. Soldiers spilled through them, heading straight for her. *That was quick!* Brie turned and careened down the corridor to the area with the ships. Shouts for her to stop rattled against her eardrums. She ignored them. Laser fire pelted the wall next to her as the guards fired warning shots. Ignoring all of it, Brie concentrated on her task. Glass doors loomed before her. She swiped Gaden's keycard, hoping it would work. The light turned green and the doors opened. Brie ran inside, shutting them behind her just as her pursuers caught up. She stared at them for a moment before turning and delving deep within the chamber. Ships of every size filled the area. A long, narrow strip down the center of the room stretched the entire length of the ship. She knew it was the runway.

Banging on the doors pulled her from her musing. Brie hurried over to a terminal. She touched it. A holoscreen flickered to life. Her fingers flew over the screen as she pressed buttons, hoping her plan wouldn't fail now.

"Come on," she hissed. "I need to send a message."

She tapped a few more keys on the screen, but nothing came up, except the prompt, "Command?"

"Communication," said Brie, thinking of nothing else to say. The screen changed and up popped a box that looked similar to an email message. Brie hit "All Channels" and then pressed a button that beeped.

An idea struck her. She pressed the button, sending a series of *dit, dit, dit, dah, dah, dah, dit dit, dit* repeatedly, forming the code for S.O.S. Brie knew that no one in this sector would be able to decipher it and would pass it off as a series of random sounds, but Solaris might notice it.

Bang!

Whipping around, she realized that they had pried the glass doors open an inch. Brie shut off the screen and ran to the first ship with an open hatch. She plopped in the pilot's seat and punched the first button she found. A missile fired, striking another ship. *Oops.* Another tremendous bang alerted her that the guards had broken in. Within moments, they surrounded her, pointing their weapon at her.

"I'm curious," said Klanor as he walked to the front with Stein close behind, "where did you think you would go?"

Brie didn't answer.

Smirking, though there was no joy in it, Klanor waved his hand and two guards seized her arms. "I give you props for courage. I honestly didn't think you had it in you."

The guards ripped Gaden's keycard from her and dragged her away. Once back in her cell, Brie tore some toilet paper off the roll on the wall. In a corner of her room, she found black dust. Using it like ink, she drew, from memory, a map of the ship, hoping that Solaris picked up her signal.

Chapter 25
A Trap

The whine of a ship droned through the peaceful forest of the planet Virdyr in the Rynirran Sector; being the furthest planet from its sun, one would think that there would be no life, but its sun was a supernova, and its intense heat stretched all the way out to Virdyr, allowing life to flourish. The serene planet had no idea why this lone ship deigned to hover over its canopy as it searched for a place to set down. The strange vessel eventually spotted a clearing and touched down on the soft, bluish green grass with Redwood trees swaying in the wind as the rear hatch opened, revealing a black hole from which five people stepped out; a woman with emerald hair took the lead.

Snap!

A thick-soled, knee-high boot trampled a dried twig, breaking it in half as a stranger peered through a pair of binoculars concealed on a ledge, observing the newly arrived strangers. A smirk appeared on his chapped lips as he studied their movements. The man lowered his binoculars, the earrings in his ear shifting with each of his movements. He brought a radio up to his mouth and flicked it on. "They're here."

"Understood," came a reply.

The stranger stalked away to his hovercraft and sped off to where to trap awaited the new arrivals.

Rynah surveyed the region with her palm-sized scanning mechanism. Tre had sent her a transmission, telling her of a signal, matching Klanor's, coming from there. "We appear to be the only ones here."

She turned off the device and hitched her belt with the laser pistol, her training in the fleet, and as a security officer, ruling her judgment. "Be careful. I don't trust this place."

"You said we were alone," said Tom.

"Appearances can be deceiving," said Rynah.

Solon agreed. "When one appears to be alone is when he should be most wary."

"Always the epitome of good advice," Tom clapped him on the back. "So where do we start looking? According to your interesting friend, Klanor should be here, but where are his ships?"

"Good question," said Rynah. "Solaris?"

"I have found nothing," answered Solaris, "however, there are readings coming about five miles north from our position."

"All right," said Rynah, "let's go." She hiked towards the woods, leaving a small trail in the waist high grass; the others followed behind her.

Birds cooed and sang a peaceful melody as they walked. The soft chirping of crickets accompanied them as they trekked through the rich and colorful (a wide range of gold, orange, pink, blue, and burgundy melded together) forest of Virdyr. The luscious green leaves tinted blue in the rays of the sun. Dried and dead leaves crunched beneath their shoes as they walked; the serene landscape portrayed little in the way of deception. The longer they walked, the more uneasy Rynah became. If Klanor had been there, there was no sign of him now. *Why would he come here, anyway?* she asked herself. She glanced around at the wildflowers that bloomed beneath the canopy of the trees; a few rays of light trickled through, dotting her face.

Click! The unnatural sound echoed through the otherwise quiet area. Usef put a hand on Rynah's shoulder, stopping her. Another click emanated from the trees. Her intuition alerted her that something was wrong and she whipped out her laser pistol. "Down!"

A string of laser fire spilled from the trees, heading for them; bits of bark rained down upon them as it pelted the twisted trunks of the trees. Rynah shot a few spurts in the general direction of the attack. The thick, wooded area made determining where the enemy was difficult. The barrage of laser fire zoomed over their heads, singeing their hair. Snapping of twigs forced Rynah to whirl around. A man stood behind her. She aimed her pistol and pulled the trigger, catching him in the chest.

"It's a trap!" shouted Usef.

Rynah cursed. She knew that Tre would not have lied about tracking a signal here, meaning that Klanor had planted it on purpose and she stupidly followed it, blinded by her desire for revenge and to rescue Brie. "We need to get back to Solaris!"

The five friends jumped to their feet and crashed through the forest in the direction of the ship; laser fire surrounded them, forcing them to duck and run hunched over. A slow, ominous creak filled the air. Rynah looked up. Above her, a giant ash tree fell towards her. Alfric's muscular arm wrapped around her waist, yanking her out of the tree's path as it smashed into the moist ground, sending bits of dirt in her direction.

A man ran for them. The Viking dropped her, swung around, raising his steel blade, and sliced the attacker's weapon in half. Dumbfounded, he stared at it, and Alfric, not believing what had just occurred. Without mercy, Alfric plunged his sword into the man and allowed him to crumple to the ground.

A laser beam nicked the steel blade. Turning, Alfric noticed another charging him. He heaved his sword above him and rushed toward his enemy with a terrifying howl. At the last second, he dropped to his knees, rolled across the earth, and brought his sword up into his opponent's abdomen.

He snatched the laser weapon from the dead man's hands.

Though he preferred his sword, Alfric listened well when Rynah had taught him the use of this strange weapon that produced deadly beams of light and put that knowledge to use, aiming at another who attacked Tom from behind and fired.

"This way is blocked," yelled Rynah. "We need to find another. Solaris!"

"Yes," answered Solaris in Rynah's earpiece.

"Can you get to us?"

"I'll try. I need to…" Solaris' transmission cut out.

"Solaris? Solaris!" Rynah ripped out her earpiece, storing it in her pocket and swearing in her native language. She scanned the area for a way to escape. Solon's frantic movements as he waved his arms stopped her.

"This way!" she yelled, pointing at him.

Solon crouched near a patch of forest that the mercenaries had forgotten about. He whistled at Tom and Alfric after he had gotten Rynah's attention. The two turned toward him. "Here!" he screamed.

Both Tom and Alfric ran for him as laser blasts pelted the jade shrubbery around them. One by one, they dove through a small opening within the brush and to temporary safety.

Solaris tried to get the link back with Rynah after having been cut off. An explosion just outside her hull shook the ground, dumping clumps of dirt upon her exterior. She performed a scan and realized that whomever had attacked them had a laser cannon, poised on a cliff, aimed at her. Her scanners watched as another blast headed straight for her, striking the ground yards from her position.

Knowing that she could not remain, Solaris started her engines. Switching off manual control, she took control of the pilot's console and ascended into the air; fire burst from her booster rockets as she rose into the atmosphere and disappeared.

The five companions ran through the forest, crashing through the brush and the trees, jumping over logs and upturned roots, and not caring which direction they went in during their efforts to escape. Their pursuers closed in, creating as much noise as them. The sound of an engine stopped them. Rynah peered through a tiny space in the entangled branches of the trees. Her heart sank as she saw Solaris leave.

"What is it?" asked Usef.

Rynah pointed.

The same sense of abandonment filled him. "Cursed ship."

Ignoring emotion, Alfric pushed them onward. "This way," he said. "We must find high ground."

The Viking took the lead, setting a fast pace as he hacked his way through the dangling vines and away from their quarry. Despite his bulky size and determined movements, he made no sound. The others trailed behind him, keeping a wary eye on the surrounding trees.

"Rynah!" called a mocking voice.

She stopped. Usef grabbed her arm and forced her onward.

"Oh, come now, Rynah, I know you are there. Klanor sent me here to find you."

Alfric continued. Judging by the man's statements, he knew that their attackers had no clue as to their whereabouts, and he intended to keep it that way.

"Who are these people?" asked Tom.

"Mercenaries," whispered Usef. "Klanor probably hired them to destroy all of you so he wouldn't have to himself."

Rynah walked in a daze, still not believing that Solaris had abandoned them—had abandoned her. Despite being a ship, she liked Solaris and had grown attached to the hunk of junk, as she sometimes called it, and wished that she had remained. Her weapon hung by her side in her limp grip as her feet plopped on the forest floor, crunching the dead leaves.

"Hey," said Usef. "You okay?"

"She left us," muttered Rynah. "She just left us."

"It's a ship."

Rynah glared at Usef.

"Sorry, but…"

Alfric shoved him out of the way. "All is not always as it seems," he said to Rynah. "Put this out of your mind. We have more immediate problems."

"I don't know if I can," whispered Rynah as the sense of abandonment took root in her soul.

"Come now, Rynah," the mercenary continued to taunt her.

Alfric silently vowed to cut out the man's tongue. "Is that what you will tell Brie when we all meet in Valhalla?"

The last statement did it. Rynah tightened her hold on her weapon as a stern expression filled her face, masking the hurt deep within. Satisfied that he had gotten through to her, Alfric continued in the lead.

Solon stopped him. "Listen," he said. "They are trying to surround us."

Alfric strained his ears, listening to every sound of the forest. The lad was right. As the mercenary leader scoffed at them, the others attempted to cut off their escape. "Cursed fool that I am," Alfric scolded himself. "This way."

They moved through the trees, keeping their voices quiet and their feet nimble. Alfric led them closer to the man who continued to throw insults and taunts their way, though always careful to remain out of sight, and managed to maintain a clear line of vision on him as he stomped among the trees calling to them.

"Why don't you make it easier on yourself and just surrender? You cannot hide," he continued.

Alfric squashed the burning desire to shut the man up. Doing so would give away their position. "Go," he whispered to the others as he kept a close eye on the mercenary.

The others squeezed past him. They found a narrow trail and followed it down a hill away from the shouts. Taking one last glance at the mercenary that taunted them, Alfric hurried away. They walked for another hour before finding a cave. The sun hung low in the sky, and without Solaris, there was no escaping the planet.

Knowing that there was little else to do, Alfric ordered them inside before locating a boulder and pushing it into the cave entrance so they would have no unexpected visitors during the night.

Each of them slumped in a corner of the cave. Silence loomed around them as their thoughts plagued their minds. Rynah kicked pebbles across the rocky ground. "I can't believe she abandoned us."

"What?" asked Tom. "Where is Solaris?"

"Don't know," shrugged Rynah. "She flew away on her own. Cursed ship!"

"So how do we get off this planet?" Tom persisted.

"There is a way," said Alfric in a steady voice.

"How?" asked Usef. "Without a ship, we are stranded here."

"No kidding," scoffed Tom. "How long did it take you to figure that out, genius?"

"Hey!" Usef rose to his feet. "It's not my fault that that useless ship got a mind of its own and took off."

"Useless ship," Rynah rounded on Usef. "You didn't think she was so useless a few hours ago."

"That was before her autopilot kicked in and she stranded us."

"Those mercenaries have ships." Solon's calm voice silenced them. Each stared at the young scholar as though they had realized something for the first time. "How else would they have gotten here?"

Rynah scolded herself for not thinking of it earlier. Of course the mercenaries had ships. If they could steal one, then they could get away. "We need a plan."

"I will scout the terrain and learn where their ships are," volunteered Alfric.

"No need," said Solon as he pointed through a slit in the opening where some light spilled in.

Alfric shifted the boulder. Lights filled the night sky, illuminating an area a few miles away.

"I guess they weren't too concerned about us knowing where they were," said Solon.

Alfric rubbed his beard as he thought. "We are here," he said drawing an 'x' in the dirt. "They are here. We will need to infiltrate their camp so as to commandeer a vessel."

"Distraction is always a useful ally," said Solon.

Usef snapped his fingers. "I got it! A couple of us will send up a smoke signal to lure them away from their camp. The rest of you will sneak in and take a ship. We can meet here." He drew another mark in the dirt.

Rynah thought about it for a moment. "Alfric, you and Tom will be the distraction. Solon and Usef, you two will be with me. We will leave in the morning."

"We should go now," said Usef.

"No," Rynah replied, "they will be on their guard for now. By morning, they will have tired of searching for us."

Solaris scanned the surface of the planet for any signs of Rynah and the others. A series of bleeps and blips echoed inside her empty interior as she searched for her friends. Nothing. Worry filled Solaris' internal components. You may find it strange for a ship to feel anxiety, but Solaris was no ordinary ship, for Marlow had constructed her to be very human-like in temperament.

More scans blazed across the planet's surface as she tried to find the people she had left behind. It's not that she wished to abandon them, she just knew that the mercenaries mustn't be allowed to board her so that her secrets would remain just that, secrets. She refused to let herself be taken over again, as when the pirates had stolen her.

Still nothing. Frustrated, Solaris snapped off her sensors and scans. "Where is she?" she yelled over the intercom, experiencing anger for the third time in her life. The first instance was when Marlow and Rynah grew apart; the second was when they had lost Brie (she should have known that Brie hadn't died); and now that she had lost Rynah. The fear that Rynah and the others had been taken captive—or worse, killed—consumed Solaris.

"I have failed you, Marlow," she said over the intercom, knowing that no one could hear her. "I have failed Rynah."

"Initiating emergency protocol," said a robotic voice, which sounded very similar to Marlow's.

A holographic image of Marlow appeared in the center of the command center of Solaris, turning around a few times before settling on a posture for which to speak.

"Hello, dear friend," said the image in Marlow's deep voice. Age filled it, and Solaris knew that he had recorded this image not long before he died. "I have initiated this recording should you ever fall into the trap of regret and self-pity. A very common emotion, and one we all fall prey to. Do not stay victim to it for too long.

"I will take a gander here and assume that you have had to leave Rynah and flee, or you've been separated and cannot find her. Do not regret your decision. She will be angry, yes, but she will understand, in time. Rynah can take care of herself. Remember the precious cargo you hold. You mustn't let anyone get it. It must be protected at all costs until the time is right.

"Now, if you have had to abandon Rynah, you must return to her. She is resourceful. She knows how to evade standard scanners so as to avoid detection. Remember the band she always wears on her wrist. Remember when I gave it to her?

"I wish I could be there with you, old friend, but, alas, this sickness has caught up with me. Remember your promise, and remember that I am always here."

The hologram vanished, leaving only silence to fill the gap. Solaris could not speak. She could not think. When Marlow had died, she thought she had been left alone, forced to live a solitary life. His message proved that he had never abandoned her, nor did he forsake Rynah.

Solaris thought about the wristband that Rynah always wore.

It had been made from a unique alloy not commonly found in the Twelve Sectors. Recalibrating her sensors, Solaris initiated another scan of the planet. A small dot appeared on her screens. It moved.

"Got ya!"

Solaris watched, in the way that only a ship can, as the tiny dot moved closer to the mercenary encampment. She knew what she had to do.

Tom and Alfric crashed through the dense forest of Virdyr as they ran for an exposed hilltop to carry out their plan. Footsteps sounded behind them as the mercenaries closed in.

"Make more noise!" shouted Alfric.

"Why don't you?" Tom shouted back.

Alfric stopped, turning around with a regal pose. Filling his lungs with air, Alfric raised his sword, releasing a huge roar while beating his chest. Once done, he fled, with Tom close behind.

If that doesn't attract them, thought Tom, *nothing will.*

They reached the crest of a hill where the pyre they had built before dawn lay. Alfric ducked behind it, yanking Tom with him. Leaves crunched under boots and twigs snapping into pieces as the mercenaries behind them burst from the confines of the trees. They slowed. Unsure of the pyre, which didn't seem to belong in this serene setting of the forest, they stared at it before approaching the pile of logs and foliage. Tom and Alfric listened as the underbrush crumpled beneath their pursuers' footfalls.

When they had passed the pyre, Alfric leaped out, thrusting his blade upward, catching one of the mercenaries in the shoulder. He twirled before slicing through the man's stomach. Alfric dove out of the way of another's blow. He swung his sword, bringing it down upon his attacker's laser pistol and rammed his fist into the man's face before finishing him.

Tom gawked at the sight for several moments, mesmerized by Alfric's fluid movements.

"Come on!" yelled Alfric.

Shaking himself free of his wonderment, Tom jumped to his feet and tackled another mercenary. The two rolled across the ground until a log stopped them. The mercenary jabbed Tom with his elbow. Winded, he noticed his quarry go for his weapon. Tom reached for the pistol, grasping it in his sweaty palms, and the two struggled for the weapon, rolling over leaves and branches, feet kicking, while Tom punched the man in the jaw. Stunned, the mercenary swayed, allowing Tom a chance to seize his laser pistol. Tom backhanded the man before flinging him off. He sat on his knees, aimed, and fired. The mercenary crumpled to the ground.

As the fight raged on around him, Tom just stared at the corpse before him as he lowered his weapon, allowing it to dangle by his side. A light touch on his shoulder jerked him back to reality. Alfric looked down at him.

"I never..."

"You did well," said Alfric. "It was either him or you. Come. Rynah is waiting for us."

Tom holstered his weapon and rose to his feet, following Alfric as he ran to the pile of brush. Alfric stuck the steel blade of his sword against a rock, producing sparks, which landed upon the dried foliage, transforming the pyre into licking flames that reached out to consume everything within their wake. Gigantic clouds of smoke billowed upward into the sky, alerting any, and all, to their presence.

A blast of laser fire singed the tree next to them as more mercenaries emerged from the trees; Alfric and Tom fled.

Rynah peeked through the branches of the bush she, Usef, and Solon hid behind. Metal forks clinked against tin cans as the mercenaries stuffed their mouths with slimy, pungent food that resembled excrement more than anything edible—such was the nature of rations on space vessels. The clinking forks made her stomach growl (considering she, and the others, had not eaten since breakfast the day before) despite the disgust she felt at the sight of their meal. Some men strolled through camp with their shirts off, revealing their broad shoulders and well-developed chest muscles. Rynah shrank back down on the ground.

"There's at least 20 of them," she whispered. "Usef, you'll go that way. Solon, you'll go the other way."

The two men nodded in affirmation.

"Hey, what's that?" shouted one of the mercenaries as he pointed to a plume of smoke in the distance.

"Let's go," said the leader, grabbing his gun belt and tying it across his waist. He darted through the trees, with the others close behind. Only four remained to guard the ships.

Rynah motioned for the others to move.

Solon scrambled over the brush to where she had instructed him to go. With great stealth, and in the manner Alfric had once taught him, he crawled over dead leaves and an upturned root, inching his way through the undergrowth until he had come upon one of the guards. Solon paused, waiting.

He watched as Usef's face appeared across from him. They locked eyes a moment, neither moving. One of the mercenaries paced in front of Usef, blocking his face for only a moment. A soft breeze prickled Solon's skin, causing goosebumps to form as he waited for Rynah's signal.

A whistle echoed in the air.

Solon sprang from his position at the exact time that Rynah and Usef did. Each pounced on a guard, pinning them to the ground. Remembering Alfric's lessons, Solon seized his opponent's arm until he popped the shoulder out of its socket. The man screamed. Ignoring it, Solon punched him in the throat and the mercenary clawed at his windpipe, gagging, until he ceased moving.

Solon looked up. Usef had already subdued his opponent. Rynah remained locked in battle with hers. The fourth approached her from behind.

"Usef!" Solon dove on the ground, snatching an abandoned laser pistol, and tossed it to Usef, who caught it, aimed, and fired. The fourth mercenary dropped to the black dirt. Together, Solon and Usef watched as Rynah wrenched her opponent's arm behind him, before bashing his face into a nearby tree.

Without warning, a fifth guard they hadn't seen burst from the trees and charged Rynah, dagger held high. Rynah somersaulted on the ground, avoiding the blow. At the same instant, Usef ran for her. Shielding Rynah from the enraged man, he fired two laser blasts. The mercenary stopped as two burning holes filled his chest; taking one last glance at them, he collapsed.

"Don't say I never do anything for you," Usef said, smiling.

Rynah grinned as that same attraction she had felt for him earlier rose up. Her eyes jerked to the ships. She stood up, her mouth hanging open as dismay filled her face. "We can't use these."

"Why?" asked Usef."

"Look," said Rynah, pointing. "They are one-man fighters. Only one person will fit in each of those ships. Tom and I are the only pilots here besides you."

Usef frowned. He jumped on the side of one of the vessels, clinging to the rungs, and hauled himself up so that he could look inside the cockpit. Rynah had been correct: only one person would fit. As Usef studied the small interior, he realized that they would never be able to fit two to a ship no matter how they tried. He dropped back to the ground. "What do we do? Alfric and Tom will be here soon."

Cursing, Rynah kicked the ground. *All of this planning for nothing,* she raged in her mind. She slammed her foot into a nearby sack, sending small round balls flying.

"Look out!" yelled Usef as he dove for the ground. Solon and Rynah did the same. When nothing happened, they glanced up.

"Damn it all," said Rynah, as she realized that she had just kicked a sack full of handheld explosive devices. "How could I be so stupid?"

Solon picked one up. He held it close as he studied it, having never seen one before.

"Careful," warned Usef.

"What is it?" asked Solon.

"Something that could have killed us all," said Usef.

Rynah grabbed one of the devices. Staring at it, she glanced at the nearby ships; an idea formed in her mind. "If we can't leave, I think they shouldn't either."

"What are you… oh," said Usef as he understood her meaning.

Rynah handed each of them a bag full of explosives. "Press this to stick it to the side of the ship," she said, showing Solon how the device worked, "and this to arm it. These are frequency activated. We'll wait until they camp for the night."

Solon took the sack of explosives, still uncertain as to why Rynah and Usef handled them with care, and a sense of fear, but trusted her judgment.

"How will you detonate them?" asked Usef.

Rynah held up her earpiece that she had used to talk with Solaris.

They went to work. Each of them took a section of the camp, placing the explosive devices on the sides of the ships where none would spot them. Within minutes, they had finished.

"We need to find Alfric and Tom," said Solon.

"Agreed," said Rynah.

They ran away from the mercenaries' camp and into the temporary safety of the trees. Rynah hoped they'd find Alfric and Tom before the others returned.

Tom and Alfric careened through the forest, jumping over hollowed, fallen trees that had rotted and holes in the ground as they fled; heavy footsteps crashed behind them. Crushing leaves and snapping branches told them that their pursuers closed in. Gasping for air, Tom looked around for an escape route. Only a small ravine caught his attention.

"Alfric!" Tom yelled, pointing at it.

Alfric nodded his head and veered towards it. He swiped a branch out of his way. One of the mercenaries attacked him from the side. With fluid movements, he dodged the attack before striking the man in the back with his sword. He continued to the ravine.

Tom pushed himself hard. His lungs burned for oxygen, but his quick movements denied them that. *Almost there*, he told himself. Gasping, he placed one foot in front of the other, determined not to quit. After one final sprint, both he and Alfric reached the small cliff with vines, the color of asparagus, dangling from the top as tree roots protruded from the hardened and red-tinted rock.

"Maybe this wasn't such a good idea," said Tom as he studied what he had thought would provide an escape route.

"Too late for that," said Alfric, seizing a vine. He tugged it, making certain it held. "Here," he shoved one into Tom's hands.

Tom took the vine, not liking where this idea led. "You can't be serious."

A laser blast struck the rock next to him, leaving a blackened mark.

"On second thought," said Tom, "race you to the top."

He grasped the vine tight in his hands and heaved himself upward as he placed his feet on the side of the cliff, using all the strength his arms held, and propelled himself upward. Tom glanced at Alfric, who had already scaled halfway up. Not wanting to be outdone, he climbed faster. Sweating and puffing by the time he reached the top of the cliff, he gave one final push. Alfric snatched his hand and pulled him the rest of the way.

Infuriated, the mercenaries at the bottom fired at them, shouting insults. One blast hit the ground by Tom's foot, forcing him to jump backward. Weightlessness took hold as the ground left him and he tumbled backward down a hill, rolling uncontrollably. The spinning ceased. Lying motionless, Tom regained his equilibrium before sitting up.

"Tom!" Alfric charged down the hill after him. "Tom!"

Shaking his head, Tom rose his feet, but his legs turned to rubber, instead of supporting his weight.

"Are you all right?" asked Alfric.

"I think so," mumbled Tom, swaying.

"Let's go." Alfric heaved Tom onto his shoulders and darted through

the woods, dodging dangling limbs and the snares of the rugged underbrush. His swift movements never faltered. The crack of a single laser
blast stopped him. Looking up into the sky, Alfric saw a flash of light
in the clear sky and recognized it as coming only from Rynah, knowing
that mercenaries would not waste their time firing straight into the air.
Changing course, he headed for it with Tom in tow.

"Do you think they got the message?" asked Usef as he, Rynah,
and Solon ran.

"I hope so," replied Rynah, her breaths coming in sharp gasps.

They hurried through the trees, hoping to catch up with Tom
and Alfric before the mercenaries caught them.

"Rynah?" came Solaris' voice, through Rynah's earpiece.

Rynah stopped. She put the earpiece back in her ear. "Solaris?
You left us!"

"I had to."

"Why?"

"No time for that. I am entering the upper atmosphere of the
planet right now. I need you all to be ready to board when I land."

"Where shall we meet you?"

"See that open space just over that next rise?"

"Yes."

"Go straight there."

"Change of plans," Rynah told the others and took off for Solaris' coordinates. As she ran, she fired another blast from her pistol
into the air. She knew that the mercenaries would see it, but she
hoped her friends would too, which they did.

Scraggly branches tore at their clothing as they charged through
the forest. A loud rip sounded as a branch tore Solon's shirt. Ignoring it, he continued his pace, not wanting to fall behind, crunching
leaves echoing around them. Rynah knew they had been found. Laser blasts pelted the trees around her, sending bits of bark into her
face. Shielding herself, she aimed and fired.

More laser fire bombarded them. Usef turned, running backwards; while he held both his weapon high, he released his own merciless onslaught of laser blasts before whipping back around and continuing the trek to the rendezvous point. Putting all of their reserve energy into their legs, the three sprinted though the tree line until they came to a small clearing. They stopped. In front of them was a cliff with a sharp drop of several hundred feet.

"Solaris!" yelled Rynah.

Trampling boots, as more dead brush crunched behind them, alerted her to another's presence. Rynah, Usef, and Solon whirled around to face their new foe. Closer the pounding came until—out popped Alfric and Tom. Relieved, Rynah relaxed.

"They're right behind us!" yelled Alfric.

Rynah raised her weapon with Usef beside her. Solon stood with his knife raised, while Tom and Alfric took positions by his side; sweat poured down their temples as they waited.

The mercenaries sprang from the foliage. "Well," said their leader, "what do we have here? You are an interesting quintet."

No response.

"I hope you enjoyed your little game because it ends here."

The thunder of engines ricocheted off the rock walls around them, whipping Rynah's flowing, emerald hair into her face as the blast of Solaris' propulsion systems reached them.

"Down!" Solaris yelled into Rynah's earpiece.

"Down!" Rynah reiterated the message, hugging the hard ground.

The others followed her movements, dropping on all fours, leaving the mercenaries to mock them.

"What's this?" scoffed the leader.

Solaris appeared over the cliff wall, guns bared. A hailstorm of laser fire escaped her cannons, pummeling the earth where their enemies stood as the mercenaries tried to escape, heading back to their ships. Solaris turned around, exposing her opened hatch to them.

Rynah leapt to her feet. "Come on!"

She backed up a few feet, steeling herself for the jump. Charging, Rynah ran, leapt from the edge of the cliff, and landed on the open ramp of the ship. One by one, the others did the same until all of them had boarded Solaris. Rynah punched the button to close the hatch before running to the command center with the others in tow.

"Nice to see you again, Solaris," she said as she sat in the pilot's seat and put the helmet on her head.

The mercenaries have left the ground in their ships, said Solaris, telepathically to Rynah.

Wait until they are in the upper atmosphere. I want them to chase us for a while.

Rynah steered Solaris into the edges of space. She wanted to lead the mercenaries to where she could watch them die.

Rynah?

On my mark, set your transmitters to frequency 650-Rir-1.

Solaris set the frequency, awaiting Rynah's command.

A cannon blast exploded just off the bow of the ship, rocking them.

"Rynah," said Usef, "whatever you're going to do, do it now."

Rynah ignored him. She steered the ship before turning around so that she could face the mercenaries' armada. "I wish to speak to your captain," she said over the comm.

Static filled the air until a voice said, "So, you wish to turn yourself in?"

"Just answer me this. How much did Klanor pay you for my death?"

"Nearly 5,000 scillions."

"A pittance," said Rynah as she waited for the last mercenary ship to appear.

"Why? You wish to double the offer? I am willing to negotiate."

"Negotiate this," said Rynah. *Now, Solaris!*

Solaris transmitted the frequency that Rynah had instructed her to. Bursts of fire erupted from the ships before them in a cascading action until every vessel had been reduced to smoldering, desultory chunks of machinery that filled the void before them. Rynah watched with an expression that could freeze steel. Alfric placed his calloused hand on her shoulder. He said nothing as no words were needed; Rynah understood his unspoken message.

Solaris, continue the search for Brie.

Rynah tore off the helmet. "Tom, you and Usef monitor the comm for now."

She jogged down the steps, hurrying through the dim corridors, seeking solitude. Once alone, Rynah slumped in a dark corner, hoping that its darkness would conceal her from the others. Huddled like a frightened child, she cried. All of the emotions, all of the regrets that she had kept locked away, deep within, poured forth in her salty tears, welcoming their release. The fires and rubble of the destroyed mercenary ships from moments before played over and over in her mind, mingling with memories of Lanyr's last hours and the family that she had almost abandoned in order to secure her own safety: small knives that stabbed her heart.

Rynah had wanted the mercenaries to be punished for agreeing to Klanor's request, for trying to kill her and her crewmates, but it only made the pain worsen, forcing her to cower in a corner, reminding her of the instances when Brie had done the same, and she had scolded her for it. Brie, how Rynah had envied the girl's innocence; as thoughts of her mistreatment of Brie flared up, Rynah wept even more. She wished she felt strong, strong enough to stop Klanor, strong enough to find the crystals, strong enough to rescue Brie, and strong enough to allow Usef the chance to offer her his friendship. So Rynah remained, huddled in the icy darkness with only her tears for comfort, but she wasn't alone.

Someone had seen her moment of anguish. She wished that she could comfort Rynah, wrap a comforting arm around her shoulders, but Solaris had no arms. She possessed nothing that would take away Rynah's heartache, except the decency to allow her friend a chance to cry in peace.

Chapter 26
MESSAGE IN SPACE

dit, dit, dit, dah, dah, dah, dit, dit, dit

Tre's snores vibrated his glass of water; little ripples formed as he slept by his computer console. Hours before, he had leaned back in his chair, propping his feet upon his warped desk as he watched the communication lines for anything out of the ordinary. His eyelids had grown heavy, and before he knew it, he had fallen asleep; a small stream of spittle escaped from his chapped lips. Another series of snores spilled from his wide open mouth.

dit, dit, dit, dah, dah, dah, dit, dit, dit

An eyelid cracked open. Shifting, Tre settled in for another long nap.

dit, dit, dit, dah, dah, dah, dit, dit, dit

Both his eyes popped open. This time, he knew he had heard

something. Yawning, he stretched his arms, sitting up, while glancing at the screen, tapping the flashing icon.

dit, dit, dit, dah, dah, dah, dit, dit, dit

Now, fully alert, Tre studied the series of sounds that repeated on his holoscreen. It resembled nothing that any of the Twelve Sectors used, but its tone and persistence told him that it had been transmitted on purpose. He typed in a series of commands to trace the origin of the signal. *Bingo*. He had found Klanor's armada. Knowing that Rynah would want to know this information, Tre opened up a comm message and hailed Solaris.

Having finished shedding regretful tears, Rynah stormed through the interior of Solaris on her way to her bunk, emotions coiled in thoughts roiling through her mind as sorrow turned to anger. She paused before her grandfather's picture, which still hung in the center of the ship. She studied his wry smile and the twinkling eyes that betrayed that he held a secret, one she wished she knew.

"What didn't you tell me?" she demanded of the portrait.

Her grandfather's portrait did not answer, nor did she expect it to. A part of Rynah wanted to smack that smirk off him. He knew about the crystals, more than he had ever let on. He knew a secret about her. He had created Solaris and never told anyone, and all with the purpose of helping Rynah.

Again, thoughts of the mercenaries and how merciless she had been while she watched them die reeled through her. Never had Rynah done such a thing, nor had she thought it was within her capability to be so callous.

"What is wrong with me?" she whispered, more to herself.

"For starters," said Solaris, "your refusal to let things go."

"Solaris, is there ever a time when you do not sneak up on people?"

"Sneaking up on others would be a difficult task for me, considering I have no feet."

Rynah slumped against the wall, releasing a heavy sigh. "I'm not in the mood."

"Perhaps not," said Solaris. "How did you feel when the mercenaries died?"

"They would have killed us all. You know that."

"Granted, but that was not the question I had asked."

Rynah grunted, annoyed at Solaris' curtness. Sometimes she seemed more human than machine. "I felt nothing."

"Nothing?"

"I don't know. I... I can't explain it. I wanted to escape and I wanted all of us to get away, but I wanted them to pay."

"Pay for what?"

"Klanor left them there to get me. He knew I would go there. How did he know that?"

"Maybe he knows you better than you know yourself," said Solaris. "You're still angry at what he did to you, but don't let that anger drive you to a place from which there is no escape."

"What are you talking about?"

"You know."

Rynah glanced at Marlow's portrait again. "What did he know?"

"Much."

Rynah snorted as she received another vague answer from Solaris. "Why did my grandfather create you? There were already dozens of computer systems he could have used to facilitate this ship, yet he created you. Why?"

"Marlow's reasons for doing anything were his own, and he took his secrets to the grave."

Rynah released another exasperated sigh. "What aren't you telling me?"

No answer.

"Solaris?" Rynah's insistent tone reverberated off the steel walls of the ship. "It isn't time."

"Time for what? Solaris, please."

"You must do something for me, Rynah," said Solaris, changing the subject.

"What?"

"Let go of your anger."

"My anger?"

"I don't ever want to see that look upon your face again."

Rynah glanced at her muddy boots, ashamed of what she had done and wishing that she could take it back. "What is wrong with me, Solaris? I am so full of anger and I don't know how to not feel loathing for what Klanor did. He betrayed me. I loved him and he betrayed me!

"I should have listened to my grandfather when he first warned me about the crystal in the geo-lab. If I had... but I hated him for what he had done and what his actions had done to us. But if I had listened to him, instead of..."

"Abandoning him," finished Solaris. She remembered when Marlow had been released from the psychiatric institution, deemed fit to return home, but still monitored by the authorities; his first act was to contact Rynah, but she had refused his calls. Solaris remembered the wounded look on his face and how much Rynah's refusal had torn his heart. That was when Marlow had locked himself in his workshop with Solaris as his only friend, but each day, he called Rynah, and each day, he received the same result: no answer.

Tears rolled down Rynah's cheeks. "I should have just answered his calls. One is all it would have taken. If I had..."

Pity filled Solaris. Once, she had been angry with Rynah, detesting the fact that Rynah had hurt her friend, but then she met Brie, a person with the capacity to forgive, and as she listened to Rynah, all she felt was sympathy for another friend.

"He loved you, Rynah," consoled Solaris, "and he never gave up on you."

Rynah stared at a dimple on the wall, not seeing it, and not hearing Solaris' words.

"You cannot hold onto your regrets. They are a poison that fill one's heart with anger, with darkness. You must let it go before it controls you, before you become the very thing that you despise."

"You've been spending too much time with Solon," said Rynah, her hollow voice just above a whisper.

"Maybe a little."

"Will you help me?"

"Of course, I will."

"Because my grandfather programmed you to?"

"No," said Solaris, "because I want to."

Suddenly feeling exhausted, Rynah longed for her lumpy bunk. "I think I'll go get some rest."

"I'll wake you if anything…" Solaris cut off.

"Solaris?"

"I have an urgent message from Tre," said Solaris. She routed it to a local computer console.

"Rynah?" His face filled the small screen.

"Yes," said Rynah, doing her best to control her breaking voice, so as not to betray the fact that she had been crying.

"Did you find Klanor?"

"It was a trap."

"Sorry to hear that, but I think I know where he is. There is this strange series of notes playing on the communication waves." Tre played the same message he had retrieved an hour before: *dit, dit, dit, dah, dah, dah, dit, dit, dit.* "It doesn't match anything the Twelve Sectors use. My guess is that it is from your friend."

"Where did it come from?" demanded Rynah.

"Here." Tre sent her a list of coordinates. "And, Rynah, he is there."

Rynah studied the screen a moment; her eyes narrowed. "How long ago was it sent?"

"Maybe a few days, hard to say. I'm not sure how long he will stay there, but my guess is that he probably thinks that his trap worked."

"It nearly did," said Rynah. "Keep tabs on him. If anything changes, let me know." She turned off the comm link. "Solaris, summon the others. It's time to bring Brie home."

Chapter 27
ESCAPE

Brie lay on her stiff cot, waiting for the man who served her meals to arrive. She had bided her time for over a week since sending the signal, having no indication that Rynah and the others had received it, nor would she ever know; she just hoped that a week was long enough for them to get to her. As the days passed, Brie knew that she had to make her escape, now or not at all. Stein and Klanor kept constant watch on her, Stein especially, but she had noticed a bit of tension, a rift, forming between them. She acted subdued, even feigning depression and hopelessness, all of which made Stein smile. Klanor's jeers seemed half-hearted, as his mind lay elsewhere. He hadn't been the same since she had tapped into his memories of Rynah.

She needed to get out of there. She didn't know where she would go, but she had watched Tom fly Solaris many times and had some idea of how to control a ship, a risk she was willing to take, determined to attempt freedom over waiting to die a prisoner. Now was the perfect time as the crew performed a systems maintenance check, meaning that not all of the security cameras would be operational.

The clank of the door down the hall echoed through the silent area of the ship. Brie scrambled from her bed to the door, kneeling by the opening, the width of a manila envelope, on its bottom, which the guard used to push the tin tray of stale food through. Willing her nerves to calm themselves, Brie waited in bated anticipation. *This is it.* She hoped her plan worked.

The latch on the small flap clicked. Readying herself, Brie waited.

Thwap! The guard raised the flap and shoved the tray through it. Brie seized the man's wrist and yanked until his head struck the door. She heaved again, bashing his head against it a second time, making certain he had been knocked unconscious. Hands shaking, Brie let go. The guard didn't move. Brie went to her bunk and pulled out one of the rods that she had worked loose and snatched a thin piece of clear plastic that she had hidden in the lining of her mattress. Rushing back to the opening, Brie placed the plastic film over the man's index finger, acquiring an impression of his print, wrapping mattress stuffing around the tip of the rod and attaching the plastic to it.

"This better work," she said to herself as she fed the pole through the small opening and toward the keypad to her cell. She had seen this done in movies and felt it worth a try. In any case, though she hoped she wouldn't have to, as the thought disgusted her, she'd cut the man's finger off, if necessary.

Straining her neck so she could see, Brie guided the pole to the keypad, flopping the end against it. Its violent beeps filled the hall, making her cringe; she hoped no one heard it. Brie tried again, doing her best to maintain control of the pole as she placed the wad of stuffing with the plastic near the holopad and rolled it across the scanner. The lock to her cell clicked.

Brie dropped the pole and opened the door. She dragged the guard's body into her cell and stripped him of his clothing, putting them on herself. Brie bunched her brown hair under his hat and snatched his keycard as she closed the door to her cell, vowing to never set foot in there again.

Brie scanned the ceiling and found the ventilation shaft. Stretching, she opened it. She placed her arms on a protruding pipe and her feet in the corner, using all of her strength to heave herself upward and into the square ducting. Once inside, she managed to turn around and shut the crate.

She pulled out the map she had made of the ship. Rechecking where things were, Brie crawled forward to the main hallway. Chilled air washed over her, but despite its temperature, beads of sweat formed on her forehead, running down her face. She wiped her eyes, but it did little good.

She came to a fork in the shaft. Rechecking her map, Brie turned right. Using her knees and elbows to push her forward, she crept through the icy metal of the ventilation and the air that whistled around her as the circulation system pumped it through. Voices trickled in from the grates she passed. Ignoring them, Brie prayed that none would hear her, as the slightest sound would be her undoing.

"You promised me that you could bring my family back!"

Stein's voice stopped Brie. Fear rose within her, clenching her throat shut. As her heart raced from the very thought of being in his presence again, Brie breathed in slow, steady breaths to calm herself. *They don't know you're here*, she told herself. She maneuvered so that she could peek through the vent grate. Her heart stopped. Without even realizing it, Brie had followed the direct path to Klanor's private quarters, recognizing the carpeting and the desk in its center situated on a hexagonal rug.

Stein stood in the center of the room with Klanor before him. Irate expressions filled the faces of both men, though each tried to conceal them.

"I said I would try," answered Klanor, "but I never guaranteed that it could be done."

"That is not how you made it sound the day you recruited me." Stein's icy tone chilled Brie to the core.

"You heard what you wanted to hear," said Klanor, "but I told you that there is much about the crystals that I have yet to learn."

"With all of the time you have spent studying that book, you should have discovered something by now."

"The ancient text is not so easy to understand."

Stein's features betrayed an underlying fury at not having his wish fulfilled. "What have you learned thus far?"

"We need six crystals, this you know, in order to complete the weapon."

"But we have the weapon aboard this ship."

"A recreation. I discovered other texts that talked about how one could make the copy of it, but the device itself lies elsewhere, hidden long ago."

Stein remained silent, waiting for Klanor to continue.

"The weapon itself appears to be located here, but it is more than a weapon. It's supposed to have the ability to rewrite time."

"But?"

"There seems to be something missing from the text." Klanor closed the volume on his desk, hiding the ragged edge of a page that had been torn out in the back of the book. Stein hadn't noticed it, but Brie did. An idea struck her.

"What is missing?" asked Stein.

"That is what I need to learn before we attempt to bring your family back."

Stein said nothing at first. Brie noticed him clench his fists in an effort to control himself. "Did you ever have any intention of bringing them back?"

"Why would you ask such a thing? I made a promise."

"Like the one you had made to Rynah?" Stein clamped his mouth shut, having blurted out what he had wanted to keep silent.

"Rynah was a means to an end," Klanor's voice tightened, betraying him.

Brie found her mind pushed back to the time she had managed to enter Klanor's thoughts. His true feelings for her still boiled just beneath the surface. She recognized the tone in his voice. Klanor still loved her, though he refused to admit it, even to himself.

"And speaking of Rynah," continued Klanor, "I received this communication from the mercenaries on Virdyr."

Klanor held up a holorecorder and played back a message sent by the mercenary in charge.

They arrived just like you said they would, the woman with the strange companions. They are proving most difficult to deal with. If you wish them dead, the bounty has doubled.

"I don't remember ordering anyone's execution," said Klanor.

Stein looked Klanor in the eyes, his face unreadable. "I thought it was implied. She has been a nuisance from the beginning."

"My orders were specific."

"You had asked me to deal with them."

"I had ordered you to have them captured and taken prisoner, not killed! At no time did I order their deaths. What use would their deaths be to us?" Klanor dumped the holorecorder on his desk, his jaw clenching as he tried to contain the emotions reeling within him.

"It would free us from their interference," snapped Stein.

"And then what? In case you haven't noticed, the others that travel with Rynah are not from any of the Twelve Sectors. How are we to learn of their home world if they are dead?"

"Does it matter?"

"There could be some value in it. The problem with you, Stein, is you fail to see the value in anything, except your own desires."

Stein's face tightened. "Earth," he said, "they are from a planet called Earth in what some call the 13th sector."

"You've been interrogating out prisoner."

"I thought it wise."

"Without my permission!"

"I am your second in command," said Stein, "it is my duty to…"

"To follow my orders! The mercenaries, questioning the girl, how often have you gone behind my back, Stein?"

"I have only ever served you."

"Have you?"

"How many chances have you had to eliminate Rynah, but failed to do so? How often have you allowed your personal feelings get in the way? I remember back on Lanyr, you seemed to have hesitated when the time came to steal the crystal. Now why is that, I wonder?"

"How dare you…"

"It appears that I am not the only one letting my personal feelings get in the way. So, I ask you again, will these crystals bring back what was stolen from me, or did you ever intend to hold to that promise?"

Klanor remained silent.

"I thought so," whispered Stein.

"I will do my best to return your family to you. It just might take some time."

Stein said nothing, steeling his face so that an impassive mask concealed his anger and his deepest thoughts.

"You may go," said Klanor. "And, Stein," he added, stopping Stein at the door, "if Rynah is to die, I will be the one to do it. Understand?"

"Yes, sir," replied Stein.

The intercom in Klanor's room beeped.

"What?" said Klanor as he answered it.

"I'm sorry to disturb you, sir," said a shaky voice, "but the guard in the detention center has not reported in."

"Well, contact him on his radio. Damn fool probably fell asleep."

"He is not answering, sir."

"Send someone down there, then."

"We have, sir, but they did not find him."

"And the prisoner?"

"Her cell is still locked."

"I'm coming down." Klanor swept towards the door, with Stein right behind him.

Once the room had emptied, Brie kicked the ventilation grate open and jumped out. Her bare feet pattered as she stepped on the varnished table. She scrambled off it and ran for the book that Klanor had left on his desk, rifling through it, making certain it was the one she wanted. Its bulky size made carrying it difficult, forcing her to search the room for a backpack she could use.

Voices sounded outside the door, laughing and joking with one another. Brie froze. Holding her breath, she waited for them to pass before continuing. She flung open a closet door. Rummaging through it, Brie started cursing, wondering how she would carry the book. Something caught on her foot. Almost tripping when she tried to move away, Brie realized that it was a strap belonging to a pack. She freed her foot and ripped the bag out of the closet. Dumping the contents on the floor, she stuffed the ancient book in it, tying it shut.

She paused. Underneath the book was Alfric's pendant. She thought she had lost it the day Klanor had captured her. *Why would he keep it?* Knowing she could waste no more time, Brie grabbed it and put it around her neck before hitching the bag onto her shoulders.

Brie ran for the ventilation shaft. Voices approached the door again. Listening, she realized that they headed straight for the room. Desperate, she flung herself inside and pulled the grate shut just as the door opened and Klanor stalked in. Not wanting to get caught, Brie hurried away to the bend in the shaft.

Rynah set the coordinates into Solaris' computer. "You know what to do."

"Yes," said Solaris. "Though I do not like the artwork you had put on my hull."

Rynah laughed. "Deal with it. If we succeed, I'll see to it that it's removed."

"I hope so," said Solaris, as she entered the area where Klanor's armada was.

"Just remember the plan," said Rynah.

"I know it by heart."

Rynah headed for the steps.

"Rynah," said Solaris with a touch of concern, "be careful."

"You too."

Rynah jogged down the steps and ran for the cargo area where she found the others. Tom and Alfric had already dressed themselves in uniforms that they had stolen from previous encounters with Klanor's men. Solon and Usef wore pressurized suits and were ready to open the door when she gave them the signal.

"All right," said Rynah, as she dressed in a pressurized suit, "you know the plan."

They all nodded.

"Tom, Alfric, I'm counting on you to find her. Remember where the lockers are because the suits will be there and you will need them."

"We will not fail," said Alfric. "On my honor, or may I never enter Valhalla."

Rynah smiled, knowing that that was the Viking's way of making a promise and that he would keep his word. Rescuing Brie was important to him, more so than the others because he felt a responsibility towards her.

"We are approaching," said Solaris.

Rynah silenced everyone.

"State your business," said someone over the radio. Solaris played the message over the ship's intercom so that the others could listen.

"Transport," said Usef.

"Transporting what?"

"New recruits," answered Usef.

"How many?"

"Two."

"Two?" The voice on the other end sounded incredulous.

"Yes," replied Usef, "I have instructions to bring them here. I can turn back, but I'd rather not explain to my superiors why I disobeyed orders. Unless you are willing to take that responsibility."

"Report to docking bay 16."

"Acknowledged."

Solaris steered to where she had been instructed to go.

"So far, so good," said Usef.

"We've only just begun," Rynah reminded him. "All of you get ready. Tom, Alfric, you won't have much time to find Brie. So make the best of it."

Solaris aligned herself with the docking station, allowing it to attach to her hull, not liking the thumps that sounded as the arm of the station attached to her and pressurized the tube. She opened her hatch. Alfric and Tom stood ready to disembark, while the others hid.

"Orders?" said an officer, standing in the entrance.

Tom handed him the papers; forged ones that Solaris had created that morning.

The officer looked them over before handing them back. "Report to section eight."

Tom and Alfric walked off, while Solaris closed her hatch and detached from the docking station of the ship. "They are on board."

"Right," said Rynah. "Now the hard part begins."

Solaris maneuvered her way through the armada and to the central part of the biggest ship, the one Klanor was on. She lined up with it, holding steady. "You only have minutes until their sensors detect us."

"Understood." Rynah looked at Usef and Solon. "Ready?"

None of them answered.

She punched the emergency button on the hatch and opened it. Each of them shot out of the ship with a bag of explosives in their hands and their security lines trailing behind. They soared past miniscule clusters of ships (small vessels, their primary function to grow food used by the armada) and bits of trash ejected from the ship's garbage chutes, but the main ship was the target. Klanor's primary vessel resembled a small space station, with bright lights emanating from its windows; landing docks lined the sides with cannons on the bow and aft of the ship, and laser weapons on both its knobby wings. Using their thrusters, Rynah, Usef, and Solon, who had received a crash course on how to use his spacesuit's thrusters only two hours before, guided themselves to different sections of the main vessel's exterior.

Solon hit the hull first, smashing into it with a grunt. He grabbed hold of the rungs and caught his breath, taking the time to look around at the stars and the empty space around him, filled only by a sea of space vessels. Nausea overtook him.

"Don't look at the stars," warned Rynah.

Solon turned back to the metal he clung to. As his stomach settled, he opened his bag and pulled out an explosive device. Adhering to Rynah's earlier instructions, he armed it, and placed the triangular thing on the ship. Once done, Solon crawled to the side and set another charge. He continued his methodical movements until his bag had emptied.

"Done," he said.

"Good," said Rynah. "Head back to Solaris."

She watched as Solon kicked off Klanor's vessel and used his thrusters and safety line to steer himself back to the safety of Solaris. She set another charge. Rynah glanced at Usef. "How are you doing?"

"Almost there."

Rynah set the last charge. Usef had finished as well. Together, they used their safety lines and thrusters to guide themselves back to Solaris; each reached her at the same time, clinging to the rungs on the side.

"Here," Usef said, holding his hand out to her.

Rynah took it and allowed him to pull her inside. "Solaris, we're back aboard."

Solaris flew away from the ship and to the meeting point.

Klanor entered his chambers and stopped when he noticed the closet contents on the rug (something he knew he had not left there), and crossing to the ajar door, looked in, his eyes taking in every detail. A soft creak caught his notice. He whirled around, but realized that he was alone in the room, though his heightened senses alerted him that someone had been there. Wondering what the thief could have been after, much less how one managed to get in and out without being noticed, he scanned the room until his eyes fell upon the desk and the bare spot upon it. The book! Klanor tore through the room to where his prized possession (even though it rightfully belonged to Rynah, as it had been willed to her by Marlow) had once been.

"*Masgontha*," he cursed, slamming his fists upon the wooden desk before punching the intercom button. "Sound the alarm. We have a breach in security!"

A thump from the ventilation made him jerk his head. Klanor ran over to it, yanking the grate open, poking his head in and looked to his right. Nothing. He glanced to the left. Still nothing. Unsure if the thief had come in this way (but knowing he was long gone), Klanor closed the opening and stormed out of his quarters, determined to get his stolen property back.

Tom and Alfric shoved their way through the throng of people darting about in the confusion of the alarms, their helmets keeping any from being able to see their faces.

"This way," said Tom as he checked a schematic of the ship on a wall.

Alfric followed him. They hurried down a flight of steps and to the detention center. The door lay open with two guards in front of it.

"Halt," said one. "We need to see your authorization."

In response, Alfric pulled free the laser rifle Rynah had made him take, though he would have preferred his sword, and rammed it into the man's middle. With one swift strike, he clonked the guard on the head with it, rendering him unconscious. Tom flung himself on the second guard, forcing him to the floor, and the two rolled around until Tom kicked him in the face.

With the guards subdued, they ran into the detention area and to Brie's cell. "I don't understand," said Tom. "She should be here."

"She's escaped," said Alfric. "That is the reason for the alarms. Where would she go?"

Tom turned to a computer console in the room and tapped the screen, bringing up image after image. "There," he said, pointing to a map of the flight deck. "That is where they keep the other vessels. She must be going there. There is no other way off the ship."

"How quickly can we reach it?"

Tom checked the maps and found a short cut. "Follow me."

Brie hurried through the ventilation shaft, as best she could, but the cramped space made maneuvering a challenge. She pulled out her map and rechecked her position. Just a little bit farther. She shoved the map back into her pocket and scrambled though the metal tube, the piercing alarm informing her that she had little time.

Doing her best to ignore the screeching alarms, Brie moved through the shaft, bumping and thumping as she went. She found her exit. Peeking through the mesh grate, Brie made certain no one was around. She kicked it open and jumped out, closing the vent before running away, securing the bag around her shoulders, and racing for the elevator.

Guards ran for her. Frightened of being caught, Brie pulled her cap lower and darted around a corner until they had passed. None of them looked in her direction. Relieved, she continued her trek to the elevator, punching the button when she reached it. The doors opened, revealing a man already in there. Brie thought about running.

"What are you waiting for?" demanded the man. "Get in."

Brie stepped inside. She pulled her hat a bit lower over her face, hoping he wouldn't notice.

"Another drill?" asked the man.

Brie nodded, tugging her sleeves over her hands to hide her white skin.

"What's the matter?"

"Don't feel like talking." Sweat poured down Brie's back as her skin flushed, wishing the elevator would reach its target.

The man looked closer at her. Despite having the collar turned up, he noticed a speck of white. "Turn around."

Brie didn't move.

"I said turn around!"

Loosening one of the straps around her shoulder, Brie remembered what Alfric had taught her about fighting in close quarters. She spun around and rammed her bag into the man's face. Stunned, he crumpled over. Brie struck him on top of the head until he fell unconscious. Winded, she slung the bag back over her shoulder and took his weapon. The elevator doors slid open. Brie rushed out, using the butt of the laser gun to break the controls so no one could use it; sparks flew as the doors sealed shut.

Bombarded by the alarms, she hurried down the corridor, ignoring any she came upon. Most were too busy to notice her. She dashed around a corner and turned another until she came to the area where the engine lay. Frosted doors greeted her. Using the pass key she had swiped, she opened them.

Brie ran inside, firing at one of the guards that stood there. She whipped around and shot another.

"What are you…" said a technician as he approached her.

Remembering everything Alfric had taught her, she struck him in the throat, silencing him. Brie hurried over to where the power cells were kept and pointed her weapon at them.

"It's her!" yelled a voice.

"Listen to me!" shouted Brie, stunned at how forceful her voice sounded. "All of you leave this room, or I fire upon one of these crystals."

"Are you insane?" said one. "You'll blow up the ship and kill yourself in the process."

Brie remained silent.

"She won't do it," said another. "It's a bluff."

Brie armed the laser pistol. "Are you willing to bet on that? Unlike you, I have nothing to lose." The stern expression on her face stilled everyone in the room.

"Everyone out! Now!" ordered the engineer in charge.

When the room had emptied, Brie shot the locks to the door, sealing herself inside. She hurried back to one of the power cells. She put on an abandoned glove and ripped it out of its housing. The engines of the ship groaned before the sound faded away and the engines stopped. Pleased that she had stalled the ship, Brie wrapped the power cell in a protective cloth and shoved it into the bag.

Bang!

She turned around. Those outside attempted to break their way back in. Knowing she had little time, Brie ran to another ventilation grate, propping it open, and tossed her bag inside.

Bang!

Straining, she pulled herself in and closed the grate behind her, crawling as fast as she could through the vent, pushing the bag before her. Stinging pain gripped her hands and knees as she hurried to the other end, but she ignored the bruises that formed. Another grate stood before her. Peering through it, Brie noticed the sign on the wall and she knew where she was. The flight deck wasn't far.

She turned a bend as her arm gave out. Losing her balance, Brie slammed against another grate, popping it open and tumbling out. Pain gripped her as she plowed into the floor, her bag crashing beside her. Two guards in helmets stood before her. Brie jumped to her feet, ramming her bag into the face of one. She noticed her weapon lying on the floor. Brie dove for it and aimed at the other guard.

"Brie?" said the one she had struck, "it's me. It's Tom."

Shocked, Brie stood frozen as Tom took off his helmet, exposing his black, and sweat soaked, skin to her, a bruise forming on his cheek from where she had struck him.

"How?" asked Brie in disbelief.

"We got your message," said Tom, as Alfric removed his helmet.

"We need to move," said the Viking.

Relieved at seeing them again, Brie lowered her weapon and rushed for them, embracing them. "The ships are this way."

"We have a better way," said Tom, pulling her in a different direction.

Together, they raced down the corridor away from the flight deck, rounding a corner to an empty hallway. A door opened. Guards swarmed out of it, heading straight for them. Tom grabbed Brie and yanked her to the left down another hallway.

Gasping for air as their lungs burned, they charged down the corridor to a door marked "Storage Locker". Brie used her stolen passkey to open it. Alfric shoved them in. When the door shut behind them, he smashed the keypad. "This won't hold for long."

Tom rummaged through the locker. Rynah had told him that the suits would be there. Doors clanged as he opened and closed them.

"What are you looking for?" asked Brie.

"Suits! Spacesuits," replied Tom.

Brie hunted around the locker room. She didn't find anything. "Do you know exactly where they are?"

"No, but they're supposed to be here."

Brie rounded a corner. A red sign above a panel caught her attention. Taking a chance, she smashed it, forcing the panel to open and reveal a set of spacesuits. She found a similar one nearby. Doing the same, Brie exposed the suits, and their escape. "Tom!"

Tom ran to her, stopping when he saw the suits, and smiled. "Oh, I've missed you."

He snatched two suits and tossed one to Alfric. Once suited up, Brie turned to Tom. "Where's the exit?"

Tom scanned the schematic Rynah had given him, while pacing the room, until he found a faint red line marking an emergency exit. "Here!"

Brie and Alfric stared at it before securing the helmets to their suits. Clang!

The door to the locker room opened a few inches. Knowing they had little time, Tom tied them together with a tether line before placing his hand over the release valve. "Ready?" he asked.

Brie gave him thumbs up, while clutching her bag close to her, determined not to lose it.

Tom pulled the lever. The emergency exit door ripped open, thrusting them, and articles of clothing along with whole lockers, into the vacuum of space. Brie screamed from the force of the pressure change. Alfric's hand found hers and clung to it. Once calmed, she looked up at the outer hull of Klanor's ship, the very place she had been kept prisoner for far too long. She stared ahead.

In front of them was Solaris with her cargo hatch open wide, and three people in spacesuits stood there, waiting to catch them: Rynah, Solon, and one she didn't recognize. Elated, Brie's heart skipped several beats as Rynah stretched her hand out to her. Brie held hers out as well, clinging to Rynah's the moment they touched, while Usef and Solon grabbed Tom and Alfric, hauling their friends inside.

"Solaris, we have them!" yelled Rynah into her radio.

The hatch closed, sealing itself as the room repressurized. They each took off their helmets.

"I'm so glad to see you," Brie exclaimed, hugging Rynah and Solon.

"So are we," said Rynah, "but we haven't time for pleasantries right now. Solaris!"

The ship jerked as Solaris flew away from Klanor's main vessel and maneuvered through the armada.

Rynah ran to the command center, followed by the others, with Brie looking all around, remarking at how nothing had changed, glad to be back.

"Are they pursuing us?" asked Rynah.

"The doors to their flight deck have opened," replied Solaris.

"Are we far enough away?" asked Rynah.

"No."

"We'll have to chance it. Detonate the charges."

Solaris transmitted a code to each of the explosives that they had planted on the side of Klanor's ship. Fire erupted as a succession of explosions took place. Brie and the others watched, mesmerized, as an entire section of Klanor's main ship blew away, exposing the inside. Solaris lurched as the shockwave reached them; debris and metallic bits surged past them in a fiery inferno.

Solaris made the calculations for hyperspeed. As her engines increased power, she shot into space, disappearing with her passengers.

Chapter 28
A Bribe and a Reunion

Stein waited just outside the supply storage area for Gaden to exit. He had observed the man going in there on previous occasions, always leaving with a few rations. The door clicked. Out walked Gaden, his arms full of freeze dried meal packets, turning down the corridor.

"Stealing from our supply stores," said Stein, his icy voice stopping Gaden.

Gaden faced him and dropped the meal packets; they clomped on the floor, covering his feet.

"An offense punishable by hanging in the old days. Now, we just eject you into space. Of course, I would have done that the moment you came aboard this ship."

"Stein, sir, I... I... didn't think..."

"You didn't think that I knew about your little habit of helping yourself to our supplies."

"I don't take much."

"Not enough to get noticed," said Stein, inching closer.

"What are you going to do?"

"Give you a chance to redeem yourself," Stein said. "You have, I'm sure, noticed how Klanor seems a bit reluctant to do away with our enemies. At times, it appears that he no longer wishes to continue our mission."

"What mission would that be?"

Ignoring Gaden's question, Stein continued. "Such reluctance has resulted in us suffering losses."

"You mean the girl's escape."

"One of many. This armada needs direction again, but my question for you is, what did Klanor promise you?"

"Nothing. To get me out of that lab."

"You hated it there?"

"I was a researcher's assistant. Unnoticed by all of them; even the security officers paid no attention to me."

Perfect, thought Stein, a man that no one notices or cares goes missing. "So, he promised you nothing? No monetary reward."

"No." The hatred in Gaden's voice told Stein all he needed to know.

"And where have you been since he allowed you on this ship?"

"Ship's maintenance," replied Gaden, with more loathing, "I am responsible for keeping the floors clean."

"He couldn't even give you an honorable position," said Stein, pretending to sympathize with Gaden. "What if I could promise you more wealth than you have ever seen and a chance to govern by my side?"

"How can you deliver on such a promise?"

"Never mind how," said Stein.

"But you serve Klanor."

"I feel that there is a change coming. Klanor is proving himself incapable of the responsibilities he has taken on, and what I want to know is, if there is a change in leadership, where do you want to be?"

"Sir?"

"Let me put it to you this way," said Stein, "if the ship were irreparably damaged and Klanor incapacitated, would you be one of those who stays by his side and go down with it, or on an escape pod?"

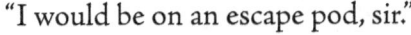

"I would be on an escape pod, sir."

"Good man," said Stein.

"What do you want me to do?"

"I have business off the ship," said Stein, "I want you to keep an eye on Klanor. Keep me informed of his movements and his moods. You will, of course, be well rewarded for this. For now, let's say that we ignore your visits to the supply area, and these meal packets, and I'll see to it that you are put in better accommodations. I hear the barracks area can be quite uncomfortable."

Gaden seemed pleased by Stein's offer. "How should I contact you?"

Stein tossed a small transmitter into Gaden's hands. "With this."

Stein left Gaden alone in the hallway, and not only did he keep silent about Gaden's visits to the supply area, but he had him transferred to a different area of the ship, where he had his own room and was given a new assignment in the command center, well away from ship's maintenance.

Everyone sat at the long table in the meeting area of the ship with a single lantern in its center providing light. A cake—at least that is what they called it, even though it looked like it had crawled out of a dumpster—sat next to the lantern. Brie eyed it, her stomach growling.

"Welcome back," said Tom as he raised his tin cup. "We kind of missed you around here."

"Thanks," said Brie. "I missed being here as well, and I have something you might all be interested in." Brie plopped her frayed bag on the table and pulled out the tattered book and crystal.

"Is that…" began Solon, staring at the crystal.

"No," said Brie, "this isn't one of the crystals we are searching for, but I heard it referred to as an energy crystal. It was in the heart of Klanor's ship and seemed to be a power source for it."

Rynah took the crystal, holding it to the light. "It is exactly as you thought."

"What is an energy crystal?" asked Solon.

"The crystals you have been searching for are energy crystals, in a way," replied Solaris. "But they are different from the one Brie brought us. This crystal is more like a battery. It starts the engines of a ship and keeps it running indefinitely by using the cosmic rays of the universe to stay powered."

"Cosmic rays?" asked Solon.

"Energy rays, if you will. They are everywhere and are produced from stars, infinite, and they can travel for an eternity. That crystal was designed to attract the cosmic rays and turn them into an energy source that could power a ship."

"Could it power something other than a ship?" asked Tom.

"Most definitely," replied Solaris.

"So you stole this," said Rynah, impressed.

"Yeah, well," Brie's face turned red, "I thought that if they needed it to keep their ship running, then me taking it would be similar to throwing a wrench in their system."

"Good thinking." Rynah handed the crystal back to her.

"Could I have it?" Tom asked.

Brie gave him the opaque crystal. "Sure."

Ecstatic, Tom took the crystal, knowing what he would do with it.

"And what about the book?" asked Alfric.

"Klanor says that this is the original copy of the ancient text," said Brie, "or about as close to the original as you can get. This is what he has been using to find the crystals."

Rynah opened the book, recognizing the scrawled lettering and characters of the ancient language, one she had studied as a child, courtesy of her grandfather. "How did you come by this?"

"Luck, mostly," Brie said.

Rynah turned the stained pages until she reached the front of the book and the inscription that marked it with its faded ink: *To my dearest Rynah.*

"This book is of importance to you," Alfric said, noting the delicate nature with which Rynah treated it.

"Of course it is," snapped Rynah. "It will undoubtedly contain information that is not in the data scans."

"That is not my meaning and you know it," said Alfric.

All eyes turned to Rynah. None of them had seen her act emotional over an object before. Scanning their querying faces, she knew she could no longer evade their questions. "This text was given to me by my grandfather."

"No way!" blurted out Tom, receiving a reproachful look from Alfric. "How did Klanor get it?"

"As you all already know we were… um… engaged."

They all leaned closer, except for Usef, who remained still, his face betraying mixed feelings.

"Sometime before he stole the crystal, Klanor must have stolen this book. It wouldn't have been difficult as we shared an apartment then." Her voice faltered. "I think I'll put this where it belongs. Solaris, when will we reach Sunlil?"

"About two days."

"See you all then," said Rynah as she hefted the torn book into her arms. Usef reached a comforting hand out to her. Rynah clasped it for a moment before disappearing around a corner.

"Maybe we shouldn't have brought up the past," said Brie.

"Yeah, really sorry about that," said Tom, his mind elsewhere. "Anyway, I got work to do, so I'll see you all later. Come on, Solon." Tom jumped from his seat and raced down the cramped corridor with Solon close behind.

"Where do you think they are off to?" asked Brie.

Alfric's grim face watched them. "Trouble."

Brie looked at Usef. "I don't think we've been properly introduced."

Usef turned away from the doorway he had been staring at for the past two minutes, remembering that he was not alone in the room. "Usef. My name is Usef."

"How did you…" began Brie.

"He has been most useful in repairing our vessel, and in rescuing you," said Alfric.

"Thank you," Brie said to Usef.

"You don't need to…"

"Yes, I do," interrupted Brie.

The lights flickered, growing dim before brightening again.

"Those fools," muttered Alfric as he jumped to his feet and stormed out of the room.

"Where are you going?" asked Brie.

"To make sure those two ingrates don't damage the ship."

Brie chuckled to herself, wondering what trouble Tom was getting into now with Solon as his accomplice. She glanced at Usef, who stared at the door that Rynah had gone through minutes before. "I know she seems a bit cold when you first meet her, but she is anything but."

"Wha… I'm not sure what you mean."

"I may have been stuck in a cell, but I still have eyes. And since we have never met until today, there are only two reasons why you are aboard this ship."

"You are most perceptive," said Usef. "I had a ship once. A crew that I was responsible for. Our ship was damaged and they died because no one would help me save them. When Rynah told me about you, I just…"

"Couldn't allow her to go through what you did," Brie finished. "Rynah has been through a lot, and what she needs most is a friend."

"Is that a warning?"

"An observation. You've heard, no doubt, that Rynah had gotten engaged right before her home planet was destroyed."

"Yes, she told me."

"What you don't know is that the man she was engaged to is the same man who is responsible for Lanyr's destruction."

Usef's eyes widened as Rynah's sullenness and distant nature made sense. She didn't just fear having her heart broken again, she blamed herself for Lanyr and for trusting the one responsible.

Brie yawned, realizing how tired she was and excused herself.

"What is the other reason?" Usef asked.

Brie gave him a quizzical look.

"You said that there were two reasons why I'm aboard this ship. What was the other?"

Brie gave a sly grin. "Solaris."

Usef chuckled under his breath after Brie had left. Everyone aboard the ship acted as though it had a personality; even Rynah had chastised him for neglecting Solaris' qualities. He had heard of pilots attributing characteristics to their vessels, but none of them had ever believed them to be living things. As Usef thought back to their time on the planet Virdyr, and how Solaris had appeared just in time to save them from the mercenaries, and how she had played a vital role in rescuing Brie, he began to wonder if there was some merit to the others' claims.

"Maybe there is something to this ship," he whispered to himself.

"You have no idea," quipped Solaris, who, being true to her nature, had eavesdropped on the entire conversation.

Tom and Solon burst into the storage room where he had been building his cybernetic life form.

"I must say that you two are acting like a couple of children during the *Festwyre* Celebration," said Solaris.

"You're excited to see it work, too. Admit it," Tom said.

"I have no comment on the matter," The eager tone in Solaris' voice betrayed her.

"Of course you don't," said Tom. "Okay, Solon, let's fire this baby up." He hurried over to the sitting robot and yanked the tarp off it, before standing back to admire his work: skin that looked lifelike and natural, and was also infused with nano-technology, violet eyes that matched Rynah's, long, flowing emerald hair that was also infused with nano-technology, and a face that could express even the deepest of emotions.

"What is it?" asked Solon.

"You got to admit that it looks pretty realistic," said Tom.

"Are you going to turn that thing on or not?" said Solon.

"Thing!" Solaris' insulted voice filled the chamber.

Solon shrunk back. "Well, it's not really you… yet."

No response.

"Solaris?"

"Gotcha," joked Solaris as she laughed, which surprised Tom because he had never heard a computer laugh before, nor did he think one capable of playing practical jokes.

Tom opened the middle compartment of the android form. Circuits and wires filled the small area in a jumbled mess, save for a small space just big enough for the power crystal. Tom wondered how to stick it in. "I guess it just goes in the slot," he mumbled.

The opaque crystal lit up. Tom stepped back. As the cybernetic life form came to life, its arms twitched and legs flailed about in an uncontrolled manner.

The lights dimmed, thrusting them into darkness before growing bright to the point of bursting. Realizing that he still had the robotic life form plugged into the ship's main circuit, Tom reached down and unplugged it so that only the crystal powered it.

"What's happening?" asked Solon.

"I think it's working," said Tom.

"But it's acting erratic," Solon said.

"Because I haven't downloaded Solaris' consciousness in there, so it has no command function." Tom switched the machine off. "This is great! It works. Now I just need to make a few modifications and connect this thing to the main computer and we download you into it, Solaris."

"Why not now?" asked Solaris.

"I want to make sure the mechanisms all work first," said Tom, "but it won't be long now. In a few days, you should be able to leave the confines of this ship."

"A few days then," said Solaris, "and not a minute later."

"Can it be a few seconds?" joked Tom.

Steam burst from the vents.

"A few days it is."

"Where is that cursed blacksmith!"

Tom cringed at the sound of Alfric's booming voice.

"I know that it is you who has doused the lights," came Alfric's voice.

"He sounds like he is in a bit of ill temper," said Solon.

"You know, you have a knack for stating the obvious," Tom replied.

Alfric burst into the storage room. His sharp eyes roamed every corner, every crevice, as he surveyed the scene before settling on a very innocent looking Tom, standing next to a tarp that covered the android. "This vessel seems undamaged."

"Why would it be in any other state?" asked Tom. "Really, Alfric, you act as though I'm up to something."

Solon watched the two, amused.

Alfric eyed Tom a moment before speaking. "I have learned that it is best to keep two eyes on you."

Tom released a nervous laugh, which put a smile on Alfric's face. The Viking took one last glance around the room and left.

"That was close," said Tom. "Where are you going?" he asked Solon when he headed for the doorway.

"Though this is most interesting, I have a… book… that requires my attention."

"Always the bookworm," Tom mumbled to himself after Solon had left.

Chapter 29
An Alliance Formed

Fredyr Monsooth hunched over his cedar wood desk (an expensive piece with braiding that wound up the legs; carved geometric shapes lined the edges, forming a diagonal pattern until meeting in the center), reading the latest communication from one of his search parties. They had failed to recover the stolen crystal. Still fuming over the theft, he slammed the report down on the smooth surface.

"Mr. Monsooth," said his secretary into the intercom.

"Yes, what is it?"

"Someone is here to see you."

"What is his name?"

"He won't give it. All he says is that he knows how you can get the crystal back."

"Send him in."

The door buzzed. Stein walked in, his polished boots reflecting the twilight as they clomped on the floor. "Mr. Monsooth," he said, holding out his hand.

Fredyr refused to take it.

Stein pulled his hand back, never faltering in his regal demeanor.

"What do you know about the theft of my property?" demanded Fredyr.

"I know who took it," said Stein as he studied the office with its lavish decorations, noting the window and exit points. His eyes scanned the desk. No pictures. In that instant, Stein understood what drove Fredyr Monsooth: a lust for power.

"So who took it?"

"Did you honestly think that I was going to tell you right away? If I tell you now, I know that you will have me killed."

"I could kill you anyway."

"True, but it would serve little purpose."

"Why's that?"

"Because you want to know what I know, and you want your crystal back."

Fredyr frowned. He knew what this man wanted. "Name your price."

"An army," said Stein.

"What?"

"You have your own private army. Everyone knows that," said Stein. His eyes roamed over the mantel and the *Kresnyr* sword (a three-pointed sword, the center blade long and narrow, with the remaining two points directly in its center, forming U-shaped curls) resting upon it; Fredyr had added his own touch by coating the edges of the weapon in gold. "I want control over it. Temporarily, of course."

"In exchange?"

"I'll take you to where not only your crystal is, but the thieves as well."

"How do you know where they are?"

"That is my business." Stein paced the office, noting the invaluable treasures (a spyglass made of pure silver, a ruby encrusted journal, and writing pens made of sapphires) on display.

"I know you," said Fredyr, recognizing Stein from the banquet. "You were at the celebration with that Klanor."

"True."

"How do I know this isn't a trick?"

"You don't," said Stein, "but I guarantee that I will take you to the thieves and your precious crystal."

"What's in it for you? You're not doing this out of charity."

"No," Stein fiddled with a whimsical display on the desk. "That, too, is my affair. I can get you what you want, but I will need command of your army."

"And your boss knows of this?"

"I work for no one," said Stein, his cold eyes bore into Fredyr, sending chills down his spine, despite the double layered, crocodile jacket he wore.

"How can I trust a man so willing to betray his employer?" asked Fredyr.

"You can't," said Stein, "but I have named my terms. Do you accept them or not?"

Fredyr rubbed his chin, distrusting the man before him. He disliked the callousness Stein emanated, but he wanted his property back. "Very well. I'll accept your offer, but know this: if you betray me, there is no place in this universe that you can hide where I won't find you and exact my vengeance."

"Why, Mr. Monsooth, I believe we have something in common. I will contact you with the details later. Until then." Stein bowed his head and whisked out of the office.

Fredyr stared after him, unsure if he had just made the right decision, or a fatal mistake.

Chapter 30
A Discovery

Alone in her room, Rynah studied the splotched writing of the text, identifying many of the verses from the digital scans she possessed, and had found nothing new. The book even contained the smudged lines that always showed up as a blob on the scans. Rynah rubbed her fingers over the smudge as she stared at the unreadable lines, wishing she could make them out. A part of her thought that the smeared ink looked deliberate, but logic told her that this was an ancient book; a few of the words were bound to be washed away by time. She touched the tender pages with care, remembering the hours her grandfather had spent poring over the ancient writing, engrossed in its myths and spectacular tale.

A memory of her at the age of 12, happening upon Marlow as he compared passages from the archaic volume with other ancient texts, struck her. Rynah closed her eyes, allowing herself to be taken back to that time. She remembered that she had just come home from school and stopped by for her daily walk with her grandfather. Each afternoon, once school was out, Marlow took Rynah to a special place near their home where four lilac bushes, the size of boulders, grew and where bees, bigger than her fists, collected the pollen, turning it into the sweetest honey she had ever tasted. They would collect the honey and eat it beneath the lilacs, reveling in the peaceful atmosphere around them.

But that afternoon had been different. Rynah thought back to how she had arrived home, but instead of greeting her in his usual, cheerful manner, Marlow had remained unaware of her presence, jumping from one place to another in agitation. That was when Rynah spotted the book. Always having been curious about it, she decided to seize her chance and have a look at what consumed her grandfather's attention much of the time. The moment the tips of her fingers had touched the opened page, her grandfather had dove for the book, slamming it shut.

"I told you never to touch this book," he growled at her, with anger she had never witnessed coming from him.

Frightened, Rynah had run away, with Marlow calling after her. Later that evening, he had found her curled up in her room and sat next to her.

"I am sorry," Marlow had told her. "I should not have acted the way I did."

"I just want to know what is so special about that book," Rynah had told him, in a small voice.

Marlow gave Rynah a warm smile. "In time, you will know, but first, you must learn its language."

"Its language?"

"That text is old, far older than any of us," Marlow had said. "It is ancient Lanyran. If you wish to understand its words, you must learn the language."

Rynah opened her eyes, coming back to her room, as she allowed the memory to fade. That day Marlow had told her to learn ancient Lanyran was the day a lot of things changed for her. She abandoned many of the activities that youth on her planet participated in and delved into the ancient Lanyran language, determined to not only learn it, but to be able to speak and read it fluently.

She glanced at the book and a thought struck her. With delicate fingers, she reached for the dusty volume and turned the creaky pages to the final one. Torn edges was all that was left of the very last page. Curious, and not remembering it being this way when it had been in her grandfather's possession, Rynah fiddled with it, studying both sides of its remnants.

"Why would someone tear out this page?" she asked herself.

She snatched a magnifying glass from her desk and focused on a watermark near the binding; its smudges made it appear as though someone had spilled coffee on the page, but Rynah noticed something that didn't belong. She peered closer. Her eyebrows arched upward in surprise as she recognized the faint watermark.

"Solaris!"

No answer.

"Solaris, get in here!"

"I'm already in here, so to speak, considering that I am the ship," replied an annoyed Solaris.

"You know what I mean. What is this?"

"What is what?"

"The watermark on this page," said Rynah, pointing at the stained, frayed edges of the page. "Why is this there?"

"I'm not at liberty to say," said Solaris.

"Don't play games with me," said Rynah. "I want to know why this mark is here on this page and why the rest of it is missing. You know why. I know you do."

Solaris remained silent.

"Did my grandfather know?"

"He knew a lot of things," Solaris replied.

Infuriated at the vague response, Rynah slammed her fist on the desk, causing the book to jump. "Why won't you tell me what this is?"

"Because you already know," said Solaris.

"Why won't you tell me what it is doing here?"

"You know the answer to that as well," replied Solaris.

Rynah glanced back at the burnt edges of the page; questions with answers she did not like filled her mind. She slammed the text shut and stormed out of her room.

She collided into Usef.

"What's wrong?" he asked, noticing the irate expression on her face. He had heard her shouts and rushed over, concerned.

"Nothing!"

"Nothing? Something is bothering you."

"None of your business!" Rynah didn't wish to speak to anyone; that image burned in her mind. What was it doing there? And why?

"I have some right to know," said Usef, not liking the way she brushed him aside.

"Do you?"

"Yes," said Usef. "I risked my life to help you and your friends rescue that girl; I nearly died alongside you on Virdyr; and I know that something is frightening you."

"I thank you for assisting me in bringing Brie back, but there is nothing more you can do here," said Rynah, trying to rein in her anger, anger she felt towards Marlow more than Usef, but Usef remained on the receiving end of that ire.

"Why won't you talk to me?"

Rynah started to walk away, but Usef's next statement stopped her.

"It's the crystal, isn't it?"

Rynah faced him, wondering how much he knew.

"At the settlement, we had heard about the destruction of Lanyr and how a man named Klanor was responsible. Even in the outlands, we knew that a crystal kept the magnetic fields stabilized for Lanyr to flourish, and without it, the planet would die. The only way Klanor could have destroyed Lanyr was by stealing that crystal. So I asked myself, why would he need it?

"Unlike others in my home, I always talk with the pilots of the supply ships; they know more than most realize. They talked about settlements being destroyed throughout the Twelve Sectors by a weapon so powerful, none had ever seen it's like before.

"Then you show up, searching for Klanor because he held one of your friends captive. That very armada of his matches the description of the one given to me by the supply ships' pilots when they talked about the destruction of outlying hubs.

"And your friends, they are not from the Twelve Sectors. Anyone can see that. I know about the poem; I've seen you reading the text."

"So are you going to betray me to him?"

"Do you think so little of me?" said Usef.

"You do not understand what Klanor has done."

"I know what he is doing to you now. If you do not learn to let go of this hatred for him, you will never learn to move on. Think of how your loathing is affecting those around you. Think of the companionship you are missing. These people, despite your treatment of them, care for you."

"How dare you!"

"You are consumed with a need for revenge. It's written on your face, and it is destroying you, Rynah."

"And why should I listen to you, a man I barely know."

"I did not help you save Brie for my own gain."

"Then why did you?" Rynah's voice had grown quiet, almost a whisper.

Usef brushed a strand of emerald hair away from Rynah's face. "I know what it means to lose a member of your crew, and it is a loss I would never wish on another."

Turmoil roiled within Rynah as she stared into Usef's eyes; not an ounce of deception lay within them. She had felt an intense attraction to Usef since she had met him, but she still held a mixture of love and hatred for Klanor. She had trusted him, even agreed to marry him, yet he betrayed her. She didn't dare trust another. Yet, should she?

"I am not him," continued Usef. "You are free to rebuff me, but don't think of me as an idiot. I know that book troubles you."

"Usef, I…"

"I will never harm you, or your friends."

Rynah started to walk away, but stopped. Something Usef had said about learning to trust others hounded her as she thought about how the four people from Earth trusted one another, yet they had never met until she had ripped them from their homes.

"I'm sorry," she said.

"I am offering you my friendship and my help with whatever it is that you are involved in."

Rynah chewed her tongue as she tried to control her emotions, but the watermark still plagued her mind. "Like you've said," she began, "most are aware that Lanyr's magnetic fields were kept intact through the use of a crystal, but what they don't know is that some on my planet believed that crystal to be one of six: powerful and deadly. Klanor was one of them. He stole the crystal and has been gathering the other five."

"What happens when he finds them all?"

"No one knows, really. According to some ancient texts, the crystals form a deadly weapon that can wipe out entire solar systems; others say that the crystals, if united, will rip a hole in space and time, thus causing untold damage. But if one was able to keep Lanyr's magnetic fields intact, I do not want to think about what would happen if all six were united."

"And so you have been spending all of this time trying to stop Klanor from getting all of these crystals, and that is how he captured your friend."

"Yes. Look, I know this all sounds…"

Usef held up his hand, stopping Rynah. "If Klanor is willing to massacre entire civilizations just to find these crystals, it doesn't matter what I believe. He does, and judging from what little I have witnessed, many have suffered for it."

Rynah blinked back tears as she looked into Usef's calm eyes, not finding any ounce of deception within them.

"I know that something other than the crystals is bothering you, and that you are uncertain if you can tell me, or anyone, but at least trust me enough to allow me to help you, and perhaps, someday, you'll accept my friendship."

"Thank you," Rynah said, "for helping us get Brie back… and for your friendship."

Rynah walked away without another word, but stopped as a thought struck her. "The answers you seek, I don't have. Yes, that book troubles me, but why I cannot say. The only person on this ship who does know is Solaris, and good luck getting her to tell you."

Usef smiled at that. He began to understand why everyone aboard the ship treated Solaris as a real, live person, and in the short time he had been there, he had learned just how secretive Solaris could be. He glanced at the speakers above him, knowing that she had been listening, even if she had been silent.

Chapter 31
SOLARIS' CONSCIENCE

While the others busied themselves, Brie had snuck up to the observation deck for some time alone. It wasn't that she didn't want the company of the others, but so much filled her mind and she needed to make sense of it. She could not stop thinking about the memories she had gleaned from Klanor, and wondered how she could tell Rynah that he did indeed love her, or if she should remain silent. Telling Rynah now might set her over the edge.

She felt restless and wanted to do something, but what? Brie spotted a loose pole from the railing of the stairwell. She yanked it free. Holding it out in a defensive posture, just like Alfric had shown her during one of their lessons, Brie arched it above her head before bringing it down. A loud clang filled the air as its tip smacked the floor.

"Brie?"

Brie whirled around when she heard Solaris's soft voice. "What is it, Solaris? I thought you were with the others."

"I was. The advantage of being the ship is that I can be any place at any time, and change locations in an instant, so to speak."

"What's wrong, Solaris?" asked Brie, detecting a note of sadness in her voice.

"I… I… I'm sorry!" Solaris blurted out. Since the day Brie had been lost to them, Solaris had carried a certain amount of guilt with her. She did her best to pretend that all was well, but Brie's loss ate at her, clinging to her. "I should have known that you weren't dead. I should have… it's my fault that you were captured. It's…"

"It's no one's fault."

"But I am partly to blame."

"Solaris, I don't blame you. I don't blame anyone. If it's forgiveness you want, you have it."

"Most would harbor ill will towards my failure."

"I'm not most people," replied Brie. "You are my friend, and I hope that I am yours as well. Please, don't feel guilty because of the past. I'm back now and I'm safe. That is all that matters."

Silence filled the void between them before Brie asked a question that had been on her mind since she had returned. "Solaris, how am I still alive? That gas should have killed me. I remember not being able to breathe."

"When you first came aboard, Rynah injected you with nanobots, do you remember?"

"Yes."

"Well, she accidentally gave you the experimental nanobots. Marlow had created them. They were meant to stop one from dying by putting them in a comatose state, but the nanobots had never been tested. I had scanned you for vital signs and ran 10 different tests, but my systems were so damaged that every test came up negative, pronouncing you clinically dead."

"It's okay."

"We didn't learn any of this until we discovered that you were still alive and in Klanor's possession."

"These nanobots, will they keep me from ever dying?"

"No," said Solaris. "Marlow once explained that they had an

expiration date, if you will, and will eventually become inert and be flushed from your system, but he never knew how long that would take. Like all living things, you will die at some point, but you may outlive most of those you know, and you might not age like they do. I'm sorry that I can't give you more information than that."

It's all right. I just wanted to know."

"Is that pole from my staircase?" said Solaris, noticing the metal pole in Brie's hands for the first time.

"Um… sorry." Brie put the pole back where it belonged.

"You know, it's bad enough that I have to put up with Tom and his untidiness, and that Rynah put a few dents in my hull. Now you're tearing bits of me apart."

Brie laughed at Solaris' outburst, as she imagined some of the things Tom might have done to anger her. "So, what has Tom been up to?"

"Building a surprise for me. Of course, I know all about it."

"What sort of surprise?" asked Brie.

"I can't tell you," replied Solaris.

"Why?"

"Because it's a surprise."

Brie smiled at Solaris' response, still amazed how human-like she was at times. "When might I see it?"

"Soon, I hope."

Again, memories of being within Klanor's deepest thoughts propelled Brie to tell someone of what she had learned, but at the last second, she stopped, unable to find the words. "Solaris, do you think people can change?"

"What makes you ask that?"

"Because… because while I was locked in that cell, I got the feeling that Klanor is not who we think he is. That there is someone worse than him."

"What makes you say that?" asked Solaris.

"Just things that happened during his interrogations. A feeling I have."

Solaris remained quiet. She wanted to ask Brie to further explain this feeling, but felt that it was best to leave it alone, instead of pushing the matter.

"Thank you, Solaris," said Brie, breaking the silence.

"For what, dear?"

"For coming back for me."

"There was never another option."

The domed ceiling of the observations deck changed as holographic images appeared with the constellations that Brie was familiar with, but in brilliant shades of red and orange, creating a warm glow upon her face. Appreciating the gesture, Brie sat on the cold floor, bringing her knees in close as she admired the images above her and the bit of home that Solaris had tried to bring to her.

Chapter 32
A Pirate and a Bottle of Rum

Obiah's sleek ship soared through the pale gold clouds of the planet Glosef as he headed for the landing strip, floating on the surface of the water of the port city of Lenel. The strip of land that Lenel rested on measured only 1,300 square miles. The port itself consisted of floating vessels (sailing ships, barges, or planks of rotted wood with splintered flagpoles stuck to them) connected by rough-hewn ropes that tied them together.

Obiah set his ship down on the landing strip that bobbed up and down with the current of the water. "We're here," he said to Merrick.

"Are you certain that this is wise?" asked Merrick. "Pirates frequent this place."

"Precisely," said Obiah. "We are looking for a particular ship, and there is no group of people better suited to find it than pirates."

"They do not work for anyone, but themselves."

"Depends on how deep your pockets are." Obiah opened the rear hatch and stepped out into the bright sunshine, taking a deep breath of the salty air with the aroma of rotted algae mixed in it.

Two men with thick hair and tentacles on their chins rowed past, ignoring Obiah's and Merrick's presence. Many came to Lenel in search of food, drink, entertainment, or rest, and they assumed that the two newcomers were no different.

"Best watch ourselves," muttered Obiah. "Come, I believe the tavern is this way."

"Have you been here before?"

"Once, in my youth, when I was still a midshipman in the Lanyran fleet. I met this woman with a rear the size of a barrel, but she played a mean game of Rocue."

For those of you who don't know, Rocue is a game that is a cross between poker, gin, and Russian roulette, and best avoided. Only the foolish, or inebriated, attempt it.

Dubious about the entire venture, Merrick stepped onto the floating walkway, which sank just a little under his weight, allowing green water to slosh over his boots, and followed Obiah. They strolled down the waterlogged path, doing their best to ignore the swaying of the sea. Obiah's purposeful movements told Merrick that he knew where he went.

They reached an oval-shaped vessel, bearing a similarity to a sailing ship of the 16th century, except that it had holographic doors and an incinerator, and walked up the barnacle-infested gangplank to the top deck. Raucous laughter surrounded them as pirates sloshed their drinks, while trying to impress the tavern wenches. Ignoring them, Obiah and Merrick strolled past, until they reached the ship's interior.

Tenebrous lanterns stretched around the room, providing murky, yellow light to the small area filled with cigar and pipe smoke that hovered over tables, which littered the chamber in a haphazard fashion, each bearing occupants who wobbled from too much drink. Obiah walked past them, with Merrick close behind, stopping at the bar in the back.

"Yer in my way!" shouted one pirate at Merrick; his sallow skin hung from his bones.

Merrick ignored him.

"Hey!" The pirate grabbed him with a worn, gloved hand.

Merrick reached around the pirate, placing his hand in the middle of his back before bashing the pirate's wrinkled face into the counter, spilling a tankard of beer.

Another pirate attacked from the side. Before he got far, Obiah lifted up his laser rifle, cocking it, allowing its high pitched hum to fill the air. The pirate backed away, grabbed his friend, and hurried off. No one paid any heed to them; such squabbles were common.

"Drink?" asked the bartender as he wiped up the spilt beer, though he smeared it more than cleaned it up, with his grungy, gray rag.

"Two rums," said Obiah.

Two mugs filled with the intoxicating liquid appeared on the bar counter. Obiah tossed two coins into the bartender's outstretched, wrinkled hand.

"Where do you suppose we start?" Merrick asked as he sipped his drink and eyed the gambling, drinking, and dancing crowd.

Obiah scanned the room. He stopped when he noticed one lone pirate seated at a table with no drink. "There."

They plopped their mugs on the sticky counter and wandered over to the pirate. "Hello, friend." Obiah sat in the seat directly opposite the man.

"You are no friend of mine," grumbled the pirate, clicking his yellowed fingernails on the grimy table.

"To business, then," said Obiah.

"And what makes you think I am here to do business?"

"You are not enjoying the festivities, nor have you bothered to order a drink," said Obiah, "so you are either here to meet a man who has not shown, or are hoping to make the right contact."

"And you are the right contact?"

"Perhaps." Obiah motioned for Merrick to move closer, and pulled out a holographic image of Solaris.

"We need to find this ship," said Obiah.

"What makes you think I know of it?" asked the pirate.

"We will pay well for any information," said Obiah.

"How much?"

Merrick tossed a pouch of coins, containing a hundred scillions, on the table. The pirate fiddled with it a moment in his hands, which looked more like scuffed leather, weighing it, before setting it down.

"A fair amount. There was talk about a ship matching the one you seek not far from here. It was last seen on the planet of Virdyr, where a group of mercenaries went missing."

"Missing?" said Merrick.

"Dead," said the pirate.

"How long ago?"

"A week," said the pirate, "maybe two."

"Is there anything else you can tell us?"

The pirate glanced around before leaning closer. "You are not the only ones looking for this ship. Another seeks it as well."

"Who?" asked Obiah.

"He didn't give his name, but he is staying at the Wayward Inn, just around the corner here. Perhaps you should speak with him."

"Perhaps," mumbled Obiah. "Anything else?"

"I've told you what I know." The pirate reached for the money.

Obiah snatched his wrist with his strong grip, pulling the pirate closer. "You best be telling us the truth. If you've lied…" he allowed his voice to trail off.

The pirate jerked free of Obiah's grasp, snatched the coins, and knocked over a chair in his haste to leave, his baggy pants swooshing with each movement.

"Do you trust him?" asked Merrick.

"No," replied Obiah, "but now we have an idea of where to begin our search."

"You said…"

"No one would lie about a group of mercenaries being killed. Come on."

Obiah and Merrick walked out of the smoke-filled tavern unaware of a pair of eyes that watched them.

The outside air wasn't much cleaner than that inside. The mildew laden planks filled the area with their unpleasant aroma. Merrick spotted the Wayward Inn and pointed it out to Obiah.

"No," he said.

"But that pirate said the man who is also looking for them is there."

"Probably a trap."

"You don't think another is interested in Rynah?"

"Oh, there most likely is another searching for her, but pirates only get specific when they are setting a trap. We should get back to the ship."

Obiah led the way down the floating wood path amidst coiled ropes and small boats tied to the pier. A tall man, with scaly skin and a tattered jacket, stepped out in front of him. Obiah and Merrick whipped around, but more pirates had blocked their path.

"What is the meaning of this?" demanded Obiah.

"Did you think I was lying when I told you that others seek the same ship as you?" The pirate they had talked to in the tavern walked up from the side. "I've done what you asked," he said to the scaly man in front of Obiah, "now where's my payment?"

The man chucked a bag of coins at him.

The pirate clasped it—greed filled his face—and ran off.

The scaly man reached into Merrick's pocket and yanked out the holographic image of Solaris. "It appears that you and I are looking for the same ship."

"What interest is it to you?" demanded Obiah.

"Much."

"It's a bit difficult to speak to a man without first knowing his name."

"By the powers, you are right," said the scaly man, his red eyes boring into Obiah's. "My name is Jifdar, captain of the Fragmyr Pirates."

Obiah and Merrick both recognized the name, but Obiah remembered Rynah's account of who had marooned her and her friends on Ikor.

"So you've heard of me," said Jifdar.

Merrick glanced around, spotting a chance to escape. While Jifdar paced in front of Obiah, he jabbed the pirate behind him with the sharp point of his elbow before snatching a pole with a hook on the end and charging the other pirates. "Run!"

Obiah punched Jifdar in the nose and took off. He careened

down the walkway, struggling to keep his balance as it swayed beneath his feet. Shouts and yells rose up behind him. Looking behind, he saw Merrick heading straight for him. They met a dead end.

Merrick pointed at a line of buoys bobbing in the gentle waves of the water. With no other choice, they ran for them and leapt off the gangway onto the buoys, hopping across them (with a surprising amount of grace) until they reached another floating path. They charged up it to a parked vessel. Pirates cut them off. Swerving, Merrick and Obiah veered to the right. They hurried up the gangplank to the deck of a vessel, past crowds of women and other pirates, who were none too pleased to have their fun interrupted, and down the other side.

Two of Jifdar's men blocked their path. Merrick leapt from the plank and grabbed onto a hang bar; he swung through the air until he kicked the pirates into the water behind them. Obiah snatched his arm just in time to prevent Merrick from falling into the water as well.

"There!" shouted a pirate.

Merrick's and Obiah's boots stomped on the hollowed, wood planks of the walkway as they ran and headed for their ship. Obiah knocked a stack of crates over behind him.

"Hey!" yelled the man who owned those crates.

They jumped to another floating walkway. Together, Obiah and Merrick raced down it until they stopped. Jifdar had blocked their path. Turning around, they ran in the other direction. More pirates blocked their way. A rope hung from a crane. Obiah and Merrick clung to it, sailing through the air, and landed on another walkway.

Jifdar's angry shouts reached their ears. They paid little attention to him as they jerked to the left and jumped into a boat drifting nearby before leaping to another floating walkway. Their feet pounded the planks as they hurried away. Barrels fell from a net above them, smashing through the walkway and into the ocean below, while water splashed and sloshed in response, spraying them and soaking their clothing.

"I want them alive!" Jifdar scolded the pirate that had dropped the barrels.

Obiah and Merrick both turned to run. A stinging pain gripped Merrick's leg as an electrical jolt seized him from a stun-dart. He dropped to his knees. Obiah rushed to his side. "Go!" said Merrick.

Refusing to leave him, Obiah put Merrick's arm over his shoulder and lifted him to his feet. They had made it three feet when a stun-dart struck him in the back. Gripping it, Obiah dropped Merrick as he, too, fell to the ground.

Slow, steady clomps approached him. "If you are done with this running around," said Jifdar, "I would like to get down to business."

"What do you want?" hissed Obiah.

"The same thing you do apparently. That ship."

"I don't know where it is."

"That much is evident; otherwise, you wouldn't be asking questions about its whereabouts. I am curious about your interest in it."

"Do what you will with us and be done with it," spat Obiah.

"Such animosity," said Jifdar. "Why?"

"You left Rynah for dead on that ice planet."

"So that explains it," Jifdar beamed. "You do know her and you are looking for her. Well, my friend, I am afraid you have misunderstood my intentions. I do not wish to harm the occupants of that ship. I wish to negotiate an alliance with them."

"An alliance?" said Merrick, with doubt. "What game is this?"

"No games," replied Jifdar.

"Why would I trust you?" demanded Obiah.

"Does the name Klanor mean anything to you?"

Obiah's and Merrick's irate faces indicated that it did.

"Well, I am very interested in finding him and I know that this ship"—Jifdar held up the holoimage of Solaris—"is the key to that end."

"Perhaps we should take this indoors," said Obiah, knowing that, for now, it was best to listen to the pirate captain's proposal.

Chapter 33
USEF'S INSIGHT

Usef paced back and forth in his room. It had simple accommodations (a bed, toilet, and a sink), much like the other rooms
on Solaris. His mind remained focused on what Rynah had told
him about the crystals. A part of him wished to return back to the
settlement; after all, this business with the crystals was none of his
concern, but then Rynah's face filled his mind. He had offered her
his friendship and his help, and what sort of friend would he be if
he turned and ran? He wished they could be more, but despite his
desires, Usef understood her reluctance.

The more he thought about it, the more he remembered his
own misfortunes. The men under his command, who had trusted
him, who he was unable to save, and who died before his eyes. He
couldn't bear to tell their families, to look them in the eyes and
allow them to see his shame. So he ran away, and stumbled upon
the settlement by accident. He liked it there, its peacefulness, but
realized that it was never home to him. He loved the stars and relished flying among them.

Regret and shame are what filled his nights, and he knew that they filled Rynah's dreams as well. If time was what she required, then time is what he would give her.

A scream pierced his ears. Usef charged out of his room and into the one next to him, which was Brie's, where he found the girl huddled on her bed covered in sweat.

"It's okay," she said. "It was only a dream."

"Are you sure?" asked Usef, concerned.

"Come closer."

Usef moved next to the cot.

Brie stared into his worried eyes for several seconds until a small smile rested upon her lips. "Yes, it was only a dream. I'm sorry if I scared you."

"That's quite all right. Was it bad?" Usef thought back to the nightmares he had had, constant reminders of his failure. "You don't have to tell me," he said when Brie remained silent. "I understand if you'd prefer to tell one of the others."

"For a moment, I thought I was back in that chair," Brie said, staring straight ahead of her. "Klanor would have me strapped to a chair and wearing a helmet that linked us telepathically, the same way we are able to link our minds with Solaris, and he would make me believe that I was back home. For a while, I started to believe the hallucinations, and I guess I was afraid that my being back here was another of his games."

"How were you able to tell the illusion from reality?" asked Usef.

"People's eyes," Brie replied. "In the illusions, their eyes were hollow, devoid of anything that makes them human. Yours are definitely not empty."

Usef now understood why Brie had asked to look into his eyes. "What did you see?"

"Pain," said Brie, "the same torture that Alfric and Rynah carry in theirs, and I have to wonder, whom did you lose?"

Silence filled the space between them.

"Sorry," said Brie, "you don't have to tell me."

"It's not so much a question of whom I lost, but what I failed to do."

"Failures can be fixed."

"Not this one."

"What do you mean?"

Usef turned away, but something about Brie's calm nature and genuine interest forced him to face her again. "Men died; men whose lives I was responsible for died because I was unable to do as you had, to risk everything to save them. And those who were supposed to help me never came."

"And Rynah?" asked Brie. "I know you are attracted to her and I think I know why. You both have so much in common. And don't deny it. She likes you too. She looks at you when she thinks you aren't paying attention."

"How do you…"

"Solaris told me. She's a regular busybody."

"Probably listening to us right now."

"Most likely."

"You should go back to sleep," said Usef. "Klanor can't hurt you now."

"It's not him I fear," said Brie.

"Why's that?"

"He has the same tortured look in his eyes."

Usef stared at Brie's silhouette in the shadows, realizing something about her for the first time. She had the capacity to understand others, to give them another chance even when they wouldn't give it to themselves. "I'll see you in the morning."

Usef left Brie's room, allowing his feet to guide him back to his own, his mind focused on what she had said about Klanor and Rynah.

"You have much on your mind," said Solaris.

Usef groaned. "Is there ever a time you do not spy on people?"

"I get asked that a lot," said Solaris.

"I wonder why," Usef mumbled.

"I am the ship. I am connected to everything on this ship. For instance, I know that Tom has just spilled green slop all over my pristine counters. I had just cleaned them this morning. That little runt is going to hear about that.

"I know that Solon is busy in his room, studying a book he found on Neblar, while Alfric is in the cargo hold, practicing with his sword, and you were comforting Brie just now. Or was it the other way around?"

"I think you know the answer to that," Usef replied.

"So, what is on your mind?"

"I think you already know what troubles me."

"I would say she is about 5'9", green hair, heliotrope skin… am I on the right track?"

"Quite perceptive."

"You should just tell her how you feel. It's written all over your face. Even I noticed it."

"I'm beginning to think there isn't much you don't notice."

"You're right about that. Rynah was never one who easily trusted others. The two people she loved most betrayed her."

"Two people?"

"Her grandfather," said Solaris.

"He…"

"Marlow did not mean to, but the result was the same."

"Do you think she would listen to me?"

"Does it matter what I think?"

An annoyed expression crossed Usef's face.

"I know Rynah better than she knows herself. She does care for you; that is why she has erected a wall between you both. Besides, no one leaves here without my permission."

Usef noticed a bit of sarcasm in her voice, something he never thought an artificial intelligence could portray. "I still…"

"What you need to do is clear your head," said Solaris. "Perhaps a walk."

"Where would I go? This is a ship."

"The observation deck is always a nice area."

"Maybe I should just go to the kitchen."

"I wouldn't," said Solaris.

"Why?"

"Because I'm about to commit a murder in there—now he has dumped red liquid all over my freshly mopped floors! Does he not know the importance of cleanliness?"

Hiding a chuckle, Usef was glad he was not in Tom's shoes right then as Solaris grumbled to herself.

"You go to the observation deck. There is a quite a view there. Oh, and put on a clean shirt." Everything went silent, giving the impression that Solaris had left.

Usef remained where he was.

"That wasn't a suggestion, numbnuts," said Solaris, growing impatient with his sluggishness.

Knowing he would never win an argument with her, Usef changed his shirt—the moment he did so, the door to his room slid open—and walked to the observation deck. He decided exercise would do him some good. Once he reached the top step to the deck, he saw a shadowed form standing there, staring out at a rose colored planet surrounded by a golden glow and rings that reminded one of sunset.

"Rynah?" he said.

She jumped, having been startled by his appearance.

"Sorry," he apologized, "I did not realize that anyone was up here."

"No, it's… it's okay. I was just leaving."

Usef caught her arm just as she tried to walk past. "Stay. If I am intruding, I can leave."

"No," said Rynah, "you're not."

As Usef stared into Rynah's violet eyes, he realized that Solaris had set up the meeting. "I was just taking a walk and trying to clear my head."

"This is the place to do it."

"Quite a view."

"Yes, it is. I often come here to think when my mind is troubled."

"What troubles you?"

"You know," said Rynah. Her distant demeanor was absent, being replaced with a more vulnerable persona.

"I'm sorry for my outburst the other day. I had no business…"

"You were right," said Rynah. "I will never be able to forget the past, but perhaps I can move on and have a better future. You remind me of Klanor, in a way, but you're more gentle and caring. You helped me save my friend and I never thanked you for that."

Unable to hold back any longer, Usef kissed Rynah, who, instead of shrinking away, returned it.

"Don't you turn your back on me!" came Solaris' shrill voice from below.

"Well, it's not like you have a face," came Tom's reply. "I don't know what it is you are so upset about."

"You left green—oh, whatever it is—smeared all over my counters. Then, you spilled your drink and didn't clean it up."

"I wiped it."

"More like, smeared it! For the last few months I have been putting up with your greasy fingerprints and crumbs from your meals. No more!"

"I better get down there before she kills him," said Rynah.

She and Usef hurried down the stairs where Tom remained locked in an argument with Solaris over the importance of being tidy.

"Will you two stop it?" Rynah interrupted them.

"He…"

"Enough, Solaris," said Rynah. "I'm certain Tom did not mean to be so careless."

"What? I…"

Rynah's glare stopped Tom midsentence.

"I'm sorry," he said, "I will do better in the future."

"Solaris," said Rynah.

"Accepted," groaned Solaris. If she had arms that she could have folded, she would have.

"Right, well," began Tom, "I think I'll go now."

Tom walked off to the storage area where he kept the cybernetic body he had been building for Solaris.

"And don't even think about giving it orange hair," Solaris called after him before going silent.

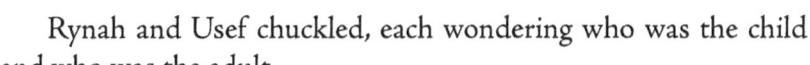

Rynah and Usef chuckled, each wondering who was the child and who was the adult.

"I should probably go back to the command center," said Rynah.

"I will," Usef offered. "You should rest."

"But..."

"You don't have to do everything," said Usef. "I can handle it. I am a pilot, you know."

Rynah gave him a warm smile and headed for her quarters.

Gaden watched as the security detail changed shifts, making note of how many remained at each station. Since Stein had enlisted his help, he had spent every hour listening to those on the ship, making a list of those who voiced discontent towards Klanor's leadership. He had kept tabs on Klanor's movements as well, noting how distracted the man seemed, just as Stein had described him. Once he had finished making his notes for the day, Gaden sought out a secluded area to make his transmission to Stein.

"Yes?" came Stein's harsh voice from the communicator.

"It's me," whispered Gaden, "I have what you wanted. Am sending it now." Gaden placed a chip into the communications device. It flashed yellow as it sent the information to Stein.

"Well, done," said Stein. "You will be well-rewarded. See to it that you are assigned to the same detail that is charged with protecting Klanor."

"How..."

"Don't you worry about that. My men will be in place. Just see to it that you are in yours."

The transmission ended. Gaden left his secretive place and mingled with a group that had walked past him, pretending to be interested in their conversation. Stein had upheld his end of the bargain in giving him a better assignment aboard the ship far removed from the tubes; it was time for Gaden to keep his, knowing that he would be well rewarded.

Chapter 34
NAVIGATING THE LABYRINTH

Alfric stood upon the observation deck of Solaris—like the others, he appreciated its solitude—looking out at the approaching planet of Sunlil, watching the glowing orange (with black splotches encasing it that moved in gradual circles) planet. It reminded him of one of the tales he had often heard as a child and told his own sons.

"Hey," said Brie as she walked up from behind.

"Brie," greeted Alfric, "is there something you require?"

"Always so formal," laughed Brie. "No, I wanted to thank you for coming back for me. I wish to thank all of you in person, but I am having difficulty finding Tom and Solon right the moment, but…"

"You do not need to thank us," said Alfric. "It was the honorable thing to do."

Brie reached into her pocket and pulled out Alfric's talisman that he had given her when they had thought she had died. "I thought I would give this back," she said, holding it out to him.

Alfric wrapped her hands in his. "Keep it. It was a gift."

"You thought I had died."

"It doesn't matter," said Alfric. "It was a gift nonetheless. Perhaps it will bring you luck. Gróa would have been honored to have you wear it."

Brie placed it around her neck, knowing that when the Viking had made up his mind, there was no changing it. "Who's Gróa?"

"My sister," replied Alfric.

"Where is she?"

"Dead."

Brie bit her tongue, scolding herself for bringing up a painful memory.

"Have you ever seen such a sight?" asked Alfric as he turned back to the window, changing the subject.

"No," said Brie, "it kind of looks like Vulcan to me."

"Vulcan?" Alfric gave her a quizzical look. "Is this a place where you are from?"

"No," said Brie, almost laughing, "it's part of a story, a tale in my day, *Star Trek*. Or Mustafar from *Star Wars*. Another great tale of my time."

Alfric grunted. "You must tell me these stories."

"Someday."

The two stood together, watching the systems float by as Solaris steered them towards their new destination, and the final crystal.

"Hey," said Rynah as she appeared, "we will be landing soon."

"Very well," said Alfric.

"Have either of you seen Tom and his partner in crime, Solon?" asked Rynah.

"No," replied Brie.

Rynah frowned. She knew where they were. "Meet me in the shuttle bay."

Rynah hurried away, rounding corners and crossing corridors as she went to the storage room that Tom had taken over and turned into a tinkering room, or as Rynah like to call it, a disaster area. She heard his and Solon's voices as she neared the doorway. "You two," she said.

Tom snatched a sheet and flung it over a very humanoid looking object.

"What's going on in here?" asked Rynah.

"Nothing," said Tom.

Rynah eyed him, not believing him.

"Really! It's a surprise," Tom said.

Rynah groaned. She didn't have time for this. "We're nearing Sunlil. It's time to go."

Tom's playful expression turned serious. He nodded at Solon, who snatched a holopad, and they hurried out of the room.

Usef, Alfric, and Brie waited for them when they entered the shuttle bay. Rynah checked her weapons and handed one to each of her companions. "Solaris," said Rynah, "you know what to do?"

"Yes," answered Solaris. "I will watch the skies, while you six look for the final crystal."

"Everyone in the shuttle."

The others obeyed, climbing into the small craft and fastening their safety harnesses. Rynah jumped in the pilot's seat. "Ready?"

"Launch doors opening," said Solaris over the intercom.

"We'll be back soon, hopefully," said Rynah.

"I'll be waiting," said Solaris.

"Take care of yourself," Rynah said, as a touch of affection for the ship struck her.

She engaged the engines and pressed the throttle, guiding the small craft out of the ship and into open space. Rynah's bravura showed as she guided the shuttle into the planet's atmosphere and the volcanic plumes of ebony smoke that saturated the air around them, making navigation difficult. Using her guidance system, she steered them to a landing area she had found earlier while aboard Solaris.

Lava flows lined the surface of the ground, forming molten rivers of death where she maneuvered the ship. Double checking her readings, Rynah placed the shuttlecraft on solid ground. "Be careful when exiting," she said. "This planet is known for its volcanic eruptions."

"Just another day in paradise," quipped Usef as he unfastened his harness.

They exited the shuttle and stopped short, staring out at the massive river of lava that flowed several miles ahead of them. Brie tugged at her collar from the heat, wondering where anyone could have hidden a crystal in this inhospitable place.

"Okay," said Rynah, "the crystal is supposed to be somewhere on this planet." She pulled out her handheld holopad where she had downloaded a copy of the ancient text. "We need to look for the *Mesir's* head."

"The what?" asked Brie.

"It's a bird of sorts," said Rynah.

"I suggest we head for higher ground," said Usef.

"What makes you say that?" asked Rynah.

"Because birds always nest in high places. The *Mesir* is a majestic bird known as the king of the skies on Lanyr."

"It is logical," said Alfric. "I think there is a trail over there."

The others looked where he pointed.

"It's settled then." Rynah pocketed her holopad and headed in the direction Alfric had pointed, taking the lead like she always did.

They trekked over the solid ground, a blackened planet made so by the soot that formed a fine, yet gritty, silt that creeped into the crevices of their shoes as ash floated around them, hovering in the air and filling their lungs as they coughed; their resolve to locate the crystal drove them onward. Embers danced in circles around them, mimicking fireflies.

The trail led up a steep incline. Using their hands, each hoisted themselves upward. Despite the sharp rocks that cut into their skin as they climbed (Solon's especially, forcing him to wrap cloth around them for protection), they continued onward.

In the lead, Rynah paused, looking back as her companions struggled to move up the slope. Her foot slipped. Pebbles clacked against the rock as they clattered to the uneven ground below them. Usef's hand appeared. Thankful, Rynah took it, allowing him to help her regain her feet, and gave him a wry smile.

"Thanks," she said.

"No problem."

Below them, Brie climbed upward at a slower pace. Soot covered her pasty skin, painting her with blackened streaks as it mingled with the sweat that streamed down her neck, smearing the ash that had collected upon her. She reached for a protruding rock. Grabbing it, she heaved herself upward, her now strong muscles having little difficulty.

"Place your foot here," said Alfric, pointing to a secure space, still feeling the need to protect her.

Brie did. Using the leverage Alfric provided, she pushed herself upward until she reached the top of the trail where the others stood. Tom reached down for her. Brie took his clammy palm and he heaved her to her feet. Regaining her composure, she glanced out at the landscape below them.

"Whoa," said Brie.

"I know," muttered Tom.

From their vantage point, each saw the river of crusted lava; sparse leafless trees, resembling charred sticks, surrounded it with a massive expanse of grassland (which, to their surprise, was a rich and dark gold in color) grew, regardless of the gurgling volcano nearby. The ground shook beneath their feet, warning them that danger was not far away.

"This volcano isn't going to erupt anytime soon, is it?" asked Tom.

"It's always spewing lava," said Rynah. "The chances of a cataclysmic eruption is minimal. However, you will find that this planet constantly suffers from earthquakes."

"That's nice to know," Tom mumbled.

Rynah shook her head and continued onward as the others followed her. Each step they took strained their already tired muscles, even though they now walked on flat land; the soft ground formed casts around their feet.

Gentle roars rumbled around them as the volcano burped more of its molten core in sporadic bubbles of noxious gas; the ash decorated it the way a light snow dusts the ground. Alfric looked back. He wished to remember this moment as it mirrored his impression of the underworld.

"What is it?" asked Brie, seeing a side of Alfric she had never observed before, the side of a man that appreciated the beauty around him, while ignoring the need for honor.

"Look at it," said Alfric.

Brie turned and observed the mountain behind them. Darkened orange streams of molten lava snaked down its sides amidst black clouds of ash—lightning streaked through them, sending electrical shocks that struck the ground and scraggly sticks for trees—that enveloped it, save for a small hump sticking out of its sides, basking in the burnt rays of the red-orange sun.

"I shall have tales to tell when I return home. You will as well," said Alfric, taking on the role of mentor again.

"Well, for now, let's concentrate on finding the crystal," said Brie.

They both hurried after Rynah and the others, the earth rumbling beneath their feet as it swayed before stilling once more. Usef tripped over a rock poking out of the ground. He reached down for it and pulled it out; it turned to ash in his hands. Frowning, he looked around him, not liking the situation, hoping that Rynah was right about the volcano.

"Look!" Tom pointed at a boulder in the distance.

The others looked at it. It seemed to be a rock that bore a remarkable resemblance to the head of a bird.

Rynah pulled out her binoculars. "That's it!"

They ran for it. Excitement coursed through them as they neared the rock. Once there, they stopped cold. A dark cave loomed in front of them.

Usef noticed an inscription above the opening. "'*The labyrinth traps all in its lair. None enter who aren't caught in its snare.*' What does that mean?"

Rynah pulled out her holopad and looked up the same lines in the poem. "I think this is going to be more difficult than we thought."

"Yeah," joked Tom, "because it has been so easy up until now."

Rynah gave him a reprimanding look.

Alfric pulled out his sword, raising it before him. "Onward, I say. We have a quest to complete, and failure will not be tolerated."

Sharing the Viking's sentiment and wanting to get the ordeal over with, Brie stepped inside the cave, no longer fearing the unknown. "I did not escape Klanor's mind games just to be stopped by some warning posted thousands of years ago. We get that crystal, we stop him. That's all that matters."

"Alright, let's go," said Tom, following after Brie. "Besides, we did not come all this way for fun and games."

Alfric harumphed in response.

"Solon," said Rynah, "what do you say?"

"It is a fool that embarks on a journey, only to turn back when they have neared its end," Solon replied. "I agree with the others."

"Solaris," said Rynah in her earpiece, "the trail leads underground."

"I'm not sure how long we will be able to maintain communications. The rocks are full of iron and graphite, which might inhibit our ability to stay in touch."

"Understood. If we're not back within 48 hours, leave without us."

"Acknowledged," said Solaris.

"Everyone watch your step," said Rynah. "We've no idea what awaits us in there."

One by one, they entered the dark opening as it beckoned them to come inside. Rynah popped a glow stick, allowing its yellow light to illuminate their path. She handed more to the others. "Use these sparingly," she said. "I haven't many."

They walked down the sharp gradient of the lava tube (red, fuzzy moss covered the walls where water trickled down it), delving deep within the maze underneath the volcano. Blackened rock, with a ragged, knife-like edge, protruded from the sides, snagging their packs and clothing. Brie swiped her arm on one and it sliced her; Alfric grabbed her arm and wrapped a torn cloth from his shirt around the cut.

"It's just a scrape," she said.

"This will keep it clean," he said.

"I'll be fine. I'm not going anywhere this time."

Alfric released a huge sigh. "I know. I have taught you well, but twice in my life I have lost people I considered to be my family. Only one has been returned."

"Who was the other?" asked Brie.

"My sister, Gróa," Alfric replied. "It is because of me that she died. Each time I look at you, I see her. You have her eyes and…"

Brie placed a comforting hand on Alfric's arm. "I'm sure she forgives you."

"And you are just like the father I never had," said Tom, with a bit of sarcasm; he had overheard them. "You know, every time I look at you, I see major machismo."

Groaning, Alfric nudged Tom out of the way, hurrying after Rynah and Usef, while Brie chuckled.

"What?" Tom called after him. "I thought we were all having a moment."

"You really shouldn't tease him so much," Brie said.

"But it's so much fun," replied Tom.

"And a bit of a dangerous proposition," added Solon, who had watched the entire incident.

"We're on a planet that is covered in lava and has an active volcano," Tom said, his voice echoing through the tunnel as they all ran to catch up with the others.

Droplets of water fell from the ceiling, filling the tunnel with a hollow echo. Curious, Solon touched a small trickle of water that streamed down the rock wall before wiping the burning liquid off his skin. Tom hurried over to him. He sniffed it and backed away.

"It's acidic," he said. "The water is full of sulfur and acid from the volcanic activity on this planet. Best stay clear of it."

"Indeed," said Solon. He observed a small bit of red moss growing on the ceiling. "But apparently its poison does not kill everything."

Tom looked at the moss. "Odd."

He reached up and touched it, exposing a small round button

that was as black as the rock around them. Allowing his curiosity to get the better of him—he never could resist pushing buttons—he pressed it. Thunder rumbled around them, vibrating the tunnel.

"What was that?" asked Usef.

As though in answer to his question, the walls and floor around them trembled with violent jerks, causing pebbles to rain down around them; the cave floor suddenly turned smooth and slick, tipping and forming a steep slope, a slide. Tumbling, they careened downward, deeper into the planet's core (Usef and Tom being the only ones laughing and enjoying the ride), bumping into one another and smacking into every bump and crack, until they tumbled out at the bottom; their shouts and screams echoed around them. Crashing into the ground below, they rolled across it, only stopping when they struck a wall. Moaning, each of them sat up, rubbing their sore spots.

"What was that?" demanded Usef.

Alfric rose to his feet and stared up at where they had been. "Odin is testing us."

"Did any of you touch something?" asked Usef, rubbing his sore head.

"No," said Tom, "not a thing."

Rynah, Alfric, Solon, and Brie all turned in his direction, each giving him a nonbelieving look.

"Odin is indeed testing us," grumbled Alfric. A sharp noise forced him to turn around and he gasped at what he saw. Before him, stood a maze of volcanic rock and stone with spewing lava in small rivers, its orange glow providing the only light in the depths of the planet. "We must navigate our way through to prove our worth."

The others rose to their feet mesmerized. "It really is a labyrinth," breathed Rynah.

The grumbling of liquefied rock rose around them until a plume of lava spewed from a vent, creating a molten waterfall. Each watched, entranced.

"How do we navigate through?" asked Tom.

Rynah pulled out her holopad and brought up the ancient text she had downloaded onto it. She read the verses aloud.

> Far from home are you now.
> Cross the bridge to the maze's bow.
> What eyes have seen do not trust.
> Only the wise will find the invisible crust.

Tom groaned. "Can't they ever just write in plain English what they want us to do? There is no bridge!"

Rynah put the holopad away. "Well, there has to be one around here somewhere." She examined the edge of the rock cliff they stood upon and the river of lava flowing beneath them. "Everyone spread out. See if you can find anything that will let us cross."

Searching, each took a different part of the area. They studied the rock wall and the edge of the cliff, but none found anything.

Solon stepped away from the others. He scuffed his shoe across the cave floor. Bits of dirt fell, but stopped as though it hovered in midair. Intrigued, Solon knelt down to look closer. The dust had landed on rock when it should have continued its descent to the lava below. Remembering a time when he and his brother had hiked through the back hills near their home, he thought about a strange rock bridge they had found. It blended in with the landscape so well that none ever saw it, unless they stood upon it. It was sheer luck that they had discovered it at all.

Solon jumped to his feet. Realizing what he had to do, he stuck out his foot and stepped off the cliff.

From the other side of the chamber Rynah saw him. Horror filled her face as she watched the young man jump. "Solon!"

She and Usef dashed for him, but stopped.

Solon's feet landed on a hard surface. Regaining his composure, he turned around and realized that he stood upon the bridge to the other side: the invisible bridge. "I found it," he said.

"Well, I'll be damned," said Usef. "It really was invisible." He stepped a few paces to the left and right studying the crossing. "It blends in perfectly with the cliff and lava flow. How did you…"

"I remembered something," answered Solon.

They darted across the land bridge to the entrance to the maze. Once on the other side, a set of steps led them downward. Rynah took the lead, reading the poem.

> The maze you've entered, its path must be tread.
> Stray, but a little, you will all be dead.
> Let the philosopher's wisdom be your guide;
> tempered by love, you'll reach the other side.

"How does this book know everything?" asked Tom.

"What do you mean?" said Brie.

"Well, this entire trip, it's as though whoever wrote the poem knew everything we would do, or would need, to the last detail. It's just strange."

No one argued. Tom's statement voiced what they all thought.

"Philosopher's wisdom be our guide," said Usef. "Who…"

"I think it means me," said Solon.

"But how can you guide us through here?" asked Usef.

Solon pulled out another holopad, which Solaris had downloaded the text of the book he found onto. "When we visited that planet with the ruined buildings, I found this book. It intrigued me, so I took it. Solaris helped me translate it and put it on here."

"What was this book?" asked Rynah.

"It spoke of a labyrinth beneath a volcano."

"And now we stand in one that is beneath a fiery mountain," said Alfric. "Fortune has smiled upon us."

"It gets tricky, but it is in poetic verse as well." Solon tapped the top right corner of the holopad, turning it on and bringing to life the three-dimensional image of the book. He turned its holographic pages and read its text aloud.

Let thy feet take you left
to a bend and a narrow cliff.

"I guess we go left then," said Brie. The others stared at her. "Why not? What do we have to lose?"

"I'm in," said Tom. "It's not like some poem is going to make us walk off a cliff. Oh, wait—it just did!" Tom looked at Solon. "Lead the way, my good man."

The others glanced from one to the other until Usef said, "What other choice do we have?"

Rynah shook her head. She had learned to quit questioning the ancient text. It always proved correct. "Lead the way," she said to Solon.

A bit hesitant, Solon turned left, taking them through a narrow tunnel. He followed it as it twisted and turned until a giant opening greeted them. Solon stopped. They stood upon another cliff.

"Does anyone else get the feeling that these ancient texts are trying to kill us?" asked Tom as he leaned over the ledge, looking at the lava below. "Now what?"

Solon checked the text in his hands as he tried to figure it out. "We need to cross."

"Is there another invisible bridge?" asked Usef.

Solon read the text.

Hands and feet on the wall,
must like an insect crawl.

"Oh, yeah, that's really useful," scoffed Tom. "What?" he said when Rynah gave him a piercing stare. "It's just… I'm sick of these lyrical rhymes!"

Rynah laughed, understanding Tom's frustration. She, too, had grown tired of them.

"Guys?" said Brie, pointing at the rock wall next to them that stretched from the cliff they stood upon to the other side. Small bulbs poked out from it, providing hand and footholds for any who dared to climb across. "Looks like you have to move sideways like the way a bug crawls across the wall."

An ear-piercing roar filled the space around them as its echo quaked their hearts.

"Are there monsters down here?" asked Tom.

"I believe we are in Hades' domain," said Solon.

Rynah grasped her laser pistol as her eyes roamed the area. "There is no telling what manner of creatures live here. Keep your eyes peeled and your ears open."

Alfric moved to the wall.

"What are you doing?" asked Usef.

"I will cross."

"We should…"

"I will go," said Alfric. He pulled out a small knife and handed it to Usef. "In case I don't come back."

Usef took the blade without a word. His sober expression said it all.

Studying the wall, and the bits of rock protruding from it, Alfric lunged, gripping the jagged surface with all the strength his fingers and arms held. Bubbling lava rippled below him. Alfric reached out and grasped the next handhold. His heavy boots clacked against the stone as he felt for a foothold, snaking his way across like a spider. The gurgling lava below him reminded him of his fate, should he fail.

Sweat greased his palms as he reached for the next hold; his fingers scraped the ragged rock as he seized it. His hand slipped. Dropping a couple of feet, Alfric clutched the wall as best he could, the rough edges scraping the skin off his fingers, before stopping his descent. He remained where he was, catching his breath.

"Alfric!" yelled Brie, worry in her voice.

He glanced over. The others watched in frightened anticipation. Searing heat from the molten river burned his flesh as more sweat poured down his neck and back. Sending a silent prayer, Alfric studied the faces of his companions. His eyes settled on Brie's. So much like his sister. For a moment, the painful memory of how he had abandoned his sibling to her death gripped him, motivating him. Determined not to fail, Alfric heaved himself upward. His muscles strained as the sinews appeared beneath the skin with each effort he gave. At the pace of a snail, he scaled the wall.

Only a few feet left to go. The droning roar of the lava filled his eardrums as it tried to mask the throbbing of his heart. He seized another rock. With a grunt, Alfric hauled himself sideways as he hugged the wall. *Almost there.* His foot found another hold. Placing his weight on it, Alfric grabbed another and another until he had reached the end. He jumped off the wall and onto the other side, his feet plopping on the smooth stone.

He roamed the area, searching for anything that could be used as a way to cross. Nothing. Frustrated, Alfric let out a howl as he tore the place apart. *How are the others to cross?* he asked himself. He slammed his fist into the side of the wall. A rope dangled before his face. Cautious, he took it, studying the strange fibers as he had never seen a rope made of such material.

Alfric whistled. "Catch this!" He swung the rope at them.

Usef reached out and caught it. Tugging on it, he realized that it would hold no more than one. "Right. One at a time. Brie, you first."

Stepping forward, Brie took the line, unsure of what to do.

"Just jump and hang on," said Usef.

Brie wrapped her fingers tight around the rope. Taking a deep breath, she leapt. Sweltering, moist air rushed her face, singing in her ears as she swung to the other side. Alfric's strong grip seized her. He pulled her up and sent the rope back across.

Tom appeared, followed by Solon. The ground shook. Ryan and Usef stepped back as cracks appeared beneath their feet. Their jagged forms stretched up the walls and around the ceilings. More splits appeared, forcing Rynah and Usef to dance around them in an effort to avoid their snares. Steam burst from a fresh crack, missing Usef by inches as he dove out of the way. A low rumble echoed beneath them.

"The lava is shifting!" shouted Usef.

A piece of shale, the size of Rynah's head, crashed next to her feet. Startled, she jumped back only to find that another crack had appeared. Scalding heat spewed from it, forcing her to leap away. Usef grabbed her. He looked across the way at Alfric.

The Viking chucked the line to them. Usef grabbed it. He and Rynah locked eyes for a moment.

"It won't hold the both of us," she said.

Coiling the cord around his arm, Usef wrapped his other arm around Rynah's waist, squeezing the air out of her. "It'll have to."

As another split tore the ledge they stood upon, sending bits of molten liquid upward, Usef dove with Rynah. The rope strained under their weight as they swung to the other side. Hands reached for them, but failed to catch them. They arced back toward the ledge they had left, which lay covered in lava.

"Usef!" screamed Rynah.

He tightened his grip on both her and the rope as they swung back towards the others. The rope lurched. Looking up, Usef noticed that it had begun to fray. As the other side drew near, he glanced at Rynah and she read the message within his eyes.

He let go.

The two of them plunged as the momentum of their descent propelled them forward. Both Rynah and Usef slammed into the rock wall of the cliff the others stood upon. Usef's hands gripped the rock. A yelp alerted him to trouble. He noticed Rynah below him, hanging on with one hand. Her grip slipped. Usef reached for her, seizing her wrist before she fell into the lava flow below. Another hand snatched his and Alfric pulled them both to safety.

Sighing with relief, Rynah clapped Usef on the shoulders in appreciation. "I don't ever want to do that again."

"Agreed," said Usef.

Another quake shook the ground, causing Solon to tumble over. Tom dove for him, grabbing him before he rolled over the edge.

Clink. Clink.

Solon's holopad skipped over the ledge.

"No!" yelled Solon, lunging for it, but Tom held firm. "You don't understand! It has the way through! I need it!"

Solon rose to his feet and paced the area in frustration, afraid that he had let the others down. Brie placed a gentle hand on his shoulder, but he shook it off. "You don't understand. On that thing was the way through. I spent countless hours studying it. Without it, I don't know how to navigate this maze."

The others watched in silence as Solon hunkered in a corner with a despondent look on his face, seeing a side of him they had never witnessed.

"What do we do?" asked Usef.

Rynah silenced him. She understood Solon's frustration; she had been there herself. She pulled out her own holopad and chucked it into the lava below.

"What the…" began Usef.

Rynah's glare stopped him. She understood at that moment that they didn't need the holopads. All the time she had spent reading the ancient text, she had memorized it. She just didn't realize it until then.

Rynah walked over to Solon and placed a tender hand on his. "Solon, we don't need it."

"But without it, I don't know how to guide us through here."

Rynah lifted his chin so that her eyes bore into his. "I, too, have spent hours reading the ancient text, and in all of that time, I never realized it, but I had inadvertently memorized it. We rely too much on technology and not on our minds."

"I…"

"You spent hours upon hours studying that book."

"Yes."

"Then be the scholar I know you are."

Solon looked at her. His mind silenced as the same cognizance hit him that Rynah had just touched upon. All his life he had been able to memorize what he read in the scrolls at the library. He just never had any faith in himself, but she had faith in him, and that belief forced his mind to remember what he already knew.

"There should be a solid wall through there. It's a doorway."

"How do we open it?" asked Rynah, with patience.

"You have to step on the mark of the scorpion."

"Okay then," said Rynah, "let's find this scorpion."

"It's not a real scorpion, is it?" asked Tom in a worried voice. He feared scorpions; his fear dated back to the time in grade school when one of the older students stole a scorpion from the biology lab and placed it in his sandwich during lunch as a practical joke.

Ignoring Tom's question, Rynah helped Solon to his feet. All of them walked through the narrow tunnel to the dead end that Solon had spoken of. A metallic door blocked their path. Using another glow light, Rynah lit up the area. "Spread out."

Each took a corner, looking for anything that might resemble a scorpion. Cobwebs hung low, ensnaring them with their stickiness. As they rummaged around, particles of dust mixed with ash floated around them. Tom's foot bumped something. Kneeling down, he brushed away soot and black dirt, revealing a small square peg with the depiction of a scorpion. "Hey!" he shouted.

The others gathered around. "You found it," said Brie.

"Step on it," said Usef.

"Solon should do it," Tom said, pushing Solon closer to it.

Solon lifted his foot, allowing it to hover a moment before stepping on the scorpion-shaped stone. Grinding filled the air as giant rollers dropped and a door opened, revealing a dark interior. Each walked through, unsure of what lay beyond. The door closed behind them, sealing them inside.

They whipped around.

"Locked," said Rynah.

Having no other choice, they walked onward across the new chamber and to the archway at the other end. A low growl echoed around them.

"Are there animals down here?" asked Tom.

"The dark has many creatures," said Alfric, pulling his sword free of its scabbard.

Rynah and Usef clutched their pistols. "Be careful," she said.

Rynah strode to the other end where in opening appeared. "Come on," she said, waving the others through.

Brie, Solon, and Alfric walked through the doorway. A swish filled the air as a panel shut, separating them from the others. Frightened for their safety, Rynah hurled herself into the metal door, her fists banging it in a vain attempt to open it.

On the other side, Alfric struck the metal door with his blade; sparks flew with each swing. "We are sealed in here."

Another low growl sounded; this time, it was right behind them. Dreading what they would find, they turned around. In the center of the cavern, crouched a creature with spiked fur on its back and claws the length of Brie's foot. It spat at them, saliva dripping from the sides of its open mouth.

"Solon," said Brie, a quiver in her voice, "what did the book say about this?"

Solon thought about it, but the only words he remembered were:

Trust not thy senses. They deceive.
Mercy's gift thee must give to receive.

The creature lunged. Alfric shoved Brie and Solon out of the way. Both crashed onto the stone surface and rolled across the ground, while Alfric and the strange creature circled the room, facing one another. It attacked. Alfric swerved to the side, missing a crushing blow from its claws. He whirled around. The creature jumped at him. Alfric raised his sword, clipping the animal on the side of the neck, drawing a trickle of blood. With rage, the creature howled. It shook its head in vehemence as it pranced around the chamber before stopping; a bone chilling glare filled its eyes.

"Does it look bigger to you?" asked Solon.

Alfric and Brie looked at the creature. It had doubled in size. They each swore in their native tongue. It lunged for them again. Brie pushed Alfric out of the way, while she somersaulted beneath the creature's belly, ripping out the dagger that the Viking had given before leaving Solaris and poking the beast in the shin. Roaring, it faced her. As Brie eyed it, the creature grew in size once more as saliva dripped from its razor fangs, drawing closer to her.

Alfric jumped on it, landing on its back. As the creature tried to fling him off, it backhanded Brie, sending her flying across the room. She slammed into the wall, slumping to the floor.

"Brie!" Solon charged the creature, while Alfric hung onto its back. The animal danced about in a frenzy, but the Viking's grip remained firm.

Dazed, Brie sat up, shaking her head. As the fog cleared, she noticed glowing eyes staring back at her from a hole in the wall. She looked closer. Three cubs huddled in the small space. One growled at her, its fur bristling. Brie glanced at Alfric and Solon, who still battled with the creature and understood the beast's aggressiveness towards them.

She found a lone rock. Scooping it up, Brie flung it at the animal to get its attention. The beast turned around. Its expression changed from anger to fear as it realized where she stood.

Seizing his opportunity, Alfric jabbed his sword at one of its legs. The creature lifted it up in pain, losing its balance and toppling over. Both Alfric and Solon jumped on it, pulling its head back to expose the tender flesh of its neck.

"No!" screamed Brie, stopping them.

"Brie," said Solon, "this thing almost killed us."

"Look!" She pointed at the small hole in the wall and the three cubs within. Remembering the lines Solon had repeated, Brie continued, "She's just protecting her cubs."

Alfric raised his sword.

"Please," Brie pleaded.

Alfric stopped. He lowered his weapon and stood back, releasing the creature.

Brie stepped forward, her arms held out in a submissive posture. She knelt next to the animal, placing a gentle hand upon its fur; the softness of it surprised her. "We are just as scared as you. We just wish to pass through and mean you no harm."

The creature stood up. Alfric's grip on his sword tightened, but Brie's hand stopped him. The animal sniffed Brie's mop of hair, its nose rummaging through it, taking in her scent before turning away. It vanished. Surprised, Brie jerked her head towards the hole in the wall. The cubs had gone as well.

The lock on the door popped, and in rushed Rynah, Usef, and Tom.

"I don't understand," said Brie. "Where did they go?"

"They?" asked Usef. "They who?"

"We encountered a foul beast," said Alfric, "but it has vanished like the spirits."

A zap drew Usef's attention. He walked over to it and pulled out a small box. "It's a holo emitter," he said, "used to produce holograms." He pressed a button and the creature appeared again. Everyone jumped, but Usef turned it off.

"That was a bit too realistic," said Brie.

"Probably supposed to be," said Usef. "There is something strange about this entire place. The walls and ground look and feel like stone, but the doors are metal, and this holo emitter has no business on a volcanic planet."

"This whole thing is weird," said Tom.

In silence, Rynah agreed. She didn't like how the tunnels of a volcanic planet seemed to resemble a ship, but one she had never seen. "We should move on."

"Why?" asked Usef.

"That crystal is here somewhere," said Rynah. "I can't explain it, but the ancient poems have described everything we have done in perfect detail. The book Solon found has proven invaluable. I don't know why that is, or why this cavern seems to be made of metal, but I do know that Klanor is on his way here. He will not stop to ask about this place. He only wants the crystal, and I aim to stop him."

"So, what do we do now?" Tom asked Solon.

Solon thought a moment as the next lines of verse entered his mind.

> Think on the path thee has tread.
> Treat like a riddle to move ahead.

> Far thee has come and heavy is the load.
> Creatures that you've seen are your code.

"You know," said Tom, "I am getting really tired of all this poetry."

The others agreed, but remained silent, each wondering what the lines Solon had recited meant.

A panel the size of an index card slid open, revealing a holopad.

"A code? Of course," shouted Usef. "We need to type the code into here."

"What code?" asked Tom.

While the others discussed what Usef had mentioned and what they should type into the pad, Alfric pondered the verses Solon had told them. It hit him. "This is a puzzle, a riddle."

"What?" asked Tom.

"This labyrinth is a puzzle," Alfric stated again. "What must you enter on that thing?"

"These are numbers," said Rynah, "and it looks like it takes three."

Alfric thought some more. *Creatures that you've seen.* "How many beasts have we met in this place?"

"Beasts?" asked Usef.

Solon understood Alfric's meaning. "There was the creature we fought."

"And its three cubs," said Brie.

"Any others?" asked Alfric.

"That scorpion," said Usef. "The carving of the scorpion."

"So one scorpion, one monster, three cubs," said Tom.

Rynah typed in the numbers 1, 1, 3. The pad turned off as clamps released, but they saw nothing.

"Now what?" asked Tom.

Solon recited the next verse.

Upward thee must rise
And cast off the final disguise.

A series of snaps and bangs filled the air, bouncing off the stone walls as the floor moved in a circular motion while rising upward. Each of them jerked in an effort to maintain their balance, wondering what was happening. Picking up momentum, the floor rose into the air with them upon it as they moved up through the cylindrical cavern and to the ceiling.

"Now this is just creepy," muttered Tom.

The rotating floor stopped as it reached its end. A domed ceiling loomed above them, allowing the orange glow from the volcano to fill the room. Tom touched an upturned office chair that crumbled beneath his fingers. He looked around at the computer terminals that looked both archaic and technologically advanced.

Smoke rose from the crater of the volcano. Rynah studied it, not liking what she saw. She riffled through items on the desks, wondering what that place was. "I do not recognize this technology."

"Neither do I," said Usef.

Brie's foot bumped something. Looking down, she noticed what appeared to be a stick poking out from underneath a pile of rubble. She removed the blocks of concrete, revealing a skeleton. Stifling a surprised shriek, Brie summoned the others over.

"What?' asked Rynah, stopping the moment she saw the remains. She reached down and picked at the patch on the corpse's clothing, its well-preserved state astounded her. The emblem matched the mark scratched on one of the crystals they had found earlier.

Words of the ancient poem echoed through her mind.

> You'll know the path by its mark.
> Twice you've seen it in the dark.

Rynah dropped the patch. Questions filled her head.

"Guys," said Tom, summoning them over to a corner of the room.

"What is it?" asked Usef.

Tom pointed at a raised platform. "I've been studying this thing and I think it might be a teleportation device."

"A what?" asked Solon.

"In your stories," said Tom, "the gods can appear and disappear quickly—vanish, basically."

"Yes," said Solon and Alfric together.

"This device would allow someone to do the same."

"That kind of teleportation does not exist," said Usef. "We've only been able to go small distances. You're talking about some much bigger."

"That you know of," said Tom, "but I knew someone back at the academy that was fiddling with the idea and believed that one day we would be able to cross whole solar systems. Besides, how did Solaris bring us here?"

Rynah thought that was a good question. She never questioned Solaris when she insisted on summoning the four heroes from the myth. Somehow, she had transported them across time and space. Could she—Rynah shook such thoughts from her head. Now wasn't the time.

"What does he mean brought them here?" asked Usef.

"Solaris somehow managed to transport them from their own planet and time to here," said Rynah. "I never thought much of it then, but I think Tom might be right; but this place looks old—ancient almost."

"Ancient with some modern-like, and futuristic, equipment," muttered Brie.

"Exactly," said Tom. "This place reminds me of the pyramids of Egypt, yet it has desks and chairs like in our world. I might be able to get this thing working."

"How?" said Usef. "There's no power."

Tom kicked something and lights around the platform flickered on, while a hum filled the air. A grinding noise reverberated around them. Whirling around, they watched as a door, disguised as part of the wall with shelves built in, slid open, revealing an enclosed space.

"I wasn't expecting that," said Tom.

Each treaded with care as they walked inside the secret chamber. On a pedestal, in the center of the room, rested a lone crystal with a rose-colored light emanating from it. Rynah noted the same mark upon it. She raised her hand to grab it, but jerked it back.

"What are you waiting for?" said Usef.

Upon his encouragement, Rynah wrapped her thin fingers around the crystal. Warmth spilled from it. She held it close, thinking of Marlow.

"What does the text say to do now?" asked Brie.

"That's where it gets a little strange," replied Rynah as she recited the verse.

Coveted treasure you now possess.
Thieves upon you, they will transgress.
Lost will your prize be,
yet gain another from the sea.

Fire surrounds you from within,
while enemies trespass your glen.
A friend you'll lose, but one you'll gain;
reborn in body, but spirit same.

"That doesn't make much sense," said Tom.

"We should get back," said Alfric, his nerves on edge. Something felt off and he wished to be rid of that place.

"Agreed," Rynah said as she turned to exit the chamber, but stopped. In the doorway stood Klanor with Stein and a room full of soldiers.

"Leaving so soon?" said Klanor; the gloating in his voice had a fake air about it, but Rynah never noticed as her anger towards him boiled to the surface.

"How'd…"

"It wasn't difficult," interrupted Klanor. "You see, while you six were busy navigating the maze, we just followed the bread crumbs you left. I must say that this is an odd place to hide such a valuable item. I'll take it now."

Rynah hugged the crystal as daggers flew from her eyes at Klanor.

"The crystal. Now." Klanor held his hand out.

Though reluctant, Rynah held it out to him, knowing she was in no position to argue. He seized it; greed, and woefulness, filled his face. "At last," he breathed. "I now possess them all."

Brie noticed the same coveting expression on Stein's face, but it was more sinister, more frightening than Klanor's, and it unnerved her.

"Take this," said Klanor to a soldier, "to the ship. We have a weapon to test, and what better place to do it than here?"

"We could test it at Dirthe," said Stein.

"That planet has over 8 billion people living there," Klanor replied, aghast.

"Precisely," Stein said, "what better place for the universe to see your might?"

"We test it here," Klanor said, his voice firm.

"Should I lock them all in the room?" asked Stein, displeased with being contested.

"Everyone, but her," said Klanor as he pointed at Rynah. "She's coming with us."

"She has openly defied you at every turn," challenged Stein.

"You have my orders," Klanor said.

Stein inclined his head in obedience.

While the others watched the exchange between Stein and Klanor, none noticed Solon moving closer to the soldier with the crystal. The young philosopher caught Tom's eye and he understood Solon's intent. With lightning speed, Solon snatched the crystal from the guard, flinging him to the floor. He tossed it to Rynah, who caught it. At the same instant, Tom shoved Rynah and Usef, because he was closest, onto the transport pad and punched the execution key. Lights flared up, surrounding Rynah and Usef as the transporter came to life. When the lights had faded, Rynah and Usef had gone, and the machine died, having used the last of its power.

Infuriated, Klanor backhanded Stein. "I want that crystal! Do not return without it!"

Stein rubbed the welt on his cheek as he eyed Klanor with murderous intent. "Yes, sir," he hissed before stalking out of the room.

Chapter 35
SUNLIL

In the howling, ash-filled winds of the volcano, Rynah and Usef materialized. Tiny streams of lava snaked past them. Rynah looked around, but found no signs of Klanor's men. "Usef, what happened?"

"I think we've been transported to the side of the volcano," replied Usef. "I see the shuttle right down there."

Rynah looked at where he pointed and spotted the small craft nestled at the base of the mountain in a small clearing. She didn't see any of Klanor's men nearby. "Come on," she said, "we need to get back to Solaris."

"What about the others?"

"We can't help them here."

Rynah trotted down the side of the volcano, clutching the crystal in her fist, her feet slipping and sliding on the smooth surface as black pebbles clacked downward. Together, they crab-walked down the mountain as silt shifted underneath their feet. Usef caught Rynah as she started to lose her footing.

A bit of rock broke underneath him. Usef rolled down the volcano's side, bumping into every sharp stone as he fell. He neared a ledge;

he reached for it and caught the edge, his bloodied fingers scraping against the rock. As he dangled in the air, Usef glanced around at the white particles that waltzed in the wind. Plumes of lava seeped out of the ground, reminding him of the danger he and Rynah were in. He grabbed the ledge with his other hand.

Rynah's hand seized his. Staring into one another's eyes, each read the unspoken thoughts within them. Heaving, Rynah's muscles strained as she pulled Usef to safety and both leaned back on the edge, catching their breaths. The shuttle lay just below.

POP!

Laser fire struck the lava cinders next to Usef's hip. Scrambling to their feet, both tottered down the hill half sliding, half jogging as they went. Klanor's men stood above and below them, firing upon them. Ducking as they ran, Usef and Rynah reached the shuttle, hunkering behind it.

"How do we get inside?" asked Usef.

"Cover me," said Rynah, as she darted to the hatch and punched in a code. Pings echoed around her as laser blasts struck the craft. The door opened.

"In!" shouted Rynah.

Usef sprang from behind the shuttle, firing two shots at the armed men that surrounded them before darting inside.

Rynah jumped into the pilot's seat and started the engines. Without waiting for them to reach full power, she pulled back on the throttle and propelled them into the air, heading straight into space. "Solaris, we're coming in hot," she said into the comm unit.

"Understood," said Solaris.

Rynah increased their speed.

"Easy!" yelled Usef, as she swerved to miss one of Klanor's ships.

Rynah paid no attention. Another headed straight for them. She jerked the controls, banking to the right before veering to the left. Punching the afterburners, Rynah raced through the upper atmosphere of Sunlil, away from Klanor's armada. She spotted Solaris.

"I see you," said Solaris. "The shuttle doors are open, but you'll have to slow down to dock properly."

"No time!" Rynah shouted.

Cannon fire exploded near them, jockeying the small vessel. Hands tight on the controls, Rynah concentrated only on reaching Solaris. She lined up.

"Rynah!" shouted Usef.

She ignored him. With one last burst of acceleration, she steered the shuttle into the heart of Solaris before shutting off the engines and extending the flaps. Screeching metal attacked their ears as the ship scraped across the floor of Solaris before crashing into a wall.

Soon after Tom had activated the transporter, a laser blast struck the console near his head, destroying it and any ability to use the device. He dove to the ground, somersaulting as he rolled away. Lights blew as sparks rained upon them in dazzling fashion; smoke rose from the transporter pad.

Solon whistled at Tom. Reading his message, Tom waited for Solon's signal. Together, they jumped on one of Klanor's men, dragging him to the floor and wrestling his laser pistol away from him. Tom punched him in the jaw. He took the pistol and tossed it to Brie, who caught it with ease. Solon ripped the laser rifle from the man's shoulders. He glanced at Brie. Focused on the armed men before her, Brie never noticed the one that snuck up from behind. Solon aimed the rifle at the man, remembering everything Rynah had taught him about such weapons. Holding steady, he fired. His shot struck the attacker in the neck, causing him to collapse next to Brie.

Startled, Brie jumped before nodding her head in appreciation. She crept to the doorway, hunkering behind the corner as laser fire zipped by her in all directions, and fired off two shots. More whizzed past her head in response. Peeking around the corner, Brie noticed that Klanor's men attempted to set up a laser cannon, aimed right at them.

"Alfric!" she called, pointing at it.

The Viking turned around and looked at the weapon. Understanding what she wanted, he bashed the hilt of his sword into his opponent's face and charged through the door, bolting through it, past Brie and the others. Dodging laser fire, Alfric ducked and turned on his heels as he jabbed his blade upward, catching one unsuspecting soldier. Without pause, he ran forward, ramming his sword into another. His constant movements made hitting him impossible. He noticed a man with a laser rifle aimed at Solon. Alfric punched him, wrestled the weapon away, and fired twice at the soldier before tossing it to Tom and the others.

He had almost reached the weapon. Charging forward, he focused only on the task at hand. Searing pain gripped his shoulder as a laser blast scraped him. Ignoring it, he willed himself onward. Two guarded the weapon. Alfric slammed into one, knocking him to the floor. He turned on the other, using his sword to swipe the laser weapon from his opponent's hands. With one swift strike, he killed the man. The click of a pistol hit his ear.

"Drop your weapon," said one of Klanor's men as he pointed his laser pistol at Alfric.

The Viking stared at him with a callous expression. He swung his blade at the man, cutting him down with ease.

"Alfric!" Tom tossed a ball of what looked like wax at Alfric.

He caught it. Not knowing what it was, but understanding what Tom wanted done with it, he placed it on the device and ran away. Ignoring all else, Alfric squeezed past Brie and the others, ducking behind cover just as an ear-splitting explosion filled the room, causing it to quake. Silence loomed as the fire and bits of debris dissipated. Solon peered around the corner of the doorway. Klanor's men lay on the ground, unmoving.

"We need to secure that outer door," said Brie.

"I might have an idea," Tom said as he ran for the door. "Just keep those guys off my back."

Alfric, Solon, and Brie followed after him, taking their positions just inside the outer door. A laser blast struck the entryway just as Solon poked his head out. Jerking back, he turned to the others. "I believe they have returned."

"No kidding," mumbled Tom. "I never should have taught you sarcasm." Tom fiddled with a panel near the door. "I need a screwdriver, or something, to get this thing off."

Alfric pushed Tom back. Raising his sword high above his head, he smashed it into the paneling, knocking it free. The metal plate thudded on the tile floor, showing its new dent.

"Thanks," said Tom.

Alfric said nothing as he took his place beside Brie.

"Here," she said, handing him a laser pistol. "This might work better than your sword."

Alfric stared at it. He preferred his blade over the alien weapon. Seizing a knife, he flung it at a charging soldier, striking him in the neck. "Keep it," said Alfric as the soldier fell.

Brie smiled at his stubbornness. She fired two shots at another of Klanor's men. More gathered in the hall, drawing closer. "Tom, now would be a good time."

"Almost there." Sweat dripped from Tom's chin as he worked with the wires of the door's locking mechanism, his hands moving at a furious speed. He held two in his fingers, a red and a yellow one. If he combined the wrong wires together, he would ensure that the door stayed open.

Laser fire pelted the walls around them, leaving blackened scorch marks. In retaliation, Alfric seized the panel he had ripped from the wall and thrust it into the hallway at the oncoming soldiers. The heavy panel slammed into them, forcing them to tumble over. Brie and Solon fired their weapons at the oncoming soldiers.

A yelp forced Brie to jerk her head in Solon's direction. He had taken a shot to his leg. Without thinking, she ran to him, pulling him into the room and behind the safety of the doorway. One of Klanor's men attacked her, having been able to sneak up from the side. They rolled across the floor, the pistol flying from Brie's hand. The man hit her in the stomach. Gasping, Brie struggled to maintain consciousness as the pain threatened to overtake her. She rammed her knee into her opponent.

Brie crawled over to the weapon on the floor, but the man had seized her ankles, yanking her back. She kicked him. Undaunted, he flipped her over, straddling her, his hands wrapping around her throat. Desperate, and choking, Brie flailed her arms at him. Something poked her side. Remembering the dagger that Alfric had given her before leaving Solaris, Brie grabbed it, freeing it from its sheath and plunged it into the man's side. His grip relaxed. Forcing him off her, Brie dove for the laser pistol and fired two shots in his chest.

With no time to think, she hurried to Solon, who clutched his bleeding wound. Brie fired five shots from the laser pistol and placed the searing hot tip on Solon's wound to cauterize it; he screamed in pain. Once done, she tore a piece of her shirt and wrapped it around his leg to protect it until they could administer medical treatment.

"I'm all right," Solon said.

"Course you are," replied Brie. "Tom!"

"Almost there!" shouted Tom.

A huge battle cry escaped Alfric's lips as he lifted one of the attacking soldiers into the air and threw him into the hallway. His massive form made him a startling sight. The helmeted soldiers paused in their attack as they watched Alfric stand erect in the doorway, daring them to attack him.

"Kill him!" shouted Klanor.

Just then, the doors slid shut. Tom joined two more wires together and another set of doors sealed. "That's it," he said. "They can't get in. Well, for now, anyway."

"How long will these doors hold?" asked Brie.

"Not sure," replied Tom. "I just hope Rynah and Usef got away."

Solon's sharp intake of breath told Brie that his leg hurt more than he let on. "I need something to clean this wound."

Alfric stormed through the room, tearing things apart and rifled through the drawers, nooks, and crannies. He had remembered seeing a flask—at least, that's what he called it—and he intended to find it. His boot bumped something. Reaching down, he clutched what he searched for. Alfric pulled the cork off. The sweet aroma of alcohol told him that he had guessed correctly as to the container's contents. "Here," he tossed it to Brie.

She clutched the bottle and poured the liquid on Solon's wound.

Sharp pain seized the young scholar's leg as he gripped it tighter and clenched his teeth.

"Sorry," said Brie.

"It's okay," Solon said, as Brie removed the scrap from her shirt and wrapped a clean bandage, which she had gotten from a first aid kit, around it.

Bang!

They all turned towards the door. "What's that?" asked Brie.

"They are attempting to storm the doors," said Alfric. "How long will they hold?"

"I don't know," said Tom, "and there is no other way out."

Alfric gripped his sword as he approached the doors, ready for whatever came through them. "Then we hold this position until our dying breaths."

Stein marched into the ship that he, Klanor, and the soldiers had used to land on the surface. Fury fueled his movements as he stormed into the command center of the vessel. "Where is she?"

Eyes stared back at him as they wondered what Stein had meant by "she".

"Don't stand there like a bunch of idiots," roared Stein. "Where did Rynah and the one with her go to? Two people transported from that bunker and I want to know where they are."

"Sir," said one, "a shuttle craft is leaving the planet's surface."

Stein looked at the screen. "Track it. It's her."

While the young man obeyed his orders, Stein stepped off the ship and watched as a lone vessel rose into the burnt sky; lava bombs left black streaks in it. He touched his earpiece, which he had inserted before leaving the armada to come to the planet. "It is time. Await my signal," he said to his consort on the other end.

Usef lifted his head. He looked around as he regained his bearings. Rynah lay slumped over the console.

"Rynah." He shook her shoulder.

Groaning, she sat up. "What happened?"

"I think you managed to crash successfully."

Rynah laughed. Cannon blasts beyond the hull reminded them that they were still in danger. Rynah seized the crystal and opened the hatch to the shuttle and jumped out, running straight for the command center of Solaris; Usef was right behind.

"Solaris!"

"I am attempting to evade them, but they seem determined to capture us," said Solaris.

Rynah snaked her way through Solaris, reaching the command center just in time to see that they were on a collision course with another ship. She plopped in the pilot's seat and rammed the helmet on her head. With a single thought, Solaris jerked downward, missing the other ship by a few feet.

Solaris, target the main ship in the center.

Understood.

Solaris aimed her weapons at Rynah's intended target and fired. Red blasts of light streaked through the blackness of space, striking one of Klanor's ships. As fire spread across it, it dipped, smashing into another vessel.

"Usef," said Rynah, "I need you in the weapons array."

Usef rushed out of the command center, taking the steps two at a time. Once strapped in one of the seats of the weapons array, he placed the helmet on his head, linking his thoughts with Rynah's and Solaris'. A small fighter whizzed past. Moving the laser gun, lining up the enemy craft in his sights, Usef let out a slow breath as he fired. He watched, emotionless, as the ship burst into flames.

Klanor's armada surrounded them. Rynah dodged an incoming fighter. Twisting the controls, she banked to the left before pulling back and soaring upward. *I am going to take us past the command ship. Usef, give it all you've got.*

Understood.

Rynah zigzagged through the mass of vessels as laser blasts ricocheted past the hull of the ship. Ignoring the chaos, and the fear within herself, she kept her hands steady.

I have calculated your trajectory, said Solaris, telepathically, *I can fire two missiles at the aft of the ship.*

Do it! replied Rynah.

Closer the ship came. Rynah steered them for a collision course. As they were almost upon it, she twisted the controls, barrel rolling, before diving underneath the giant vessel. *Now!*

A hailstorm of laser fire escaped Usef's weapon as he fired upon the command ship; a rainbow of lights lit up the darkness, each ending with inferno flames. Two streaks of smoke curved away from Solaris to the command ship. Rynah watched as the missiles honed in on their target. Bursts of flame and debris stretched out to them when the missiles struck. Rynah swerved, dodging the debris as it pelted the ships around her.

A laser cannon struck the rear of the ship, causing Rynah to lose control of Solaris. The craft spun in circles as a spiral of smoke surrounded them. *Solaris, reverse your engines.*

The engines droned as Solaris switched them to reverse. At the same time, Rynah fiddled with the controls, extending and retracting flaps to put the flames out. Once she had regained control, she punched the throttled and sped out of the thick of the armada.

We have one on our tail, Usef told her.

Rynah checked her radar. A blue dot followed her every move. Jerking to the right, Rynah did a U-turn and headed straight for the fighter.

Up in the weapons' array, Usef aimed. He pulled the trigger. Laser fire burst from the giant gun, striking the nose of the enemy ship and causing it to explode.

Rynah flew straight through the remains of the vessel. *We need to rescue the others.*

How? asked Usef, telepathically.

Rynah had no answer. She only knew that she could not leave them behind. She refused to leave them.

What happened to them? Solaris asked.

Klanor took them prisoner, replied Rynah.

Perhaps we could… began Usef, but before he could finish, a laser blast struck the center of Solaris.

The ship rolled as it tried to recover from the shockwave. Rynah veered sideways, but just as she moved the ship, a missile slammed into them. The explosion rocked the vessel, tearing it apart, ripping entire chunks away. Red lights flashed throughout the ship as an alarm blared, warning them of impending danger.

Sparks zapped above Usef's head as he remained strapped in his seat. His eyes opened. A light dangled from the ceiling being held by its wires. As his mind focused, he glanced around. More sparks exploded above him. Usef unbuckled his safety harnesses and jumped from his seat, charging down the steps and to the command center.

"Rynah!" he shouted.

No response.

Unconnected wires shot jagged streaks of electricity in his direction as a broken pipe pumped recycled water onto the floor. Usef navigated around the charged liquid to the command center. "Rynah!"

Still no response.

"Solaris!"

"Sys—tems—dama—can—not—re—aban—ship," came Solaris' jumbled reply.

Usef ran into the command center. A piece of the ceiling dropped on top of him, forcing him to his knees. As he hunkered down, Usef noticed a still form on the floor, surrounded by bulkheads and pieces of the ship. He ran to it and heaved the debris off Rynah.

"Rynah?" He held up her head.

Moaning, Rynah's eyes fluttered open. Her glazed eyes looked right past him and toward the crystal that illuminated the floor. With clumsy movements, she reached for it. Usef snatched the crystal and helped her to her feet. Unsteady, and dizzy, Rynah fell over, forcing Usef to support her as he wrapped her arm around his shoulder.

"Stay with me," he coaxed her.

"Solaris," Rynah whispered.

Fires lined the corridor as Usef led Rynah into it, chunks of metal dropping around them as they walked.

"Solaris," said Usef.

Solaris managed to get her vocal processors back online. "The ship has taken a direct hit to the engines. We are dead in space."

"Is there a way to repair them?"

"Negative. You must make your way to an escape pod."

"No," said Rynah, as her mind regained its focus. "We need to get to my quarters. We need the other crystal and the book."

Knowing when not to argue, Usef changed course and headed for Rynah's quarters. Small explosions rocked the interior of the ship as they moved through the hallway. The ship jerked to the side as another blast of laser fire pummeled its outer hull. Both Usef and Rynah lost their footing, tumbling to the floor and slamming into the railing.

"Come on," said Usef as he helped Rynah back to her feet.

They wormed their way through the cluttered hallways until they found Rynah's room. Frantic, she searched through her bunk, throwing papers and junk to the already cluttered floor. "Where is it?" she screamed.

Rynah spotted a corner of a tattered book. She snatched it and the crystal that lay beside it. "Let's go."

Taking her arm, Usef pushed Rynah down the corridor and towards the escape pod. Flames burst from a panel, forcing them to duck and swerve around it. More wires and dangling lights blocked their path. Taking their time, while at the same instant, trying to hurry, Rynah and Usef snaked through the maze of wires, making certain not to touch the exposed ends. Sparks flashed at them. As sweat poured down their faces and necks, they maintained their composure until they had cleared the area.

"Solaris," Rynah coughed from the thick smoke, "we nee…"

An ear-splitting explosion rocked the ship as another missile crashed into it, forcing Rynah and Usef to tumble forward. They unlocked hands as they rolled across the metallic floor and the ceiling dropped on top of them as dust and metal shards ripped through the hull of Solaris.

Rynah regained consciousness. She seized the crystals and the book before searching for Usef in the thick, smoky fog; flashes of light escaped exposed wires, outlining a shadowy form.

"Usef?"

"Rynah," came his weak response.

Rynah looked in his direction and gasped. An entire bulkhead had landed on top of him, pinning him to the floor. Blood trickled from his mouth. She ran to him, flinging bits of metal and aluminum off him in an effort to free him.

"Rynah," whispered Usef, "go."

"No." Rynah took his hand and held it close.

"Go."

"I'm not leaving you."

"You must go."

"No!" Tears streamed from Rynah's eyes as she thought about all of the times he had offered her his help, his friendship, and she had responded with coldness, turning him away because she feared being betrayed again. Regret welled up in her as she stared into Usef's eyes and witnessed the life within them leaving. "I can't."

"You must."

"I... I can't leave you here." Rynah's voice cracked as she wished she had been kinder to him.

The pile of metallic rubble shifted, crushing Usef even more, forcing him to release a blood-curdling scream before falling silent.

"Usef..."

Usef's last breath escaped his parted lips.

Frozen, Rynah stared at his vacant eyes as she grasped his limp hand, willing it to move, willing the man she had shunned to come back to life and give her a second chance at accepting his friendship and treating him with the respect and kindness he deserved.

"Rynah," said Solaris, "you must get to the escape pod."

"Do the missile tubes still work?"

"Rynah..."

"Do they still work!"

"Yes," replied Solaris.

"Is there a way to rig them so that we can take down the entire armada?"

"Yes, but there is no guarantee that it will work."

Rynah leapt to her feet and turned to where she thought the stairs had been. She met a wall. Black smoke swirled around her, making it impossible for her to see. "I can't find my way," coughed Rynah as the smoke disoriented her.

"I will guide you, but you must take the book and crystals with you."

"To the missile tubes?"

"Yes. To the missile tubes."

Relenting, Rynah scooped the book and crystals up. "Lead the way."

"Take four steps to your left and you will be at the top of the stairs. Be careful, the railing is gone."

Rynah crept through the hall, counting her steps. When she reached the stairs, she felt with the toe of her boot before descending. "Now what?" she said as she reached the bottom.

"Go straight."

Rynah walked with more confidence, one arm stretched out to feel for any obstructions. Smoldering wood blocked her path. She stepped around it.

"Continue straight," said Solaris.

Rynah followed the instruction, trusting the artificial intelligence that her grandfather had created, and whom she now looked upon as a friend, instead of a tool.

"Turn right and there will be more stairs."

Rynah obeyed. "Am I almost there?" she asked when she stepped off the bottom step, holding the crystals and the book close to her.

"Yes," said Solaris, "just a little bit further. There is a corner up ahead. Turn right when you reach it and go straight 20 paces."

Rynah touched the sharp edge of the corner. She veered right. Counting each of her steps, she clutched the book and crystals, focusing only on Solaris' instructions and blocking all else from her mind. The swish of a door sounded behind her. Rynah spun around, dropping the book and crystals as she ran to the sealed hatch.

"Solaris!" she screamed.

She glanced around her as the smoke dissipated enough for her to make out her surroundings. Realization that she had been tricked dawned on her as she recognized the interior of an escape pod.

"Solaris!" Ryan beat her fists against the door. "Let me out!"

"No," answered Solaris.

"Let me go! You can't do this to me! I won't leave you! I can't leave another person behind."

"I am sorry, Rynah, but it has to be this way," sorrow filled Solaris' voice. "Marlow charged me with protecting you and I intend to see it through."

The latches holding the pod snapped. Rynah raced to the window and watched as the release door opened, revealing the stars and ships beyond. "Solaris, please!"

"Save the others. Tell them good-bye for me."

"SOLARIS!"

The release valve popped and the pod lurched as it was freed from its hold.

"Solaris," begged Rynah, her voice cracking, "Don't leave me. Please, do not leave me."

"I am glad that we became friends."

"Solaris, please."

"Good-bye, Rynah."

The pod jettisoned from the ship and shot out into space. Screaming Solaris' name one last time, Rynah watched in vain as her grandfather's most prized possession grew smaller in the distance. The fiery tail of a missile stretched out to it. With tears in her eyes, Rynah watched as Solaris exploded into thousands of pieces. Helpless, she stared out of the pod's window before slumping in the only seat available.

The planet's gravitational pull yanked the pod towards it. Fire engulfed the outer hull as it entered the atmosphere, heading straight for where the shuttlecraft had been earlier, homing in on the only signal it could find. Unable to slow the craft down, Rynah clutched the book and crystals as she waited for the inevitable. Clumps of earth sprang into the air as the pod crashed into the ground. The dirt drifted away, being carried by the wind as the chaos the pod had caused quieted.

Groggy, Rynah sat up as she regained consciousness. The pod had crashed into the volcanic planet with such a force that even the straps on the seat failed to prevent her from being flung to the floor. Emotions welled up within her as she remembered that Usef was not with her and Solaris had been destroyed, causing her to lose two friends in a matter of minutes. Forcing herself to control her inner turmoil, she grabbed both of the crystals and the book and hugged them close.

Fumbling, Rynah found the release valve and pulled it. The door hissed as it opened, smothering her in sulfur and smoke as the fumes filled her nostrils when she breathed in the volcanic air. Rynah stumbled out, falling to the ground. Wind whipped her emerald hair, causing strands to become caught in her long eyelashes. With one hand holding the book and the two crystals, Rynah used the other to crawl out of the crater created by the escape pod. She dropped one of the crystals the moment she heaved herself over the edge.

Before she could react, a laser rifled poked her in the nose. Looking up, Rynah stared straight into the masked eyes of one of Klanor's men.

"Well, here you are," said Stein as he approached.

Rynah glared at him.

"I'll take those."

Gloved hands ripped the other crystal and the ancient book from her grasp. Fuming, Rynah lunged for them, but the butt of a gun stopped her. She doubled over.

"If you are done trying to be a hero, I suggest we go." Stein waved his hand and two soldiers seized Rynah's arms, hauling her away.

Another tremendous bang echoed off the hollow walls of the room as a battering ram slammed into the steel doors, a bulging dent filling its center. Hunched together, the four companions watched as the dent grew larger with each strike and waited for the inevitable to begin.

The banging stopped. Curious, Alfric stood up and walked over to the door. He listened as he tried to make out what the voices on the other side said.

"What's going on?" asked Solon.

"They seem to be rethinking their tactics," Alfric replied.

"Brie," Klanor's voice spilled through the door. "Brie, I know you are in there. Open these doors."

"Why should I?" demanded Brie.

"If you don't, I'll kill your friend."

"Rynah," whispered Brie, but Alfric silenced her.

"We need proof," he said.

"How do I know you aren't lying?" asked Brie.

"Brie, it's me," came Rynah's voice. "I'm sorry. He got the crystal and the book."

All of their hearts sank.

"What do we do?" asked Tom.

"Open the doors," said Solon.

"But what if..." began Tom.

"They already have the crystal and the book," replied Solon. "They have Rynah and we are useless behind these doors. Our enemies hold all of the treasure."

"But if we open those doors, they will kill us," said Tom.

"We're dead anyway," said Brie. "We can either die in here as cowards or out there with honor."

Alfric sheathed his sword. "Open the doors."

"Well, what is your answer?" Klanor demanded from the other side.

"We're coming out!" yelled Brie.

Tom went to the locks and pulled the wires apart. The doors opened, revealing armed guards with raised weapons and Klanor in the center, holding onto Rynah's arm, while Stein and Gaden stood by his side.

"Drop your weapons," ordered Klanor.

They did.

"Where's Usef?" asked Tom.

Rynah lowered her head in answer. A low rumble moaned beneath their feet as the ground swayed back and forth, but not enough to cause alarm.

"We should kill them," said Stein. "They have been far too much trouble."

Klanor's face betrayed him. "They know where the crystal from Fredyr Monsooth is."

"If it is not with her, then it was on her ship, which has since been destroyed, but you have proven that we do not need all six for the weapon to be operational."

"But this is about more than that," said Klanor.

"Truly," said Stein. He snapped his fingers. Gaden pointed his weapon at Klanor's head.

"What is this?" demanded Klanor.

Half of the soldiers turned on the other half. A storm of laser fire filled the room as they fought with one another. Alfric seized Brie and Rynah, pinning them to the ground, while Tom did the same to Solon. A cacophony of noise rattled their ears as the conflict continued, until it ceased. Brie lifted her head. Bodies lay everywhere.

"Up," said Stein's cold voice.

They rose to their feet, observing the mound of dead bodies. Klanor hunkered in a corner. With horror, they watched as the armed men surrounding them tore off their helmets, revealing their faces, each bearing a tattoo on their cheeks, marking them as Fredyr Monsooth's men.

"Stein," said Klanor, "what are you doing?"

"Taking what you promised me. The crystal and the book, now."

One of Fredyr's men snatched them and handed them to Stein.

"You made a deal…"

"When it became apparent that you had no intention of keeping your word, I sought out Mr. Monsooth's assistance. He and I struck a bargain. It saddens me that I will be unable to deliver him the crystal you stole" —Stein glared at Rynah— "but I can deliver your death."

"No!" Klanor flung himself onto Stein.

With lightning reflexes, Stein blocked the attack and threw him to the floor, ramming the heel of his boot into Klanor's stomach.

"Pitiful. Even now, you still want to protect her." His malicious sneer chilled all of them.

The ground shook again, cracking the walls around them as a roar escaped the mouth of the volcano; lava spilled forth, covering the mountainside. Stein looked out the windows and smirked. "I do believe that this place is going to blow up. What could be more perfect? Seal them in the room."

Armed men seized each of them and shoved them into the room that they had sought safety in earlier.

Stein lifted Klanor to his feet. "You can die with your fiancé." He tossed him inside. "Lock the doors."

"What do you plan to do with the crystals?" demanded Rynah.

"Though Klanor built his weapon, it seems that the one they were meant for actually exists on a planet you might be familiar with. Let's see how welcoming the residents of Earth are."

The doors sealed before them as the locks snapped into place. No one spoke. They all thought the same thing. Again, the ground quaked beneath their feet as the volcano threatened to release its wrath upon them.

"You," Rynah charged Klanor, seizing him around the collar of his shirt and forcing him to his knees. She yanked the knife in her boot free. "I should kill you where you stand."

"If it makes you feel better," said Klanor, his voice hollow, devoid of emotion.

Rynah paused. He had always been confident, not weak like he was now. "You tried to kill me. You tried to kill all of us."

"That day," said Klanor, "in the lab, when I aimed my pistol at you, I never fired. Ask me why I didn't."

Rynah pressed the sharp edge of her knife against Klanor's neck, drawing blood, but Brie's hand appeared, taking hold of the blade.

"What are you doing?" demanded Rynah. "Go away!"

Brie looked into Klanor's eyes. All she saw was sorrow, the same sadness she had seen each time he had mentioned Rynah's name. She knew what Rynah's fury failed to see: Klanor still loved her. Despite his attempts not to give in to that sentiment, he did.

"Will killing him ease your guilt?" asked Brie.

Rynah glared at Brie and Klanor. She pressed the knife further. Rynah's muscles strained as she gripped the hilt, gritting her teeth as she struggled with her emotions, what she desired, her sense of justice, and what she knew to be morally right. She lowered her knife. "You win," she said to Brie.

Brie and Klanor locked eyes for a moment, coming to an understanding.

"Though wise to keep your enemies close," said Solon, "you should never turn you back on them."

Agreeing with that sentiment, Alfric ripped some cords free from the machinery in the room and bound Klanor's hands and feet. "If you move," he whispered in his ear, "I will kill you."

The ground shook again. Pipes above them burst, releasing steam that filled the room, making it difficult to see.

"How are we to get out?" asked Tom. "Stein sealed the doors so that I cannot open them from in here."

Smoke poured into the room. Each searched for a way out, but none existed in the windowless space. More quaking knocked them off their feet.

"I'm sorry," said Rynah. "I failed all of you. I ripped you away from your homes just so you could die here."

"No apologies are needed," said Alfric. "You have given me the chance to find honor."

"I wouldn't have missed it for the world," said Tom. "Besides, they were about to kick me out of the academy anyway."

"Brie," said Rynah, "I know you miss your family."

"Don't beat yourself up about it. I would have done the same were I in your position."

"It is foolish to hold on to regrets. They are the bane of the heart," said Solon, accepting his fate.

"Well said," added Tom, "though I have no idea what it means."

"I think I do," whispered Rynah.

As the ground jerked again, bits of the ceiling crashed around them as more steam escaped another set of ruptured pipes; smoke filled the air with its sulfuric odor, causing them to cough. The five companions huddled together, accepting their end.

A deep thud resonated throughout the chamber as the doors opened from the outside, causing them to lift their heads. A shadowed, feminine form approached them, silhouetted by smoke; tendrils of her long hair swayed behind her. They stared, dumbfounded, at the stranger and raised their weapons, ready to defend themselves from this new assailant, but their eyes widened as she stepped into the foggy light, her purple, nanotechnology infused skin reflecting it with perfection.

"I have returned," Solaris' voice filled the area, but it seemed foreign coming from the person before them.

"Solaris?" whispered Rynah.

"Yes," replied Solaris, "before the ship was destroyed, I downloaded myself into this mechanical body that Tom had built for me and escaped in the last remaining pod."

"I don't… It's so good to have you back!" Rynah ran to Solaris and embraced her in a giant hug.

The others did the same.

"So," said Solaris, breaking up the emotional moment and placing her hand on her belt buckle. She eyed the people before her and their gaping expressions, as trails of smoke wisped around them, her eyes falling on Klanor, and in that moment, Solaris knew what had happened.

"Who wants to kick Stein's ass?"

The story continues in book 3: Solaris Strays.

The adventure continues in
book 3 of the Solaris Saga

About the Author

Ms. McNulty began writing short stories at an early age. That passion continued through college until she published her first book: Legends Lost: Amborese under the pen name of Nova Rose. Since then, she has gone on to publish a mystery series, children's books, and even a dystopian series.

Ms. McNulty currently lives in West Virginia, where she enjoys hiking, being outside, crocheting, or simply sitting around and doing nothing. She continues writing and is busy working on the next book in her Solaris Series.

The Solaris Saga

*Also available
on audio.*

Solaris Seethes
Solaris Seeks
Solaris Strays
Solaris Soars

Every myth has a beginning.

After escaping the destruction of her home planet, Lanyr, with the help of the mysterious Solaris, Rynah must put her faith in an ancient legend. Never one to believe in stories and legends, she is forced to follow the ancient tales of her people: tales that also seem to predict her current situation.

Forced to unite with four unlikely heroes from an unknown planet (the philosopher, the warrior, the lover, the inventor) in order to save the Lanyran people, Rynah and Solaris embark on an adventure that will shatter everything Rynah once believed.

Get the companion coloring books.

More by Janet McNulty

The Mellow Summers Series

Sugar And Spice And Not So Nice
Frogs, Snails, And A Lot Of Wails
An Apple A Day Keeps Murder Away
Three Little Ghosts
Oh Holy Ghost   *Also available*
Where Trouble Roams   *on audio.*
Two Ghosts Haunt A Grove
Trick Or Treat Or Murder
Roses Are Red…He's Dead
Double, Double Nothing But Trouble
Ring Around the Rosy, Not Another Ghosty

Mellow Summers moves to Vermont to attend college, accompanied by her friend Jackie. They soon find themselves running into ghosts and one mystery after another.

The Dystopia Trilogy

  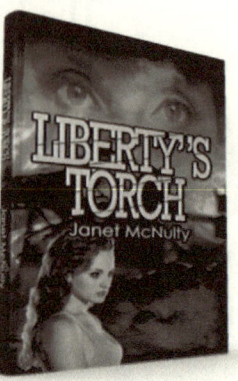

Also available
on audio.

Dystopia (Book 1)
Tempered Steel (Book 2)
Liberty's Torch (Book 3)

Imagine living in a world where
everything you do is controlled.

Dana Ginary lives in a world where every aspect of her life is controlled by the Dystopian Government. Forced to work in Waste Management, her life becomes a nightmare with hunger and survival is her only constant. Before she knows it, she is caught up in a resistance movement and exiled from Dystopia, forced to find her way in the barren wastelands. While there, she must learn to live independently and discover how far she is willing to go to live and achieve freedom.

The Legends Lost Series

Published under Nova Rose

Tesnayr
Amborese
Galdin

Enter the Lands of Tesnayr and join on an epic fantasy adventure that spans over 1,500 years.

Begin with Tesnayr, the first king of the five lands as he unites the against a savage foe bent on their destruction.

Next, Join Amborese as she fights reclaim the throne after her family was forced to flee from it.

Thinking peace has finally entered the land, follow Galdin as he returns to Tesnayr to find it greatly hanged. Barbarians, led by a mysterious sorcerer, burn and destroy as they go. And only Galdin can stop them if he chooses to accept his fate.

Visit www.legendslosttrilogy.com to learn more about the Legends Lost Trilogy.

Something for the Little Ones

The Dragon Who series

The Dragon Who was Afraid of the Dark
The Dragon Who Went to the Moon
The Dragon Who Found a Monster Party
The Dragon Who Found a Spider in His Shoe
The Dragon Who Explored the Sea
The Dragon Who Caught a Cold

The Fairy Who series

The Fairy Who Lost a Tooth

The Mr. Chili series

Mr. Chili's Chili
Mr. Chili Goes To School
Mr. Chili's Halloween
Mr. Chili's Christmas

Others

Mrs. Duck and the Dragon
The Hungry Washing Machine
Rhymes-a-lot
Are You the Monster Under My Bed?
How Do You Catch An Alien

Grandpa's Stories

My grandfather grew up in Arizona during the 1920s and 1930s. One week after the attack on Pearl Harbor he joined the Navy. During the summer of 2012, my mother visited him and recorded his stories about growing up, World War II, and his time as an employee at the Pacific Bell Telephone Company. This is the history of the 20th century as he lived it. These recordings make up this book. These are his words.

www.ingramcontent.com/pod-product-compliance
Lightning Source LLC
Chambersburg PA
CBHW020641030726
47498CB00002B/319

* 9 7 8 1 9 4 1 4 8 8 0 1 0 *